"Ms. Kress handles th̲ ̲ ̲ ̲ ̲ ̲ ̲ ̲ ̲ ̲ ̲ ̲ ̲ ̲ ̲ t
the end I found it both s̲a̲t̲i̲s̲f̲y̲i̲n̲g̲ ̲a̲n̲d̲ ̲t̲e̲r̲r̲i̲f̲y̲i̲n̲g̲.
—*The New York Times*

Why in the world would the Mafia be investing in a genetic engineering company in New Jersey? And why has Judy Kosinski's husband, Ben, been murdered only days after a job interview? FBI agent Robert Cavanaugh is sure that all this is connected, and other deaths too. But how? And why? The answer is a real killer.

Also by Nancy Kress

NANCY KRESS

OATHS and MIRACLES

TOR®

A TOM DOHERTY ASSOCIATES BOOK
NEW YORK

This is a work of fiction. All the characters and events portrayed in this book are either products of the author's imagination or are used fictitiously.

OATHS AND MIRACLES

Copyright © 1996 by Nancy Kress

Edited by David G. Hartwell

A Tor Book
Published by Tom Doherty Assocaites, Inc.
175 Fifth Avenue
New York, NY 10010

Tor Books on the World Wide Web:
http://www.tor.com

Tor® is a registered trademark of Tom Doherty Associates, Inc.

ISBN: 0-812-54473-0
Library of Congress Card Catalog Number: 95-39722

First edition: January 1996
First mass market edition: April 1997

Printed in the United States of America

0 9 8 7 6 5 4 3 2 1

FOR MY AUNT SANDY, WHO
ALWAYS LIKED THRILLERS,
AND MIGHT HAVE LIKED THIS.

ACKNOWLEDGMENTS

The author would like to extend grateful thanks to many people who assisted with the writing of this book. Thanks to:

Dr. Kishan Pandya, M.D., for sharing his medical expertise;

Jill Beves, R.N., for her assistance with medical terminology;

Robert Murphy, New York Department of Investigations, for his many helpful suggestions;

Terry Boothman, for his unique insight on Robert Cavanaugh's doodles;

Miriam Grace Monfredo, Mary Stanton, and Kate Koningisor, for their generous critiques of early drafts of the novel.

Oaths and miracles are usually followed by
deceptive statements.

—*General Rules for Statement Analysis,
Rule #9*, Federal Bureau of Investigation
Interviewing and Interrogation,
U.S. Department of Justice

AUGUST

He that increases knowledge, increases sorrow.
—*Ecclesiastes 1:18*

One

Fourteen minutes into the midnight show at Caesars Palace, the sixth showgirl descending the left side of the Staircase from Heaven tripped.

Her name was Sue Ann Jefferson, from Amarillo, Texas, although in Vegas she was known as Taffy. Her long legs had shaken throughout the 9:00 P.M. show. Under the tight blue-sequined helmet with ice-blue feathers rising two feet into the air, her face was the color of the waiter's linen. Her huge brown eyes remained wide open and unblinking during her fall, which tumbled her and her enormous blue angel wings forward into the showgirl on the step below.

That girl, the most spectacularly built of a spectacular group, wobbled. To keep her own balance and restore Sue Ann/Taffy's, she thrust her gorgeous body backward. Her smile stayed hard and false as the blue diamonds in her shoulder-length earrings. Over her shoulder she hissed, "Bitch! Stay off the junk when you working!" Eighteen steps below, the famous singer in the white dinner jacket sang on, unaware.

Sue Ann lurched upright, took another hip-swaying step downward on five-inch sequined heels, and wobbled again. This time her knees gave way. She sat down hard on her step, just as the showgirl above her, smiling fixedly out at the audience, put out her foot to descend to that same step. The foot encountered Sue Ann, not firm ground. The other girl stumbled, gave a small cry, and fell on top of Sue Ann. Both girls caromed into the spectacular body in front of them. The left side on the Staircase from Heaven crashed down the steps in a tangle of feathers, legs, wings, tassels, breasts, and earrings like flying chains.

The audience laughed and pointed. The famous singer half-turned his head, glimpsed the writhing female pile at the bottom of Heaven, and kept on singing. His eyes were volcanic rock.

In the line of showgirls on the right side of the staircase, Jeanne Cassidy watched, smiled, waved her arms like an angel, and took the next step down. She knew that Sue Ann wasn't using. Sue Ann was Jeanne's best friend. Sue Ann had been like this—shaky, glassy-eyed—for twenty-four hours now. She hadn't slept. She wouldn't eat. She wouldn't tell Jeanne what was wrong.

The fallen angels picked themselves up and backed up the left side of the stairway, lining up with those on the right. Only Sue Ann stayed where she was, sitting in a heap on the stage, staring at nothing. The line descended slowly, smiling, and walked around her. Dawn had lost one earring. Tiffany's stocking had torn and her knee bled. The jeers in the audience died slowly away as the customers, in suits and cowboy jackets and evening clothes and polo shirts with shorts, grew uncertain.

The famous singer finished his song and started another. The girls sashayed behind him, arms on each other's shoulders, a line of half-naked pelvises and long legs that blocked Sue Ann from audience view. Jeanne saw the stage manager rush out, grab the girl under the armpits, and drag her off stage left. Kemper's fat bulging face was purple.

The song finished. The audience laughed and applauded. The famous singer bowed extravagantly, his moussed hair bouncing. The curtain swept closed.

Jeanne pushed her way through the chattering gleaming bodies. When the wall of flesh proved too solid, she used her elbows. "Owww! Bitch . . ."

"Where is she? Fred, where did she go?"

"Outta here!" Kemper yelled. "A million dollars sitting in the audience and you bitches think you can go on using—"

"Taffy doesn't use," Jeanne said coldly. "Where *is* she?"

"In the can. You get her outta here, Amber, I'm telling you, outta here before Bobby gets back here, he'll have her tits in a jar—"

Bobby was the famous singer. Jeanne pushed her way to the backstage ladies' room.

Sue Ann sat on a toilet, her body stocking in place, the stall door open. Two girls dressed like mostly hairless tigers stood at the sinks. They bustled out, striped tails twitching, without glancing at the stalls.

Jeanne knelt in the narrow space. "Sue Ann? What is it? What happened, honey?"

The girl didn't seem to hear. Her eyes, huge and fixed, stared at something straight ahead and invisible.

"Susie, it's Jeanne. I'm here. What is it? Is it Carlo? Did you have a fight?"

"Carlo's dead."

Jeanne put out a hand, steadied herself on the side of the stall. Sue Ann's tone scared her more than the words. "Dead? How do you know, Sue Ann?"

"I know."

"Did you see it? What happened?"

"What do you think happened? You know what he is. Was." This was said in the same voice: calm, empty, completely without inflection. Jeanne's spine turned cold.

"Susie—"

"And now I'm dead, too."

The ladies' room door opened. Jeanne felt her heart skip. A sudden vertigo took her, like the swoop of a great dark bird, blinding. A showgirl dashed into the stall next to theirs and muttered, "Damn!" In a moment urine tinkled into the bowl. Jeanne's vertigo passed and she could see again: Sue Ann, motionless on the toilet, white to the lips.

"Sue Ann, you've got to get out of here. Now. Kemper says you're fired anyway."

Sue Ann appeared not to have heard her. "He loved me," she said tonelessly. "Carlo loved me."

"*Now,* Sue Ann."

"He did love me. He would have left his wife. Soon."

"Right. Get up. Stand up now."

"I was the first woman he really ever loved. I mean really." Her eyes stared expressionlessly at the stall door.

Jeanne got to her feet. The weird toneless monologue made her stomach lift and shiver. She heard the music start onstage for the next number. She was supposed to be in it; so was Sue Ann. Without them both the line would look skimpy. Carlo was dead. Panic turned her angry.

"Get up, damn it! Get up off that toilet!"

Sue Ann didn't get up. But she turned her face to Jeanne's, slowly, mechanically, like an automatic flower.

"Cadoc. Verico. Cadaverico."

"What?" Jeanne said. Her stomach flopped again. Sue Ann had snapped. She was standing in a Las Vegas toilet with a crazy girl marked for death. Then she realized Sue Ann was speaking Italian. Something Carlo had taught her, some lying dago sweet talk from a two-timing son of a bitch.

"It's a joke," Sue Ann said in that same flat voice. "A joke that will make me dead."

Jeanne grabbed both Sue Ann's hands and yanked her off the toilet. She dragged her out of the ladies' room and into the showgirls' dressing room. Kemper had gone. From the stage floated the music for "Somehow I've Always Known."

"Put this on." She shoved jeans and a yellow cotton sweater at Sue Ann. When the girl didn't move, Jeanne grabbed Sue Ann's headpiece and yanked. A handful of hair came off with the sequins and feathers. Jeanne shoved the sweater over Sue Ann's head, right over the body stocking and sequined pasties. The sweater stuck. Sue Ann gasped, unable to breathe, and then pulled the sweater down over her head. Without prompting, she kicked off her heels and pulled the jeans over her feathered G-string. Her face was still expressionless.

Jeanne pulled on her own clothes and sneakers and grabbed her purse and Sue Ann's. Both women still wore stage makeup. Their hair, Sue Ann's dyed platinum and Jeanne's natural red, stuck out wildly. Jeanne clutched Sue Ann's arm and steered her down the back stairway, past the stage door to the basement, through subterranean corridors stifling with boiler heat, and out a door beside a loading dock far from the casino's glittery entrance.

What if they were out there now, in the parking lot? Waiting?

She forced herself to walk normally. But nothing was normal, nothing would ever be normal again. Nothing had been normal for four months, not since she'd come to Las Vegas to be Amber, not since she'd driven her third-hand Ford Escort, a graduation present, out of her father's East Lansing driveway because East Lansing, Michigan, wasn't good enough for her, not her, not for Jeanne Cassidy who was made for fun and bright lights and excitement. . . . Her stomach flopped again and she thought she was going to be sick. Sue Ann moaned softly, the sound oddly indifferent. Jeanne had heard that sound once, from a jack rabbit caught in a coyote trap, resigned to dying.

"Keep walking," Jeanne hissed, although Sue Ann hadn't stopped.

One mile, two . . . the parking lot seemed endless. At this end there were no limos, no Caddys, no Porsches. Jeanne had left her Escort beside a wooden fence, hoping for some afternoon shade. Now the fence was a shadowed looming barricade. It could hide anything. . . .

She shoved Sue Ann into the car, locked her door,

and scrambled into the driver's side. On the highway, Jeanne suddenly felt better and then, a few minutes later, worse. Another wave of vertigo took her and the car swung to the left. She pulled it back into the lane.

"Cadoc," Sue Ann said tonelessly. "Verico. Cadaverico."

"Will you shut up with that stuff?" *A joke that will make me dead.* "Listen, Susie, where are your family? Your parents?"

"No parents."

"Sisters, then. Or brothers. Anybody."

"Nobody."

"Damn it, you must have somebody! Everybody's got somebody!"

"I had Carlo."

Jeanne wanted to slap her. Instead she kept her eyes on the entrance to McCarron Airport. A jet screamed overhead, landing. Her abdomen began grinding again and something wet and sticky slid between her legs.

Her period. *Now.*

"Susie, where can you go? With who? *Think,* damn it!"

Sue Ann's voice, for the first time, lost a little of its toneless despair. "My cousin Jolene. In Austin . . ."

"Fine. Cousin Jolene, then. Fine." She would put the ticket on Visa. If there was still room, there had to still be room, but she'd bought those snakeskin boots—

Jeanne parked in Short Term Parking and yanked open Sue Ann's door. The movement made another gob of blood spurt between her legs—she could *feel* it, oozing through her body stocking and around her G-string. Her fucking period always started at the wrong time, and it was always bad. Her stomach ground and flopped. "Come *on,* Susie—"

They hurried, wild-haired, across two lanes of cars in the brightly lit parking lot. Pain stabbed Jeanne's stomach. She faltered. "Listen, Sue Ann, I just remembered, I have Tampax in the car, and I need—"

"No! Don't leave me—"

Jeanne peeled Sue Ann off her. "Just for a minute, I

promise, I'm bleeding like a pig, and the ladies' room is always out in places like this. . . . I won't put it in until you're on the plane, I promise, but I have to get it from the car. . . . Sue Ann, let me fucking *go!*"

Sue Ann started to cry. Jeanne pulled herself loose and sprinted between two parked cars, toward her Escort. Sue Ann wrapped her arms around herself, shivering in the night desert air. It was 1:12 A.M.

The black car tore around the corner of the line of cars and barreled toward Sue Ann. Jeanne, turning at the sound, her body whirling slowly, slowly as if this were a dream, saw Sue Ann lift her face to the oncoming car, the same way she'd lifted it to Jeanne in the toilet stall. *Cadoc. Verico. Cadaverico.* Yellow floodlight gleamed on Sue Ann's white lips. Overhead a jet screamed its descent.

The car hit Sue Ann without slowing down. Her body bounced off the grille onto the hood, then flew backward. She hit another car, a green Toyota spotted with rust, and slid to the ground. The black car, a Buick LeSabre with California plates, disappeared around the lane of parked vehicles.

Jeanne stood without moving, still in that eerie slow-motion dream. When her legs did move, they carried her in a hesitant step, like a wedding procession. Everything looked too bright, as if it had been drawn by a child with new crayons. She saw, so sharp that it hurt her eyes, the rust smeared from the Toyota on Sue Ann's yellow sweater, at a precise point just above the left breast. Below the rust, a blue-sequined pasty showed lumpy through the thin cotton. Sue Ann hadn't zipped her fly all the way. Her eyes were still open.

Jeanne knelt beside the body and groped for a pulse in the wrist. She didn't know how to find one anyway. She put her head on Sue Ann's quiet chest, then yanked her head back as if it were burned. After that, she couldn't think what else to do, so she did nothing.

From somewhere far, far away, someone shouted. Then there were running footsteps, and the screech of sirens, and someone saying "Miss? Miss?" Later, there were bright lights and coffee she didn't drink and blue uniforms with gun belts and questions. Many questions. But that was much later in this queer slowed-down time, and by then Jeanne had already decided what she must not say, ever, to anybody, anyplace, anytime. Not here, not at home in East Lansing, where she was going as soon as they let her leave Las Vegas, nowhere. Not to anyone.

Not ever.

TWO

Robert Cavanaugh, FBI Criminal Investigative Division, Organized Crime and Racketeering Section, looked at the girl seated in front of him and fought off irritation. It wasn't her fault that he hated interrogating adolescent girls. And that's what this one was, no matter what her driver's license said. She was twenty-one like he was an Arab terrorist. The casinos didn't care. Not as long as they could prove it was the girl lying about her age and not them knowingly hiring children to pose half-naked at 2:00 A.M. for vacationing out-of-towners who thought they were living the glamorous high life.

"Let's go over it one more time, Miss Cassidy."

"*Ms.,*" the female LVPD uniform murmured behind him. Cavanaugh ignored her. Her presence was obligatory; her political correctness was not. And as far as Cavanaugh was concerned, this witness was a little girl.

You're only twenty-nine yourself, he heard Marcy, his soon-to-be-ex-wife, say inside his head. Cavanaugh ignored Marcy, who was thirty-five. She was good at logic, even better at external images, but bad at tuition. She was a great success in corporate marketing.

"I told you everything I can," Jeanne Cassidy said.

"I know. But I want to be sure I have it all."

"I'm so tired," the girl said, which Cavanaugh believed. She looked tired, under the garish showgirl makeup, or what was left of it after her crying. She looked tired and stunned and miserable, all of which was expected after seeing her best girlfriend killed by what the LVPD had logged as a hit-and-run. Jeanne Cassidy's weary stunned misery didn't interest Cavanaugh. But she also looked scared. That did interest him.

"You and Miss Jefferson do the midnight show. Miss Jefferson collapses halfway down the onstage staircase because she hasn't eaten anything all day."

"That's what she told me," Jeanne Cassidy said, and it was lie number one. Cavanaugh had a nose for lies. And this exhausted girl wasn't any good at it. However, there was something odd about her, something different from the usual gorgeous-but-not-too-bright kids who strutted their stuff in Vegas, mostly turning after a year or two to drugs or prostitution or dubious boyfriends. Sometimes all three. This girl was subtly different, but Cavanaugh hadn't yet put his finger on how.

"So Miss Jefferson collapses—"

"*Ms.*," the uniform said, more insistently.

"—and you finish the number. The stage manager tells you he's upset with Miss Jefferson and the show's star is going to be even more upset. Then you go find your friend in the ladies' room—"

"*Women's* room—"

"—and she says she has to go home to her cousin's house in Austin right away. Why was that again?"

"She didn't say," Jeanne Cassidy said, and it was lie number two.

"So the two of you rush out of Caesars right there and drive to the airport, without Miss Jefferson packing any bags or anything. Didn't that seem odd to you?"

"Yes."

"Did you ask Miss Jefferson why she had to leave in such a rush?"

"Of course I did!" the girl snapped. Cavanaugh poured another cup of coffee, to give her time. He didn't want her hysterical. He held the paper cup out to her but she shook her head.

"And when you ask Miss Jefferson why she has to go to her cousin's so quickly, she doesn't give you a straight answer. She just keeps repeating 'I have to go home.' Nothing more."

"Yes," Jeanne Cassidy said, and that was the big one, lie number three. But she had stuck to it for an hour now, which also interested Cavanaugh. She didn't look like she had that kind of tenacity. Unless it had been fused into her, and that took something extremely hot.

"So the two of you are running toward the airport terminal, and this big black car comes racing out of nowhere, hits Miss Jefferson while you've gone back to your car for a feminine necessity, and disappears. You never get so much as a glimpse of the driver, the license plate, the make of car, or anything else significant."

"No."

Cavanaugh drank the coffee himself. It was probably terrible, but he couldn't tell. He never could. Coffee was coffee. He drank it for the caffeine, and to give a weighty pause to what came next.

"Miss Cassidy, did Miss Jefferson have a steady boyfriend?"

"Yes," Jeanne Cassidy said, and she didn't even try to look surprised.

"Who was it?"

"Carlo Gigliotti."

"Did Miss Jefferson ever mention to you that Carlo Gigliotti might have connections to organized crime?"

"No," Jeanne said. Lie number four.

"Never, not even as a suspicion?"

"Never."

You couldn't call her cool, she looked too frazzled and weary and scared for that. So call her stubborn. But something else was there, too, the quality Cavanaugh still couldn't put a name to.

He said, in a harsher voice, "Did Miss Jefferson tell you last night that Carlo Gigliotti is dead?"

She didn't try to fake shock. Instead she just looked at him and said in that same exhausted, stubborn, something-else voice, "No."

"He's dead, Miss Cassidy. The body was found yesterday afternoon, with marks of what is almost certainly a professional job. And there's been no retaliatory activity—that's the kind of thing we watch for—which means his own organization probably disposed of him. It's not surprising—Gigliotti was a loud-mouthed stupid braggart who had his position because he was family to some very powerful people. They gave him minimal trust, and he blew that minimum, and they killed him and then his girlfriend too. The only reason they'd do that, Miss Cassidy, is if they suspected Carlo had told her something, probably to impress her, that he shouldn't have. And it's possible they will reason that she might have told you as well, which could put you in considerable danger. We can help protect you against that danger. Now think again, Miss Cassidy—is there anything you want to tell me that you haven't said yet?"

"No," Jeanne Cassidy said. "There isn't."

"Miss Cassidy—"

"*Ms.,*" the local said, and it was Jeanne who looked at her, with such a look of freezing contempt that the fool woman shut up and even Cavanaugh, despite himself, was secretly impressed.

He kept at her another hour. She wouldn't budge, not on any of it. The report on the hit-and-run vehicle came in: a stolen Buick LeSabre, abandoned in the desert, yellow cotton fibers on the hood. Finally, because there wasn't any other choice, Cavanaugh had Jeanne Cassidy sign a statement and let her go.

"But, Miss Cassidy, I want you to let the department know where you are at all times. In fact, I want you to call in every twenty-four hours for the next two weeks.

Use this phone number." He handed her the laminated plastic card.

She handed it right back to him. "I can tell you right now where I'm going to be from now on," she said, in the strongest voice he'd heard from her yet. "I'm taking a taxi from here to my apartment. I'm packing my things. At the apartment I'm making one phone call, to Fred Kemper, to resign from Caesars Palace. Then I'm taking another taxi to the airport and waiting there until I can get a flight to East Lansing, Michigan, where my parents live. I'm enrolling at Michigan State for the fall semester, and I'm living at my parents' house for the next four years while I get my degree. My father's name is Thomas M. Cassidy. He's in the book, but I'll write it down for you. If you want me, you can call me there."

Cavanaugh and the female uniform stared at her. She took a piece of paper and a pen from her purse. Cavanaugh watched her print an address and phone number. He wondered if she was smart enough to have figured out that her and the Jefferson girl's phone was probably tapped and her decision to shut up would thus be clearly communicated to the Gigliotti family. He wasn't sure she was that smart, but he was sure she meant what she said. She wouldn't tell anybody anything more, and she was going home, and she was going back to school.

He knew then, what was different about her. Unlike most of the Las Vegas showgirls, she had a strong sense of self-preservation. She was getting out.

The Carillon was one of the small motels between the airport and the Strip, neither grand nor sleazy. Cavanaugh flicked on the light in his room, set the chain on the door, and glanced at the phone. The message light blinked. Hope surged in him. Not Felders, Felders would beep him direct. Marcy?

He pressed 0 for the hotel operator. "This is room 116. I have a message?"

"Yes, Mr. Cavanaugh. The message is, 'Call in. Felders.' Shall I repeat that?"

"No," Cavanaugh said. He hung up and pulled the

state-of-the-art mobile phone from his pocket. There was no tone. He punched Felders's number: nothing. "Shit," he said, and called Marty Felders on the motel phone.

"Cavanaugh? What the hell's wrong with your mobile?"

"Probably the same thing that was wrong with the section fax machine last week," Cavanaugh said acidly. "There's not a damn piece of technology in the Hoover Building you can count on."

"Good old pessimistic Bob," Felders said jovially. Nobody else ever called Cavanaugh "Bob." He was Robert, always. And he didn't consider himself a pessimist. Why would a pessimist spend his life chasing scum? A pessimist would just assume they couldn't be caught.

"Listen, Bob," Felders said. He always began that way: listen. As if there were a chance his agents might not. "Did you learn anything useful from that showgirl?"

"Nothing. She knows, but she isn't saying."

"Well, leave your notes at the branch for Paul Garrison and catch the 6:45 A.M. United flight for Washington. Pick up the ticket at the desk. Is there anything Garrison needs to know that isn't in your notes?"

"No," Cavanaugh said. Gigliotti wasn't his case; he'd just happened to be in Vegas, finishing up a semi-important errand, when the call came. He was closest, was all. He hadn't yet been agent-in-charge on a case of his own. Felders knew how much he wanted it.

"Then come on in. And listen, Bob—what do you know about recombinant DNA?"

"Nothing," Cavanaugh said promptly.

"Well, hope the in-flight magazine has an article about it. Really, nothing? At all? It's a hot topic in the scientific world."

"Clearly we're not in the scientific world," Cavanaugh said acidly, "or we'd have basic technology that works."

"Good old pessimistic Bob. See you tomorrow."

"What about? What's the interest in recombinant DNA?"

"That's what you're going to find out," Felders said. "There's a company we should look into. See you tomorrow."

Cavanaugh hung up. *A company we should look into* meant just more routine intelligence work. Same old, same old.

He opened the desk drawer. The Carillon Motel stationery featured, for no discernible architectural reason, a medieval bell tower. He pulled out three sheets.

He always carried his own drawing pencils, in various colors. With the green one he sketched rapidly, easily: two birds with long fishlike tails. Their odd bodies contorted into odd poses. He added water and undersea plants and bottom-feeding slugs. He gave both fishbirds baffled, pained expressions. Above the picture he printed MERBIRDS DISCOVER OBSTACLES IN LIFE.

On the second paper he wrote, in his small upright hand:

> *There's a beauty to a day alone in the hotel room. You can choose to not shave over your Adam's apple. You can wear the wrong shirt with the wrong pants. You can order room service and fake a Mexican accent. You can line up all the little soaps, mouthwashes, sewing kits, and shower caps in a line across the floor and accuse them of loitering. No one knows the satisfactions I've seen.*

On the third paper he drew a military general, chest puffed out, hat at a preternaturally correct angle. Across the general's uniform marched a row of campaign ribbons with hearts and knives and tiny beds. Cavanaugh printed BATTLE STARS FOR THE WAR OF THE SEXES.

He put each sheet of paper in a separate envelope and addressed all three to Mrs. Marcia Cavanaugh, in Washington. In his wallet he found three stamps. He stacked the letters on the nightstand, beside the dead mobile and his regulation Smith & Wesson.

He'd been sending Marcy notes like these for five years, from the first day they'd met. He'd sent hundreds during their first year together. The frequency had fallen off after they married but had surged again when he'd left corporate life, which he'd hated, and joined the FBI. Then another falling off, coinciding with the slow creeping chill in their marriage, like slow-motion frost that had escaped its season to settle permanently through the entire calendar.

Then she'd left, and Cavanaugh had stopped sending the notes.

"I want more than this, Robert," Marcy had said.

"More what?"

"More *everything*. More travel, more laughter, more people, more experiences. More breadth to life."

"Maybe you only get breadth at the expense of depth," Cavanaugh had said, not even knowing if this was true, wanting to score points.

"No epigrams, Robert. No quips. I want to experience a much wider world than I ever could with you."

Cavanaugh eventually decided, after months of pain, that he'd been left for another lover: the wider world. He wished he'd thought to ask Marcy how she expected it to love her back.

Now Cavanaugh was sending the notes again. Two, three at a time, a few days every week, from wherever he was. Even from Justice at Washington. She had loved them, once. She'd laugh and shake her head: "Who would ever suspect this side of you, Robert?" He remembered her laugh. Every night now, he remembered her laugh.

He turned off the light and made his mind leave Marcy and return to whatever Jeanne Cassidy hadn't been saying. The Jefferson girl falling onstage at Caesars, and then the stage manager dragging her off, and then—

He went over it all once more, and then yet again, looking for something he might have missed. Something he could pass onto Garrison. He didn't find it.

Just before he fell asleep, he turned on the lamp and held the three envelopes to the light until he found the one that held the nasty crack about the war of the sexes. He tore it up.

Cavanaugh turned off the light and settled back into bed. A minute later he turned the lamp on again and fished the fragments of torn paper from the wastebasket. Carefully, he peeled off the unused stamp.

Three

"There are only four reasons in the world to do anything," Judy O'Brien Kozinski said to her nearly naked husband. "Because you want to, because you need the money, because you gave your word, or because you want to please someone you love."

"And which of the first three dragged you to Las Vegas?" Ben retorted. He hung his sports coat in the hotel closet. "It sure the hell isn't because you want to please me."

"Actually, that is the reason," Judy said evenly. "There's certainly no other reason I'd be here."

Ben gave her his skeptical-scientist look, its force not at all diminished by his standing there in his underwear. He had a beautiful body, Judy thought despairingly. Tapering back, sexy strong shoulders, flat belly. At forty-three. And she, despite being ten years younger, did not. Or at least, not in Ben's class. And his face, with its Roman profile and thick blond hair, was just as gorgeous as his body. Judy hunkered down in the red plaid wing chair, the hotel's idea of contemporary elegance.

"You might," Ben said, pulling on his suit pants, "just might, possibly, be here in Vegas for *your* job. Or weren't you planning to do that interview at Nellis after all?"

"Of course I'm going to do it."

"Then why haven't you left yet?"

"Because the interview isn't until four. And because right now I'm fighting with you."

"I didn't start this fight."

"Oh, no. You're just an innocent babe in the academic conference woods."

"As a matter of fact, I am. Although of course you've already made up your mind otherwise."

She watched Ben shrug into his jacket—Armani, of course, he'd be the only scientist at the entire fucking microbiology conference in Armani, and he'd love that. "Ben—"

"I'm changing clothes," Ben said with great deliberation, "because I have an important presentation to do this afternoon, possibly the most important presentation of my career. Or did that fact escape your sight?"

"Not enough escapes my sight. Certainly not your behavior at lunch."

"There was nothing wrong with my behavior at lunch. Will you stop *picking* at me?"

"If the issue is important, it isn't picking."

"The issue is not important."

"Maybe it is to me," Judy said. "Or doesn't that matter?"

He didn't deign to answer. I don't blame him, Judy thought. We sound like the kind of married couple we never wanted to be.

"Ben," she said, fighting to sound logical, "you didn't say one word to me at lunch. Not one. I sat there like an extra finial on the chair and you talked through the entire meal to that wretched girl from UC Berkeley. Ninety solid minutes. What do you suppose people thought?"

"I imagine people were far too busy with thoughts of

substance to notice what I was doing. This is an important conference, after all, Judy."

"Don't take the moral high ground with me! I know it's an important conference!"

"Then act like it." He stood in front of the mirror and fine-tuned his tie, a red-and-blue Italian silk. The blue matched his eyes.

"Did you . . . did you think she was so very pretty?"

He glanced at her swiftly, hearing the change in her voice. From anger to pleading. She heard it herself: the sound of the central fact of their marriage reasserting itself, inevitable as gravity. She wanted him more than he wanted her. She knew it, and he knew it, and she knew he knew it. God, she despised herself. She was pathetic.

Ben crossed the room to Judy's chair. "Is that what this is all about? Because that graduate assistant was pretty?"

Judy looked at him, without smiling. But she couldn't help herself. He stood there above her, in his perfectly fitting clothes, his blond hair shining in the light from the window, the strange power on him of arcane and difficult knowledge. It held a pull for her, that power. It always had, since their very first date on her twentieth birthday. On her wedding day she'd thought she'd die of happiness. Good Catholic girl that she'd been, it had seemed that the saints had answered all her prayers.

"Oh, honey, you don't need to be jealous," Ben said warmly. He said warm things very well. "Anita's just a graduate assistant. She hasn't got a third of your brains." He sat on the arm of the plaid chair and took Judy's hand.

"Truly?" she said, although of course it wasn't true, Anita couldn't be a graduate student in microbiology without being brainy. But Judy couldn't stand to continue arguing. Ben's fingers traced little whorls in her palm. He was always generous in victory, any kind of victory. Good policy. Ben believed in good policy.

Judy looked out the hotel window at Las Vegas. The hotel wasn't directly on the Strip, but that didn't help much. She'd been with Ben to scientific conferences all over the world, and she thought Las Vegas was the ugliest city she'd ever seen. Garish, cold-blooded, baking in the August heat like some bloated iridescent lizard. Even Oslo had been better. In winter.

Ben said, "I only talked to Anita for so long because she was feeling shy and out of place, a graduate assistant among the big guns."

"My husband the humanitarian."

He grinned. He liked her wry, not pathetic. She liked herself better that way, too. Didn't he ever notice that after twelve years of jealousy, wryness wore thin?

Probably baseless jealousy, she reminded herself. Because she had never known for sure. Because, of course, she had never really tried to find out.

—only four reasons to do anything. Because you want to . . .

She forced herself to say, "Who else is presenting this afternoon? Besides you?"

"Sid Leinster. From the University of Washington. I'll blow him away."

He would, too, no matter what Sid Leinster's paper was on. Ben was presenting a major research project from the Whitehead Institute for Biomedical Research at Massachusetts Institute of Technology, with all the prestige that automatically conferred. And Ben was the third most cited geneticist in the country, according to the spring newsletter of the Institute for Scientific Information, which kept track of such things. And today's presentation was in the hot area of gene therapy, which even the garbage press paid attention to. Manipulate living DNA! Cure dread diseases by altering the genes that cause them! Redesign the original blueprints from God—who after all hadn't had the advantage of a 3.5 million dollar grant from the National Institutes of Health.

But that wasn't the whole truth, Judy forced herself to admit. Even if Ben had been from Podunk University's biology department, presenting on the causes of athlete's foot, he would command attention. He had that most valuable gift for research science, an infallible nose for the next big scent. Plus the second most valuable gift, the ability to obtain funding to track that scent. And while she was counting up his gifts, she might as well throw in the third biggie: absolute integrity about his work. If Ben said this project was of world-class importance, then it was. Where his research was concerned, he never inflated, never fudged, never prematurely announced, never denied others credit, never indulged in the hundred petty misrepresentations that smeared modern government-funded science for the idealist. He was greedy for attention, yes, but his research was always honest, capable, and important.

It was one of the things she reminded herself of, lying awake in their bed hour after hour, during the nights he didn't come home.

Ben stood, still smiling at her. "Sure you won't come hear me emote about envelope proteins in retroviral vectors? Last chance, love."

"I can't. I can't. You know this is the only time Ressman would give me." Dr. James Ressman, head of the Atomic Energy Commission office at Nellis Air Force Base, seldom granted interviews to the "popular scientific press," about which he displayed much witty contempt. Judy, freelance writer for that same popular press, had worked for weeks for this interview on the latest round of horrors to come to light about bomb testing in Nevada in the 1950s. *Science Update* was paying for her trip to Vegas. No interview, no expense voucher.

Ben said, "Well, then, wish me luck."

"You won't need it. Dea Nukleia is on your side." An intimate, dumb joke: Dea Nukleia, the Muse of Microbiology. Twelve years of intimate, dumb, sweet jokes between them. Ben bent to kiss her where she sat, unmoving, in the plaid chair, and Judy thought she smelled perfume on his suit jacket. Musk, or maybe sandalwood—she herself used a light lilac scent. Then Ben straightened, and she told herself that she was probably mistaken, the scent was probably just one more unsubstantiated imagining. Her head felt heavy, the familiar feeling of having her brain wrapped in cotton wool. Unable to reason through to logical conclusions. It was a feeling familiar to her only around Ben.

Ben picked up his notes from the table: "Envelope Proteins in Retroviral Vectors: Implications for Major Histocompatability Complex Antigen Activity." Judy forced herself to smile at him. "Good luck, Ben."

"Thanks, love."

"Dinner at seven? The hotel restaurant on the top floor, what's-its-name?"

"Unless Dea Nukleia decrees otherwise."

"Just the two of us?"

"I promised, didn't I?"

"Bye."

"Bye, love."

The door closed. Judy sat unmoving in the plaid chair for another five minutes, ten. After that time, she shook her head. This was stupid. She had things to do. Brooding never helped anything. She reached for the phone to confirm her 3:00 appointment.

But instead her hand dialed the eleven digits for Troy, New York. The phone rang twice.

"Hello?"

"Dad? It's Judy."

"Judy! Hi! Mom and I were just talking about you!"

"You were?"

"We just got back from Mass, and Father gave his homily from Genesis 43:34: 'And he took and sent messes unto them from before him, but Benjamin's mess was five times as much as any of theirs.' And I said to your mother, God's at the conference with Judy and Ben."

Judy laughed. Her father could always make her laugh. Less for his wit—it wasn't really all that funny, and she didn't believe in the Bible anymore anyway—than just for what he was. Solid. Generous. There when you needed him.

"So what are you up to today?" Dan O'Brien asked.

"Interview with James Ressman at Nellis. On the NIH fallout report."

"I'm impressed," her father said, and she heard in his voice that he was. He taught physics and calculus at Cardinal John DiLesso High School. "Ask him why escort fighters get funded and science education doesn't."

Judy laughed. "Right. And get myself escorted right out of there."

They talked a few minutes more. When Judy hung up, her mood had lifted. She buttoned her blazer, watched the linen wrinkle at her sides and strain across her belly, and unbuttoned it again. God, if only she could lose twenty-five or thirty pounds. But dieting was so hard. She always got so hungry.

She turned her back on the mirror.

Judy shared the elevator with a large group of conference delegates wearing name tags. They headed past the Sapphire Room, which held Sid Leinster's presentation on excitotoxin damage to mitochondria. Judy peered in. Rows of gilt chairs, occupied by a total of five people. A nervous-looking man stood behind a podium, gazing forlornly at the empty spaces. Poor Dr. Leinster.

The Topaz Room was doing better. Crowds thronged the aisles, and uniformed hotel employees carried in more chairs. Judy peered at the topic on an ornate gilt easel: "Patenting Gene Fragments: Ethical Issues, Legal Concerns, and Commercial Opportunities." Well, that figured. Patenting genetic discoveries was a hot topic. Making money always was.

She chided herself for being cynical. After all, the Garnet Room across the hall was doing just as well with "Cell-Cell Adhesion Mediation by Tyrosine Phosphatase: Experimental Outcomes," which didn't sound like something anybody could get rich from. The group Judy had seen on the elevator headed toward the Garnet Room. They looked eager. Wait till you hear Ben's presentation, she thought, and smiled to herself.

She threaded her way through the elevator contingent. Three of them were women. One was pretty, a diminutive Asian with shining black hair.

Dea Nukleia and Ben. The first-string team. Her husband.

Hers.

The Asian scientist had a bright red mouth and tiny waist. One hundred ten pounds, at the most. Judy caught the scent of sandalwood.

She walked out of the hotel in the glaring heat and drove to Nellis Air Force Base.

By 7:30, when Ben still hadn't shown up at the Top Hat Bar, Judy started to get angry.

She sat alone at a tiny table near floor-to-ceiling windows, watching frantic neon blink green and red and blue and gold. It wasn't pretty, just hysterical, but if she turned away from the window she'd have to wave and smile at the conference participants passing through the bar to the dining room, who might then feel sorry for her, all dressed up and stranded by her husband. They might even know where Ben was, and with whom.

No. That wasn't fair. Probably he'd been delayed in some intense argument about epinephrine receptors or cytokines. It had happened before. She should stay calm, give him a chance to explain, not jump on him just because *her* day had been a bust. Ressman had given her nothing. Furthermore, he'd been testy and short, just this side of rude. Judy knew she was good at patiently digging for the political aspects of science that scientists never wanted to disclose, but Ressman had proved even better at not giving them to her. She hadn't even gotten a decent quote.

At 7:45 the waiter threw her a significant look. Judy ordered another glass of California Chardonnay.

At 8:00 she saw the Berkeley graduate student, Anita, pass into the dining room with Sid Leinster. Anita wore a clinging red sheath. Until that minute, Judy had thought well of her own black knit, a dress that made her feel almost slim. Anita had a gardenia in her glossy hair.

At 8:10 Judy shoved her chair away from the tiny table and jerked to her feet. This spilled the rest of her wine. Ben walked into the bar.

"Judy! I'm so sorry I'm late."

"You're always sorry," Judy snapped, mopping at the table with a cocktail napkin. "I've been waiting an hour and ten minutes, Ben."

"I know. I know. But there's a good reason. Come on, let's go."

"Go? Go where? Ben, I'm starving!"

"Up to our room. We'll order room service. We need privacy to talk."

Judy looked at him more closely. His eyes shone feverishly. His tie had been loosened, and there was a spot on his collar. She leaned forward. Not lipstick.

"Ben—did your presentation go all right?"

"The what? Oh, the presentation. Yes, fine. Great. Come on, Judy, let's go."

He grabbed her hand and pulled her from the bar. In the elevator he stared at the flashing floor lights as if they were genetic code.

Once, in fifth grade at Holy Name Elementary School, Sister Joseph Marie had refused to tell Judy what Judy had done wrong. Sister had merely waved her to the corner stool, where Judy had sat in flushed disgrace for thirty minutes, not knowing what her sin had been. The ignorance was worse than the disgrace. "You see?" Sister had said softly, afterward. "Not knowing kills the spirit. So why wouldn't you tell Peggy what page the math assignment is on when she asked you?" "Because I didn't want to," Judy had answered, furious that little sneak Peggy had tattled. Sister hadn't argued, only smiled sadly. But at recess Judy had given Peggy all the answers to the social studies homework, plus the candy bar from her lunch. *Not knowing kills the spirit.*

She looked at Ben, studying elevator lights, and her heart started a slow, methodical thud against her ribs.

"Judy," he said in their room, "how would you like—"

"I'd like to order dinner," she said firmly. Buying time.

"This is too important to . . . oh, all right, order for us both." He disappeared into the bathroom.

She ordered shrimp cocktail, steak, baked potatoes, sautéed zucchini, wine, coffee, and Black Forest torte. Ben came out of the bathroom with his shining blond hair freshly brushed and his tie straight. As if he were going to make a presentation. She settled herself in the plaid wing chair and clasped her hands in her lap.

"Judy, how would you like to live in New York, closer to your folks in Troy? In a nice big co-op on the Upper East Side, with a live-in housekeeper? And also be able to afford to start our family?"

Judy's breath whooshed out of her. Whatever she'd expected, this wasn't it.

"How . . . who . . ."

"I've had a job offer." Ben sat on the edge of the bed and grinned at her. His blue eyes shone brilliantly. "A once-in-a-lifetime chance!"

"You'd leave Whitehead? But it's the most prestigious genetic research institute in—" She stopped. But, no, the offer couldn't be from the Centre d'étude du polymorphism humain. He'd said New York, not Paris.

"Very little would make me even consider leaving Whitehead. But this isn't very little. In fact, it's everything. I'd have complete control over all research, a virtually unlimited budget, a percentage of profits, and the *salary*. . . . It's at a biotech company."

Judy blinked. The commercial biotech firms had been springing up ever since the Human Genome Project started mapping the broad outline of human genes. Most of them were engaged in large-scale sequencing, refining the maps the Project had pioneered. The more traditional ones worked on ways to fight disease. But she knew that a few were pushing the envelope, moving into uncharted territory in search of whatever large-scale applications might emerge from the latest discoveries in microbiology. Especially since the Supreme Court had ruled that genetic discoveries could be patented. "Research privateers," Ben had called them.

She said, "But you said you'd never take any position that—"

"Let me finish. With this company, I'd be able to conduct experiments for their own sake, go wherever the research takes me—they're interested in long-term results. And I could work without accounting to an NIH grant board for every test tube and gene sequencer. I could design research without arbitrary controls, in an environment dedicated to pure—"

"If it's so pure, how come they're talking about percentage of profit?" Judy said acidly, hoping to slow Ben down. It didn't work.

"They're talking about percentage of profit because there eventually will *be* profits. There have to be. Biotech companies are the future, I've *told* you that, honey—the genome project is only the infrastructure, the roads and sewer lines. The commercial companies will build on that infrastructure, and some of it will be billion-dollar skyscrapers. Why else do you think ninety million dollars was invested in genome-related private companies last year alone, up 35 percent from the previous year? Wall Street smells money."

"You sound like a PR release," Judy said. She was getting dizzy. These weren't the kinds of figures Ben usually had at his fingertips. "Ben—"

"Hear me out, honey. This is *big*. And not just financially big—scientifically big. Important. Companies like Verico—"

"Like what?"

"Verico. That's what this outfit is called."

Verico. Truth company. She clasped her hands more tightly.

"Anyway," Ben rushed on, "Verico and commercial enterprises like it will be where the next big scientific breakthroughs happen, away from government bureaucracies and away from crusading congressmen who object to spending money on anything but themselves and away from animal-rights lobbyists who want to set all the lab mice free and away from—"

"Wait!" Judy cried. Ben stopped. She took a deep

breath. "Just slow down, Ben. Don't give me the prop-aganda, just tell me what happened. From the beginning. Verico approached you—"

For a moment Ben's blue eyes glittered. He never liked being interrupted. But then he sat on the arm of her chair and took her hand. It was the same pose he'd taken this morning, when he told her he wasn't going to lay that girl from Berkeley. Judy wished he'd shift position, but she didn't want to risk angering him.

"Okay, honey. From the beginning. I gave my presentation and answered questions. This representative from Verico, who'd been sitting in the back taking notes, hung around until I was ready to leave. After introductions—"

"Is this representative male or female?"

"Male," Ben said evenly. "You had to ask, didn't you? This *male* representative, a Dr. Eric Stevens, introduced himself as the president of Verico. He's a biochemist himself, undistinguished record, strictly second-rate but at least he knows it. They want a first-rate talent to conduct research in areas adjacent to my work on envelope proteins. He spent an hour outlining their general thrusts, the facilities, budgets, and so on. Stevens showed me a summary of their current work. Uninspired, but in all the right areas. They're working on T-cell antigen recognition that—"

"Don't tell me the technical side yet," Judy pleaded. "Just what it means to *you*."

"What it could mean to me is the chance to finally do the work I really want to. Without petty accountability, with adequate resources, and with the rewards that I— that *we*—are entitled to for doing it."

"Such as a big salary. How big?"

"Half a million a year."

It took her breath away. For a second she stared at Ben, who smiled triumphantly.

"But, Ben, nobody gives researchers that kind of money . . ."

"Verico will. Plus a percentage of eventual profits. Don't look like that, Judy. God, your New Yorker suspiciousness! After I finished talking to Stevens, I called Paul Blaine."

Paul was their accountant, and an old friend; Judy respected him. He'd been best man at her and Ben's wedding.

"I caught him at his office, he was working late. That's why I was late meeting you. I was waiting for Paul to do some checking and call me back. Verico is a private company, so there's no public financial documents. But Paul verified that Verico was founded two years ago by a wealthy entrepreneur, Joseph Kensington, whose great-grandfather made the family money over a century ago in New Jersey real estate. This Joseph is his namesake, and only surviving heir. He owns a couple different companies, apparently well managed. He invested the family fortune well."

Judy heard the admiration in Ben's voice; he admired people who invested well. At least she tried to tell herself that was the part he admired, and not the family-fortune part. Ben's own family had been the sort that moved to avoid paying back rent. Judy had always thought that her own family was one reason Ben married her.

Ben continued, "Kensington apparently regards science as a sort of spectator sport. Like you, honey."

She said quietly, "Don't patronize me, Ben."

"I'm not. Anyway, he founded Verico, and he's searching for top talent to make it successful, and he's shrewd enough to recognize that top talent costs money." Ben's voice was flat now. He'd run out of patience with Judy's resistance.

"Ben, you always said you'd never leave Whitehead—"

"Things change," Ben said in the same flat voice. A knock sounded on the door.

"Room service."

Ben let in the waiter and tipped him. Sizzling steak, steaming coffee perfumed the room. Judy found she wasn't hungry after all. She rose from the plaid chair and positioned herself by the window.

"Ben, I know things change. I just don't see what's changed here. Other commercial biotech companies have approached you—"

"Not with an offer like this."

"Granted. But you're happy where you are. We've made a life in Boston."

"And we'd make one in New York. God, Judy, how many people do we know there already, not even counting all your cousins? Besides, I haven't made up my mind yet. I wanted to talk with you, although that doesn't seem to have been particularly productive. And I certainly want to fly down there and look Verico over." He stood with his arms folded across his chest, on the other side on the serving cart. Neither of them moved toward the food.

Judy said, "So you've already agreed to a recruitment interview? Flying there straight from Vegas, I bet."

"Yes."

"Without so much as consulting me."

"I'm consulting you now. And regretting it more by the minute."

"We're supposed to go to Gene Barringer's daughter's wedding on Saturday."

"Make my regrets."

He had on his stony face. Judy said, "You always said you'd never leave Whitehead—"

"You keep *saying* that, as if it was some religious vow! Look, Judy, things change, even if you don't want them to. I like Whitehead, but there are a lot of constraints on me there, I don't run the show, and I'll entertain any reasonable offer."

"This isn't exactly an offer from a recognized research center, and furthermore—"

"Every important research center was unknown once—"

"—*furthermore,* saying you'll entertain anybody makes you sound like a hooker."

"Don't pin your medieval notions of sin on *me*," Ben said furiously. "That's just your Catholic upbringing clouding your judgment again!"

"My Catholic upbringing was supposedly one of the things you loved about me! Remember? Stable family life, spiritual center, lifelong marriage—"

"Like I said, things change," Ben said coldly.

Judy didn't answer. Ben walked out of the room.

By the time she finally fell asleep, close to 5:00 A.M., he hadn't returned. The table from room service sat untouched, the fat on the steaks long since congealed into cold slippery ridges the color of maggots.

Four

Wendell Botts stood outside the electrified barbed
wire fence of the camp of the Soldiers of the Divine Covenant and whispered a prayer.

The prayer just sort of mistook him—he didn't know
he was going to say it until it was too late and the prayer
was out. Wendell scowled and spat on the ground. His
praying days were over, that was for damn sure. He'd
prayed and prayed, and where the fuck had it got him?
Standing here, outside the camp, looking at a lot of rusty
barbed wire threaded with double 110-volt lines.

Not that he'd minded the wire when he'd been inside,
a Soldier himself. Going to Bible class six days a week
and chanting at Mass and helping out in the dining hall
and kneeling every night to pray with Saralinda and
Penny. The wire had seemed good then, keeping them
all safe inside, safe on sacred ground, away from the
temptations and misery and blood sins of the world.
He'd really believed that, about the sins and all the rest
of it, stupid fool that he was. He'd really believed it. And
so he'd liked the wire, circling the camp in the foothills

of the Adirondack Mountains, cheap land too rocky for farming and too isolated for jobs and too dirt poor to interest much of anybody except the kind of desperate religious nuts who'd follow their desperation to Cadillac, New York.

Cadillac. This place was barely a rusty Corolla.

Two men opened the iron gate set between high brick posts. The gate was strong but plain, and so were the men, dressed in the dark work clothes Soldiers of the Divine Covenant favored on weekdays. On their breast pockets was hand-embroidered the red silk *C*. Wendell measured both men. Over six feet, maybe 195, 200 pounds each, not much of it fat. But Wendell had been a marine, and in prison he'd lifted weights for hours every day, and still worked out regularly.

"Saralinda doesn't want to see you, Wendell," the taller guy said. Wendell didn't recognize him. He hadn't been here when Wendell had been a Soldier.

"Tell her she's got to see me. That I got a right to see my wife and my kids."

"I told her, Wendell. She says no."

He felt his temper rising, the steam building up inside him, and he tried to push it down again. He couldn't lose his temper again. Then Saralinda would never come out.

"Tell her I said please, it's real important to me, and I—"

"She said *no*."

Who did this guy think he was? Wendell kept his palms flat against the legs of his jeans, to keep from making fists. Beyond the two men he could see the camp buildings baking in the sun: flat, low, plain. Painted with red *C*s.

"Then let me see my kids. I got a right—"

"I'm sorry." The taller man turned away, and the other followed.

Wendell said, "I saw a lawyer. If Saralinda and my kids don't come out here and talk to me, he says we can get some kind of court order to let me come in there and see them!"

That stopped them. He knew it would. No one who wasn't washed clean by baptism could go inside the camp. It would pollute sacred ground, earth once trod by the feet of a saint. Wendell had been clean once, but he sure the hell wasn't now. He added, bluffing, "I'll come back here with my lawyer and papers. I'm sick of this runaround shit!"

"Wait here," the taller guy said.

Both men disappeared. They were gone a long time. Maybe they called the Elders together, that group of crazy old men who ran the place, who never left sacred ground because they didn't need to work outside like the young men and childless women. Wendell had to laugh every time he saw one of those stupid TV shows about religious cults with some crazy charismatic leader who fucked all the women and lived high on the hog. The Soldiers of the Divine Covenant weren't like that.

They followed the secret ways of St. Cadoc, who'd left the world to start a monastery and then left the monastery to travel around the world, holy and poor, until he died. Twice. The camp was run by five old men who lived plainer and barer than anybody else, for the greater glory of God. They ate rice and beans and slept on the floor, even in winter and never fucked nobody. That was the way to be really holy.

Wendell'd known even when he was inside that he'd never be really holy.

Yeah, that was what they were doing, calling together the Elders. They didn't care that they kept him outside in 92-degree August humidity with no shade closer than two hundred feet and the inside of his pickup like an oven. Did they think he'd give up and go away? Not a chance in hell. Not this time. He wanted to see his kids.

Twenty minutes later, his heart leaped. Three people walked toward the gate, the two tall men and a small figure between them, a woman dressed in jeans and a loose, dark blue work shirt with the red C. Saralinda.

The men unlocked the gate, pointedly left it open, and stood spaced equidistant just inside. Saralinda walked out slowly, in that hesitant way she had that always looked so feminine. Wendell made himself hold still, so she'd have to walk over to him, out of earshot of the Soldiers.

"Hello, Wendell."

"Saralinda." Christ, he was going to cry. She looked just the same, long straight shining brown hair around that small thin face. Big soft brown eyes. No, he wouldn't cry, he couldn't, she'd think he was a wuss. To keep the tears back, he scowled. "Where are the kids?"

"Inside."

"I want to see them."

"That's not a good idea, Wendell."

"I don't give a flying fart whether it's a good idea or not! They're my kids!"

"I know they are," she said. She turned to look over her shoulder at the gate, maybe to make sure the two Soldiers were still there, and he forced himself to lower his voice.

"They're my kids and I want to see them. Is that a crime?"

"You can see them, Wendell. When the divorce decree says."

"Once a month, with that social worker stuck to them like glue!"

She looked at him quietly, not smiling. She'd never been one for smiling much. "That's what the judge decided. You did a robbery, Wendell. And you hit me. And Penny."

"Once!"

"Twice."

"Saralinda . . ." His voice choked up and he tried again. "What I did was wrong. I know that now. I was drinking so hard, and I lost my job, and I was so confused about the Soldiers—"

"No confusion is necessary about the Soldiers," Saralinda said quietly, and he forced himself to let it go by because he couldn't afford to upset her, couldn't afford to get angry himself, this was too important.

"I was wrong. But I haven't had anything to drink for five months, I swear it. I go to A.A. every night, you can ask my sponsor, I'll give you his phone number. I'm different now. Saralinda . . . they're my kids. And you're—were—my wife. Saralinda—I want you back. I still love you, and I want us to be a family again."

There. He'd said it. Without anger or blame. He'd said it. He waited, his heart in his mouth.

She turned again to glance over her shoulder at the two men standing in the gateway, and it seemed to Wendell when she turned back that there was a little shine in her brown eyes. His breath caught and held.

She said, almost shyly, "You still love me?"

"God, yes! I can't tell you how much. And the kids, too."

"You stopped drinking?"

"I swear it, honey."

"You're working?"

"Andrews Construction Company outside Albany. Here, I got a pay stub right in my wallet, I can prove it to you—" He fumbled for his wallet. Saralinda stopped him, putting her small hand on his wrist. Her touch made a deep sweet flood open under his ribs.

"I believe you, Wendell. And you'd come back, to the Covenant? Be reinstated as a Soldier of Truth?"

He stared at her. She gazed back, and the shine in her eyes dulled like somebody wiped them with sandpaper. She took her hand away. "Oh. Oh. . . ."

"Saralinda . . . I can't come *back*."

"If the Elders held a special meeting—"

"I won't go back inside that fucking place! Not ever!"

"Don't talk that way about the Lord's work."

"The Lord's work! Memorizing Bible verses and praying to a dead saint and sacrificing woodchucks for the sins of the world and waiting for fucking Christ to come save us all—"

Saralinda turned to go.

"No, wait, I didn't mean that, don't go, Saralinda, you're my *wife*. . . ."

"No. Not anymore."

"And whose idea was that? I never wanted this divorce, I only wanted you and David and Penny and—"

"Then you shouldn't of broken Penny's arm."

"It was an accident! I swear to God it was an accident, I told you and *told* you but you fucking never listen to me! Not to me, just to those five dried-up so-called holy men with their fucking animal sacrifices to atone for the sins of the fucking world—"

" 'For the life of the flesh is in the blood: and I have given it to you upon—' "

"Don't quote Bible at me, I know it as well as you do, I fucking had to learn enough—"

" '—the altar, to make an atonement for your souls: for it—' "

"I said stop it, I'm warning you, Saralinda—"

" '—is the blood that maketh an atonement for the soul.' Leviticus 17:11."

"Stop it!" Wendell screamed, and it was exactly the same as it used to be, he felt like he was drinking again, even though he hadn't had a drop in five months. What he told her was no more than the goddamn truth. But she never listened, nobody ever listened to him, not even when he was right, and he *was* right about that dangerous stinking camp. It was unhealthy, it was fucking *unclean*—

"Good-bye, Wendell," Saralinda said.

"Don't you keep my kids from me, bitch! I'll get another lawyer."

She faced him. "We already did lawyers, Wendell. And they didn't change anything that really matters."

Wendell stared at her. His anger drained away again and the empty feeling followed, the way it always did, eventually. Sometimes, during the end of their marriage, he'd kept the anger going just so he wouldn't have to feel the empty feeling. It was so much fucking worse.

"Saralinda—don't go, don't go back inside, don't keep my kids away from me—"

"They have a good life inside. They have clean friends, and schooling that teaches them to live Godly lives, and a simple healthy diet without no blood. They learn about the lives of the holy men, Jesus and St. Cadoc and Père Cadaud and the rest. Penny and David are happy here, Wendell. You know that's true. They're both happy, and living without fear."

Fear of him, she meant. And because he couldn't bear that, he seized on what else she'd said. "Without blood, sure, how healthy is that, all vegetables and cheese so they don't make no mistake and swallow a drop of blood—"

"Acts 15:20—"

"Being taught that people can come back from the dead, fucking *ghosts*—"

"You know St. Cadoc was only raised as Père Cadaud because the New World needed a sign that—"

"And watching those old men sacrifice woodchucks and rabbits and—"

"You know children aren't allowed to watch—"

"And if something happens to them, you telling the hospital they can't even have a blood transfusion, it's better to let them die—"

"Acts 21:25—"

"*Die* rather than get a transfusion because five crazy starved old men decided that a transfusion is eating blood, so if *my* kids are lying there in a fucking hospital bleeding and hurting—"

"The only time they've been hurting in a hospital," Saralinda said, "is when *you* put Penny there."

There was a long silence.

"Saralinda," he finally said, and at his tone she took a step backward, "I been reading the *Cadillac Register*. The death notices. Another name I recognized from inside died two days ago. Are the Elders doing some kind of human sacrifice?"

Her eyes went wide. Then, for the first time, her small thin face broke up. "How dare you!" she spat at him. "You know better than that! You know the Soldiers revere human life! Mrs. Evanston died of a heart attack, and do you think her obituary would be in the newspaper otherwise? We've got used to the world being full of anti-Christs doing the devil's work and trying to smear the Truth with mud—but *you*, Wendell Botts, you know better! You!"

She turned to march away, and Wendell grabbed her. He caught her arm and started to drag her toward his truck. Saralinda screamed. He heard the real fear in her scream and it turned him sick inside. He was just about to let her go when the first of the two Soldiers clamped his neck from behind.

Wendell released Saralinda. His rage boiled into a tremendous bellow and he threw the guy over his shoulder. In a second all his Marine training was back and he'd delivered an expert kick to the fallen man's head and turned to take on the other one. But the kick never connected. The fallen man hit the ground rolling, got to his feet in one smooth fluid motion, and charged Wendell, and he knew immediately that his first throw had been blind luck, happening only because the guy hadn't been prepared. In thirty seconds Wendell lay bloody and gasping for air, puking out his guts on the ground, and the two men, undamaged, were hustling Saralinda through the gate and slamming it hard.

When he could see again, he eased himself off the ground. Nothing was broken. But he'd been whipped like a dog and that's how he crawled off, like a whipped dog, his blood in the dust. In front of Saralinda. Behind the wheel of the pickup he sat gasping a long time before he could drive away from the wire and the camp and the kids he hadn't got to see after all, and all he could think of was that he wanted a drink as bad as he'd ever wanted anything in his whole fucking life.

He was five miles down the highway before it occurred to him to wonder about something. The Soldiers of the Divine Covenant were peaceful, because three hundred years ago Père Cadaud had been a peaceful fucking wimp who let himself be tortured to death on this very spot by a bunch of Indians he was trying to convert. The Soldiers were supposed to live like Père Cadaud. They didn't believe in going to war or owning guns or taking life except in holy atonement.

So how come they had camp guards so good that one could take down a twenty-six-year-old ex-marine in superb shape without the guard's buddy even turning a hair to help?

He didn't have a drink.

It was a triumph, a fucking triumph, every time he didn't have a beer. That's what A.A. said. Maybe they were right. But it sure didn't feel like a triumph tonight.

Wendell sat in front of the TV in his motel apartment in Gloversville, nine miles from Cadillac. Outside, traffic honked and droned on Route 29A. Inside, all in one room, were a sagging bed, a sofa with loose springs, a TV on a metal stand, a coffee table with deep knife cuts, a dresser, and a combined sink-refrigerator-stove unit with no counter space. A toilet and mildewed shower had their own room. One hundred twelve dollars a week, because he was saving his pay for a nice two-bedroom apartment if Saralinda and the kids came home.

When Saralinda and the kids came home. He wasn't beat yet.

He sat on the bed, holding ice against his ribs where the bastard had kicked him. In twenty minutes he had to get up and drag himself to A.A.

They had sayings for everything, A.A. "Fake it to make it." "One day at a time." "I'm not okay and you're not okay but that's okay." "It takes what it takes." Which goddamn saying would they use for a guy going to a meeting with a broken rib?

Because broken or no, he was still going. This night and every night. He'd seen a counselor at Legal Aid in Albany, a place you could walk in and get one free counseling session to tell you what rights you had. The woman lawyer, a smart little Jew, told him that his best shot at regaining visitation was to "document." That meant he had to show a judge written records that he was working and sober and saving money, for at least six months straight. So he was going to A.A., tonight and every other fucking night. They wanted documentation, they'd get documentation. He had a drawerful of pay stubs and a bank book with bigger numbers every week and a perfect A.A. attendance record marked down in a little notebook by his sponsor, Lewis P., who was a fucking *court bailiff*. Let Saralinda and her Soldiers fight *that*.

He moved the ice pack and winced. Maybe he should see a doctor. No, he didn't have any health insurance and an office visit would cost maybe fifty bucks. That'd be fifty bucks less in the bank account to show the judge.

He had to get Saralinda and his kids back. He *had* to. Not just because his life was worth shit without them, either. For their sake. Even forgetting all that shit about Père Cadaud really being St. Cadoc raised from the dead. Even forgetting all that crazy ghost stuff. There was worse.

There were Bible verses that you could use to make human sacrifices sound all right. He could think of half a dozen verses himself, just sitting here, if you stretched meanings like the Elders did. And the ground underneath the Divine Covenant camp was honeycombed with limestone caves. Howe's Caverns, a big tourist attraction, was only fifteen miles away, on the other side of the Thruway. Branches and offshoots on the underground caves were all over this part of the state.

The Divine Covenant camp prepared some of their underground caves like bunkers, stocking them with food and beds and candles, for the great holy war of Armageddon that was supposed to turn up soon.

They could easily hold human sacrifices of blood atonement down there. Wendell had been down in those caves. They were cold, and dark, and they had tons of natural limestone. Break it up and shovel it over the bodies in some deep little offshoot tunnel, and nobody'd find them in a hundred years. So maybe Naomi Evanston had had an obituary and died in a hospital, all regular, but who else in the camp was missing? With defiled scum like him forbidden on holy ground, and the government calling it private property, who'd ever know?

And his kids were there. Inside. And Saralinda . . .

It takes what it takes.

He drank off the last of his club soda, gingerly buttoned his shirt over the bruised ribs, and went off to attend Alcoholics Anonymous.

Five

What the hell are you doing?" Felders said. "We don't pay you to do that."

Cavanaugh looked up from the pieces of coffeepot spread over the formica table. "Apparently we don't pay anybody else to do it either. Damn thing's broken. I've been working on it for twenty minutes."

"So get some coffee in the lounge. I know you'll drink anything anyway."

"That's not the point," Cavanaugh said patiently. "This coffeepot is just fourteen months old. Barely out of warranty. It *shouldn't* break down on me yet."

Felders grinned. "On you, personally?"

"Yes," Cavanaugh said. "I take it as a personal affront. For which, I might point out, there is good reason: I paid for it. This is my personal nonfunctioning coffeepot."

"Just like your personal nonfunctioning mobile and your personal nonfunctioning fax."

"No, those are sectional malfunctions, although not completely unrelated. Marty, it's this building. Bring a machine anywhere into the Federal Triangle—here *or* at Justice—and it's dead."

"No, Bob, its not the Federal Triangle—it's you. Machines just plain don't like you. I can't imagine why. You're so likable. Listen, grab some coffee in the lounge and come down to my office. We have something bigger than dead Mr. Coffees."

"Dead people?"

"No," Felders said. "At least, not yet."

A man waited in Felders's office. Younger even than Cavanaugh: twenty-five, twenty-seven. Expensive dark gray suit, rep tie, Ivy League haircut, a certain self-conscious precise look that Cavanaugh recognized instantly. A new Justice attorney, trying to look older and more important than he actually was. Hired after spring graduation, they bloomed in August, like ragweed.

"This is Assistant U.S. Attorney Jeremy Deming," Felders said. "Robert Cavanaugh."

The two men shook hands. Deming didn't smile. He said pompously, "Thank you for coming, Agent Cavanaugh. We have something very interesting to discuss with you."

"Yes, we *do*," Felders said.

Felders didn't like attorneys. That was, Cavanaugh thought, an odd trait for an FBI supervisor; most of Felders's superiors and some of his counterparts were attorneys. But Felders had come up a different career path: He was an ex-cop. He still looked like a certain kind of cop: wiry, feral, seldom motionless. Fingers tapped, foot jiggled, arm twitched. When he paced his office, talking rapid-fire to Cavanaugh about fake-tough lawyers who'd never busted down doors, he looked like a cartoon of a New York detective on double speed.

Felders assumed that Cavanaugh didn't like attorneys, either, maybe because Cavanaugh's career path had been even weirder: English major to corporate sales to the FBI. But Felders was right. Too many of Marcy's snobbish friends were attorneys. Cavanaugh, like Felders, preferred lawyers across the street, at Justice, trying cases after the Bureau had solved them. It was neater that way. Like Felders, he kept this opinion within the confines of Felders's office. Assistant U.S. Attorney Jeremy Deming looked like a good example of the reason why.

"Shoot," Cavanaugh said. He settled into Felders's padded visitors' chair, leaving the straight-backed one to Deming. Felders perched at the edge of his desk, foot tapping.

Deming passed Cavanaugh a folder. "This is the case initiation report on what we hope will eventually be an REI." He sounded as if he were announcing the Second Coming. "It contains both long-term strategic intelligence and more immediate investigative items. Maybe I should begin with some background, gentlemen. We're hoping that under Section 1962 of Title 18, United States Code—"

"I think we're all familiar with the RICO statutes," Felders said easily. Cavanaugh admired his restraint.

Deming said, "I thought Mr. Cavanaugh was fairly new to the section—"

"Mr. Cavanaugh has an extensive background in FBI strategy, plus years of the closest kind of investigative work."

"Sorry," Deming said perfunctorily.

Cavanaugh blinked. He'd had two years in Intelligence, the Bureau's single most boring section, and less than a year with the Criminal Investigative Division, much of it spent sitting in cars watching people go in and out of buildings. Routine surveillance. Felders must be really offended by this pompous young ass. But if this really *was* a chance to work on an REI . . .

A Racketeering Enterprise Investigation was their most effective tool against organized crime. In traditional cases, Justice prosecuted the Relatives one by one—this one for loan-sharking, this one for murder, this one for narcotics. Overall, it made no difference whatsoever. The convicted felon, often a foot soldier, went off to prison, *omertà* intact, and somebody else moved into that slot on the organizational chart. To go after the real power, the Relatives at the top, you needed the Racketeer Influenced and Corrupt Organization statutes. Under RICO, it was a separate, federal offense to even belong to an "enterprise" that was engaged in a "pattern" of racketeering. It let law enforcement go after organized groups that engaged in crimes for profit—even if the top members couldn't be directly linked to the specific crimes that made up the pattern. An REI needed authorization from the director, with written notice to the attorney general. It meant a commitment of money and manpower. It was big.

But Deming had only said he "hoped" this would become an REI. So what was it now?

"Deming, what exactly do we have here?" Cavanaugh asked.

"I'm trying to *tell* you. It's been my privilege to assist in preparing the case against Carl Lupica et. al., for which a grand jury returned a RICO indictment last week. You may have read about it in the papers."

No, Cavanaugh wanted to say, because Deming was such an asshole, but of course he had. The entire nation had read about it in the papers. Cavanaugh had Deming pegged now. Deming had been a legal go-for on the case, an utterly unimportant round peg the prosecuting team had used in easily identifiable round holes, and Deming knew it. It stung. He was trying to make himself feel better by throwing around his utterly negligible weight across the street from Justice. Cavanaugh wondered who Deming knew to have gotten his job, and how long he'd keep it.

More important, nobody at Justice would have trusted him with anything important. Which meant this "case" was either marginal, merely a routine check on peripheral data, or very preliminary. Cavanaugh hoped for preliminary. Maybe he could do something with preliminary.

He wanted a case of his own.

Deming continued, "The predicate acts of the Lupica enterprise included bribery, extortion, wire fraud, mail fraud, obstruction of justice, plus separate counts of money laundering and continuing criminal enterprise. Briefly, gentlemen, and at the risk of over-simplification, the defendants have been indicted in the Southern District of New York for misuse of the pension fund of the International Longshoremen's Association. In particular, the fund has allegedly been used to provide the ILA with secret ownership in real estate and in various legitimate businesses."

The guy talked as if he were writing a brief. Maybe he didn't know any other way to talk.

"As part of the investigation," Deming said, "Title III electronic surveillance was utilized, yielding over five hundred hours of taped conversation in both English and Italian. If you'll turn to page sixteen of the initial case report, you'll find one very brief section of the aggregate transcript. The speakers are Frank Cinelli and Mark 'Marco D.' Denisi. 'Northwood' refers to real estate since seized under criminal forfeiture."

Cavanaugh turned to page sixteen, which was a welcome contrast to Deming's diction:

CINELLI: All accounted for?

DENISI: Yeah, all of it.

CINELLI: And Jimmy delivered all right?

DENISI: I would of personally put his eyes out if he fucked up.

CINELLI: Yeah. All right. Did Lupica say anything to you about Northwood?

DENISI: It's all set.

CINELLI: What? All set? Already?

DENISI: They got it done fast.

CINELLI: What about that other thing? Verico?

DENISI: No, that's not on this deal.

CINELLI: It's not? Says who?

DENISI: Lupica.

CINELLI: It's separate?

DENISI: It's separate.

CINELLI: God damn it, nobody told me! I'm supposed to be told things like that! Especially when it's that important!

DENISI: Listen, a lot of people aren't getting told important things. Like with Jimmy last month. It's Mascaro. He's an asshole.

CINELLI: I'd like to fucking kill him. I should of been told.

"The focus here is the reference to Verico," Deming said. "As you can see, the transcript clearly establishes that it was not part of the same illegal use of funds as was Northwood, and thus has not been included in the criminal forfeiture proceedings. We don't have probable cause for a subpoena duces tecum, but both speakers use the word 'important' when referring to Verico. This, combined with a—"

Cavanaugh interrupted. "Will Cinelli talk more about Verico? Or will Denisi?"

"No, they—"

"Has either been given grand jury immunity?"

"They have," Deming said, offended. "Both flatly deny that they ever heard of Verico. They maintain that the tape was mistranscribed."

"To be expected," Felders said. "They have this odd preference for not ending up at the bottom of New York Harbor. I don't understand it. Do you understand it, Bob?"

"I don't understand it," Cavanaugh said.

Deming said frostily, "This transcript, combined with other intelligence I'll explicate in a moment, has attracted the attention of Justice's Organized Crime and Racketeering section. Pages one through fifteen contain known background on Verico, Incorporated. It allegedly is—"

"Why don't I have a crack at the summary," Felders said. He smiled at Deming, out of either exasperation or remorse. Cavanaugh couldn't tell which.

"Verico is a biotech company," Felders said to Cavanaugh, "two years old. Incorporated in Elizabeth, New Jersey. It's solely owned by one Joseph Kensington. Your basic eccentric multimillionaire. He inherited the money, which is all legit. Until a few weeks ago, when this report was prepared, anybody would have said Kensington was legit, too. Dissipated wastrel youth, drugs in the sixties, dropped out of Yale. Straightened out in his mid-thirties and settled into increasing the inherited fortune. An American success story."

"And then a few weeks ago..." Cavanaugh prompted. Felders liked audience participation.

"And then a few weeks ago we get the photograph on page seventeen, a picture of one Vincent DiPrima being admitted to Kensington's house on Long Island, by Kensington himself, on July 28 at three in the morning. We had an agent watching DiPrima, who was flying around the country making calls on people on behalf of the Relatives. One of the people he called on, so late at night, was Joseph Kensington. This seems very odd, what with Kensington being such an upright citizen and all."

"Odd indeed," Cavanaugh said.

"The info went into the computer, and came up a match with the Cinelli-Denisi reference to Verico. Justice requested a background check, including a tax check, which you have in your folder there. No, don't study it now. Five years ago Kensington's income tax returns reported loss after loss, from what the analyst says are amazingly stupid investments. In fact, she says you have to be almost trying to lose money to make investment choices that bad."

"Or else panicking because the money's running out."

"Bingo," Felders said. "Of course, he could have all kinds of extra stashed away in Swiss accounts or something. The fact that he lost a lot of money and then started two businesses within a year doesn't necessarily prove he had crooked help."

"Two? What's the other business?"

"A chain of Caddy dealerships. Honest as the day is long, and believe me, Justice checked. Kensington's making money by the Eldoradoful."

Deming winced. Cavanaugh gave himself the luxury of ignoring the attorney. "A car dealership and a biotech firm," he said thoughtfully. "Both businesses that take a lot of up-front capital."

"And Verico's losing money, which I'm told is par for the course for a biotech company for the first few years. They've filed for three patents, all on what I'm told are things with limited commercial potential. But the equipment and salaries and operating expenses are taking mucho cash. So where's it coming from?"

"From Vince DiPrima's Relatives?"

"There is as yet nothing to establish that link," Deming said primly. "But even though Justice lacked probable cause for electronic surveillance, and although we—"

"What *Justice* did do," Felders said, before Deming could wind up to deliver another subordinate clause, "was deepen the background check on the nine people employed at Verico. The list's on page twenty-seven. The analyst must have been some enterprising kid, eager to make his mark. He or she checked out everybody's gardeners, their wives' bridge clubs, whatever. See— there, at the bottom of page thirty. Dr. Eric Stevens, Verico's president, was once married to Mary Staller, née Falacci, whose sister Janice was once married to Frank Mascaro. The information is marked Top Priority."

"This is marked *top priority?*"

Felders grinned. "Like I said, the analyst's eager. You know these newly hired hotshots."

Deming shifted in his chair.

Cavanaugh thought a minute. "Still . . ."

"I know, I know. Contact has been made in more tenuous ways than that. It's just possible that Stevens, who knew Kensington at Yale—that's in the background report—was the means for one of the New York or Boston or Las Vegas families to offer Kensington financing in exchange for an impenetrably legitimate front. Frank Mascaro is part of the Gigliotti family; Mary Falacci's father has ties to the Callipare family. More significantly, Christopher Del Corvo, a lab assistant at Verico, is Stephen Gigliotti's nephew."

An ELSUR tape mention. A photograph. Out-of-pattern tax returns. Possible social and blood ties. "Pretty thin," Cavanaugh said. "What else have we got?"

Deming said, "Two additional items. First, Dr. Eric Stevens is living considerably more lavishly than his reported income would appear to justify. The Tax Division report is in the folder. They're holding off on an audit pending a decision about a RICO investigation. Second—"

"This is more our bailiwick, counselor," Felders said, too pleasantly. "Bob, look at page fifty-four. It's a letter addressed directly to Duffy."

Patrick Duffy, head of the FBI Criminal Investigative Division, had once been an attorney, but Felders respected him anyway. He'd been a good prosecutor and he was now a good division chief. Duffy didn't look like an attorney. He looked like a liquor-ad model, cool and elegant. He also believed in judicious economy. On the whole Cavanaugh admired this, except when it came to law enforcement equipment. He turned to page fifty-four.

There was no letterhead, salutation, or closing:

I apologize for my anonymity, but I am concerned for the safety of myself and my family. Nonetheless, I'm compelled to advise you of a serious, potentially dangerous situation unfolding at Verico, Inc., a commercial biotechnology firm in Elizabeth, NJ. The research at Verico is terrifying, and made more so by links to organized crime. An investigation into both research and staff should be an FBI top priority. Also, it would be enlightening to contact those whom Verico is currently trying to recruit. I understand that Dr. Benjamin Kozinski will be approached at the microbiology conference in Las Vegas.

"No fingerprints," Felders said. "Hewlett-Packard printer, standard CopyMaster sixteen-pound paper and

Mead envelope, postmarked Denver but could have been written anywhere in the United States. Addressed to Duffy, by name and correct title."

Cavanaugh said, "Not the wording of your standard-issue nut. A disgruntled employee?"

"Nobody's left Verico. In two years. But our scientific expert tells me that's not unusual at a biotech company. They hire carefully, pay well, keep their staffs small to cut down on communication errors. People stay."

"You already have a science advisor on this?"

"Breezed it past her. She's just that, an advisor, not an investigator."

"You said two final items. What's the other one?"

Felders began to pace, jingling the change in his pocket. Cavanaugh was used to this. Deming, from his expression, was not. Across the street at Justice, they were less peripatetic.

"Yesterday I asked an analyst to check airline tickets from the microbiology conference. Dr. Kozinski, who's a big cheese in genetic research at M.I.T., changed his reservations two days ago. Instead of going home to Boston with his wife, he flew into Newark, and then to Boston the next day. The Vegas-Newark trip was on the same flight as Dr. Eric Stevens. Adjoining seats. Your background information on Kozinski starts on page sixty-two. Solid-gold professional reputation, but apparently an arrogant sort. Not likely to give a second-rater like Stevens the time of day, under ordinary circumstances."

"I didn't know that!" Deming blurted, surprised into simplicity. Felders smiled at him.

Cavanaugh considered. It was a collection of circumstances, not really a case. Deming was hoping it would become something more because he wanted it to be more. So did Cavanaugh. He was tired of field surveillance. He wanted a case.

And this was the sort of "case" he'd have to start with. Even if it wasn't pleasant to be on the same level as Deming. Cavanaugh was already starting late. In a few months he'd turn thirty.

But he was—or would be—a good agent. He *knew* it. He knew what investigations took: a certain graceless, dogged persistence. Cavanaugh also knew that he possessed this quality because Marcy, his soon-to-be-formally-ex-wife, had told him so. Often.

"Jeremy, how interested is Justice in pursuing this?" Felders asked.

Deming looked Felders directly in the eye. "I have authorization to be here. Obviously."

Which told Cavanaugh nothing. Did Justice really believe this off-shoot of the year's most spectacular RICO case could become important in its own right, or was Justice just tying up loose ends? Deming couldn't tell him and Felders; Deming wouldn't know. But Duffy *had* approved the initial case report. Because the case was real, or as a political favor to somebody? That was the kind of thing an agent almost never found out.

Cavanaugh wanted this. He could taste how much he wanted it.

Felders smiled faintly. "Thank you, Jeremy. Agent Cavanaugh will take on this matter. Thank you again for your cooperation on the initial case report."

"You're welcome," Deming said, not even realizing he was being parodied. God, Felders was good.

When the attorney had left, Felders looked at Cavanaugh. "Well, it's yours. Scurry on down to Disbursement and pick up your vouchers. You better go on up to Boston and talk to Benjamin Kozinski."

"Yes," Cavanaugh said. "I'll get a late afternoon flight. I've got a lot of paperwork I didn't get done before I left for Vegas."

"This afternoon, good," Felders said. "Don't want to be too much the eager beaver. Then you'd have to end up in law school."

"Not funny."

"Sure it is. I can just see you, good old pessimistic Bob, complaining that the court stenographer's machine is broken."

"Marty—what do the Relatives want with a biotech company? That's way off their usual style."

"To put it mildly. I have no idea what they want with Verico. That's what you're going to find out."

"Thanks, Marty. For the chance."

The phone rang. Glad for this reprieve from gratitude, Felders seized it. He listened, and his smile faded.

"Right," Felders said, "okay," and hung up. He sat thinking deeply. Cavanaugh didn't interrupt.

"Listen, Bob, you'll have to leave right away after all. I'll have Carol call for tickets while you're on the way to Dulles, and page you there. The situation's changed."

Cavanaugh waited.

"Benjamin Kozinski's dead."

At the airport he headed straight for the gift shop, even before making sure of his tickets. There was a big rack of magazines, many more than the usual *Time* and *Playboy*. He leafed through *Scientific American:* nothing. Then through *Science Update:* nothing. Wasn't recombinant DNA supposed to be a hot topic? Why wasn't anybody covering it?

Then he remembered that this was Tuesday; the Tuesday *New York Times* included the *Science Times* section. He bought it, leafed through. He was in luck. A big article on gene therapy, written for scientific ignoramuses.

Next, the Quik Kopy. Usually they had fax machines. He'd tried the section fax, but of course it hadn't been fixed yet. Quik Kopy, designed to make money rather than spend it, kept their machines repaired.

"I'd like to fax this," he said to the teenage clerk, whose hairdo was wider than her shoulders.

She said doubtfully, "This?"

"Yes. That."

"Is this the area code?"

"Yes. It is. That's why I didn't write down a different area code."

"Only this *one* sheet?"

"One sheet," he said. "Inspiration is stingy." She didn't look at him as she loaded it into the machine.

He'd written the note on the plane from Vegas, in

purple ink on the back of a paper airlines-food-tray liner:

> *The highways and fields and rivers below make lines. He addresses the lines, salutes them, entreats them. He changes them. They become straighter, sharper, more orderly: direction transposed into virtue distance made grace.*
>
> *But after all, she is right. She has always been right. The altered lines lack something. He concentrates on them, willing them to deconverge and reassemble. Slowly, they do. They form a sparrow, whose head touches a cool river, whose wings palpate in questing flight.*
>
> *It is Euclid's sparrow, he thinks and realizes that such a bird deserves a grander geometry.*

The note whirred through the fax, on its stationary way to Marcy's office.

But it was all he could think of to do. And maybe it would help. Maybe Marcy would read it and recall how she had felt about him once, when such notes had been a regular part of their life together. Maybe.

"Two dollars, sir," the girl said. Cavanaugh paid her, and went to pick up his tickets for Boston.

On the plane he unfolded the *New York Times* and read the article on gene therapy. He read it slowly, backtracking when he didn't completely understand something, moving back and forth between the text and a helpful printed diagram.

Gene therapy didn't involve, as he had first naively supposed, altering the genes in a sick person's cells. The human body had too many cells for that—about ten thousand billion—and each cell had a hundred thousand genes. Instead, gene therapy was aimed at diseases in which the body wasn't making enough of some protein, or wasn't making the protein correctly, or wasn't making it at all. For diabetes, the proteins that control insulin manufacture didn't work right. For a disease called severe combined immunodeficiency, SCIDS, the body wasn't producing a protein called adenosine deaminase (ADA). You had to have that to fight off other illnesses.

Gene therapy apparently put new cells into your body that *could* make the missing proteins. These new cells were injected with a hypodermic needle, just like some medicines. Once inside, the new cells divided and reproduced, as well as immediately making whatever protein was needed.

The hard part of gene therapy, Cavanaugh gathered, was making these new cells. The scientists started with a virus. They removed part of the virus's own genes and substituted—"spliced in"—new genes that would direct the manufacture of the new protein. Part of the material they removed from the virus were the genes that would let the virus go on making its own proteins, most of which only poisoned the human body. Instead, the altered viruses—called "vectors"—could only act as delivery vehicles to get the desirable new genes spliced into the body's cells.

"A beverage, sir?" the flight attendant asked.

"Coffee, please." He wondered if coffee could be considered a vector to get caffeine into his cells. Probably not. He returned to the *Times* article.

So the vectors entered a patient's very cells, spliced the new genes right in with the person's old ones, and then the virus withered away. Every time the cell divided and reproduced, the new genes divided and reproduced right along with it. And all the copies of the new genes kept on making the missing protein, curing the disease.

Sort of, he thought, like frantically breeding terriers inside an infested barn. Pretty soon you didn't have any more rats.

So far, it only worked for a few diseases, for which scientists had been able to figure out where the right genes were, how to splice them into viruses, and whether the single protein they made would in fact cure the problem. Information on all these matters, Cavanaugh gathered, was still scarce. It was a new, experimental field, and by no means a sure thing. There were enormous questions, enormous unsolved problems, major setbacks occurring every day.

Uncertain at best.

Not, by itself, a lucrative or certain investment. Not yet. Maybe not ever.

And not the kind of thing the Relatives got into. Or was it? There was a new generation coming to power now, whom their elders tended to consider too Yuppie. More and more, the old men at the top imported illegal-alien great-nephews and fourth cousins from Sicily—"Zips"—who still respected the old ways. And who didn't have American rap sheets or fingerprints in NCIC. The younger American-born wiseguys laughed at the Zips, with their pointy patent-leather shoes and jackets worn over their shoulders. Was Verico a bid for diversification by some college-educated, designer-suited hotshot of forty who felt frozen out by the old men who still ran things? But it was still a weird choice for a target industry: too uncertain, too esoteric, too slow.

Cavanaugh sipped his coffee and read the article again, trying to see another angle, trying to discover what else this gene therapy could be used for. To poison a human body? Yes, of course, but anybody who wanted to do that could do it now, with considerably less trouble. Just inject whatever toxins the proteins made, instead of injecting altered cells. Or—simpler yet—just inject cyanide. There had to be something else.

He didn't find it.

The seatbelt sign flashed on. Cavanaugh folded his newspaper and prepared to land in Boston.

Six

By the time Cavanaugh reached the place Benjamin Kozinski had been killed, the body was already gone.

Cavanaugh had expected this. Kozinski had been killed in the parking lot of an all-night Stop 'n Shop on Route 135, between Natick, where he lived, and Boston. His skull had been bashed in with a hammer. He'd been killed at around 3:00 A.M. and the body dragged into some brush, where it had readily been spotted at first light, around 5:30. It was now past noon. The body was awaiting autopsy.

Cavanaugh learned all this at the Natick Police Station from Lieutenant Piperston, the detective assigned to the case, a very short, bald man with intelligent gray eyes. He had a faint accent that Cavanaugh couldn't place, a slightly formal phrasing. He studied Cavanaugh carefully.

Cavanaugh looked older than he was; that would help. But he was less experienced at street police work than Piperston would assume. Felders, the least tactful of mentors, had impressed on Cavanaugh that cops scorned bumblers who didn't happen to be their own bumblers. *If you're going to fuck up,* Felders said, *at least don't fuck up right after you meet somebody. Wait until later.*

"If you don't mind my saying so, Agent Cavanaugh," Piperston said, "this is not the kind of case Justice is usually concerned with. A man stops for cigarettes or whatever at a convenience store, some junkie knocks him on the head to steal his wallet—this is not the stuff of organized crime."

Cavanaugh ignored the invitation to provide information. "Was it cigarettes he'd stopped for? Did Kozinski smoke?"

"No." Piperston didn't seem put out by Cavanaugh's evasion. Good. He wasn't interested in a territorial struggle. "We don't know what he stopped for. He was killed before he went into the store."

"Could I see the initial reports?"

"They aren't written yet," Piperston said, without undertones. He seemed to lack the belligerence of many short men. "There hasn't yet been time." He went on studying Cavanaugh, as if the sheer penetration of his gray gaze would cause Cavanaugh to leak information. Probably, Cavanaugh thought, that worked for Piperston with a lot of people. The detective seemed good. That would help.

"When the reports are typed up, can I see them right away?"

"Certainly. The ident team collected evidence from all possible sources. The ground, Kozinski's car, clothing, the hammer—"

"The perp left the hammer?"

"Yes. He took Kozinski's wallet, left his keys and loose change. We're taking casts of every tire track within two blocks. Likewise footprints, although that doesn't look helpful—the weather has been dry here."

"Witnesses?"

"So far, none. Nobody saw it. The woman who found the body was just stopping in for morning coffee on her way to her factory job, as she has apparently done every day for fifteen years. She parked her car in the lot behind the store, next to Kozinski's Corvette. Everybody else stopping between 3:00 A.M. and 5:30 was just after cigarettes or beer and they just left their cars running out front while they dashed in."

Cavanaugh said, "Kozinski drove a Corvette? What color?"

"Red."

"Pretty flashy for a research scientist."

"It does seem an unusual choice," Piperston said, without expression.

"What was an important scientist doing on the road at 3:00 A.M.?"

"Apparently he often went into the lab to work at night. Although not usually so late. He'd had a nasty fight with his wife, stormed out of the house."

"You talked to her? You, personally?"

"Yes," Piperston said. "Would you like some coffee?"

"Thanks," Cavanaugh said. He watched Piperston pour coffee—from a fully functional Braun coffeemaker—into a thick white mug. Actually, he'd been surprised not to be offered coffee as soon as the introductions were over. Evidently Piperston held back this courtesy until he was sure he felt like offering it. Cavanaugh must have passed some kind of test.

The coffee was properly hot. Cavanaugh sipped it and immediately felt more confident. "What did Mrs. Kozinski say the fight was about?"

"Another woman. She'd gone through her husband's files while he was out of town interviewing for another job. Apparently he made the decision to interview in the other city without even consulting her, and she was angry enough to force a showdown on some long-standing hot topics. She found credit card receipts for motels, expensive lunches, flowers. The receipts were locked up, but she took a hammer to his file cabinets."

Another hammer.

"Not a temperate woman," Cavanaugh observed.

"Doesn't seem to be. Although," Piperston added,

"it's maybe not a fair time to judge. She was shocked and hysterical about his death."

Cavanaugh's respect for Piperston's judgment rose. He asked quietly, "Is Mrs. Kozinski a suspect?"

"Formally? Of course."

"But not seriously? Despite the hammer? Does she have an alibi?"

"No," Piperston said. "She could have followed him, I suppose. We're checking her car and clothing. But no, she's not a serious suspect at this time."

The way he said it, Cavanaugh knew it was an intuitive call on Piperston's part, and that Piperston trusted his own intuition. He said only, "Is there anything else I should know before I talk to her?"

Piperston didn't answer right away. He poured himself another mug of coffee and gestured toward Cavanaugh's mug. Cavanaugh shook his head. Piperston seemed to be considering whether he should say something in particular. Cavanaugh saw the moment he made his decision. "Are you Catholic, Agent Cavanaugh?"

The question surprised Cavanaugh. He shook his head. "Not much of anything, I guess."

"Like most people. Well, Judy Kozinski is. Or at least, she was raised one. In fact, her father is a noted lay scholar, the author of an important book on seventeenth-century heresy. I've followed his career very closely. Judy Kozinski would have had a particular kind of Irish Catholic middle-class girlhood: sheltered childhood, Catholic schools and colleges, intense idealism, orderly educated lives. I don't know what she believes now, but I do know that girls who grow up like that develop a strong sense of moral order. Usually they don't even know they have it. But they hold deep, hidden, fierce ideas about how the world is supposed to operate for people who play by the rules. When they find out it doesn't always work that way, they can go wild."

Cavanaugh didn't understand. "Are you saying," he said carefully, "that discovering her husband's infidelities may have made Mrs. Kozinski go wild enough to kill him?"

"No," Piperston said, and Cavanaugh saw that he'd made a mistake. Piperston had expected him to understand and Cavanaugh hadn't, and now Cavanaugh had fallen a notch in Piperston's estimation. "I'm not saying that at all. I'm saying that Judy Kozinski has had a terrible shock to her good-Catholic-girl view of the way the world works. It will affect her. I don't know why Justice is interested in this case, but if you're going to be watching Judy Kozinski, you should be aware of this."

Cavanaugh finished his coffee, thinking. Piperston went on leaning against the front of his desk, neither offering more information nor signaling that the interview was over. His intelligent gray eyes gave away nothing. Cavanaugh decided to take a risk.

"Are you Catholic, detective?"

"I'm Lithuanian," Piperston said, which told Cavanaugh nothing. However, he had the uneasy feeling it was supposed to tell him something and he was just missing it, so he didn't reply.

The rest of the interview was logistics. Cavanaugh arranged to have Piperston fax the initial reports to the local FBI office. Piperston agreed to not open Kozinski's file cabinets, brought in as evidence, until tomorrow, when Cavanaugh could be present. Then he drove to the Stop 'n Shop where Kozinski had been killed.

The ident team was still there, with local uniforms keeping away gawkers. An unhappy-looking couple who Cavanaugh guessed were the franchise owners sat at a weathered picnic table out front. They kept glancing at the CLOSED sign on the door.

Cavanaugh introduced himself and took a long look around. There was absolutely nothing to see. Bushes, asphalt, poorly maintained frame building, outline where the body had lain. Body, car, murder weapon, and everything else of remote interest had already been removed. The measuring was all finished, but the ident team was still taking blood and soil and leaf samples from every conceivable place, labeling everything carefully, hoping some of the blood or fibers or hair belonged to somebody else besides the victim. Cavanaugh already doubted that.

He'd analyzed dozens of reports of murder sites during his two years with Intelligence. Most had been the killing of somebody connected to the Relatives, probably by somebody else connected to the Relatives. This was different. This was the killing of somebody who did not count murder among his daily possibilities, who did not spend his life glancing over his shoulder or sitting in restaurants with his back to the wall. In Ben Kozinski's world, people assaulted ideas, not skulls.

He wondered what the scientist's last thoughts had been.

On the way back to Natick, Cavanaugh passed a small plaza with a bookstore. He stopped, turned around, drove back. The store stocked mostly best-sellers and diet books, but in the back was a small reference section. He found a two-volume desk encyclopedia and looked up "Lithuania." The third paragraph stated, "The majority of Lithuanians are Roman Catholics." The copyright date was 1983.

"Did you want to buy that, sir?" a clerk asked brightly.

"No," Cavanaugh said, and put the encyclopedia back on the shelf. He had an encyclopedia at home, bigger and newer than that one. Cavanaugh was offended by this dated reference work's still being for sale. Information, like machinery, should be kept in shape.

Back on the highway he considered carefully the information Piperston had given him, taking the words apart, examining each, the way he would a defective coffeepot. Religion had never mattered much to Cavanaugh. He didn't see why it should matter here. "Catholic moral order," whatever that was, didn't stop the Relatives from doing much of anything. And Irish Catholic politics right here in Boston didn't show much history of expecting the world to work in an orderly way, not without considerable unsavory behind-the-scenes oiling. Of course, Piperston had been careful to confine his remarks to "a particular kind of Irish Catholic girlhood." How would Piperston, a Lithuanian male, know? And what kind of Lithuanian name was "Piperston," anyway?

Still, there was something solid about the small detective. Cavanaugh carefully separated Piperston's information from Piperston's speculation, and filed each in a separate place in his mind.

Then he drove into the driveway of the woman who had attacked her husband's filing cabinets with a hammer, hours before the husband himself was attacked with another hammer. But who, Piperston insisted, was not a serious suspect.

Cavanaugh hoped Piperston was right. He'd just as soon hope that this lead to Verico wasn't a raving, maniacally jealous amateur murderer.

The house was nice but modest, a Georgian in a slightly shabby neighborhood. Kozinski apparently spent his money on other things besides real estate. Bright flowers bordered the walk. Cavanaugh didn't know much about flowers, although he could recognize marigolds and pansies, but he was struck by the colors. All orange and yellow. Somebody had chosen the plants for their colors, and the colors for their flashiness.

The door was opened by a heavyset woman who had been crying. She looked too old to be married to Kozinski, who'd only been forty-three. Cavanaugh decided she was either Kozinski's mother or his wife's mother.

"Hello, ma'am. I'm Robert Cavanaugh, investigating the death of Benjamin Kozinski." He flashed his badge, but as he'd hoped, she didn't look closely at it. He'd rather pick the time to tell Mrs. Kozinski he was a federal agent.

The older woman frowned. "But a detective was already . . . oh, all right. But try not to repeat any questions you don't absolutely have to. She's understandably upset."

A teacher, Cavanaugh guessed. Elementary or junior high. It was in the way she issued orders: firm but exaggeratedly reasonable. As if it were important to not only secure compliance but also demonstrate the virtues of reasonableness.

He followed her through a living room furnished with a long row of bookshelves, houseplants in hand-thrown pots, furniture with clean lines, wooden animals that looked like they'd been carved in more primitive countries. A sixtyish man sat on the sofa reading a book. To his right opened a hallway lined with doors, more bookshelves set between the doors. The only open door led to the bathroom.

"Judy?" The woman rapped on the door. "May we come in, dear? There's another police officer to see you." Cavanaugh heard no answer, but the mother opened the door.

He had braced himself for tears and hysteria. But Mrs. Kozinski sat quietly on a small sofa against the near wall of a home office. A handsome desk, teak or mahogany, and a huge brown leather chair dominated the room, taking up two-thirds of the floor space. Jammed into the rest was the sofa, some pine bookshelves, and a computer table. Two rectangles of squashed-down carpet showed where file cabinets had recently been removed.

Judy Kozinski, like her mother, was short and overweight. She had smooth dark hair cut in a short cap, hazel eyes, and a small upturned nose. Her eyes were red and swollen. She wore jeans, an oversized T-shirt, and an incongruous gold pendant shaped into two spirals set with colored stones.

There was no second chair, and Cavanaugh didn't like to pull Kozinski's huge leather chair around the desk. He sat at the far end of the sofa.

"I'm Robert Cavanaugh, Mrs. Kozinski. I know this is a bad time for you, but I'd just like—"

"No other time would be any better."

He thought about that and decided she was probably right. No time was going to be good for her for quite a while. "Can you tell me what happened? I know you already told Detective Piperston, but in case something was—"

"I was angry with Ben," she recited. Her voice was soft, muffled, and inert, like something dead wrapped in layers of cotton. Cavanaugh had the impression that just now she would do whatever she was told, and the further impression that this docility wouldn't last. This was the eye of the emotional storm.

"I was angry with Ben because he'd agreed to interview with an out-of-town biotech firm without even telling me. He—"

"And that firm was . . ." Cavanaugh prompted.

"Verico. In Elizabeth, New Jersey."

"How did your husband learn about the position at Verico?"

"He was approached by their acting head while we were at a microbiology conference in Las Vegas. He flew right to Newark from Vegas, after staying away from our hotel room all night. I think he was with a woman."

Her tone remained calm and muffled. Cavanaugh saw what this was going to cost her once that false calm passed, and he was shamefully glad that he wasn't going to be here when it did. He said gently, "And was he? With a woman?"

"I don't know. I never found out, at least not about that particular night. But after I flew home I went through his files and found out he'd been having an affair with his colleague and chief research assistant, Dr. Caroline Lampert. For at least two years, which is as long as Ben kept charge card records."

"And so you—"

"At least two years," Mrs. Kozinski said quietly. She picked up a sofa pillow and crushed it against her. "And I never suspected. Not Caroline."

"And so then you—"

"She isn't even pretty."

He waited. Her face stayed calm; all the upheavals were going on far below the surface. It was eerie to watch. He began, dimly, to see what Piperston had meant. This woman was profoundly shaken by more than just anger over an infidelity. Something in the tectonic plates of her personal ground had shifted.

"When Ben got home, I showed him the MasterCard receipts, the romantic cards she'd sent him, all of it. He couldn't deny it. He didn't try. In fact, he didn't even really listen to me. That's how unimportant this was to him."

Cavanaugh found he'd backed away from her, even though he was still sitting down. The sofa arm pressed hard into his side.

"He had just blown my life to bits, and he couldn't even take time to discuss it. He didn't even think it was worth getting angry about, and Ben always got angry when you criticized him. Always. It was the only thing that had slowed down his professional career: He got angry when you criticized him. Or sometimes even if you disagreed with him. His superiors didn't like that. His colleagues didn't, either."

She put down the sofa pillow, placing it carefully and precisely on the floor, as if it were a bomb that might go off. Her voice became even softer, more muffled.

"All he would say was, 'Judy, I've been through a lot in the last two days, I can't discuss this now.' Just that, over and over.. Without getting angry. 'Judy, I've been through a lot in the last two days, I can't discuss this now.' "

She fell silent. Cavanaugh said, "And you went on trying to discuss it . . ."

"I went on crying and yelling and pleading," she said calmly. "I was a crazy woman. I wasn't sane. Finally Ben left the house. He didn't even yell back. It just didn't matter enough to him."

Cavanaugh doubted that. He suspected that Kozinski had had something else on his mind, something so overwhelming that any domestic problem would take second place. But Cavanaugh didn't interrupt her.

"He went out to the garage and opened the door and started his Corvette and drove away. Here, come look at this."

She rose from the sofa and walked to a bookshelf. Cavanaugh was surprised at how small she was, no more than five-two. Seated, her weight had given her a more substantial feel. She returned with a map of Greater Boston.

"See? This was the route Ben took." It was marked in red Magic Marker: local roads to Route 135, 135 for several miles. The marker ended at the Stop 'n Shop. "His lab was here, in Cambridge. His last words to me were, 'I can't stand any more. I'm going to the lab.' But he wasn't driving to Whitehead. Not by this route."

Cavanaugh leaned over to study the map. She was right. Past Wellesley, Route 135 turned southeast, toward Boston but away from Cambridge.

"Ben was going somewhere else. Here, right by this intersection in Needham, is where Caroline Lampert lives. That's on the route he was taking. He was going to her house."

Cavanaugh studied the map. "Did you tell Lieutenant Piperston this?" He spoke as gently as he could. Her quiet despair was starting to affect him. The dead man's study felt stifling, even though the house was air-conditioned.

"No. I just figured it out about a half an hour ago. 'I can't stand any more. I'm going to the lab.' But he wasn't. When he couldn't stand me anymore, he went to her."

Cavanaugh stood. It was almost involuntary; suddenly he was on his feet. That bothered him, because he didn't like his body to do involuntary things. But she was going to erupt any minute now, and he didn't see anything to be gained by being here when she did. Just one more question.

"Mrs. Kozinski, do you have any idea who might have wanted to kill your husband? I know his wallet was taken, but on the outside chance it wasn't a simple robbery, do you know of anybody who might have had a reason to kill him?"

She looked up at him. Her hazel eyes were so clear and guileless that for a second Cavanaugh had the awful feeling he was tumbling into them. He couldn't imagine a worse fate. She said, "Only me."

He was startled. Suspects never said that. Inevitably,

they became indignant that they were suspects at all.

"Only me," she repeated, and now her voice was completely, almost preternaturally clear, each word carefully enunciated. "But I didn't. I couldn't have, because despite everything, I still loved him. Despite everything."

And Cavanaugh believed her.

He got out of there as fast as he could, before the storm broke.

Seven

Wendell Botts moved the dollhouse from the floor of his motel apartment to the coffee table. But up there it made the Fisher Price bulldozer look too small. He put the dollhouse back on the floor. When he moved it the second time, several pieces of miniature plastic furniture fell over. Wendell bit back his curse, lifted the dollhouse to the coffee table, and glanced at his watch. 1:56. They'd be here in four minutes.

He got down on the rug and reached inside the dollhouse, carefully righting the furniture. There was a green sofa of molded plastic, two blue chairs, and a blue coffee table. In the kitchen was a yellow molded table with four chairs, and in each of the two upstairs bedrooms a pink bed, purple dresser, and blue nightstand. The rest of the furniture was just painted on the cardboard walls: stove and fireplace and bookshelves and a grandfather clock. But the rugs in each room were real: bits of cloth Wendell had cut to fit. They hadn't come with the house. Neither had the doll family, which he'd had to go to three different stores to find. Wendell eyed them doubtfully. The mother and father dolls were half an inch too long for their plastic beds. Would Penny mind?

He was surer about the bulldozer. Strong bright plastic, and the bucket really lifted when you turned the shiny black steering wheel. The rubber tires went around, and the wooden peg-shaped driver smiled eternally at his loads of dirt. Wendell had filled a shallow box from the grocery store with sand and set it beside the coffee table. He'd even added some stones he'd found in the motel driveway. Davey could bulldoze to his heart's content.

Time: 1:59.

Should he have gotten chocolate cookies instead of peanut butter? David liked chocolate. But sometimes it gave Penny hives.

At 2:00 a knock sounded. Wendell, who'd been expecting it, jumped as if he'd been shot.

They came in slowly, David carried in the social worker's arms, Penny clinging to the hem of the woman's skirt. Despite himself, Wendell glanced out the door before he closed it. No one else waited in the car.

He'd bet that Saralinda hated the idea of the court-ordered social worker as much as he did, but for different reasons. "Unclean."

"David had a little nap in the car," Mrs. Weiss said, "so we might be a bit grumpy for a few minutes."

A few minutes. But all he had with them was two hours. . . . Couldn't the damn woman have kept David awake in the car? Wendell fought down his scowl. His palms were damp.

"Oh, that's all right. Come to Daddy, Davey boy . . ."

David buried his head in Mrs. Weiss's shoulder. He wore red rompers and tiny red sneakers. At least there were no Cs on his clothing.

"Penny, honey, come see what I got you! A doll-house!"

Penny looked at him without smiling. She wore a blue dress, and her brown hair, the same color as Saralinda's, was tied up in two ponytails high on her head. Wendell's heart pulled sideways. How much did she remember about him, about that awful night he'd been so drunk and . . . He was careful not to touch her. Let her get used to him first. Oh, God, if she remembered . . . He'd give anything to live that night over, make it come out different. Anything. Just that one night. . . .

Penny stared at the dollhouse, her hand still clutching Mrs. Weiss's skirt. She was four, wasn't that too old to hang onto strangers like that? If only the damn woman would go, give him a chance with his own kids. . . .

"Isn't that dollhouse pretty," Mrs. Weiss said. "I especially like the grandfather clock in the living room."

Penny glanced at her doubtfully, then moved closer to peer into the living room at the clock painted on the back wall. How, Wendell wondered, had the woman even known it was there?

"A clock keeps time, Penny," he said. God, he was an idiot. She *knew* that. Didn't she? What did a four-year-old know?

Penny said, "It says three o'clock."

Wendell was so grateful he almost cried. She'd said something. She'd said something about his clock. Quickly he knelt beside her and thrust an arm into the dollhouse. "See, there's a bookshelf, and a stove, and see, you can move the beds around anywhere you want. . . ."

"I don't want to move beds," Penny said. She stared at Wendell with flat eyes.

"Well, then, we won't! We'll just leave the beds where they are, Penny, honey!"

She didn't answer.

He felt the emptiness start, the cold terrible emptiness. A mistake. The dollhouse was a fucking mistake, like everything else in his life, every other worthless thing he'd ever touched. . . . He wanted to smash the fucking thing. Rip up the cardboard, mangle the cheap plastic furniture in his bare hands.

"Truck," David said. "Mine truck."

He pointed at the bulldozer. Wendell leaped up from the floor. He brushed the dollhouse and it shuddered. "That's right, Davey! That's your truck, Daddy got that truck for you! Come to Daddy and we'll make the truck go vroom vroom vroom—"

He reached for David. The two-year-old let go of Mrs. Weiss and went into his father's arms. Something sweet and warm flooded Wendell, and he turned so the social worker couldn't see his eyes.

He sat on the floor with David. "See, the truck can go, you push it like this, vroom vroom . . ."

"Vroom vroom," David said.

"And this goes up and down . . . what's that for, Davey boy?"

David looked at him doubtfully.

"It digs! It digs in the dirt! See, we have dirt right over here."

Wendell vroomed the bulldozer to the box of sand. David followed. Wendell showed him how to work the bucket to scoop sand and stones.

"David do it! David do it!"

"You're the best bulldozer driver in the county, Davey! You're the man!"

The child made the bulldozer go up and down. His whole rosy face shone. He laughed when the sand dumped outside the box onto the worn motel carpet.

Wendell glanced over at Penny. She was righting all the dollhouse furniture he had knocked over when he jumped up. Her thin face between the bobbing ponytails was serious, intent on getting each plastic chair directly under the wobbly yellow table.

Wendell squeezed his eyes shut. Before he knew it, the prayer was out.

Thank you, St. Cadoc.

After they left, Wendell sat on the floor, his back against the bed frame. Something metal pressed into his back, but he didn't move.

Two hours. Two fucking hours, and they were gone.

"That which is crooked cannot be made straight: and that which is wanting cannot be numbered."

Ecclesiastes some-fucking-number. One of Saralinda's favorites—she said it all the time. The worst thing about having been a Soldier was all the bits of Bible verse you couldn't get out of your head. They stuck like glue. Gummed up your thinking.

Just two fucking tiny hours.

He wanted a drink. He couldn't get up off the floor, and he wanted a drink. They were his kids, weren't they? Nobody should be able to take away his kids like that. He was sorry for what he'd done, he'd paid for it. Twice—by doing time, and by losing Saralinda. He'd paid, and they should at least give him his own kids for longer than two hours. What was he, some fucking child molester? Some murderer? He'd made mistakes, and he was sorry, and he wasn't making those mistakes any-more. He was trying. Even that bitch Mrs. Weiss, who wouldn't leave him alone with his own kids, had admit-ted he'd been trying. "This was a big improvement over last time, Mr. Botts."

A big improvement. Like she had the right to judge him. He was a good father now, he cared about Penny and David, and he had a right to be with them. They were *his*. Blood of his blood, bone of his bone.

David had taken the bulldozer home.

Penny had finally let him put the dolls to sleep in the plastic beds.

He wanted a drink.

To distract himself, he edged across the floor and turned on the TV. Four o'clock on Sunday afternoon, maybe there was pre-season football. But all he found were reruns of black-and-white movies, and a show with some guy explaining how to replace drywall.

But then he came across a news show. Wendell edged back to the bed and settled against a different spot, where no metal pressed into his spine. Somebody was interviewing a woman senator. The senator wore a red suit with a little gold scarf at the neck. Wendell snorted. You didn't see men senators strutting around wearing red and gold. They knew what was respectful for the United States Senate. "Suffer not a woman to teach, nor to have authority over a man." Paul. Oh, yeah, Wendell remembered that one. Too bad he hadn't recited it to Mrs. Weiss.

"And just what is it that disturbs you, Senator Doan, about the Supreme Court decision?"

The camera closed in on the senator. Wendell snorted again. God, he wanted a drink!

"If we allow public-funded institutions, such as schools, to be dictated to by religious groups, then we break down that important separation between Church and State. The founding fathers deemed that separation important because—"

Same old blather. Wendell considered turning it off, but he was too tired to move again. Kids wore you out. No, it wasn't that, it was that he hadn't slept very well last night. Too nervous about today. And last night's A.A. meeting, that old fart spinning on and on about how he couldn't have turned his life around without the help of a Higher Power. . . . That was the worst of A.A. All the talk about a Higher Power. If those guys saw what a Higher Power did in the Divine Covenant camp, taking a man's kids away from him and turning his wife against him just because he no longer believed a dead saint got raised a thousand years later just so he could die again to fulfill a holy covenant. . . . It was the Divine Covenant that was all to blame here. If it wasn't for them, Saralinda would come back to him. She didn't have the guts to hold out against him all by herself. She would come back, and Wendell would have his kids all the time, the way a father should, not just two hours every other Sunday with a fucking social worker there watching every minute. It was the Covenant's fault.

"—disturbed by the continued seepage into public life of religious beliefs that encourage intolerance of others. Those that believe theirs is the only true way to worship are certainly entitled to believe that, but not to impose, however subtly—"

What the hell did she know about intolerance, in her red suit and stupid gold scarf? Intolerance was not being allowed to be a daddy to your kids, because—unlike a fucking saint—you once made a mistake. And he would never have hit Penny if he hadn't been drinking so hard, and he would never have been drinking so hard if the Divine Covenant hadn't been driving him crazy with their rules and their Bible verses and their animal sacrifices to wash away the sins of the believers.

"—certain that the majority of religious believers recognize the dividing line between Church and State. But those who do not, or will not, put us all at risk of—"

Risk. That bitch didn't know what risk *was*. He, Wendell Botts—he'd taken more risks than any lady senator could ever dream of. He'd risked his fucking sanity in the Divine Covenant camp, and he'd beaten the odds and come out sane and sober.

But Penny and David were still in there. Instead of with their daddy.

The interview ended, and the news show jumped to a fire in some Texas oilfield. Wendell punched off the TV.

He had postcards. He'd bought them in prison, to send the kids when he found it too hard to fill up a whole letter with writing. The postcards had pictures of zoo animals on one side and room for the address on half of the other side, which only left half a side to think up things to say. Well, what had been good enough for Penny and David was good enough for lady senator Jill Doan. He picked a postcard with a giraffe eating leaves off a tall tree.

> Dear Senator Doan, I saw you on TV talking about the danger of religion to the US of A. You don't know half the story. There's a Soldiers of the Divine Covenant camp in Cadillac, New York. It practices animal sacrifice. I think it practices human sacrifice too. Congress should look at that because there are kids in there including mine. This sacrifice is true even tho I can't prove it.

He ran out of room. There was just enough space at the bottom to squeeze in his name. Did he want to sign it?

No. The whole fucking government was tied together

by computers. The senator might tell the people who controlled child custody, and who knew what they would do? They might take away his two Sundays a month with Penny and David. Better not let his name get into anybody's computer.

In the remaining space he printed, in capital letters, YET. *I can't prove it YET.*

The postcard made him feel better. He was doing something, not just sitting around on his ass waiting for that bitch of a social worker to report that he'd been a good boy. He was a taxpayer, he was a voter, he would damn well get the government on his side for a change, investigating what went on at the Covenant camp. In fact, he had a lot of postcards. He'd just write to the president. His congressman. The FBI. The attorney general. Why not? It might help. And it would give him something to do to fill in the time until he could go to the A.A. meeting at 7:00.

He chose a postcard of an elephant squirting water from its trunk. *Dear Mr. President . . .*

Eight

The pendant was heavy, heavier than it looked. Even the chain was heavy, thick gold links that had felt pleasantly substantial around her neck. At the bottom of the chain the double helix hung gravid: two intertwined strands of weighty gold, one set with tiny sapphires and the other with tiny rubies.

Judy Kozinski, fully dressed, sat on her bed and stared at the pendant dangling from her fingers. She had been sitting in the same position for twenty minutes. It was four o'clock in the morning.

"What is it?" her mother had said.

"A double helix. A wedding present from Ben. He just gave it to me."

"What's a double helix?"

In the half-light from the hallway the gold pendant gleamed dully. The bedspread on the wide, king-sized bed was undisturbed. She hadn't been to sleep, hadn't even been able to lie flat. On the Queen Anne chest with the elaborately carved legs lay Ben's hairbrush, deodorant, cologne. He'd liked elaborate furniture. He thought it looked rich. It had taken careful managing for Judy to keep up with the credit-card payments.

"What's a double helix?"

"Oh, Mother, everybody knows what a double helix is! The shape genetic material has in your cells!"

"For a wedding present?"

The sliding door to the closet stood open. In the cave-like gloom Judy could just make out the shape of Ben's suits: empty sleeves and dangling pants, 40 long. Earlier she'd gone through all the pockets. The shoes were lined up underneath, wing tips and Docksiders and Gucci loafers. She couldn't actually see them, but she knew they were there.

There had been nothing in any of Ben's pockets. Not so much as a forgotten scrap of paper.

The police had taken his file cabinets and the contents of his desk drawers.

There was nothing between the pages of his books: not a picture, not letters.

"For a wedding present?"

"I think it's a wonderful wedding present! He's a scientist, after all!"

"But, honey, you're not a scientist. You're a bride."

Judy slipped off the bed. Her foot had gone to sleep and she staggered, caught herself by grabbing a bed post. Her legs trembled. She hadn't eaten anything for two days.

Slowly she wobbled toward the door, avoiding the mirror. Two steps creaked. Downstairs, she put on her sneakers. The front door clicked loudly behind her.

Outside it was still fully dark, and cool. Dew clung to the grass. She shivered, but didn't go back for a sweater. Her mother would hear, or her father. As it was, they'd probably hear the car start. The police had returned Ben's Corvette. It sat in the driveway, while her Toyota and her parents' Ford were in the garage. She didn't want to have to open the garage door.

The red leather felt cold under the worn seat of her jeans. It surprised her, a little. Ben had sat here every day, drove the car, pressed his body into the leather. It

should be warm from him. Something should be warm
from him.

She was so cold.

The car leaped forward at her first touch on the gas;
she wasn't used to power steering. Her hands shook on
the steering wheel. She made herself slow down, drive
carefully, not get stopped. She was three blocks from
home before she realized that the pendant was still in
her right hand, dangling from the steering wheel, slap-
ping heavily against her thigh.

"But, honey, you're not a scientist. You're a bride."

*"So what should he give me? Some clichéd heart? With
an arrow in it?"*

"Please don't be angry. I wasn't criticizing Ben's gift."

She drove east on Route 135 because it was the only
route she knew. When she passed the Stop 'n Shop, she
turned her head away. The Corvette swung sharply
right, onto the shoulder. She yanked it back and got
steady on the road again and by that time the Stop 'n
Shop was past. Her neck prickled. There was a curious
tightness around her skull, not exactly physical pain, but
the promise of pain.

At Needham she turned north off Route 135. It was
getting light now, the first pale stain in the east, not yet
any identifiable color. She pulled into the driveway of
the townhouse complex and opened the car door. Again
her legs almost gave way. She leaned against the Corvette, breathing hard.

There were flowers in the front yard, close against the
townhouse. Yellow marigolds, yellow chrysanthemums,
orange trumpet lilies on tall stalks. Judy stared at the
flowers until they blurred into one bright smear.

She leaned on the doorbell hard enough to hurt her
finger.

It took a long time for Caroline Lampert to come to
the door. When she did, her eyes widened.

Judy said, without preamble, "Did my husband plant
those flowers with you?"

"What?"

"You heard me. Those are the colors my husband always planted. Did he plant those flowers with you? Because if he did . . ."

Something surfaced in Caroline's eyes, raw and painful. She stood a foot taller than Judy, slim but with no curves, like a rangy boy. She wore a faded green terrycloth bathrobe. She said uncertainly, "Judy, it's four-thirty in the morning. . . ."

"Not an appropriate time to call? But it was an appropriate time for my husband to visit you, wasn't it?"

Caroline put her hand over her eyes. The theatrical gesture filled Judy with contempt, and the contempt strengthened her legs so they didn't tremble.

"You thought I wouldn't suspect, didn't you? Plain reliable Caroline Lampert, the perfect research assistant, always there for any drudgework necessary, good old Judy would never suspect Caroline—"

"Don't," Caroline whispered.

"Don't what? He was my *husband!* And you know what, you were right, I didn't suspect, not you, not Caroline, bringing her famous dried-tomato pesto to parties and running lab columns late at night so we could go away for the weekend and always . . . how could you, how *could* you—"

She was shouting. A light came on next door.

Caroline sobbed, "I loved him, too."

"Love?" Judy screamed. "*Love?* You call that love, sneaking around to fuck on lab tables, taking somebody else's husband—or isn't that supposed to matter anymore? No, it's not, adultery is natural—now it's no big deal—it's smart and sophisticated, but not for me! Do you hear me, Caroline? We're not that kind of people, Ben and me, we believe in more than that, we chose to be married—"

A light came on in the townhouse on the other side. Behind Judy a car pulled into the driveway. Judy went on screaming, her fists balled at her side, tears streaming down her face.

"We're different than that, do you hear me? Ben and I believe in something, we believe in our marriage, it's not perfect but it's real and then for some bitch like you to just . . . what am I doing?"

Caroline sobbed hard, head in her hands. The belt of her robe had loosened. Under it, her nightgown was faded flannel. A door opened, slammed. Judy could barely see. Waves of blackness passed over her, the worst kind of vertigo, like motion sickness that goes on and on without the relief of vomiting. She reached for something to hold onto, but the porch, just a covered stoop, had no posts. Her hand hit Caroline's shoulder. A figure started across the driveway from the townhouse next door.

"Judy," someone said quietly.

"Caroline, do you need help?" a male voice asked.

"Go away," Caroline sobbed at Judy. "Just go away, leave me alone. . . ."

Clearly and calmly, more clearly than she had said anything else, Judy said, "I don't do this."

"Just go away!"

"Miss, I don't know who you are, but I think you better leave—"

"I don't do this," Judy repeated, in the same calm, clear voice. In the cold air the words rang a little. Her vision cleared. She looked at Caroline, who had crumpled, sobbing, against a strange tall man. Where had that man come from? "I'm not the kind of person who does this."

"Judy," a voice said behind her. She turned. Her father stood there, his eyes sad.

"Whoever you are," the tall man said, "for God's sake, get this crazy woman out of here. My neighbor's had enough shock already this week. Her boss was killed in a robbery, and now this!"

Judy ignored the tall man. She ignored her father, too. She went on looking at Caroline, who was sobbing uncontrollably. More lights came on down the row of townhouses.

"I'm sorry," Judy said quietly.

"N-n-no, I'm sorry. I'm so sorry," Caroline sobbed. Judy frowned. The words didn't make sense. She was the one who had come here, who had come to say . . . what? To accomplish what? There had been something. . . . Suddenly her legs gave way and she nearly staggered.

Her father put an arm around her. "Come on, baby."

She pulled away a little, despite the trembling legs, to face him. "I don't do this."

"I know you don't, baby. You're not yourself just now. Come on with me."

"I'm sorry," Judy said again to the sobbing Caroline. The tall man scowled at her. Judy let herself be led away.

On the front seat of her father's Ford, she started to shiver. He turned up the heat, but it didn't help. She was shivering down to her bones, down to her marrow. Her fingers were like ice. Only the ice was in them, was something she was holding, something cold and solid. A double helix on a chain.

"Please don't be angry. I wasn't criticizing Ben's gift."

"Then what the hell were you doing, Mother?"

"I was just wishing he'd chosen something related to you instead of to himself. That's all."

"That's all," Judy said. Her father glanced over at her. They were pulling into the driveway of her and Ben's house in Natick. How had they got there? She couldn't remember the drive home. Where was Ben's Corvette? Did the police still have it?

Her father's lips moved. He was praying, she suddenly knew. For her.

"Daddy—"

"What is it, baby?"

She couldn't speak.

"Judy?"

"Daddy, I don't think I'm all the way sane right now."

He parked the car, got out. When she didn't move he went over to her side, opened the door, and lifted her to her feet. His body was warm. She clung to him, his old wool shirt scratching her cheek.

"I think," he said gently, "that you should come to Troy to stay with your mother and me. Just for a few weeks, baby. Until you're yourself again."

Judy didn't answer. She just clung to his shirt, and felt her hair stir on her forehead where his lips moved in silent prayer for her. She didn't know if she wanted to go to Troy or not. She didn't know anything. Ben was dead, and he'd been unfaithful to her, and she loved him so much she was going to die, except that death only came when you didn't want it, not when you did. She knew that now. A light went on in the house, and her father led her inside, gently, as if she would break, Ben's double helix clutched in her hand, heavy and cold.

Nine

In his Washington apartment, Cavanaugh woke with a cold. His head ached, his nose felt stuffy, and his throat closed even before there was anything for it to close around.

"Shit," he said aloud, giving his throat a syllable to strangle. Of all minor diseases, he hated a cold the worst. You weren't sick enough to stay in bed and you weren't well enough to do a full day's work. You ended up sniffling your way through a pallid imitation of work, just another malfunctioning machine. It was inefficient. It was a waste of the taxpayer's money. It was an indignity that it happened to him.

"You're mortal, too," Marcy used to say to him, not jokingly. "Just like the rest of us, Robert. Even if you actually think you might die for our sins."

"Not yours," he'd always answered patiently. The patience hadn't helped.

Well, he wasn't going to give in to a stupid cold. He dragged himself into the bathroom, coughing and sneezing. He showered and tried to shave. His electric shaver buzzed, gave a sharp burst of static, and stopped working.

Cavanaugh stared at it balefully. This one was only two years and four months. He had the warranty, knew exactly where it was in his warranty-and-instructions drawer. This time he was following through: writing the company, demanding a refund, letting them know just how shoddy their product was. It was a disgrace. The entire manufacturing sector was falling apart.

Standing at the mirror in his underwear, coughing and hacking, he began shaving with a Gillette disposable. Which was damn well what he'd be using from now on. The phone rang. Felders, most likely. Mentoring had its price—the man was a one-person alarm-clock company. Cavanaugh walked back to the bedroom, half his face covered with foam, and picked up the phone.

"Hello?"

"Robert? You sound terrible."

Marcy. Abruptly Cavanaugh sat down on the edge of the bed. "I just have a cold."

"Sounds more like double pneumonia. Have you seen a doctor?"

"Not yet." Marcy believed in doctors. Cavanaugh did, too, in theory, but he never visited one. "But I will, if you recommend it."

"Sure you will. Since when do you listen to anything I recommend? Robert, I'm calling about these notes."

"The notes," he got out, and covered the receiver to sneeze. He'd faxed her three more in the past week, the last one just last night. It had been a drawing of a voluptuous, scantily clad Marcy arranging a rabbit on her head, with the caption MARCIA CHANGES HER HARE STYLE.

"The notes. Robert, please stop."

"Why?"

"*Why?*"

"Yes, why?"

"You're the only man I know who would ask that. Anybody else would *know* why. Because we're divorced. Because I no longer love you. Because it's painful to

receive notes in the same style as when I did love you.
And because it's embarrassing for the office fax to publicly receive a picture of the VP for Marketing dressed
in a bikini and wearing a rabbit on her head.''

"Why do you no longer love me?" Cavanaugh asked.
His head felt like soggy wool.

"Please, Robert, no dogged questioning today. No
tracking down facts to package in neat efficient bundles.
And no more notes."

Cavanaugh sneezed. Foam splattered over the floor.
His eyes watered. When he could see again, he said, "I
won't fax any more notes to your office."

Marcy's voice scaled upward. "Or anyplace else! No
letters, no faxes, no e-mail! Give up! For once in your
life, give up!"

"It's harder to do drawings with e-mail," Cavanaugh
said, and hung up on her before he promised anything
else. He could live with no faxes to her office. That
wasn't much.

He took the phone off the hook so she couldn't call
back. Then he sat on the edge of the bed staring at it,
half-shaven and sneezing, for ten minutes before he finished getting dressed.

"Listen," Felders said, sticking his head around the corner of Cavanaugh's cubicle, "you have a two o'clock appointment with the science advisor at NIH. Her name is
Dr. Julia Garvey. She's finished with Kozinski's files."

"Okay," Cavanaugh said. "Two o'clock."

"You sound terrible. Are you contagious?"

"Yes."

"Well, see a doctor. And don't breath on me." Felders's head disappeared.

Cavanaugh went back to the papers stacked in orderly
blocks on his desk, preparing to read them again, just in
case he'd missed something. Although he didn't think
he had.

The first stack was from the Natick police. The autopsy showed that Dr. Benjamin Kozinski had died of
subdural hemorrhage following three blows to the head

with a hammer. Based on incomplete rigor mortis, stomach contents, and insect activity at the time the body was discovered, Kozinski had died between 3:00 A.M. and 4:00 A.M. The death was ruled a homicide.

No surprise there.

Judging from the angle of the blows, the killer had been about five foot ten. From the force of the blows, the killer was probably, although not conclusively, male.

Not short Judy Kozinski in a jealous rage. Not unless she stood on a ladder in the middle of the Stop 'n Shop parking lot.

The crime-lab report stated that there were no fingerprints on the murder weapon, and no prints except Kozinski's inside his Corvette. In fact, there were no prints anywhere—not on any patch of ground, not on the body, not on debris in the bushes where the killer might have lurked waiting for a victim. There were no footprints from shoes or boots to check against the computerized data file. There was no foreign matter under Kozinski's nails. Hair was found on his clothing—in fact, three different strand types. But all were female. Fibers found on Kozinski's body and in the bushes were all cotton denim, of a kind used in clothing sold everywhere, to everyone. Kozinski's wallet had not been recovered. There were at present no leads and no suspects.

There were two possibilities, Cavanaugh thought. One was that Kozinski had been killed by a deft or lucky amateur, or maybe a semipro hired by a jealous girlfriend or outraged husband or unpaid plumber or whatever. In which case the Bureau wasn't interested. Piperston could solve the murder—or not solve it—and Cavanaugh was out a case.

The other possibility was that Kozinski *had* been killed by a professional belonging to, or hired by, the Relatives. If so, the wallet would never be recovered. The fibers would lead nowhere. And Cavanaugh might have a racketeering enterprise investigation.

So, for the sake of a working hypothesis, assume the killer was a pro.

Cavanaugh stepped out of his office to the glass-partitioned area where the analysts worked. He was in luck; Jim Neymeier sat hunched over his computer keyboard, looking like a thin curved plant yearning toward a technological sun. Cavanaugh liked to work with Neymeier whenever he could. Neymeier was new, but he was thorough and careful, and he didn't twit Cavanaugh about his background in English literature.

"Jim. I need something."

"Yo," Neymeier said. He communicated in brief, expressive syllables, and Cavanaugh liked that, too. While working, Neymeier confined himself to the essentials. But he wasn't juiceless. He cared.

"Check up on whatever we know about the movements of whatever professionals we think we've identified." Neymeier grinned; he shared Cavanaugh's skepticism about their ability to actually track a good professional. Not if the professional was really good. "Cross-file the dailies to find out who might have been in Boston on August 11, and who they might have been working for if they were."

"You got it."

Cavanaugh went back to his cubicle, blew his nose, and thought some more.

Whoever had written that anonymous note to Duffy instructing the Bureau to investigate Verico, had known that the biotech company had approached Benjamin Kozinski. That pointed to an insider: inside Verico, or inside the Relatives, or inside Kozinski's personal life, or maybe just inside the world of microbiology. Who?

Reason it out. Anonymous notes were usually based on either fear or revenge. It wasn't completely unknown for members of one crime family to alert the law to the activities of another family—but it was pretty damn rare. *Omertà.* And, more practically, retaliation. They were all more afraid of each other than of the Bureau.

So maybe the note came from somebody inside Verico but not connected to the Relatives. Cavanaugh consulted the staff list. Six names. Dr. Paul d'Amboise, scientist. Joseph Doyle Bartlett and Miriam Ruth Kirchner, research assistants. Karlee Pursel, Elliot Messenger,

Nicholas Landeau, lab technicians. Maybe one of them realized what was going on—the "terrifying research" of the note—and got scared. Scared enough to hope somebody would step in and ask questions. Which Cavanaugh was going to do, but not just yet. He didn't want Stevens moving records, destroying evidence.

What evidence? All he had so far was speculation.

All right, then, go on speculating.

Suppose the letter writer wasn't at Verico, but was someone in the world of microbiology. Then how did he or she know about the "terrifying research" at Verico?

Because they'd seen it. As—maybe—Benjamin Kozinski had.

Kozinski had come back from Verico very upset, even before his wife added her anger about his infidelity. Upset enough so that he didn't get mad when she attacked him. And Kozinski always got mad when somebody attacked him; Mrs. Kozinski had been right about that. Everyone else Cavanaugh had talked to had agreed, even Kozinski's lover, Caroline Lampert. She'd agreed reluctantly, but she had agreed. Kozinski had a short fuse for criticism.

Except for the night he was killed. Because he had been too scared to have any energy left over for anger?

Cavanaugh blew his nose, and stared at the piles of papers on his desk. Police reports, autopsy report, background reports on everybody, financial reports on Verico, surveillance reports, supplemental reports, interview reports, report reports. And none of it with the information he really wanted. Nothing that would establish Verico under RICO as a "vehicle used to perpetuate a pattern of crimes."

Well, then, if all you had was a hypothesis, go with the hypothesis. Somebody else, as scared as Kozinski, wrote that letter to Duffy—and wrote it before Kozinski interviewed at Verico. Somebody who'd also interviewed at Verico and who was their first choice for brilliant scientist. Somebody who was probably at a university or government lab because the salaries were lower than the new biotech companies were paying, and the somebody could be tempted by an astronomical salary and great perks. Somebody competent to run a risky and somehow—how?—terrifying genetic research project, which probably meant somebody already receiving data from the Human Genome Project funded by the federal government.

Cavanaugh sniffled his way back to the analysts' area. "Jim, something else. Get me a list of everybody connected with every university or government lab that receives money from the National Institute of Health for anything connected with genetic research."

Neymeier said, startled, "Everybody?"

"Too many, huh? Okay, then, not technicians. Just scientists with a Ph.D. after their name. Then crosscheck that against airline reservations to see who might have flown into Newark, New Jersey, between July 1 and August 10."

"Not soon," Neymeier said dubiously.

"As soon as you can. It's important."

"Yo," Neymeier said. He turned back toward his terminal as if toward a magnet. Cavanaugh shook his head slightly. That kind of attraction. For a *machine*.

He returned to his desk, and his hypothesis.

Verico's first-choice interviewee had said no. No thanks, I don't want the job, I'm happy where I am. So Verico asked Kozinski. And they told him something that terrified him right out of his usual narcissistic preoccupation with his own perfection and right out of his usual narcissistic anger whenever that perfection was attacked. Something really terrifying.

But why hadn't Verico told this terrifying thing to the other scientist they'd interviewed first?

They had told him. Or her; it was important to remember it might be a her. That's why he/she had turned the job down and written to the FBI.

Why hadn't he/she signed his/her name?

Shit, that was easy. This was the Relatives, after all. They'd scared their interviewee into silence. But this scientist was also ethical, and he stewed about it a while, and then he decided to risk an anonymous note to Justice, to salve his conscience. It was surprising how many people did that. Some days Justice looked like the thick "Anonymous" section of the *Oxford Book of English Poetry*.

But if all this conjecture was true, then why hadn't the Relatives also killed the first interviewee, as they had Kozinski?

Because they had a better hold over the first one. The first interviewee was more solid, less flamboyant than Kozinski. He/she had more to protect. And just to be sure, the Relatives had followed First Interviewee around for a while, the way they'd been following Kozinski after his trip to Verico. They'd tapped First Interviewee's phones. They'd let him know he was being watched. And First Interviewee had been careful not to do anything or go anyplace that the Relatives interpreted as threatening.

But Kozinski had. He'd left the house at 3:00 A.M. and he wasn't taking the route to his lab at Whitehead Institute. He wasn't behaving solidly. He was going someplace unpredictable, to talk to someone unknown, and the Relatives didn't like unpredictable and unknown. They often eliminated unpredictable/unknown, for safety's sake. They knew Judy Kozinski hadn't been told anything by her husband because the Kozinski house had undoubtedly been bugged, and the bug removed before the cops arrived. But Kozinski had been fleeing along Route 135, which was the route to his mistress's house but was also the route to the state troopers, as Cavanaugh had clearly seen on the map Judy Kozinski had shown him. It was possible Kozinski had been on his way to talk to the cops when he'd been killed.

First Interviewee, on the other hand, had presumably behaved in quiet ways that had not alarmed the Relatives' professionally and so was still walking around somewhere, terrified into almost-complete-silence by some very persuasive threat.

Cavanaugh went a third time to the analyst's area. Neymeier still yearned toward his computer.

"Jim, add another variable to that search of scientists.

Give me data on who has kids. Ages, schools, whatever. You probably can't find out how much their daddies and mommies love the kiddies, but give me anything that indicates strong family ties."

Neymeier stared at him. Cavanaugh felt like a fool. It was this damned cold; nobody could think with a cold. Neymeier said, "Find out how much *love?* In data banks?"

"Do whatever you can," Cavanaugh said. He retreated to his office. The tissue box was empty. His nose dribbled. He searched around for another box of Kleenex, which he didn't find, while the dribbling increased. Finally he blew his nose on Kozinski's autopsy report. It was useless anyway. And Lieutenant Piperston would have another copy.

In the men's room he took a wad of toilet paper and jammed it in his pocket to serve as tissues. He washed his hands; the autopsy report wasn't very efficient at absorbing nose dribble. The automatic warm-air hand-dryer didn't work.

"Jesus J. Edgar Christ."

Waving his wet hands, Cavanaugh made his way to the Nut Dump.

That was Felders's name for it, of course. All the mail containing threats to people already dead, "hot" tips on foreign enemy activity, "inside" information on communist conspiracies and secret international Jewish cartels and hidden Japanese nuclear submarines and UFO plans to kidnap Madonna—all of it made its way here, to the Nut Dump. Here triage was performed, separating what looked like it should be investigated from what looked like a waste of time. But everything, investigated or not, was logged in on computers. It was cross-filed sixteen different ways, providing a perfect picture of American neurotics who still believed in the Post Office.

The Nut Dump was presided over by Victoria Queen. Over the years Victoria Queen had heard so many jokes inverting her name that she refused to even talk to anyone who made one. Cavanaugh was careful. Victoria Queen, after a decade of running the Nut Dump, could tell from just glancing at someone if they were contemplating a name joke. The funny thing was that as the years went by, she was starting to look like Hanoverian royalty: thick bushy eyebrows and receding chin.

"Vicky, I need something."

"God, Robert, you sound terrible. Have you seen a doctor?"

"Not yet. I need—"

"I'd make you a cup of tea but the microwave quit."

"Yes. Of course. Listen—"

" 'Listen'? You been hanging around Felders too long."

Cavanaugh started again. Graceless persistence, Marcy had always said. She'd hated that quality in him. But where would his job be without it?

"Vicky, I need to know about any more anonymous letters about any scientific research connected with microbiology, recombinant DNA, or gene splicing. Duffy got a letter like that in July, addressed directly to him. But I want a wider search—anything related to biological science in the last three months."

"Biological science..." Victoria Queen muttered. She turned to her computer. "Not much there...now if you wanted physics or astronomy...Let's see..." She stared at her terminal screen. Cavanaugh waited.

"Item 16-42-0563, postcard, July 14, claims the president is an alien from Arcturus genetically altered to resemble a human being. Unsigned.

"Item 16-42-3473, letter, August 3, claims the Center for Disease Control in Atlanta is part of a feminist plot to secretly poison the nation's water supply to attack only cells with Y chromosomes. Unsigned.

"Item 17-23-8503, letter, August 7, claims AIDS virus is biological warfare against this country's artistic community by a jealous Japan. Signed, Christopher J. Walker, Seattle. That's about it, Robert...and, oh, this just came in today. Molly brought it to me because she thought I'd get a kick out of it."

She handed Cavanaugh a postcard of a grinning baboon, addressed to the Attorney General, although not by specific name. It was unsigned.

Dear Attorney General, You should know there's a Soldiers of the Divine Covenant Camp in Cadillac, New York. It practices animal sacrifice. I think it practices human sacrifice too. You should look into this because there are kids there including mine. Isn't there a law? This sacrifice is true even if I can't prove it YET.

"Isn't that a trip?" Victoria said. "I love the baboon."

"What's it got to do with microbiology?"

"Nothing. It would get d-based under 'animals,' 'religion,' and 'murders.'"

"Oh," Cavanaugh said, studying the postcard. It depressed him. God, the lost people wandering around out there.

"You're certainly in a bad mood, Robert. I just thought this might amuse you."

We are not amused, Cavanaugh thought of saying, but he knew better. He looked at the postcard again. Human sacrifice. Kids in the camp. God, what a world. And who would name a town after a car that was manufactured someplace else?

"Thanks, Vicky," he said. "Will you keep me posted if you do get anything else concerning microbiology or genetic research? No matter who it's addressed to."

"Will do," Victoria Queen said. "I'll put a flag in the program." Which at least wasn't anything a nineteenth-century monarch would say. Thereby removing temptation.

Cavanaugh sneezed, blew his nose on purloined toilet paper, and left the Nut Dump.

Ten

Dr. Julia Garvey's laboratory swarmed with sick rats. Cavanaugh hadn't expected that. Actually, he had driven out to Bethesda, five days after Kozinski's murder, not knowing what to expect, but visualizing something vaguely like a cross between a hospital and the war room at NORAD: computers, medicinal smells, quiet antiseptic efficiency. But Dr. Garvey's lab, once he'd been led to it through a huge labyrinthine building, looked more like his high-school biology lab. The computers were there, but half-buried under fantastic jumbles of boxes, notebooks, vials, syringes, racks of glassware, small machines he couldn't begin to guess the uses of. And rats. Cages and cages of them, smelling like the sewers of hell. Cavanaugh forced himself not to gag.

Dr. Garvey didn't even seem to notice the smell. She looked around sixty, a trim brisk woman in a white lab coat. Her manner was formal. She led Cavanaugh past counters and shelves and sinks and high-tech machinery to the back of the lab, where two stools flanked a white table. Behind the table were stacks of rat cages.

"Sit down, please," Dr. Garvey said.

Cavanaugh sat. He was now at eye level with several cages of white rats, some of whom stared at him from flat pink eyes that seemed to him full of rage. The back of the closest rat was covered with oozing purple sores. The rat in the next cage had pulpy lumps all over its head. The smell was overpowering, the sweet-sickly odor of rotting flesh.

"I've gone through Dr. Kozinski's records, and I've spoken at length with his research assistant, Dr. Caroline Lampert," Dr. Garvey said. "She was reasonably cooperative."

"That's good," Cavanaugh managed, although Dr. Lampert wouldn't have had any real choice. Kozinski's work had been done on a government grant, which included the provision that all files be opened to any Justice Department investigation. The rat with oozing sores moved in its cage, twitching its tail. In the next tier down a rat crept to the front of the cage, twitching its nose. Its eyes were filmed with purplish growths.

"Now tell me, Mr. Cavanaugh, just exactly what you want to know. Dr. Kozinski's work was complex, but I can try to summarize it if I know specifically what you're looking for."

Cavanaugh felt a sneeze coming on. He caught his breath and held it, forcing the sneeze back up his nose until his eyes watered. The deep breath smelled so foul that once more his gorge rose.

"We're not . . . not exactly sure what we're looking for. Could you summarize the main thrust of Dr. Kozinski's work, and then maybe I'll know what questions to ask."

Dr. Garvey pursed her lips. She looked like a strict nanny about to render judgment on some misbehavior. Cavanaugh seized gratefully on this image; it had nothing to do with rats.

She said, "Dr. Kozinski was working with the envelope coating of retroviruses. Do you know what retroviruses are?"

"You inject them into the body," Cavanaugh said,

grateful for the *New York Times.* "They carry altered genes. Then the new genes start multiplying like mad, making proteins that cure disease."

"Well...not 'like mad,'" Dr. Garvey said, pursing more, "and curing diseases isn't quite that simple. But you're essentially correct. Do you know about the coding regions of the retroviral RNA?"

"Nothing."

More pursing. "All right. Then let's start at the beginning." She took a piece of paper from the cluttered table and drew a circle studded with knobby projections. It reminded Cavanaugh of a snow tire he'd had for his first car, a '76 Chevy. Inside the circle she drew a long curvy snake, divided into six sections of varying widths:

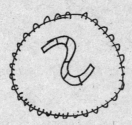

"This is a virus. These knobs are the envelope proteins. Inside is the RNA, which will become DNA when the virus enters a human body cell and starts dividing there. This shows RNA genes that perform six different functions"—she tapped each of the curvy sections with her pencil—"long terminal repeat, which influence the activity of the viral genes and facilitate the insertion of viral DNA into cellular DNA. Next is a coding region, e-n-v, which specifies the proteins of the viral coat— that's the knobs. The next two sections specify proteins of the enzyme reverse transcriptase and of the viral core. This fifth section, psi, is crucial to the inclusion of RNA in viral particles. In gene therapy, the psi is deleted, which means the virus can't reproduce itself, only the altered DNA. Then the last section is another noncoding long terminal repeat. Is this clear so far?"

"Yes," Cavanaugh said. It wasn't, not all of it, but he could ask specific questions later. After he knew what Kozinski had actually been trying to do. And after his stomach stopped fluttering. A rat stared at him through its bars.

"Good," Dr. Garvey said. "Ben was working with the e-n-v coding region. He was interested in the exact mechanisms by which viruses inject themselves into healthy cells inside the human body. See . . ." She drew next to the snow-tire-with-snake:

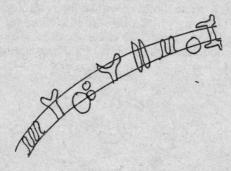

"This is the wall of a human cell that's about to be infected. All *these* are various structures embedded in the cell wall. The virus binds onto a receptor site, breaches the cell wall, and invades the cell. Ben was studying exactly how that happens: what proteins are released as signals, what genes regulate their production, how the receptor sites recognize which—Mr. Cavanaugh, are you all right?"

Cavanaugh was not all right. A young man with his hair in a ponytail squeezed past Cavanaugh with an apologetic smile and opened a cage door. He reached in for a rat, pulling it out by its tail. Simultaneously, Cavanaugh felt another sneeze coming on.

"F-f-fine!"

Dr. Garvey looked dubious. "Well, then, the specific proteins Dr. Kozinski was working with are called—"

The pulled-out rat twisted and squealed at the ends

of the pony-tailed researcher's fingers. Soft pulpy sores covered its hind quarters. It smelled of rot. Cavanaugh's sneeze—a monstrous sneeze, the grandaddy of all sneezes—exploded. It was followed by a second, and a third. His nose ran. His throat closed up like a valve.

"Oh!" The research assistant looked appalled.

"I'm sorry," Cavanaugh gasped. "Just a cold. The wood shavings—"

Both researchers stared at him in horror. Finally Dr. Garvey said, "You have a *cold?* Don't you realize you could infect the rats?"

"Infect—"

"The *rats,* yes. Colds are viruses, Mr. Cavanaugh. These are experimental rats—"

"They're already infected!" Cavanaugh said, and broke into another round of sneezing. Dimly he felt Julia Garvey take his arm and pull him away from the rats, but he shook her off and fumbled blindly—his eyes were watering like faucets—for a tissue in his pocket.

The pony-tailed research assistant said icily, "But they're not infected with *your* virus. All viruses are different, and you're contaminating—"

"Contaminating the contaminated," Cavanaugh tried to say, as a joke, to show he was being a good sport about the looks on both their faces. But before he could get the words out, the rat dangling from the researcher's hand gave a mighty twist and its flailing body brushed Cavanaugh's fingers. At the same moment his vision cleared and he noticed, half-buried under papers on the table, the remains of somebody's lunch. A ham sandwich, oozing mayo. Lipstick on the bite marks.

His gorge finally rose and he vomited. While sneezing.

Then he was being led firmly by Dr. Garvey. Out of the lab, into the hall. Pushed into the men's room door. He leaned against a urinal, praying for death.

When he finally emerged, washed and sheepish, Dr. Garvey waited. Her lips were no longer pursed, but neither was she smiling. He guessed that she was unwilling to be his particular nanny any longer.

But he'd underestimated her. "In here, Mr. Cavanaugh."

It was a conference room with a long polished table, ridiculously large for two people. It was also dark. "Unfortunately, the lights are temporarily broken, which is why I didn't suggest this in the first place. Also, I assumed..."

She'd assumed a special agent for the FBI would have a stronger stomach. Cavanaugh smiled and sneezed.

"I'm sorry about the rats, Doctor. I didn't realize I could... could..." Another sneeze.

"I really think you should be at home in bed with that cold," she said, proving him wrong yet again. Nannyness was deeply embedded. "We can reschedule this briefing session."

Rescheduling sounded wonderful. Anything that got him away from here sounded wonderful. But that wasn't the way it worked. Not for him. "Just a few more questions.... You said Kozinski was working on how viruses alter the proteins in their coats in order to invade cells. In your expert opinion, could this work, even remotely, be applied to biological weapons?"

Dr. Garvey frowned. "I don't see how. Oh, of course, biological warfare could use viruses as well as bacteria to infect people. But you don't need to understand genetic mechanisms in order to do that. You just use them. And if you were working on some new virus, something really deadly..." She paused. He could see that she didn't like this line of thought; she preferred to think of gene work as dealing in life, not death. "Well, then you'd concentrate on the viral core proteins, the toxins a virus makes when it's not genetically altered. The proteins of the coat wouldn't be of great interest."

"And there's no way Dr. Kozinski could have been working on something really bizarre?"

"Like what?" The pursed lips were back.

He felt a fit of coughing coming on. In the gloom of the unlit conference room, her face and lab coat were pale slabs.

He said desperately, "Cloned rats carrying disease. Cloned dinosaurs. Cloned soldiers."

She looked at him distastefully. "The National Institutes of Health are not comic books, Mr. Cavanaugh. And neither was Benjamin Kozinski's work at Whitehead."

"No, I just wondered—"

"Please call when you're feeling better so we can reschedule the briefing session."

A door opened in the hall, and the smell of sick rats again overtook him. He thought longingly of escaping from the Institute of Health. "No, let's finish this now, Dr. Garvey. There are still things I don't understand. I'm staying here until I do."

By the time he got back to the Hoover Building, everyone was leaving for the day. The usual traffic choked the streets around the Federal Triangle. Cavanaugh fought his way through, parked, and sneezed his way to his office, where he checked his messages. Nothing from Neymeier. Well, the kid had said the data search would take a while. He sat at his desk, opened the case of tissues he'd bought, and put a fresh box on his desk. The other twenty-three boxes he stacked neatly beside his file cabinet. Then he pulled out a clean sheet of paper.

On the drive back from Bethesda, he'd thought hard about everything Julia Garvey had told him, boiling it down into manageable, possibly relevant bites. Now he listed those bites on the paper, numbering them neatly:

1. K. was working on proteins that are on the outside of viruses.
2. Those proteins do things—release chemicals that cause other changes—when the virus is getting ready to enter a healthy cell, while it enters a healthy cell, and after it enters a healthy cell.
3. The reason K. was doing this was that gene therapy makes altered genes enter healthy cells, to cure disease, and scientists aren't

happy unless they know not only that something works, but how it works.

Cavanaugh considered this point. On the whole, he
approved. It was true it took a lot of government money
to understand something that apparently would work
just as well even if you didn't understand it. On the other
hand, scientists wanted all the facts, arranged into a co-
herent model that made sense. Just like intelligence analysts.

4. K. had identified various molecules that are
   key to a virus entering cells. He had also identified the whole chain of reactions that this
   causes, and he could make them happen.
5. Some of his work related to why virus cells
   prefer to enter some kinds of cells rather than
   other kinds. This has to do with how viruses
   bind onto "receptor sites," which are sort of
   receiving docks on the outside of cells. Some
   receiving docks apparently have less security
   than other docks. The viruses have an easier
   time with the break-in.

Cavanaugh tapped the pencil on that point. Dr. Garvey hadn't liked that analogy: receptor sites, she'd said,
were not "receiving docks." They were far more mole-
cule-specific than that. And a viral infection was not a
crime, as "break-in" seemed to imply. Cavanaugh let the
wording stand. *He* knew what he meant, and these were
his notes, not part of a case report.

6. K's work was important. Dr. Garvey was excited about it (for her). Her excitement
   seemed to be mostly because the work explained how things happened that everybody
   already knew were happening.
7. Dr. Garvey saw no way K's work could lead
   to criminal activity that couldn't proceed just
   as well without it.

8. Dr. Garvey has read the few articles published by two scientists at Verico, including Eric Stevens. She said they were both mediocre work, and completely unrelated to anything K. was working on, even by wild stretches of the imagination.

Another inconclusive end—like the crime-scene report, the interviews with Judy Kozinski and Caroline Lampert, the attempts to link Verico financially to the Relatives. He still had nothing that would justify classifying this case as an REI, with resources allocated to "discerning the composition, structure, and activities of racketeering enterprises."

Cavanaugh filed his notes alongside Julia Garvey's drawing of DNA snakes inside cellular snow tires. He took a box of tissues from the neat pile alongside his filing cabinets, to keep in his car. On the way out of the building he noticed that the section fax had been fixed and was whirling away, receiving dailies for genuine cases in which something might actually be happening.

Outside it was a perfect late-summer evening. Washington's usual mugginess was gone, leaving air so sweet and clear and limpid it was like a caress. Long cool shadows slanted down Constitution Avenue. The waning sunlight was pale gold and the evening smelled, mysteriously, of invisible flowers. Even through Cavanaugh's cold.

He stood on the shallow broad steps and briefly closed his eyes.

He went back inside. The fax had stopped receiving. He wrote on a piece of memo paper in his clear, small hand:

In such a night,
Troilus methinks mounted the Trojan walls,
And sighed his soul toward the Grecian tents,
Where Cressid lay that night

He looked at this for a long time. The debit of having once been an English major.

Then he tore up the paper. On a second paper he printed FISH TALK ABOUT WATER:

Old joke: You can wonder what fish talk about, but you can bet it ain't water.

ISTIOPHORUS: There's something out there.
HYPSYPOPS: Out where?
ISTIOPHORUS: There.
HYPSYPOPS: Out *where*? Where's there?
ISTIOPHORUS: Everywhere.
HYPSYPOPS: What the hell are you talking about?
ISTIOPHORUS: Look, just take a breath.
HYPSYPOPS: A breath of what?
ISTIOPHORUS: Of what's there!
HYPSYPOPS: What?
ISTIOPHORUS: This is ridiculous. I'm getting out.
HYPSYPOPS: Out of what?

Cavanaugh signed this, in even smaller letters, "a fish out of water." He sent it to Marcia's home fax. Then he went back out of the Hoover Building, sniffling and sneezing, into the heart-breaking summer night.

NOVEMBER

We keep making gains and they keep getting moved backward. If we take back the labor unions, the legitimate businesses, eventually they become just another street gang. Spiritually, they've always been just a street gang.

—*Rudolph Giuliani, U.S. Attorney, 1988*

Eleven

Jeanne Cassidy stepped off the curb into the street, her textbooks clutched to her chest. Around her stretched the ugly campus of Michigan State: redbrick building after redbrick building, flat-roofed and monotonous. Even the bright autumn foliage hadn't helped much, when there'd been autumn foliage, and now that the last of the leaves had fallen the campus looked even worse. Although today was warm, for November. Students had left their coats in the dorms, their scarves draped over chair backs or drawer pulls. A few people, hopeful or exhibitionist, wore shorts.

Jeanne hurried across the street, her oversized gray sweatshirt bouncing over her baggy jeans. Her hair was cut very short, shorter than most boys', and dyed dull brown.

"Hey, Jeannie! Wait up!"

Jeanne turned. Her roommate Carol Keating, a heavy girl from Toledo, bustled across the grass. Carol smiled, showing her huge, blindingly white teeth. It seemed to Jeanne that Carol was always smiling. She wore a flippy green miniskirt, a green poncho, and a baseball cap.

"What on earth were you doing just then, roomie?"
Jeanne flushed. "Just when?"

"Just *then.* While you crossed the street. I watched
you. You stood there for about five minutes until the
street was like totally empty, and then you rushed across
like you expected a Mack truck to come barreling along
and knock you into tomorrow. I called to you and you
didn't even—Jeannie! What is it? God, you're white as
a ghost!"

"N-nothing . . . I don't feel so good. Maybe a touch of
the flu."

Carol studied her. Jeanne glanced away. Carol had a
real good bullshit detector. But all Carol said was, "You
want to, like, go to the infirmary?"

"No. I can't. I have soc." She had learned to pro-
nounce it "soshe." Sociology 101. Where she was learn-
ing, God help her, about the tension between the
individual and a given group's collective power.

Carol continued to watch Jeanne closely. Jeanne
laughed. "Hey, why are you eyeballing me like that? Do
I look *that* sick?"

"Jeannie—why don't you ever wear any makeup? Or
grow your hair, or wear anything but baggy clothes?
God, if I had a figure like yours . . . but it's like you go
out of your way to look, I don't know, unglamorous."

Jeanne said coldly, "Don't you think you're being a
little personal?"

"Personal? Shit, we're roomies. And I thought we're
friends."

"We are," Jeanne said. She walked faster, her books
held tightly against her chest.

"But you don't, you know, really open up to anybody.
Not even me. And sometimes at night I hear you talking
in your sleep. . . ."

Jeanne stopped dead. "Talking? In my sleep? What
do I say?"

"Well, it's not real clear, just sort of—"

"What do I say?"

Carol stared. "No words. Or if there are, I can't make

them out. Just moans, and 'no, no,' and stuff like that."

Jeanne started walking again. Carol scurried to keep up. The big girl's voice was finally angry.

"Okay, so I'm out of line. But we're *friends.* Jeannie, if something really bad has happened to you, you could talk to the campus shrink. He's good, I hear it from everybody who's gone to him. If, like, you were abused as a child or something, and that's why you try so hard to dress drab, you could—"

"Don't try to use cheap psychoanalysis on me, Keating."

Carol stopped walking. "Okay, okay, you're above it, you're above all of us. The self-sufficient Jeanne Cassidy, who doesn't need any friends."

"That's right. I don't need any friends."

"Fuck you, Cassidy." Carol strode away, the ends of her green poncho flapping.

Jeanne watched her disappear around the corner of a boxy redbrick building. Good riddance. Carol wasn't much of a friend, anyway, always eating, coaxing Jeanne to eat, nagging her, really, on and on. . . . Jeanne would have to get a single room next semester. That would cost more money. But if she really muttered in her sleep . . .

Cadoc. Verico. Cadaverico.

Jeanne squeezed her eyes shut until her heart quieted and the throbbing in her temples went away. Sometimes it took whole long minutes. Sometimes people spoke to her while her eyes were jammed shut, and she didn't even hear them.

When it was over, she walked on to soshe, without crossing any busy streets.

Twelve

Wendell Botts tugged off his left glove by biting the index finger and throwing back his head. His right arm cradled groceries in flimsy plastic bags which threatened to split open. It was all the fucking canned goods. They were too heavy, and the checkout bitches couldn't be bothered to double-bag. Too much fucking trouble. Nobody ever considered the other guy anymore. Nobody treated anybody else with respect.

He fumbled with his bare hand for the truck keys in his pocket. By wedging the grocery bags between himself and the right fender, he got enough maneuverability to unlock the truck. He eased the bags along the fender and onto the passenger-side floor.

It was snowing again. Only mid-November and already there was a foot of the stuff on the ground. Not good snow, neither—this was the heavy wet stuff that was just a little too cold to melt and just a little too warm to powder. The parking lot of the Cadillac Grand Union was slushy dirty ruts between rock-hard mounds of snow that not even four-wheel drive could get through. The

sky was gray, about two feet above the trees. Wendell
wanted to smash something.

The fucking court said Saralinda got Penny and David
for Thanksgiving.

Wendell turned the ignition key. The truck sputtered,
died. He tried again. On the third try it caught, rasping
and wheezing. He should get a tune-up. But maybe he
could get by with just another can of dry gas.

In his crummy motel apartment, he put away the groceries: a dozen frozen hamburgers, two packages of
hamburger buns, cans of beans, chili, soup, stew, peanut
butter, corn curls, ravioli. The kids weren't coming this
weekend, so he didn't buy the apples and fresh vegetables Saralinda insisted he give them.

At the bottom of the grocery bag—that bitch had put
it on the *bottom*—was the *Cadillac Register,* which
served not only Cadillac but all the small towns west of
Gloversville. Wendell unfolded it and opened to the
obituaries. His hands trembled.

Harden, Muriel. November 17. She is survived by
her husband, Alfred; her children, Michael, John,
Roberta (Mrs. Samuel Stern), and Pauline (Mrs.
Douglas O'Shea), all of Cadillac—

No. Nobody with that much local family. Soldiers of
the Divine Covenant all came from someplace else, and
not in big families.

Montilla, Raymond. November 18, at age 82. Pre-
deceased by his wife, Theresa (Skoler) Montilla.
Survived by his niece, Mildred (Stamps) Burton;
and nephew, George Stamps; several grandnieces
and nephews. Funeral Mass at 10:00 A.M. Saturday at Church of Our Lady of Perpetual Sorrow—

No. No one at the Divine Covenant camp used the
local Catholic church. They said their own masses in a
"purer" brand of Catholic, with lots of extras thrown in

to get everybody holier, like speaking in tongues and prayers to St. Cadoc and cleansing rituals.

Diffenbach, Brittany, age six years . . .

Oh, God. Six years old. The paper felt clammy under Wendell's fingers.

Diffenbach, Brittany, age six years. November 18. Survived by her parents, William and Cynthia Diffenbach; one brother, Timothy; paternal grandparents Titus and Alice Diffenbach, of Ames, Iowa; maternal grandmother Beverly Miller, of New York City; aunts, uncles, and cousins. In lieu of flowers, friends may contribute to the Children's Cancer Research Fund—

No. Thank God, no. Some form of childhood cancer. Not the Soldiers.

Morreale, Ramon. November 19. Suddenly. Survived by his brother, Carlos De Los Santos, of Puerto Rico. Private internment.

That was it. Sudden death; the only relative a brother—half brother?—far away; no public service, maybe even a cremation. Someone nobody would miss. But wait a minute—maybe somebody *had* missed the guy. Why a newspaper notice at all? Why not just let Ramon Morreale disappear into the limestone caves under the camp?

Something here didn't add up right.

Wendell punched the phone pad. He knew the number by heart.

"Soldiers of the Divine Covenant. May God bless you this day."

He gritted his teeth. "This is Detective John Miller of the Cadillac Police Department. I'd like to speak to Mr. Newell, please." Saralinda had said that old Newell was still a high mucky-muck Elder.

The male voice grew cautious. "May I ask what this is in reference to?"

For a minute, that stopped Wendell. Soldiers didn't talk like that when he'd been there. For that matter, none of them sounded like this guy: careful. But still ready to hang up.

"It's about the Ramon Morreale case."

"I thought Detective Paxon was handling that."

Wendell slammed down the phone. So there *was* some sort of investigation of that sudden death!

The number for the local police was pasted onto the motel phone, along with fire and ambulance.

"Cadillac Police Department," a woman said.

"Let me talk to Detective Paxon."

"Detective Paxon isn't here right now. Can I help you?"

"Yeah. I'm Ramon Morreale's old neighbor. I talked to Detective Paxon already, and I just wanted to know what's happening now."

"You'll have to talk to Detective Paxon directly," the voice said. Tight ass.

"When will he be in?"

"Maybe this afternoon."

"What did the autopsy show?" Wendell said.

"You'll have to talk to Detective Paxon directly." The phone clicked. She didn't say there'd been an autopsy—but she didn't say there *wasn't*, either. What did that mean?

Frantically, Wendell paged through the paper for the Police Beat column. A stolen car, a bar fight, a burglary, three DWIs . . . no arrests for murder. Besides, if anybody had been arraigned for murder, the story would be splashed all over, and not in the *Cadillac Register*, either. The *Albany Times-Union* would have it.

So the autopsy didn't show nothing. If there'd *been* a fucking autopsy. But when you did a blood sacrifice, you slit the throat, holding the animal's neck tipped way back, and you drew the knife, sharp as you get, across the skin. . . . Wendell had been there. It was the only time the Soldiers let blood flow. They'd let their kids die of some awful disease before they'd let a doctor give them a transfusion, and they'd probably die themselves before eating a steak or even a fucking chicken, but they'd slit the throat of a squealing rabbit or woodchuck and let the blood flow out on the ground to honor God. And the noise the terrified animal made as the knife went in—if you heard it once you never forgot it.

Wendell wadded up the newspaper and threw it into a corner, on top of a pile of cardboard boxes from Domino's Pizza. The pile toppled.

Nobody had come to investigate as a result of his postcards. *Nobody.* The president didn't send nobody, or the attorney general, or the FBI, or Congress, or even the fucking Child Abuse and Maltreatment Reporting Center. Wendell knew nobody came because he'd spent a lot of time hanging around the gates of the camp, shivering in his truck, running the engine for ten minutes on the hour to keep warm. Watching. He had the time to watch, now that construction had slowed down with the bad weather. The only people who went into the camp were people who'd gone out of it earlier the same day. Nobody who could be feds.

Wendell smacked the rickety coffee table with his closed fist. Nobody would fucking *listen.* And Penny and David in there, with that going on . . .

With what going on? Something. Something really wrong.

The last time he'd seen Saralinda, waiting at the gate when he brought the kids back, she'd looked thinner and littler and paler than ever before. Hell, she'd barely had the strength to smile at him.

David had clung to Wendell's neck. He didn't want to go in. Babies *knew,* didn't they? Some kind of sixth sense. They knew when a place was bad.

"Calm down, Wendell," his sponsor, Lewis P., had said at Wednesday's A.A. meeting. "You're full of bottled-up rage."

He could still feel David's warm hands clutching his daddy's neck. How warm kids' hands were! The smell of David's soft hair, and Penny's little smile . . .

"Calm down, Wendell."

He flung himself into a chair. The TV remote fell off the arm onto his lap; he flicked on the TV. Sometimes he just let it all wash over him, sitcoms and news and talk shows and police dramas and cartoons and reruns of things like "The Brady Bunch," things he remembered watching when he'd been Penny's age. Those were the most soothing.

"You're wound up tighter than a spring, Wendell," Lewis had said. "That's how people start drinking again."

No. Not him. Not now that he had his kids back. Only he *didn't* have his kids back—

And nobody understood how hard that was. Nobody was willing to help him. Nobody.

On-screen, credits rolled for some black-and-white movie. Wendell had no idea what it had been, even though he'd just finished staring at ten minutes of it. Lush 1940s music swelled; flowers scrolled past, surrounding actors' names. The commercials started.

I shall lift up mine eyes to the hills, from where my help cometh. Yeah. Sure. There was no help. Nobody fucking helped.

Now an audience, panned over by a camera, was applauding wildly—for what? The camera switched to a fake living room, the kind with white couches that never got dirty and a low coffee table with a bowl of fresh flowers low enough not to hide the women's legs. A talk-show hostess and two guests grinned like hyenas. Wendell didn't recognize her. Local, not national, probably out of Albany.

The program can help, Wendell. Work your program. Take it one day at a time. Right.

Now the talk-show hostess stood out in the audience, carrying a microphone. People waved their hands wildly to be called on.

The Lord helps those who help themselves.

A man stood beside the hostess, beaming like he just won the lottery. Everybody laughed. The hostess thanked him prettily and carried her microphone to somebody else.

"... wouldn't never have *gotten* that inheritance if I hadn't fought both my sisters like—"

"And so you're here to tell us what?" the hostess interrupted. "What should we know about protecting our future inheritances?"

"You need to get yourself a really, really, really good lawyer," the guest said. "You can't get probate justice alone."

You need to get on a talk show.

The words seemed to come to Wendell from outside him. Almost, it seemed, like they were spoken aloud. He jumped and looked around the dirty room. Nothing like that had happened to him since when he was inside. It had happened then, all right. He'd even done speaking in tongues, once, a thing so weird he'd hoped to St. Cadoc it never happened again. Of course, he'd been drunk. But he wasn't drunk now and he wasn't at no hopped-up mass. And this time his cause was a real one, and good.

Wendell clicked off the remote. Into the sudden silence he whispered, "Thank you."

Then he put on his duffle coat to go buy some good paper. Postcards wouldn't do for this. For the government postcards were good enough, but not for this. He had an important story to tell, a real story, a story directed to TV by that Higher Power that A.A. always talked about. For this, he needed good heavy paper, cream-colored, the kind with little bumps on it like gooseflesh. And a new pen with black ink.

This was his last legal chance.

Thirteen

At 3:27 A.M., Judy Kozinski woke up, afraid.

It was nothing new. She woke every night between 3:15 and 3:45, and she was always afraid. The fear was oily, viscous, like black tar sliding through her chest and belly. It hurt to breathe.

She wasn't afraid of dying, as Ben had died. In fact, there were times, lying rigid in the cold hours before dawn, when she thought that dying would be a relief. Then it would all be over: the pain, and the loss, and the crippling fear. Nor was she afraid of being alone. She *wasn't* alone. She was in her parents' house, safe in the bed she'd slept in as a child and young girl, wrapped in her mother's concern and her father's sorrowful, steady calm. She had been here over two months. She wasn't alone.

So what was she afraid of? Night after night she asked herself that, trying to do as her father urged and face squarely what frightened her most. It's never as bad, he said gently, after you face it without evasion. Without lies to yourself. "That's what Jesus meant," Dan O'Brien told his daughter, "when He said, 'Fear not, and there is nothing covered that shall be revealed, and nothing hid that shall be known.' It's the same thing Carl Jung meant when he said, 'Neurosis is always a substitute for legitimate suffering.' Don't substitute, honey. Face what you fear, and the fear will lessen."

So Judy tried. She really did. She tried to listen to her father, to do the things he urged her, without pressure, to do for herself. She wanted to stop waking at 3:27; she wanted to stop walking like a zombie through her days; she wanted to stop feeling like someone had reached inside her chest and yanked out her heart. She wanted to get well. So she tried to listen, and tried to eat, and tried to sleep through the night, and tried to face whatever she feared so much.

Only she didn't know what it was.

Nothing in her life had ever hurt as bad as Ben's death, and this black fear that followed it.

She lay stiffly until the illuminated bedside clock said 3:49. The bright red figures added "A.M." in the lower right-hand corner. In case she didn't know this was early morning, in case she had somehow confused it with 3:49 P.M. when the sun shone and normal people went about their normal, unshattered lives.

No use. She wouldn't get back to sleep now until past dawn, which in November came late. She sat up, switching on the bedside lamp. Immediately she felt dizzy. What had she eaten yesterday? A bagel, half a banana. It was hard to get food to go down, and when it did, it sometimes didn't stay down.

"When you can't sleep," said the crisis therapist that her mother had insisted she see, "don't try. Get up and do something: exercise, or write in your journal, or read." The therapist had been sensible, but Judy had stopped seeing him after a few sessions. He couldn't touch the fear.

What was she so afraid of?

Once more, wearily, she went over it in her head. The night Ben had come home from Verico. *"Judy, I've been through a lot in the last two days. I can't discuss this* now." And his not getting angry. Not yelling back, even when she called him a faithless son of a bitch. *"Judy, I've been through a lot in the last two days. I can't discuss this now."* Walking through the kitchen door to the garage. Not slamming the door. His last words ever to her, his wife, the words by which she would have to remember him forever: *"I can't stand any more. I'm going to the lab."* The sound of the automatic garage door opener, and then the red Corvette backing slowly—too slowly for Ben—down the driveway. *"Judy, I've been through a lot in the last two days. I can't discuss this now."*

The furnace went on, thumping and knocking. It was very old. As a child, lying warm in her bed, she had heard the furnace during the night and thought of it as a friendly big bear, guarding the house from cold. Keeping her safe.

Only there was no safety now. There would never be safety for her again. *"Judy, I've been through a lot in the last two days. I can't discuss this now."*

The bedside lamp was only 40 watts. It cast strange shadows in the corners of the bedroom. Her discarded dollhouse was a humped, deformed intruder, crouching in wait. Her brush on the dresser was shadowy, hard, was a hammer ready to bash in Ben's head—

Judy gasped and put her hands over her face. The tears started again, the tears she hadn't been able to control for nearly three months now, like some shameful incontinency at the wrong part of her body.

"Judy, I've been through a lot in the last two days—"
What had he been through?

Slowly, Judy lowered her hands from her face.

She had always assumed that he meant their argument in Las Vegas, plus the stress of a job interview that obviously hadn't gone well. Ben hated rejection. It made him furious. But he hadn't been furious that night, and he hadn't actually ever said that Verico had rejected him. And only technically had their private argument been within the last two days: forty-seven hours earlier.

"I can't stand any more." Any more *what*? Again, she

had assumed that Ben meant he couldn't stand any more of her. Any more accusations, any more yelling, any more of what he always called her "relentless drilling." Well, she had been drilling, all right, but he hadn't been listening. Not really, not to her. He'd been listening to something else, something she couldn't hear, something she hadn't even known was there.

Another woman, inside his mind? Caroline Lampert?

No. That affair had been going on for two years (even now, thinking that, Judy felt the terrible band tightening around her chest.) A two-year-old affair wasn't fresh anymore, wouldn't have that middle-of-the-night urgency. Not, Judy guessed, for Ben.

Another woman, then. Whoever he'd spent that last night with in Las Vegas?

No. *"Judy, I've been through a lot in the last two days. I can't discuss this now."* If it had been a new woman, Ben would have been evasive, yes, but not so quiet. He would have done what he always did when he'd displeased Judy: become supercharming, in the hope of distracting her. As he had been in Vegas when they'd fought over the Berkeley graduate assistant. But not at home, that last night. He hadn't tried to be charming. Whatever voices Ben had heard inside his head, they didn't belong to any woman.

What had actually happened at Verico?

The furnace stopped knocking. In the abrupt silence, Judy heard her own breathing, quick and hard. She felt her own blood race through her veins, her own flesh warm—as Ben's would never be again—under the down quilt. Her fingers, lying in front of her on the quilt, curled and uncurled: pink-fleshed, blue-veined.

Her breathing. Her blood. Her fingers.

All at once, she knew what she was so afraid of.

Quietly she climbed out of bed. The dizziness came again, but she held onto the headboard until it passed. She pulled her nightgown over her head and put on underwear, socks, jeans, a warm dark-blue sweater. The jeans and sweater gaped on her; she had lost a lot of weight in three months of not eating.

From under the bed she pulled her suitcase. As quietly as possible she packed clothes and toiletries. The suitcase snapped shut loudly, and she winced.

When her parents had brought her home to Troy the day she'd confronted Caroline Lampert, Judy hadn't been in any shape to drive. Both her Toyota and Ben's Corvette were back in Natick. Judy reached for the bedside phone and called the taxi company, hoping the number hadn't changed in all these years. It hadn't. Dialing it brought back the long-ago Friday nights when she and her high-school girlfriends had pooled their money to "hit" the bars favored by the fascinating "older men" of Rensslaer Polytechnic Institute. Calling the number now gave her a strange feeling.

I am a person with a good head for numbers.

In the hall she eased her coat out of the coat closet. Her mittens were in the pocket. She pulled on her boots and carried the suitcase toward the kitchen, the exit farthest from her parents' bedroom. From there she could circle around the left side of the house and intercept the taxi before it turned into the driveway.

I am a person who finds out facts. For the science sections of newspapers. For journal articles. For myself.

Crossing the living room, she saw her mother's shopping list on the small table under the window. A streetlamp cast a dim glow over "apples, cheese, lamb chops @ 3.49/lb." Judy set the suitcase on the carpet and scrawled at the bottom of the list "Don't worry about me. Gone home. Will call." She had intended to call from the Amtrak station, but this was better. No confrontation.

I am a person who plans and acts. Not just drifts.

She crept into the kitchen. It was darker here, facing the backyard instead of the street lamps.

"Hello, Judy."

She gasped and switched on the light. Her father sat at the kitchen table, dressed in his old plaid wool robe, his onyx rosary in his hand.

"Oh, honey, I'm sorry—I didn't mean to scare you! I

heard you moving around in your room and thought you might want to talk."

Judy looked at her father. His gray hair was wild, and his robe was misbuttoned. But his face—deeply lined, puffy from sleep, as well remembered as her own in the mirror—was serene as always. Only a slight working of flesh up and down over his pajama collar gave him away.

She said carefully, "I'm leaving, Dad. I've called a taxi."

"So I guessed from your suitcase."

"You can't stop me."

He said quietly, "When have I ever tried to stop you, Judy?"

It was true. She didn't know why she'd said that. They stood in silence for a moment. Dan O'Brien's fingers moved over his rosary, and Judy knew he was praying for her safety and strength.

"Daddy...I know what I've been so afraid of. I know, now."

He said, very gently, "What, baby?"

"I've been afraid of losing myself."

He didn't answer, and at first she thought he hadn't understood. How could she explain it to him, when she hardly understood herself? But then Dan O'Brien nodded, his face grave, and she saw that his wonderful gift for understanding had held once again, as it had so many times before when people came to him in trouble. As they did, all the time, seeking help or comfort: his students, his fellow parishioners, his friends.

Words came to her. "This person I've been while I've been here with you and Mom—crying all the time, not eating, not sleeping, not even able to think about anything except Ben"—she stumbled over the name, went on—"that's not *me*, Daddy. I'm not like that. I'm...I do things, fix things, investigate things. Remember you used to call me Little Brenda Starr? I hardly recognize the person I've been the last three months, and I don't... I don't want to be her."

"Honey, you've had a terrible shock..."

"I know. And I'm not over it. I feel like I'll never be

really over it." The tears again, the incontinency. She blinked them back. "But I want to feel like myself again. And I can't even begin to do that here. You and Mom are so good to me, *too* good to me...." She stopped, lost. What did she mean?

Dan O'Brien knew what she meant. "We've made you a child again."

"Yes," she said. "Yes. And you know what even the Bible says: 'When I was a child I understood as a child, but when I became an adult, I put away childish things.'"

Her father smiled slightly. Judy never quoted the Bible. Since she'd stopped believing in God, at thirteen, she usually pretended that she hadn't learned any Bible verses, didn't remember them, hadn't in fact had the intensely serious Catholic upbringing she'd had. Dan O'Brien knew this. He didn't argue with her; argument wasn't his style. He just waited, sure that one day she would return to Mother Church. Judy knew she wouldn't. Ordinarily they avoided the subject, each not wanting to cause the other pain. But this wasn't "ordinarily." A murdered, unfaithful husband wasn't "ordinary." Not to the O'Briens.

Her father said, "Well, I certainly wasn't going to push any more scripture at you. But since you opened that door, I'll allow myself just one. Fair enough?"

Judy said, because she couldn't say anything else, "Fair enough."

"This is Solomon again, honey. In Ecclesiastes, Solomon the old man who's seen it all, done it all, investigated it all, and found out he can't really fix anything important: 'All things I have seen in the days of my vanity: there is a just man that perisheth in his righteousness, and there is a wicked man that prolongeth his life in his wickedness. Be not righteous over much, neither make thyself overwise; why shouldest thou destroy thyself?'"

"Well, that's a hell of a set of advice," Judy said, with more spirit than her voice had held in months. "He's saying just let the bad guys get away with whatever they're doing!"

Dan O'Brien said mildly, "Then you do think there are bad guys, plural, involved here?"

Judy stared at him. She'd been set up. Outside, a horn honked.

"Dad, the taxi's here—"

"Wait a minute. The taxi won't leave without you. Judy, I think that one police officer who spoke to you, not Lieutenant Piperston but the one who came here only once, was from the Justice Department."

She sank onto a kitchen chair. "How do you know?"

"I don't, for sure. He showed your mother a badge but she was too upset to look at it closely. She doesn't even remember his name."

"Robert Cavanaugh," Judy said, and when her father frowned, she had to laugh. It came out tinny and small. "You thought I wouldn't remember. But that's the kind of thing I *do* remember, Dad. Facts. Details."

"The point is, if there's something going on that the Justice Department is interested in, it could be dangerous. Oh, baby, we love you so much. . . ."

Again the incontinent tears. Her father was the only one, of all her friends' parents, who had ever said outright, "I love you." She had grown up wrapped in that warm security, as her girlfriends and dates and colleagues had not. As Ben had not, with his two alcoholic parents and appalling childhood. She'd tried so hard to make it up to him, that childhood, and somehow she never really had.

The taxi honked again. Judy got to her feet, picked up her suitcase.

Dan O'Brien whispered, "Be careful, Judy."

She nodded, blundered toward the door, turned back to kiss him. He smelled of fabric softener and pipe smoke and hair oil, a unique blend that had somehow never changed, not since she was four or five and first noticed it. As she went out the kitchen door she caught a last glimpse of him, lips moving as he fingered the onyx rosary.

The outside air was cold, gray, sad. Judy hurled her suitcase into the backseat of the cab—even in Troy cabdrivers no longer helped with luggage—and climbed in after it. "The Amtrak station in Albany, please."

The driver studied her in his rearview mirror. "You all right, miss?"

She thought what she must look like: unwashed hair, tear-smeared face, puffy eyes. A sudden sharp pain tore through her: *Ben. Is dead. Is really dead.*

"Yes," she said to the cabdriver. "I'm fine."

He shrugged and backed out of her parents' driveway.

Fourteen

s the Amtrak train moved south along the Hudson River, it became more and more crowded. Judy would have thought these towns were way too far up the Hudson for people to live there and commute to work in Manhattan. But if this trainful of people weren't commuters, then what were they? Men in Burberry raincoats over business suits, women in sneakers and socks over nylon stockings, high heels peeking over the tops of expandable leather totes. Everybody was reading the *Wall Street Journal*. Judy caught a glimpse of a headline about IBM, another about the Ukraine. She found she didn't care about either.

The only things she cared about were Ben's murder and what had happened at Verico.

She found a seat next to a middle-aged woman in a green wool suit and good haircut, who moved as far away from Judy as she could without going out the window and into the Hudson River. The woman was eating a croissant. Judy's stomach turned over.

Penn Station was jammed with frantic commuters, all

of whom seemed to be late. Judy felt detached from them, as if they existed in some other reality, hundreds of miles removed from hers. Without in the least meaning to, Judy found herself saying softly aloud, " 'I have seen all the work done under the sun, and all is vanity and vexation of spirit—' "

She frowned savagely. None of *that.* Three months with her father and she regressed. Three months with a man who prayed with conviction, who believed in angels, and who was actually writing a life of the saints—

A life of the saints! Judy, who had been an English major, wrote articles about supercolliders while her father, who taught physics, wrote a life of the saints. That wasn't even a genteel, old-fashioned, nineteenth-century occupation—it was a ninth century one, when monks sat in drafty stone cells and drew letters with a pen by the light of their burning faith. Dan O'Brien had missed not only his century but his entire millenium. What did the ideas of such a man—saint though he might himself be— have to do with a world in which people spliced genes, hurtled through the air at seven hundred miles per hour to distant continents, and killed each other for a machine-stitched leather wallet full of plastic credit cards? Nothing. Nothing at all. Three months with her father had made her worse, not better. That's not who she was.

She fought her way through the crowds (remembering sixth-grade Catholic school humor: "Give us this day our daily bread, and lead us not into Penn Station . . .") and bought a ticket on the next train for Elizabeth, New Jersey, putting it on her MasterCard. The train left in twenty-five minutes. Judy took two hundred dollars from an ATM, and found a phone booth. She put the calls on her MCI card.

"Directory Assistance. What city, please?"

"Washington, D.C."

"Go ahead."

"I'd like the number for the Justice Department."

"Wait a moment." Something pinged, and then a mechanical female voice gave the number with hypernatural clarity. Judy pressed it.

"Department of Justice."

"I'd like to speak with Robert Cavanaugh."

"Just a moment, please," the voice said, making the Justice Department politer than the phone company. Judy waited, watching frantic commuters race past.

"Sorry to keep you waiting, ma'am. Could you spell that last name?"

"C-A-V-A-N-A-U-G-H," Judy spelled, guessing.

"I'm sorry, but we don't have anyone listed by that name."

"Maybe it's spelled with a K. Try K-A-V-A-N-A-U-G-H."

"No, I'm sorry..." The voice trailed off in what sounded like genuine regret.

"Look, I'm certain he must be there. I'm a witness for a case the Department is prosecuting"—What was that big case in the papers called?—"the Carl Lupica case, and Mr. Cavanaugh said to contact him if I have any more information, and I do."

"Just a moment, please."

It suddenly came to Judy that her father could be wrong. He'd only said that he *thought* Cavanaugh was from Justice. Maybe he had just been another local detective, a colleague of Lieutenant Piperston's, taking over because Piperston had booked a vacation at Disney World or something. What did her father know about government lawyers? He was writing a life of the saints, and his idea of useful crime advice was to quote Ecclesiastes.

A male voice came on the line, gravelly and authoritative. "This is Paul Sanderson. Can I help you?"

Judy hung up.

What would Cavanaugh have told her, anyway? The Justice Department was in the business of gathering information about criminals, not disseminating it to whoever happened to phone up. And Cavanaugh wasn't even with Justice. So much for that.

She dragged her suitcase to the ladies' room to make

whatever repairs were possible in less than fifteen minutes. In a stall she balanced the suitcase across the toilet and opened it. Her mother had been doing Judy's laundry, which now made her ashamed of herself, but at least nearly everything was clean. On the other hand, she had thrown things in at random the awful morning she had attacked Caroline Lampert. All she had with her were more jeans, sweaters, T-shirts, and a track suit.

And the black dress she'd worn to Ben's funeral.

Slowly she pulled it from the suitcase. A Liz Claiborne knit, it didn't wrinkle much. She had black heels and stockings. Judy locked her jaw, stripped, and put on the dress.

She was shocked at how it hung on her. Had she lost *that* much weight? She fished around in the suitcase until she found a leather belt, which unfortunately was brown. She had to poke a new hole with her nail scissors to make the belt tight enough. The dress bunched around the waist, but it would have to do.

There wasn't much time left to do her face at the sink and mirror. Hastily she splashed cold water on her eyes, brushed her teeth, combed her hair, and put on blusher and lipstick. Better. Although she still looked like she'd just survived a train wreck. And wearing her old parka over the black knit dress didn't help.

On the train to New Jersey, which at this hour was nearly deserted, she opened her suitcase once more. She added small gold earrings and a red cotton scarf tied over her shoulders.

At the Elizabeth station she looked up Verico's address and caught a taxi, her heart pounding and her empty stomach queasy. Which, she figured, at least meant she was still alive.

It didn't look like much. A large, low cinderblock building, painted white. Small parking lot. A few outlying buildings for a backup generator and maintenance equipment, the uninspiring whole surrounded by a chain-link fence. Judy looked closely at the fence. Yes, she could see the sensor wire, less obvious and more sophisticated than electrification.

The front gate had a speaker box. Probably a surveillance camera, too, although she didn't see it. She pressed the box.

"Yes?" A male voice, impersonal and very clear. The equipment was quality.

"I have an appointment with Dr. Eric Stevens. My name is Mrs. Benjamin Kozinski."

"I don't show an appointment for you, Mrs. Kozinski."

No hint that he'd recognized her name. But, then, he probably hadn't. She said firmly, "Dr. Stevens will see me. Please tell him I'm here."

"Just a moment."

She waited, longer than a moment. A cold wind gusted over the surrounding lots, which mostly seemed to hold warehouses or factories. She'd left her parka in the waiting taxi, not wanting to look like a bag lady. The red scarf around her shoulders flapped in the wind. Judy wrapped her arms around herself and shivered.

"Come in, please." The gate swung open.

Her heels slipped on the walk, which was badly shoveled. Didn't women work here? Yes, but not in high heels. Female researchers wore sensible shoes. The guard opened the front door for her and asked her to sign in. He gave her a paper badge saying VISITOR and didn't blink at her coatless, blue-lipped, goosefleshed state.

"This way, please, ma'am." She hoped the walk down the white corridor would be long enough to let her warm up before she had to face Stevens.

It wasn't. He waited in an impressive office, lined with books, dominated by a huge mahogany desk. Not a test tube in sight. Ben had taught her that scientific offices that looked like this one belonged to third-rate scientists, more interested in show than in research. Judy had refrained from pointing out that Ben's home office had looked like this one. After all, Ben's office at Whitehead certainly had not.

Ben . . .

Stevens walked toward her, holding out both hands. "Mrs. Kozinski."

"Dr. Stevens."

"We were so shocked to hear of your husband's death. An irreplaceable loss to the entire scientific community."

"Thank you." As soon as she decently could, she pulled her hands from his. Eric Stevens looked like his office: glossy and third-rate. Thinning brown hair he combed straight across his scalp to disguise the bald spot. Medium height, medium build, expensive suit over a pot belly. You could meet him five times and not recognize him the sixth. He had the manners, or the indifference, not to register any reaction to her survivor-of-a-train-wreck appearance.

"Sit down, please."

"Actually," Judy said, sitting in an oversized leather club chair, "it's my husband's death that I'm here to discuss." She watched Stevens carefully: no reaction. But what did she expect? That he would go all shifty-eyed and start to sweat?

"Is there any way we can help? Unfortunately, I never had the privilege of working with Dr. Kozinski—"

"But he interviewed here the day before he was killed."

"And everybody on staff is sorry that he wasn't interested in the position," Stevens said smoothly. "We did what we could to lure him here, offering what I think was a quite generous salary and benefits. He must have discussed these with you."

"Yes. He did." She tried to make the words sound meaningful.

"Then you know how outstanding the package we offered was. And of course, not just money—we offered Ben full autonomy, unlimited research budget, whatever he needed to make Verico profitable. Since, as I'm sure he told you, it isn't profitable now."

Stevens didn't seem to be watching her especially closely. He half-sat on the front edge of his big desk, looking at ease. Nor did he probe to find out how much she knew. Was he so sure, then, that Ben had told her nothing about what was going on at Verico?

Was *she* so sure that something was?

She sat and waited, unsmiling but alert: an old reporter's trick. Most people found silence uncomfortable and would try to fill it, often with more information than they intended. This time, it didn't work. Stevens said gently, "Can I get you some coffee? You look cold."

"No, thank you. What I wanted to say was . . . I mean, because Ben was here the day before he was killed and he came home seeming a little upset . . . I wondered if . . . that is, what . . ." Another journalist's trick. Start something key, trail off, and see how the subject finishes it.

Stevens said, "We, too, thought he seemed a little upset while he was here. In fact, I was looking for a tactful way to ask you about his health. Had he been well?"

"Perfectly well."

"Oh, then . . ." Steven said, and his small apologetic smile said that Ben's upset had then probably been domestic, and Stevens apologized for prying.

Judy felt a surge of hatred that startled her.

"Dr. Stevens, did anything happen here that might have made Ben uneasy or angry? Because he was neither when he left Las Vegas to interview with you, and he was both when he arrived home late Wednesday night."

There. She'd shot her wad. She watched Stevens carefully.

He shook his head, his face wrinkled in friendly concern. "No, nothing happened *here*. We showed Ben over the place, filled him in on the direction of our research— frankly, most of it pretty lackluster so far—and told him how much we were willing to extend ourselves to have him come to us. He seemed interested at first, but then when he started talking about his own work at Whitehead—and of course, we're all familiar with it, given who he is—*was*—"

"At first he was interested," Judy managed to get out.

No incontinence of the eyeballs now, please God. Not now.

"As I say, when he started talking about his own work, he seemed to catch renewed fire, if you know what I mean. I think I knew then that he wouldn't leave Whitehead. Nor," he added silkily, "his staff there."

Caroline Lampert. Frozen, Judy stared at Stevens—had he known about Ben's affair with Caroline? Did the entire fucking microbiology *world* know? How much of a laughingstock was she? *Poor Judy, it's been going on for two years, she's absolutely the only one who doesn't know. . . . How could she not? Maybe she doesn't want to. How pathetic. . . .*

She pulled herself together. "Certainly Ben was intensely involved in his work on viral envelopes. He knew how important it was, and I'm not surprised he didn't want to leave it. Tell me, Dr. Stevens, have you interviewed anyone else for the directorship? Either before Ben was killed, or after?"

For the first time, she thought that Stevens looked a little disconcerted. His eyes narrowed slightly. Was he wondering how much she knew? Ben knew everybody in the genetics world; he might easily have introduced Judy to people who naturally gossiped about the life there. That Ben had not done this, because keeping his wife at arm's length made it easier to conduct his extramarital affairs, evidently wasn't something Stevens was sure of. He smiled primly.

"I'm afraid that's confidential Verico information."

"Really. But of course people talk—"

"They're entitled. But we don't talk *about* candidates. He smiled. She'd made a mistake: in tone or wording or something. He'd decided she didn't know about any other interviewees, after all.

But what did the other interviewees know?

"I'm afraid we haven't been very helpful to you about what was on your husband's mind, Mrs. Kozinski. Is there anything else I can do for you?"

"No, thank you." She knew defeat when she saw it. "I appreciate the time you've given me."

"Would you like a tour of Verico?"

If they were offering it, there was nothing to see. Yet Ben had been different when he came back from this place. *"Judy, I've been through a lot in the last two days—"*

"Sure, why not?" she said.

The tour took forty-five minutes. She saw the same things she'd seen at Whitehead: computers and lab animals and expensive equipment and refrigerated cultures and unrefrigerated cultures and notebooks and enough glassware to water Ethiopia. Stevens introduced her to everybody. Everybody was affable and consolatory. *So sorry to hear about your husband . . . such a loss to the scientific community.* Only a few of the women appeared to even notice her funeral outfit, with its bizarre brown belt and red bandanna scarf.

The taxi had not waited. Stevens said the guard had paid it, first reclaiming her parka. He called her another taxi, chatting amiably, pressing hot coffee on her. Tea? Maybe cocoa? It was so cold out, this promised to be a very snowy winter. . . .

And this, Judy thought, is what it means to be choked with hatred. To feel it clogging your throat, turning your esophagus into one more strangled drain.

She took the taxi all the way back to Manhattan, leaning back and closing her eyes. She needed to think. What did she have?

Not much.

But something *had* happened at Verico to upset Ben. After his interview there he'd been quiet, distracted, preoccupied—and Ben only became those things when he was frightened. She knew him. And she knew her own intuition, a journalist's intuition, which was that something at Verico was very wrong. A journalist's intuition shouldn't be ignored.

She was a journalist.

She was Judy O'Brien Kozinski. Bereaved, haggard, in tremendous pain, choked with rage—but once again herself.

She was back.

Judy opened her eyes, fished paper and pencil out of her purse, and began jotting down names of scientists whom Verico might have interviewed. People worthy of a position Benjamin Kozinski could have occupied. People who, she'd heard, from a careless word dropped by Ben or anybody else at the Vegas conference, might have considered moving.

People who might know something about what had killed her husband.

By the time she paid off the cab at Penn Station, Judy had a list of twenty names. She studied them as she walked down the staircase to the Amtrak waiting area. She didn't notice the man in the plain dark suit who folded his newspaper, checked his watch, shifted his nondescript briefcase, and followed her down the stairs.

Fifteen

S he did *what?*" Cavanaugh said.

"Showed up at Verico." Neymeier kept his eyes on the report in his hand, fresh off the fax. "This morning. Thought you'd want to know."

"Oh my God. Let me see that thing."

He studied the terse report, filed by the latest in a series of watchers assigned to discreet surveillance of Verico, a series of watchers Felders hadn't wanted since early October. Not cost-effective. Better use of field personnel. Difficulty of constant unnoticed surveillance in an office-park setting. Nothing happening on the case to justify allocation of resources. Division head Patrick Duffy, "Duffy the Thrifty," was squeezing Felders, and so Felders was squeezing Cavanaugh.

And Cavanaugh had argued back, hanging on with dogged persistence. This case was potentially much larger than it seemed. Not a single murder, but a pattern of organized crime involvement in biotech research. Hottest and most controversial field today. An intuition. This could be one of the big ones. An REI. Patience, all would be justified, secrecy essential so as not to alert the Relatives.

Cavanaugh suspected Felders was as sick of the argument as he was. It had taken on a low-key, monotonous rumble, background noise in team meetings. Of which one was scheduled to start in ten minutes. But so far Felders hadn't pulled the plug.

He was giving Cavanaugh his chance.

And now Judy Kozinski had shown up at Verico, disappeared inside for fifty-seven minutes, and been put into a taxi by Eric Stevens. Looking, according to the field agent, "distraught" and "shaken." By what? More important, what had she said that might shake Stevens? Had she told him that federal investigators had questioned her about Verico? Or that she herself suspected something dangerous at the biotech company? Had she implied to Stevens—hell, had she said outright (she had struck Cavanaugh as a woman capable of any hysterical speech)—that she thought Verico had had her husband murdered and she was going to get even?

If she had, her own life might be in danger. And the Relatives' sense of safety, their knowledge that no one was watching Verico, was blown. Cavanaugh had been counting on the Relatives feeling safe. People were easier to watch when they didn't know they were being watched. And now—

"God damn it," Cavanaugh said. Torpedoed by an amateur.

Neymeier coughed discreetly. "Something else."

"Something *else?* Okay, hit me with it. What have you got?"

"Not me. You. Process server on his way up to see you."

Cavanaugh stared at the weedy analyst, who determinedly studied the floor. There was no case going to trial for which Cavanaugh was expecting to testify. There was no reason for a process server to be on his way up to Cavanaugh's cubicle. Nor for Neymeier to know about it if there was.

"Ran into him in the men's room," Neymeier said.

He coughed again. "Asked directions to you. Thought you might want to know."

He moved off, his long legs covering ground unusually quickly. The process server passed him in the doorway.

"Robert James Cavanaugh?"

"Yes," Cavanaugh said. The process server was young, younger even than Neymeier. He went through his ritual as if he was still impressed to find himself part of the legal system. Cavanaugh opened the envelope.

It was a restraining order, signed by a D.C. judge.

TEMPORARY ORDER OF PROTECTION

A petition of the Family Court Act having been filed in this court alleging that ___Robert James Cavanaugh___ of ___145 Crescent Way, Apt. 3C___ has ___harassed by means of unwanted mail, phone, and facsimile machine___ the petitioner of this court, ___Marcia Suzanne Gordon___ of ___4360 Sycamore, Georgetown___ and it appearing, upon good cause shown, that a temporary order of protection would serve the purposes of this Act,

Now, therefore, it is hereby ordered that ___Robert James Cavanaugh___ shall observe the following conditions of behavior in that ___he___

1. shall stay away from the home, school, business, or place of employment of the victim(s) of the alleged offense;
2. shall refrain from harassing, intimidating, threatening, or otherwise interfering with the victim(s) of the alleged offense.

THIS ORDER CONSTITUTES A TEMPORARY ORDER OF PROTECTION. YOUR WILLFUL FAILURE TO OBEY THIS ORDER MAY, AFTER COURT HEARING, RESULT IN YOUR COMMITMENT TO JAIL FOR A TERM NOT TO EXCEED SIX MONTHS, FOR CONTEMPT OF COURT.

Harassment. Marcy. The notes.
He had sent the last one three days ago:

*Lovers and fools walk in where angels fear nothing
but fear itself. The frost is on the pumpkin eater;
the center holds none but the brave, the cowards
never started, the weak died a thousand deaths. Let
he who is without sin cast his bread upon the waters, and depend on the kindness of strangers, and
wonder whether 'tis nobler to have yet begun to
fight with arms against a sea of love. She only regrets that a fly buzzed when she died, and that she
has but one life to pursue without him but with
liberty through the slings and arrows of the winter
of her discontent.*

Two days before that, it had been a drawing of three
ovals floating over a city, one of them hatching the
Goodyear blimp, the whole labeled THREE EGGS OVER
DALLAS.
The last time she'd called him, she'd screamed over
the phone. Marcy. Who never raised her voice.
*. . . refrain from harassing, intimidating, threatening, or
otherwise interfering with the victim . . .* The victim! She,
who had thrown him out of their marriage!
Cavanaugh slammed the door to his cubicle. The glass
shivered. He dialed Marcy's office.
"I'm sorry, Ms. Gordon is in a meeting."
"Then you tell Ms. Gordon, who is still legally Mrs.
Cavanaugh—did you know that interesting fact?—tell
Ms. Gordon that this legal action—"
"Let me transfer you," the voice said, sounding fright-
ened. Why frightened? How did he, Cavanaugh, sound
to her? In the sudden silence he pulled himself together.
Marcy came on the line.
"Robert, how dare you shout at Karen. Don't you—"
"I wasn't shouting."
"You were *shouting*. And don't you realize you can't
call me like this anymore? That's what the restraining

order is for. Read it, Robert. I'm hoping that it will finally get through to you, since I can't."

She didn't sound frightened or upset. She sounded calm and in control, which was one of the things he had loved about her. She was a competent, calm, capable woman. Marcy could always cope.

Even, it seemed, with him.

He had a sudden picture of her, sitting at her office desk in the dark red suit he liked so much, looking groomed and controlled and stylish. The picture grew smaller and smaller, as if it were suddenly receding down the wrong end of a telescope. Smaller and smaller . . .

"*Marcy—*"

"Give up, Robert," she said, and hung up.

He hit redial. While the phone was giving out leisurely clicks, Felders opened the door and stuck his head in. He looked grim.

"Listen, you joining us for the meeting, Bob? Or aren't we on your social calendar this afternoon?"

"I'm coming. Just a minute—"

Felders's expression changed. He could look feral when he thought something was breaking: needle-eyed, prick-eared, a wolf scenting prey. "Got something?"

Cavanaugh thought of getting Marcy, or her frightened secretary, on the line with Felders standing there, listening. The restraining order lay, faceup, on the desk. Cavanaugh hung up. "No. Nothing important."

"Well, the meeting *is*."

Cavanaugh went to the meeting.

"I don't see," Natalie Simmons said patiently, "why we can't replace all the JVCs with Nagras. I had an informant wired just last week, and the sound quality of the JVC is so lousy that I know the judge is going to throw the tape out of court. An important case—"

"We can't have Nagras because nobody's *making* Nagras," Felders said, equally patiently. "The Swedish manufacturer went bankrupt, Natalie. You already know that."

"But something *like* Nagras. Surely somebody's making something of comparable quality. When you consider what's at stake here—"

Cavanaugh stopped listening. He was on Natalie's side, of course—the JVCs were lousy—and in fact ordinarily he'd be fighting the Equipment Wars right beside her. The Bureau needed new wires, new remotes, new PCs, new vans—just about everything updated except weapons. Which were used only a tiny fraction of all the rest of it. But weapons were something budget makers understood. The NRA approved. Congress approved. Congress was generous with weapons. It was law enforcement they never seemed to understand.

What had Judy Kozinski found out at Verico?

"Bob?" Felders said, in a tone that meant he'd said it at least once already. "What do you think?"

"I think I need more agents on Verico."

Natalie Simmons blinked. Jerry Mendolia looked away. Ralph Papanau rolled his eyes. It seemed they hadn't been discussing Verico yet. Of course they hadn't been discussing Verico—he, Cavanaugh, was the only person who still thought it was worth discussing.

Knew it was worth discussing.

"Could we maybe finish with my case first?" Papanau said, heavy on the sarcasm. "If nobody minds?"

"I don't mind," Cavanaugh said, and Papanau rolled his eyes again.

"I think," Felders said, "we'd better take the Verico discussion off-line."

A bad sign. That was what Felders did when he wanted to pull the plug: see the case agent privately in his cubicle. Less blood, less chance to stir up opposing opinion. Well, the hell with that.

"Marty, I need another full-time agent on Verico. Plus a dedicated analyst with a strong science background."

"Ask and it shall be given," Papanau said. "Don't be so coy, Robert. Blurt it right out."

Cavanaugh ignored him. "I really need this, Marty. It's important."

"Listen," Felders said, "Duffy wants to wrap this one. Nothing's happening, and the links to the Relatives are just too weak."

"Now," Cavanaugh said. *"Now* they're weak. But they won't be. I know it. We need an agent to watch Judy Kozinski, in addition to the team watching Verico, and a really good scientific analyst to track all genetic engineering publication. All of it. Consistently."

Felders didn't blink at Mrs. Kozinski's name. So he'd already seen the field investigator's report, even though Neymeier had brought it to Cavanaugh hot off the fax. How did Felders see everything so fast? *His* machinery was always working.

Felders said, "See me after the meeting, Bob."

"But, Marty, the reason it's so important is that this scientific field—"

"After." One word. But it was enough, in that tone of voice. Cavanaugh shut up. He watched Papanau smirk. Prick. Cavanaugh hoped all his far-distant grand-children were genetically engineered with the heads of camels. The kind that spit.

He picked up his pencil and doodled on his notepad. A camel, with a hump shaped like a Venus flytrap. He sketched himself falling into the flytrap. On the camel's side he wrote, in elaborate curly script, "Marcy."

At the end of the meeting he crumpled the paper and threw it away.

"All right," Felders said in his cluttered office. "Shoot. Convince me. How do you figure it?"

Cavanaugh recognized his last chance. He took a moment to arrange his thoughts.

"Suppose that I've been right all along. Verico is on the verge of something big, some way to use a genetically engineered virus to make really big bucks, probably on the underground market. *Really* big bucks. And—"

"That scientist at NIH didn't spot any implications of Kozinski's research—"

"Because they're not obvious implications," Cavan-

augh said. "Dr. Garvey had no way of knowing what
Verico is actually pursuing, because all they're publishing are small, unrelated articles and patents. But suppose
the patents are deliberately unrelated, so as not to tip
anybody to what they've got. Suppose Verico is close—
maybe real close—and there's just some last technical
problem or missing scientific breakthrough that Stevens's staff can't crack. So they start looking around for
somebody who can, somebody really brilliant. Only it's
risky, because there's no way they can recruit a top scientist like that without revealing the nature of the project."

"Which we haven't a clue about," Felders said, not
without sarcasm. Cavanaugh ignored Felders's tone.

"Which we haven't a clue about *yet*. I'm coming to
that. So the Relatives okay top-level recruitment in the
scientific community, under their own careful eye."

"Whose careful eye, do you think? Which family?
Callipare? Gigliotti? Bonadio?"

"Unknown so far," Cavanaugh said. He could see that
Felders was getting interested, despite himself. "Sometime last summer Verico approaches a genetic scientist,
gets him to come to New Jersey, offers him the moon,
and brutally lays out what's involved in terms he can't
mistake. Or she. The scientist is horrified—"

"Your analyst couldn't find any top scientist with
transportation booked to New Jersey all last summer,"
Felders objected.

"So he drove. Or he came on a commuter train from
New York or Boston. About a third of the country's
biotech labs are located within easy distance of New Jersey. Anyway, the guy sees everything and is horrified.
He says, No way. Stevens applies pressure. The guy is
ethical, and refuses to work on whatever Verico is working on. So Stevens, maybe with backup, terrifies him into
silence. They don't want to kill him unless they have to,
because important scientists aren't some other families'
foot soldiers—they're missed, they're connected, people
investigate. So the Relatives threaten to harm his wife,

or his kids, or to expose some dirt they've got on him. The scientist agrees to silence.

"But his conscience bothers him. So he risks one note to Duffy: 'Investigate Verico, head off Kozinski.' Only Kozinski is killed. And Verico's first choice is out there somewhere, knowing we are investigating. Or at least hoping to hell we are."

"How many genetics scientists did you say you talked to, Bob?"

"Seven. I really wanted to keep Verico quiet, but I did talk to seven who fit the profile and who I felt wouldn't talk about our conversation. Charles Goldberg at Cold Spring Harbor National Laboratory. Peter Hufford at Harvard. Keith Wolfe at UC San Francisco. Anne White at Brookhaven. Mark Lederer at Boston Biomedical. Jeffrey Woodcock at Cambridge. And William Myers, head of the Center for Human Genome Research at NIH. Nobody knows anything."

"Or else you analyzed right and one of them is *really* good at keeping secrets," Felders said. He did not comment on Cavanaugh's ability to reel off microbiology's most important names. "Go on. I'm still waiting to hear something new."

"Be patient. After they strike out with their first choice, whoever it was, Verico approaches Kozinski at the Las Vegas conference. He agrees to interview. He flies to New Jersey, is just as horrified as the first candidate, says no. But then, the first night home, he runs. The Relatives don't know where to. To blab to his mistress, another scientist? To the police? It's the middle of the night, after all, and he's not driving in the direction of the lab. The professional they have watching him makes an on-the-spot decision: the danger from Kozinski is greater than the danger from killing him. So the pro takes him out."

"Old stuff," Felders said, lounging in his chair. "Old, old, old."

"Then the Relatives, and Verico, wait. It's been over three months since the murder. Nothing's happening. Routine FBI inquiry, then nothing. Local cops have nothing. No questions are being asked by the scientific community. It looks safe. So they get ready to recruit again."

"And then Judy Kozinski walks into Verico asking questions."

"Right," Cavanaugh said. "And that leaves Verico with three choices. One, assume she's a danger, an amateur blundering around who nonetheless might have been told something by her husband or who in her hysterical thrashings might alert authorities to something they wouldn't otherwise get. If they assume that, they might kill her, too. Choice two, assume killing her is too dangerous, would attract too much attention. In that case, they ignore her, wait for her to go away, and postpone recruiting. Choice three, they also ignore her but go ahead with recruiting because the project, whatever it is, is close to completion."

"So which do you think it is?" Felders said.

"I'm hypothesizing they might go ahead with recruitment anyway. I think Stevens may be feeling boxed in. He has to know that the Relatives don't have a long attention span for something they understand as little as biotechnology. There's bound to be capos in the family—whichever family it is—that are old-line conservative. Stick to what you know: gambling, drugs, liquor, transport, labor unions. Biotech is bound to strike them as suspicious: egghead, esoteric. You know the Relatives."

Felders nodded, frowning.

"So what I need is an agent to watch Judy Kozinski and keep her from alarming anybody any further. Plus a really good analyst to watch all the perturbations in the genetic-engineering community. Not just who moves where, but who's publishing what, to find any patterns close to what Kozinski's specialties were. The patterns might not be obvious to us nonscientists. But if we can identify a recruitment target *before* he or she is approached, we can approach first."

Felders nodded again. "I see how you mean. But, listen, Bob—Duffy doesn't see it this way."

"You could make him see it."

Felders stopped lounging and sat up straight in his chair. "Damn it, Bob, I'm not sure I *want* to sell it to Duffy. What you've got is sound speculation, but it's still only speculation."

"The Cellini-Denisi tape that mentioned Verico months ago isn't speculative. Neither is a dead body. We were warned about Kozinski's going to Verico, and the next day he's knocked off by a pro. And you know it was a pro, Marty. So does Duffy. No fingerprints, no fibers, no attempt to use the victim's credit cards, no trail—no nothing. He wasn't knocked off by some desperate junkie or some enraged husband."

Felders smiled. "And you know because you checked all the enraged husbands."

"Plus everybody at Verico. You saw the report on the staff." Christopher Vincent DelCorvo, research assistant, whose mother was Maria Gigliotti DelCorvo, deceased; the son was possibly an associate in the Gigliotti family. Alfonso Ardieta, also a research assistant, with blood ties to the Callipare and Bonadio families. The trouble was that even to the Relatives, blood ties didn't mean what they once did. The offspring born in the 1960s and 70s were La Cosa Nostra, all right, but they were also born in the 1960s and 70s. They had their generation's sense of entitlement and individualism, two senses that didn't sit well with the old men who had grown up during the Depression, taking the oath "Loyalty above all." No wonder those old men turned increasingly to the Sicilian-born Zips who understood the old ways, who entered the United States so easily and, despite the best efforts of Immigration, who stayed there so invisibly. Christopher Vincent DelCorvo and Alfonso Ardieta had competition. There was no guarantee, despite their family ties, that they were LCN.

"I saw the report," Felders said. "But, Bob, there's nothing new. Nothing substantive has been added to this case since August, and it's now November, and we have better use for the manpower. I told you, every new IRS—"

"I know, I know. Every new IRS revenue agent repays his salary and overhead on an average of eight times. Whereas FBI agents just cost the taxpayers money, and so expenditures must be weighed against results." What Felders had actually said was, *No shooting, no shekels.* "But, Marty, this isn't your usual REI. It's—"

"It isn't an REI at all, Bob. And I don't see any promise of it becoming one."

"Not just *yet,* but—"

"No buts. Facts. Do you have facts or circumstances that 'reasonably indicate that individuals or individual'— I'll settle for just one individual, Bob—'have been or are currently or will be involved in a racketeering enterprise'?"

"No, but we—"

"Do you have any predicate acts committed by this nonenterprise? Money laundering, bribery, extortion, toxic waste dumping, fraud? I'll take anything, Bob."

"No, I—"

"Do you have enough for an affidavit that Verico was both acquired with illegal funds and is engaging in activities which affect interstate commerce?"

"No," Cavanaugh said.

"Proof of conspiracy?"

"No." Cavanaugh twisted his neck to loosen the muscle tension. Felders was moving down the list in order of easier-to-prove: for conspiracy, you didn't even need a substantive offense to have been committed yet. Only planned to commit. Cavanaugh couldn't even show that.

"Does Deming say that you, or Justice, has enough for a criminal forfeiture of Verico's assets?"

"No."

"For a civil forfeiture?"

"No." Civil forfeiture of property didn't even require "beyond a reasonable doubt" proof—"a preponderance of the evidence" standard was enough. More likely true than not.

"Can you," said Felders, his fingers drumming on his desk, "even convince a U.S. Attorney to convene a grand jury for purposes of investigation? Can you, Robert?"

Felders had called him by his full name. This was bad. The investigative grand jury, with its broad powers to subpoena persons and documents, was Justice's single most powerful tool against organized crime. You brought in lower-echelon and petty associates, gave them immunity, and questioned them about higher-ups in the enterprise. If they refused to answer, you threw them in jail for contempt of court until they did answer. Most never did—*omertà*—but a few did, especially those who weren't made men and never would be. The associates, the hangers-on. A grand jury was the rototiller of law enforcement, turning up all sorts of unexpected things in fertile ground. But you had to show reasonable credentials to be allowed to rent one.

"No, Marty. I don't have enough to convene a grand jury."

Felders stopped drumming his fingers. Lying still on his cluttered desktop, his hands looked suddenly delicate, long-fingered and empty. "Bob, an important quality of a good agent is knowing which cases have a reasonable chance of being solved. I don't see—"

"Just let me make my argument here, Marty. Five minutes."

"You got it." Felders was always fair.

Cavanaugh leaned forward in his chair. "First point— the whole thrust of an REI is to figure out the composition, structure, and activities of racketeering enterprises. That's often—in fact, usually—a long-term goal, possible only with long-term strategic intelligence gathering. As opposed to tactical intelligence for some immediate specific use. True enough?"

"True enough," Felders said.

"Second point—in the past, we've missed opportunities because we've failed to commit enough manpower to an investigation. Sometimes we've missed really tremendous opportunities. True enough?"

"True enough. But you're just spouting broad generalities. You haven't—"

"Bear with me. Third point—when RICO was first passed, it took us—and Justice, too—several *years* to really figure out how to structure an REI around them, right? At first we just went on investigating and prosecuting individual crimes one after another, the way traditional law enforcement still does. It took us a while to see that an REI is an entirely different animal, with different habits and watering holes and tracking turds."

"I love English majors," Felders said. "The metaphors."

"But what I said about developing a new approach is true enough?"

"True enough."

"And the time it took to do that?"

"True enough."

"All right then," Cavanaugh said, and took a deep breath. This was it. "What we have here is another new phenomenon, just as untried as RICO was twenty-five years ago. Not a new investigative approach, it's still an enterprise, but a new kind of enterprise. High-tech science just isn't something organized crime has ever shown the slightest interest in. The LCN doesn't run NASA the way it does the Teamsters. Racketeers don't strong-arm Microsoft. The Relatives have shown zero interest in cloning or fiber optics or dating dinosaur bones. Or in genetic research.

"Until now."

"Listen, Marty. We have the photograph linking Vincent DiPrima and Eric Stevens—"

"Hell, we have photographs linking Frank Sinatra to half the mob, and we aren't indicting him, either," Felders said.

"—and the taped mention of Verico by an indicted capo. We have Kozinski's murder, too close to the anonymous note to chalk up to coincidence. And we have a chance here to stop the Relatives before they move into gene-splicing, a new area of small, potentially lucrative, highly exploitable companies with the potential to maybe someday change everything about how human cells are structured. I've been reading about recombinant DNA, Marty. This is only the beginning. The next century is going to be the century of biotech, the way this one was for discoveries in physics. Advance after advance after advance. We don't see now the potential for money and control, no more than anybody saw it in airports on the day Orville and Wilbur Wright took off at Kitty Hawk. But now the Relatives own the air freight industry at LaGuardia, Kennedy, and Newark—we *know* they do. And they could one day own recombinant DNA, all legitimately, if we don't commit to stopping them *now*."

"You sound like a PBS special," Felders said. But he was listening.

"Do you know what this gene-splicing could do? Find a cure for cancer. A cure for getting fat. For looking old. All patentable. What do you think those things would be worth on the open market? How much money would there be in altering the cell deterioration that causes disease? It's brand new and wide open. I know we don't have a lot on this case. But we do have something, and keeping it going is the first step in blocking the LCN from a whole new area of enterprises. An area that *nobody,* not even its own top scientists, knows what the future will be. We have to keep this investigation open. Take it away from me, if that's your best judgment, but keep it open!"

Felders sat thinking, fingers still quiet on his desk. Cavanaugh waited, not breathing. Felders really did look feral, like some skinny rodent whose delicate bones belied the sharpness of his teeth. Naturally Felders didn't want to sink those teeth into Duffy, his boss. But if Felders said no . . .

"Okay, Bob. If I can get Duffy to agree, you can have one more agent, plus Tamara Lang. She's green, A.B.D. in molecular biology from Stanford, but she's supposed to be good."

"What's A.B.D.?" Cavanaugh said, out of relief. Felders was going to let him continue the case.

"And you with a degree in English. She's 'all but dissertation.' Did all the coursework for her doctorate and then changed her mind about a life of research. Decided she wanted to be an officer of the law."

"Why would she—"

"Why did you? Stop quibbling, Bob. You get what you want: an agent to watch Judy Kozinski and a science advisor to watch genetics research. Now go justify them both."

"I will," Cavanaugh said, and suddenly hoped to hell that was the truth. He rose to leave.

"Oh, and, Bob—"

"Yeah?"

Felders didn't look at him. "Stay away from Marcy. It doesn't look good to have Justice investigators served with domestic-problem court orders. Give it up."

"Right," Cavanaugh said.

Sixteen

The radio station wasn't what Wendell Botts had expected.

To start with, they didn't even recognize his name at the reception desk, which was just that, a desk in a tiny crammed storefront office with the dirtiest window he'd ever seen. Here he'd gone and bought a new suit, paying fifty fucking bucks for it, and shined his shoes, and put on a tie. He'd skipped his A.A. meeting, too, which up till now he had a perfect attendance record for. And the bimbo behind the desk didn't even recognize his name.

"Who?"

"I told you—Wendell Botts. I'm going to be *on the air.*"

"Oh." She shoved a three-ring binder at him, the kind kids used in junior high. "Sign in and have a seat."

The lined notebook paper was smudged and torn. Wendell signed at the bottom. Under "Host" he printed THE RICK ABRAMS HOUR in big capital letters.

They'd been the only ones to respond to his letters.

Forty-two fucking letters, and this Albany station was the only one to answer. Wendell had called them up right away and said yes, he'd come, he had an important story to take to the American people. Finally, somebody would really listen! But then he'd listened to "The Rick Abrams Hour" a couple of nights, and he wasn't so sure. The guy was really snotty to his guests. Wendell had almost changed his mind.

But nobody else had answered his letters.

The girl behind the desk ignored him. Wendell sat on a sagging director's chair, hands on his knees, waiting. Outside the dirty window, a neon light with three dead tubes blinked on and off: G–N– –EE. Half an hour went by.

"Hey, shouldn't I go in soon?"

"Oh, they don't want you until nine o'clock. You're the last segment."

"Then why did they tell me to be here by eight?"

The girl shrugged. Bitch. Glaring at her, the dyed big hair and heavy makeup and tight sweater, Wendell thought of Saralinda. Saralinda's clean, sweet-smelling brown hair, her thin serious face, her slow hesitant walk, so feminine . . .

This radio show felt like his last chance to make Saralinda come home.

There's never a last chance, they said at A.A. Swell. Great. But what did they know, a bunch of drunks? About the Soldiers of the Divine Covenant, A.A. didn't know jackshit.

A door behind the receptionist's desk opened and a woman came out. This one was middle-aged, well-dressed, and furious. She snatched a fur coat off a second sagging director's chair and stomped outside, slamming the outer door hard. A gust of cold night air blew across Wendell's knees.

"You can go in now," the girl behind the desk said.

Just like a fucking doctor's office.

Wendell lumbered around her desk and opened the door. He walked into a tiny room packed with electronic equipment. A guy wearing headphones took up most of the space. Beyond a glass window was a second tiny, dirty room—there didn't seem to be any other kind here—with another guy wearing headphones, this one sitting at a table with two chairs. Crushed paper cups littered the table.

The man closest to Wendell motioned him through without so much as looking at him. Wendell decided there must be a commercial on the air; he was proud of figuring this out for himself. A little hard ball of excitement bounced in his belly.

The second room was walled with soundproofing, gray spongy stuff like what came in packing boxes. Wendell squeezed himself into the vacant chair, which was so close to the wall he barely had room to fit. Across from him, Rick Abrams had his eyes closed. Was the guy *asleep?*

Wendell studied Abrams. He didn't look like his voice. The voice was deep and rich, but Abrams was a tall, skinny guy with arms like spaghetti. Wendell could've taken him with one hand. Abram's long, reddish hair was tied in a sloppy ponytail, and he wore a red sweatshirt. He looked like some kind of hippie wuss.

Abruptly Abrams opened his eyes and motioned for Wendell to put on his headphones.

"Our next guest, all you people out there with nothing better to do than listen to neurotic drivel, apparently doesn't have anything better to do with *his* time than spew it for you. And drivel I suspect it is. But we'll give the guy his fair hearing—hey, don't we always?—his FCC soapbox, his Warhol allotment of fame, right to the nanosecond before the gong sounds. With us tonight is Wendell Botts, local construction worker, sometime religious nut, who's here to talk about—are you ready for this one?—human sacrifice at a Waco-waiting-to-happen right here in upstate New York. Join with me in welcoming Mr. Botts, sound of furious applause, so what's the story, Wendell?"

Wendell stared, confused. Abrams said so many stupid things, and he said them so fast—

"Well, ladies and gentlemen, it appears we have a

problem in the front office, they're booking mutes on the show. Must be a form of labor protest. Classier than picketing, what? But take your time, Mr. Botts, there's still fourteen minutes and ten seconds on the Warhol meter."

The what? Panicked, Wendell glared at Abrams, who was smiling across the table. No, not smiling . . . *laughing*, without noise. The prick was laughing at him!

"My name is Wendell Botts," he said, and stopped at hearing his own voice in the headphones over his ears.

"So we've established," Abrams said. "Points for positive I.D., Detective Botts. Now what's the collar?"

"I . . ."

"C'mon, spit it out, there are tens of inquiring minds out there wanting to know."

"I think they're practicing human sacrifice at the Soldiers of the Divine Covenant camp in Cadillac, New York." There. He'd got it out. It would be better now.

Abrams tilted his chair back against the wall and propped his feet on the table. There was a lot more room on his side of the table than on Wendell's. "Human sacrifice. Right. And how do you know this, Goodman Botts?"

"I was a member of the Soldiers of the Divine Covenant. For almost three years."

"Ah. And you personally witnessed this human sacrifice."

"No, but—"

"What buts, Botts?"

"A lot of people have died inside the Soldiers' camp."

"People always die, Wendell. And worms eat them, as the poet so appetizingly reminds us. What makes you think these dead Soldiers were victims of unspeakable religious ritual?"

"The Soldiers sacrifice animals! I seen them! They believe Leviticus Seven—"

"Spare us the Fundamentalist chapter and verse, and cut to the chase. What evidence do you have?"

"I know how the Soldiers think. They—"

"You know because you were one. And now you're

a dropout, or a flunkout—were you expelled from Leviticus, Wendell?—and so you're out to do the grand exposé thing, and make all the other religious nuts sorry they ever messed with you. Isn't that right?"

"No, I—"

"It's not right? You're not out to expose the Soldiers of the Divine Covenant? But your letter to this radio station, which I have right here—and a charmingly written missive it is—says, that you *do* want to expose your old pew-mates. So which is it, Wendell?"

"I can't—"

"Which is it?"

"Shut up!" Wendell roared. His own voice shrieked in his headphones. Abrams smiled. Looking at him over the tops of his cowboy boots, still propped on the table, Wendell saw that smile and he felt the old surge in his guts. Smash. Smash the smiling fucking face, the prick, the motherfucking bastard—

" 'Shut up,' " Abrams said in a sweet voice. "The perfect answer to all rational challenge that might—"

Wendell stood. He locked his hands under the table and heaved it up with him. Abrams and his chair crashed to the floor, and the table crashed on top of both. Wendell stood panting beside the wreckage, scowling at the engineer in the sound booth, who was frantically pushing buttons.

"Don't you dare take this off the air!" Wendell yelled. "I got something to say and I'm going to say it! You hear me!"

The sound engineer nodded. Abrams struggled up from under the table, his ponytail untied, flailing his skinny arms. Wendell ignored him. He stood in the middle of the tiny room lined with sound baffles of dirty foam, and he fought to keep his voice under control.

"I was a Soldier of the Divine Covenant for four years. I ain't proud of it now, but I know why I went in. It's because the world treated me rotten, the way the world always treats poor people who don't have nothing, not even a high school diploma. I couldn't get work because the government said there was a recession and there wasn't no work. It's always that way for people like me. We're the first to get fired when things go bad, and nobody cares if we can't pay the rent, or buy shoes for our kids. There's a lot of people like me and my wife out there, who've about given up hope.

"The Soldiers offered us some hope. They seemed to care what happened to us. They gave us milk for our baby daughter when all the rest of the world wanted to give us a kick in the ass."

Wendell paused to collect his thoughts. Abrams was on his feet now, and his face had changed: gone narrow-eyed, suspicious. But he didn't try to touch Wendell—good thing for *him*.

"People without no religion don't ever understand why poor people join such weird religions. It's because you can get caring there you can't get nowhere's else. Sometimes it's weird caring, though. I know that now. I didn't know it then. Me and my wife Saralinda became Soldiers, and we lived in the camp in Cadillac. Our little boy was born there. David.

"When I was a Soldier, I saw the animal sacrifices. Hell, I *helped* with them. The Elders would bless a woodchuck or a rabbit, and the helpers would stand away in a circle, and then the Elder would cut its throat. I can't tell you the sound that animal would make. Sort of a squeal, but not really. It makes your blood run cold. Once they used a cat—"

"A cat? Somebody's pet?" Abrams said, in Wendell's earphones. Wendell saw him glance at a black plastic board labeled PHONE LINES. Red lights blinked the length of the board.

"Maybe somebody's pet," Wendell said. "The kids weren't supposed to watch, but sometimes they did. I saw them. 'Like the twig is bent, the tree grows.' It was a blood sacrifice, you see, to wash away the sins of the congregation. Even the kids' sins. It's the only use for blood that's allowed. No eating meat, no blood trans-fusions."

"Even if, say, a kid is dying?" Abrams asked silkily. Somehow he'd got the two chairs upright and the table, which now had one busted leg, shoved out of the way in the corner. He motioned to Wendell to sit down. Wendell sat, hardly noticing what he did. He felt a great urgency to get it all out, tell the whole story. It almost felt as if the words were jammed up there in his chest, and the sheer pressure was forcing them out without him even thinking what to say.

"Even if a kid was dying. No blood. But they shed it in animal sacrifices, because the Bible said to, and now I think they're killing human beings too, because the Bible shows that death is the way to punish members of the congregation who fuck up. Or maybe their kin. Thirteen people have died inside the camp in the last nine months—"

"How do you know that?" Abrams said sharply.

"Some from the obituaries in the newspaper. Some from my wife. Even some from my little girl. Penny is almost five, kids have to go to funerals. To get them to accept God's ways. Thirteen—but I think there's more!"

"Why is that, Mr. Botts?" For the first time, Wendell noticed how Abrams's voice had changed. It was quiet, respectful. Abrams glanced again at the row of blinking red lights.

"Because there's limestone caves all under the camp, it would be so easy to hide a body in there, and the Soldiers are ... they're hard." That wasn't the right word, and Wendell frowned. Then the right words came to him. "They're without mercy. Like the marines. Leastwise, they're without mercy when they think the Bible wants them to do something ... *and my little kids are in there!*"

It came out different than Wendell expected. He didn't know he hurt like that. No, yes, he did know, of course he did, but he didn't know that words could carry that much of the hurt. Not *his* words. He blinked and glanced around the tiny recording booth. God, he sounded like some bleeding heart pansy. . . .

But Abrams was saying, "The callboard is lit up like L.A. gridlock, so let's take our first caller. Go ahead, please."

"This is *terrible,*" a woman's voice said. "I never listen to you, Mr. Abrams, because your show is so dirty and nasty, but I'm glad I did tonight. Those poor kids—why doesn't the law do something? Even if there's not human sacrifices going on in there, it's bad enough to think that precious innocent children are being forced to watch pet cats murdered because of—that's *not* what the Bible intends, Mr. Abrams! Jesus is love! You did right to put poor Mr. Botts on your show—"

"Which you'll of course listen to from now on," Abrams said drily. "Next caller, please—"

"Botts, your predicament only underlines what I've said all along. The religious right in this country possesses a low cunning, using people's legitimate need to be self-supporting in order to brainwash us into unthinking subservience. What's interesting is that as long ago as 1943 Ayn Rand warned us in *The Fountainhead*—"

"Oh, God, spare us the Randians," Abrams drawled. He winked at Wendell. "Talk about unthinking brainwashing . . ."

The caller started shouting. Abrams shouted back: insulting, smiling. The callboard blinked frantically. More people called, all excited. They seemed to think Wendell was fighting a good fight, that he was right to get his kids out of there. Abrams let Wendell talk to some of them, and he told them to write their congressmen and the FBI. Abrams rolled his eyes, but by that time Wendell didn't care. These people thought he was right! They thought he should have Penny and David back! They *listened* to him!

Only one man was skeptical. Wendell hated his voice as soon as he heard it: cool, dry, snotty. He hated it even more when the man said he was a doctor. "What makes you think, Mr. Botts, that the so-called deaths by ritual sacrifice wouldn't have been detected instantly in an autopsy?"

"Maybe there weren't no autopsies!"

"But you've indicated that you learned of several of these deaths through the *Cadillac Register* obituary column, and you said that some of those were 'strong healthy people with no reason to die.' In such a case, the local authorities would automatically order an autopsy. Death by ritual throat cutting is pretty easy to spot, Mr. Botts. It's the deep bloody gash under the chin that does it."

Abrams grinned. Wendell said, "I don't know about that, but—"

"Obviously not."

"I want my kids outta that place!" Wendell shouted. Abrams glanced at his sound engineer, and Wendell hated Abrams all over again: for his snotty stuck-up college-hippie attitude. He'd like to knock Abrams's teeth down his throat. . . . But the next caller said warmly that Wendell was a hero, the greatest heroes were always those who fought hard for their kids, and she just knew that Wendell's daughter was a beautiful little angel like her own precious girl, with blond hair and blue eyes. Wendell started to describe Penny.

He wondered if maybe, by some miracle, Saralinda was somehow listening.

She wasn't of course. Soldiers of the Divine Covenant would never listen to something like "The Rick Abrams Hour." But here were all these people listening to *him,* and the longer he talked the more terrible details of life in the camp he remembered.

And then, the radio show was over and Abrams hadn't even got a chance to stick in all the commercials he was supposed to, so many people wanted to talk to Wendell. The sound engineer let him back into the dingy reception room. The bimbo receptionist was gone, but a man stood outside the locked front door, tapping on the glass. Wendell grabbed his duffle coat and opened the door. The man tumbled inside, shivering in the November wind. There was snow on his jacket. His handshake was firm, and his young face had the go-getter look Wendell remembered from marine recruits who wanted to make corporal faster than anybody else.

"Hello, are you Wendell Botts? My name is Jake Peterson. I write for the *Albany Gazette.* I'd like to talk to you, Mr. Botts, about your children and the camp of the Divine Covenant."

It takes what it takes.

"Sure, Mr. Peterson."

"Let's get a drink," Peterson said. "I want to hear all about your problem."

Seventeen

Barbara? This is Judy Kozinski."

"Judy! Oh, you're back . . . how *are* you?"

Judy, standing in her kitchen in Natick, held the phone away from her ear and grimaced. At the same time, her eyes filled with tears. People always said the exact same words, and in the exact same tones. First came her name in a startled voice, as if it were completely amazing to hear from her—as if, in fact, it was she and not Ben who had died, and she was now calling from beyond the grave. Then the voice always dropped to a hush, with an anxious little emphasis on the second of the three predictable words: How *are* you? And woven through it all were the undertones of guilt, because Judy was calling them instead of vice versa. People, Judy had discovered, were embarrassed by death, and their embarrassment made them defensive, and their defensiveness made her cry.

She blinked back the tears. "I'm fine. How are you?"

"Oh, great," Barbara McBride said. "I mean, not great, of course, we're still reeling from Ben's . . . nobody knows quite what to do and you were at your parents' so long, but if there's anything I can do, anything at all, even though of course I know nobody can—"

Judy took pity on her. "Actually, Barbara, there is something you can do."

"Anything," Barbara said, warmly and with misgivings.

"Invite me to the big party you always have the Saturday after Thanksgiving."

"Judy! Of course you're welcome, my God you come every year, you and . . . The only reason I didn't send you an invitation was that I didn't know if you—actually, when you told me at the funeral you were going to be away for a while, I . . . oh, dear."

This was a lot of dithering even for death embarrassment. Judy frowned. She could picture Barbara in her big sunny kitchen in Newton, holding the phone and gazing distractedly out the window at the bare raked yard. Barbara's husband, Jon, worked—had worked—with Ben at Whitehead. Ben had kept his colleagues and his wife in two separate parts of his life, so the two couples had seen each other only three or four times a year, mostly for concerts or plays, plus official occasions. Judy and Barbara weren't really friends, but they were friendly. And Barbara was one of those women convinced that their entertaining was an important help to their husbands' careers. Her big parties included everybody who was important in microbiology that she could entice to come. It would be a good place for Judy to start asking questions. But Barbara sounded so flustered. . . .

"Barbara, is there a problem with my coming to the party?"

"Oh, no, it's just that . . . no, of course not! Please come, Judy. Everyone will be so happy to see you again. Eight o'clock."

"What can I bring?"

"Oh, you don't have to bring anything!"

Judy said, slowly and distinctly, "Barbara, I always bring something. Everybody always brings something.

That hasn't changed—I'd still like to bring something.
Are curried nuts okay?"

"Oh, wonderful!" Barbara said. "See you then!"

Now what, wondered Judy, was all that dithering
about?

She hung up the phone. It was 10:00 A.M, the Sunday
before Thanksgiving. She had, she realized, nothing
whatsoever to do. Nada. Zip.

Not that she'd been doing all that much since she'd
returned to Natick. Mostly she'd been spending her time
in the library, "researching." Yeah, sure. Right. She'd
read every published reference to Verico—all three of
them. "ANOTHER BIOTECH START-UP." "MOLECULAR
BIO MAJORS ENJOY EXPANDING MARKETPLACE." "NOT
ALL BIOTECH FIRMS ON THE ROAD TO PROFIT." In each
of the last two articles, Verico had rated a single sentence.

She'd used the Internet to research Eric Stevens, and
to skim his two published articles. Neither the man nor
his work had any distinguishing implications. She'd gone
farther, checking on Stevens's police, real estate, and
family records in the county files. Nothing. She'd con-
tacted Yale, where Stevens had gone to school, and the
State University of New York at Stony Brook, where
he'd briefly taught. For both calls, Judy had pretended
to be a prospective employer checking references. Nothing. Stony Brook had confirmed Stevens's employment,
but the department chair had only been with the university four years and didn't remember Stevens personally. Neither did anyone at the hospital where he'd done
his residency.

Eric Stevens was a publicly blank individual, and Judy
was a privately frustrated amateur.

Still, she wasn't giving up. The public databases were
only background. Verico had talked to somebody before
they'd interviewed Ben, and that was where the real information would come. Starting with Barbara McBride's
party.

But that was six days away, which meant six days to
get through. Thursday morning she would drive down
to Troy for Thanksgiving with her parents, driving home

again Friday night. Saturday she could sleep late, spend the afternoon making curried nuts and maybe some cheese puffs as well, and getting ready for the party. But that still left today, Monday, Tuesday, and Wednesday to get through.

Four days.

Abruptly Judy put her hands over her face. God, she *hated* this. She'd never been the kind of woman who killed time, scrambling frantically for ways to make it pass until there was a party or a trip to fill the empty hours. She'd despised such women, in fact. She—Judy Kozinski, *her*—had always had more than enough to do. Interesting things, vital things. She'd researched science articles, and spent happy hours at her computer writing them, and done volunteer work for the homeless, and had a wide circle of friends, and loved Victorian prose, and accompanied Ben to his scientific conferences . . .

Every time she sat at the computer her mind went blank, a peculiar fuzzy blankness in which specks floated glaringly clear, and the specks were memories of Ben. Every time she opened a novel, the same thing happened. And the one time she'd tried to report to the homeless shelter, her chest had started pounding so hard she'd barely made it back to the car.

That was the part about murder that nobody told you: That it wasn't just your life with the dead man that was lost. It was everything about your life, everything you used to do, every reaction you used to have. All changed, all gone. You didn't just lose your husband, you lost everything.

No. That couldn't be true. It wouldn't be. She would fight it, struggle as hard as she could, to be Judy Kozinski again. Herself.

And didn't that sound brave? All right, then, she was brave. Judy Kozinski, daily heroine, struggling to survive and hang onto her identity. Strike up the band, alert the media, award her a Purple Heart. Only, how was she going to fill up the next four days? This day? This hour?

She would clean.

Despite herself, Judy laughed out loud. That was her

mother's solution, her grandmother's solution. When in despair, clean. Feminist with a master's degree, and she had progressed no further than her immigrant grandmother, Kathleen O'Malley, who had spat on sidewalks to ward off the evil eye and who always used plastic forks during a thunderstorm to prevent lightning attacks in her kitchen.

Who the fuck *cared.* If it would take her mind off her own dreary self, then she would clean. And after she finished cleaning, she'd dye her hair. Red. Be somebody else. Why not? She'd already been made into somebody else by events she couldn't control. Red hair she could control.

Cleaning she could control.

She got a bucket from the laundry room, marshalled Spic and Span, Windex, and Murphy's Oil Soap. For the first time, she noticed how really grimy the house actually was. Nobody had cleaned since early August, before . . .

She decided to start with the living room. The bedroom, and Ben's study, might both be harder to take. Hauling around furniture to vacuum underneath, chasing pennies and crumbs under sofa cushions (God, the disgusting stuff that accumulated in the cracks of upholstery!) actually made her feel better. She finished the living room and moved into the dining room. Opening doors in the bottom of the china closet, she pulled everything out to dust thoroughly, and she found the notebook.

The police had searched the house after the murder—not just Ben's study, but the whole house, with her consent. Judy had given them Ben's diary, his calendar, his address book, the journals he kept under the bed to read before he fell asleep. She'd never suspected there might be more.

No. That wasn't true. She *had* suspected. And she knew what this was even before she opened it.

Not a personal diary. None of his girls would be in here to pierce her to the heart. Ben was too cautious for that. Cautious, but—she'd always known it—vain.

The first entry was two years old.

> *A scientist's notebook. Sounds pretentious, I know—but I feel a need to set down my emotional reactions to the work we're doing in the lab, reactions that don't really belong in either the project notebooks or my diary. Science is so much more than equations and experiments—it's a map of truth, and how we who do science feel about the truth.*

Judy winced. This was Ben at his worst: self-conscious, heavy-handed. Posing for posterity. This notebook was intended to be turned over, some distant day, to his biographer. It would have been turned over with a great show of reluctance, she knew, but there was no doubt it would have been turned over. That was why Ben had kept it. He was documenting his own lofty thoughts, constructing the mirror in which he would be reflected. Not least, to himself.

But why was it in the china closet, between tablecloths they never used? That was easy. Ben had insomnia. When he couldn't sleep, he liked to come downstairs, heat himself a cup of warm milk, and drink it at the dining room table. Often she'd found the empty cup there in the morning. He must have used the time to write in this notebook.

> *Today was one of those days when we seem to be going backward. Nothing came out right. Caroline said to me, "Do you think Dea Nukleia has deserted us?" Dea Nukleia, the Muse of Microbiology. And I said—*

Pain lanced through Judy. She dropped the notebook. Dea Nukleia—her and Ben's joke. Or so she'd thought. But he'd shared it with Caroline, maybe it even had originated with Caroline. . . . Oh, damn him, damn him to hell. . . .

. . . significant progress on the MHC problem . . .

*. . . can't be sure what applications this might have,
I don't suppose any scientist ever is. This all reminds me of the great Pasteur, who . . .*

*. . . the computers went down just then. The curse
of depending on technology to drive the technology
we need to create the technology . . .*

And then, at the very end, the notebook changed.
Even Ben's handwriting was different: bigger, less careful, looping across the page. The ponderous general-
izations disappeared. There was more real science,
equations and gene code, interspersed with terse, exuberant questions. Sometimes a scrawled entry would
have a huge question mark drawn under it, sometimes
an exclamation point. Ben wasn't posing anymore— he
was on the trail of something, and his excitement was
genuine.

The last two pages exploded in high-spirited doodles.

The Lone Ranger, a half-figure with black mask and
Stetson, shot a silver bullet from his gun. Ben was no
artist, the figures were badly drawn, exuberant, a pure
expression of nonartistic excitement. The huge bullet
was labeled EHRLICH! The facing page was covered with
bullets, of all shapes and sizes, firing from a weird as-
sortment of guns: rifles and revolvers and cannons and
strangely shaped pieces whose unrecognizability was due
either to their nonexistence or to Ben's insufficiencies as
an artist. Each bullet had a name: PETEY. THE BRONZE
DANDELION. CASSANDRA. PRINCESS GRIMELDA. And on
the bottom of the page, written in block letters filled
with exploding stars, the word EUREKA!!!

Judy stared at the page. EHRLICH would of course be
Paul Ehrlich, the famous turn-of-the-century bacteriol-
ogist who had won the Nobel Prize. He had postulated
the idea of a "magic bullet," a drug that would kill only
the cells that cause a disease, without touching any other

cells in the body. Judy knew from Ben that Boston University Medical Center had done good work in creating a genetically engineered "bullet" aimed at AIDS, starting from diphtheria toxin. The altered fusion-toxin molecule could enter a cell only at a given receptor site that existed only on HIV cells.

Ben and Caroline had been working on how the envelope proteins of retroviruses fit with receptor sites. Had they suddenly realized that their work might lead to a magic bullet made out of genetically altered viruses, rather than from toxins? A magic bullet for something like, say, cancer?

Judy wished suddenly that she had gone to hear Ben's last presentation, in Las Vegas.

But what about that facing page, covered with all those bizarrely labeled bullets? Who were Petey and Cassandra and Princess Grimelda? And what kind of name was "The Bronze Dandelion"?

A sudden thought took her. She scrambled to her feet and called the lab at Whitehead. No answer; it was Sunday morning. She flipped through the phone book and found another number.

"Greg Harkins, please ... Greg? This is Judy Kozinski. Dr. Kozinski's wife ... Thank you. Yes, it was a great loss. Look, I'm sorry to bother you at home on a Sunday, but you were one of the graduate students assigned to my husband's lab last summer, weren't you? Do you remember what the lab rats were called?"

The young man on the other end hesitated. Judy couldn't remember what he looked like, if he was married, anything about him. Of all Ben's staff, only Caroline Lampert burned in Judy's mind.

"Well, Mrs. Kozinski, officially the rats just had numbers. You know, the experiment number and subject number. But among ourselves we gave them names. Just dumb stuff, you know. Fooling around."

The terrible seriousness of the scientific young. They thought everything playful had to be apologized for. "What names, Greg?"

"Let me think ... there's been a lot of rats since then.

Last summer. There was one called Madonna, I remember, and a Father Jones, and a Petey. And Cassandra, because it always looked so woeful. Oh, and The Bronze Dandelion—that was some joke between Dr. Kozinski and Dr. Lampert that I wasn't in on."

His voice held nothing but regret that he had been excluded.

"Thank you," Judy said. "I appreciate it. Sorry to interrupt your Sunday."

"No problem. Glad to help."

Judy went back to the dining room. She picked up the notebook and stared at the bullets, exuberant missiles of healing aimed at unseen lab rats that, like her husband, were already months dead.

Eighteen

On Thanksgiving day, Judy bent over the page proofs that cluttered her father's desk. From the kitchen came the smells of turkey and spiced cider. Somebody laughed, probably her awful cousin Maureen, judging from the high screechy sound. Why had her parents invited Maureen to Thanksgiving dinner? Because Maureen was family. Because they always invited Maureen to Thanksgiving dinner. It was the twelfth commandment, right after "Thou shalt not sulk on holidays."

If you were correcting page proofs for your father's book, you couldn't be accused of sulking.

Not that anybody would ever accuse her directly. *Let Judy be, it hasn't been very long, she's still in mourning, poor girl* . . . The bereaved didn't sulk, they mourned. Even if they went around snapping at everybody, which is what she'd been doing since she arrived, it was called mourning. And nobody was more bewildered by this behavior than Judy herself, the woman who had always loved family holidays, who had taken Ben to them proudly. *I love your folks, Judy,* Ben always said. *Even their religious folkways are so soothing.*

In the kitchen, Maureen screeched again.

Judy turned again to the page proofs. Her father had worked on his life of the saints for eight years, and finally a Catholic university press was publishing it, in a handsome layout with full-color reproductions of Renaissance art and large, pseudomedieval capitals starting each saintly biography. St. John the Almoner, the Patriarch of Alexandria, who sat on a bench outside the church every Wednesday and Friday, listening to the grievances of the poor. St. Bernard of Menthon, succor of travelers and namesake of dogs. St. Boniface. St. Christopher, good Lord she was only up to the C's; there were twenty-three more letters' worth of goodness to proofread. So much fucking goodness, leading directly to a world here where her husband had been murdered outside a Stop 'n Shop while on his way to see his mistress.

The door opened. "Judy? I brought you a glass of wine."

"Thank you, Maureen."

Her cousin advanced into the room. "You should come out and have hors d'oeuvres. There's a fabulous crab dip."

"I'm not hungry."

"Weeeell . . . I don't want to be the one to say this, Judy, but you're losing too much weight."

Judy looked at Maureen, a successful stockbroker wearing an expensive plaid jacket, gold shoes, white tights, and a size eighteen skirt. "I am?"

"You're all skin and bones. Have you talked to your doctor about anorexia?"

When Maureen had been ten and Judy four, Maureen had put Judy in a tree and left her there, wailing and terrified, for a half hour. Judy said, "Well, it's nice of you to be interested, but I don't think I'm exactly flirting with anorexia."

"How much have you lost?"

"I don't know," Judy said indifferently. She hadn't been on a scale since July.

"Weeeeell . . . I don't like to say this, Judy, but a rapid weight loss plays hell with a woman's skin. Take you, for instance. That pasty look you have now, especially against that red hair. I hate to be the one to tell you, but your natural color was much more flattering. That red is just a shade too brassy."

"I think I will come into the kitchen," Judy said. She left the page proofs in neat piles—*St. Pelagious, who erroneously believed you could achieve salvation through good works alone, leaving out the concept of grace*—

"Good," Maureen said. "You make an effort. Although I hope you realize that in many ways you're very lucky, Judy. You had Ben for ten years. It's not like what happened to me."

Maureen's fiancé had deserted her two days before the wedding. He fled all the way to Barbados, which Judy figured was just barely far enough.

"Don't forget your wine, Judy. I mean, I did get it for you. God, look at you standing up. That dress is really too big on you now. But maybe your financial situation doesn't permit too many new clothes?"

In the kitchen, Dan O'Brien lifted the turkey from the oven. Twenty-four people ooohhed and aahhed. Judy watched silently. What was she doing in this nest of happy celebrators? She didn't belong here, she only belonged somewhere that people shouted at each other in the middle of the night and then were taken to view corpses and then spent their emotions on revenge. She didn't belong here, in this cozy family party. She was too furious to be here.

With the turkey there were stuffing and gravy, squash and mashed potatoes, creamed onions and puréed turnips, fennel and red pepper gratin, green beans with roasted hazel nuts, cranberries both jellied and whole, yeast rolls and Parkerhouse rolls and popovers, cheese tarts and pumpkin mousse and apple pie. Judy felt her stomach turn over. Wine flowed, ruby red in the candlelight, pale gold, sparkling clear.

"Let us all hold hands," Dan O'Brien said, "and give thanks to the Lord."

A huge plywood board had been placed on top of the dining room table, to fit everyone in. Neighbors had loaned chairs. Judy sat between Maureen and her cousin Joe's little boy, a sticky-faced four-year-old named Matthew. His small hand clutched hers trustingly. From across the table Judy's mother watched her; Theresa's face was flushed from cooking, creased with concern.

Her father said, "On this day, Lord we remember to thank you for your material bounty, set forth in front of us in such overflowing abundance. But even more, dear Lord, we thank you for your spiritual abundance. For the love that surrounds us. For the chance to know You and Your grace. And we thank you as well, Lord, for the most invaluable of Your gifts: the chance to make our lives a spiritual quest, and so give them meaning beyond eating, drinking, and even loving.

"For we all seek the spiritual truth, whether we know it or not, and it is the reflection of this truth in Your world that makes us so thankful on a day like this, surrounded by bounty and love. The spiritual journey is a quest for truth, just as much as science is a quest for truth. Both seek to understand the unseen order of things that lies all around us. Neither quest is easy, and the obstacles along the way can loom large. But we thank You for those obstacles, dear Lord, because without them we would not grow. We thank You for unanswered questions, which compel us to look for answers. We thank You for mystery, which compels us to search below the surface of life. And we thank You for the most difficult and misunderstood of Your gifts, suffering, without which we would not see how little we understand. Suffering may not always seem like a gift, yet it—"

"*Bullshit,*" Judy said.

Every head turned toward her: slow and yet jerky, like unoiled machinery.

"It's bullshit. All of it. Suffering isn't any kind of fucking gift!" Her voice had scaled upward. Matthew pulled his small warm hand from hers and started to whimper. Across the table Great-Aunt Patricia's pale broad face pulled downward like warm dough collapsing.

"You sit here feeling safe and protected and beloved by some Eternal Labor Leader in the Sky, and all the while . . . all the while here in the real world . . . all the while . . ."

Her father's arm was around her shoulders, lifting her from her chair. She shook him off, glaring, but she followed him from the dining room to his study. Behind them was dead silence. The rows of faces, identical pale blobs, seemed to have nothing to do with Judy. She thought she'd never seen anything as stupid as those faces, lips greasy with rich food, broad Irish brows lined up like targets in a shooting gallery. Never. Not as long as she lived.

Her father closed his study door and looked at her.

"No, don't touch me, Daddy. I'm fine. I'm sorry. I shouldn't have said it. I should have just sat there and smiled and pretended to eat and said 'Please pass the salt' and not made an ass out of myself. I'm sorry."

"We shouldn't have invited everyone this year. Your mother said . . . I should have listened to her. And I shouldn't have said that about suffering. It was my fault, honey. You're not ready."

"I'm never going to be ready for your sanctimonious hiding from reality through religion!"

"Maybe not," Dan O'Brien said calmly. "I never asked that of you."

"I think I better go home tonight."

"Please stay. You don't have to come back to dinner if you don't want to. You can stay in here and read. You can even correct more page proofs." He grinned, a tired grin so full of pain that her rage vanished as suddenly as it had appeared. That frightened her. These days her emotions came and went so fast, they didn't even seem like hers. Like her. She was somebody else, not in control of what she felt or how long she felt it.

"No. I think I better go," Judy said. "Will you explain to Mom?"

"Yes, honey. I will. Will you at least eat something first?"

"I can't, Daddy. I can't."

"Okay."

She went into his arms. "I'm always sneaking out of this house. I'm sorry."

"It will get better, Judy. You won't always hurt like this."

Not because of anything you and your God can tell me, Judy thought, but she didn't say it out loud. She'd already caused enough disruption in his house.

There were other, better places to disrupt. That deserved it much more.

I will find out who killed him, Judy thought, and recognized that it had the force of a prayer.

The moment she walked into the McBrides' annual winter party, Judy understood why Barbara had dithered so about inviting her. Standing against the far wall of the living room, holding a glass of white wine and talking to Mark Lederer of the Boston Biomedical Research Institute, stood Caroline Lampert.

Judy hung up her coat in the McBrides' hall closet. Her hands were steady. She nodded at a few people she didn't know and headed into the crowded dining room, where the food was spread over a table denuded of chairs.

"Judy! I didn't see you come in! How *are* you, dear?"

"I'm fine, Barbara. And you?"

"Oh, you know how the holidays are, hectic hectic. Thanksgiving was such a mess, I wanted to kill somebody . . . oh! I mean I . . . you look marvelous! I love your hair! And how much weight have you lost?"

"I don't know." She hadn't been able to face buying a new dress for the party, after all. But in the back of the guest room closet she'd found a black velvet skirt that she hadn't been able to squeeze into for three years. It was nearly as baggy on her as her black silk blouse. She didn't look marvelous, but she was at least presentable.

Barbara said, "Come over here, there's somebody I want you to meet!"

Anybody, Judy thought. Anybody at all.

"This is Julia Garvey. Julia, Judy Kozinski. Julia came up for the party—she's at NIH."

"I know," Judy said, smiling. She took the older woman's hand. Julia Garvey, like Mark Lederer, was on the short list of scientists she'd compiled in the taxi from Verico. It was unexpected luck, meeting her here. Two birds with one stone.

"Oh, here come the Fieldings," Barbara said. "Excuse me, you two . . . I'll be back."

Judy said, "My husband was a great admirer of your work, Dr. Garvey."

"Call me Julia. As I was of his, of course. His death was a great loss to us all."

"Thank you," Judy said. She watched Julia Garvey intently. Sixty, maybe, smooth gray bob, little makeup but not dowdy. Her teal dress was becoming and expensive, and it brought out her bright blue eyes. The woman had presence. The blue eyes, however, didn't meet Judy's directly. Dr. Garvey's gaze shied slightly away— or was Judy imagining that? She probed.

"Did you know Ben well, Julia? I ask only because he traveled so much, and so did I, for my job—I'm a journalist—and I'm afraid I didn't know all his colleagues as well as I wished."

"Not well, no," Dr. Garvey said, and this time Judy was sure: The woman's gaze flickered away from her own. Julia Garvey was hiding something.

For a single painful moment Judy wondered . . . but, no. Dr. Garvey was at least sixty. Although Caroline Lampert wasn't young and pretty, either . . . but neither was Caroline *sixty*. Judy glanced at Julia Garvey's left hand. Wedding ring and heavy, old-fashioned engagement ring, a diamond set in a circle of rubies. And there was a straightforward air about her, an almost prim rectitude as old-fashioned as her ring. No. Not her and Ben.

Which meant that Julia Garvey's uneasiness came from something else.

"My field of research wasn't identical to Ben's," Dr. Garvey said. "But I served on a peer review for two of his papers. Brilliant work."

"Yes. He was very happy at Whitehead. Although just before he died, he was looking at a position with a biotech firm."

"Really," Dr. Garvey said. She sipped her drink, something brown over ice.

"So many microbiologists are, aren't they? You must feel places like NIH can't compete with the salaries and perks the biotech firms offer."

"Yes, we do sometimes feel that. Although there will always be good people for whom the salary is secondary, fortunately. NIH offers a wide sphere of influence, including, indirectly, over Congress."

Dr. Garvey had regained her composure, Judy saw. Whatever that slight uneasiness had been, it had retreated below the surface of her professional manner. Which meant that Judy had to strike now, fast, before it had burrowed so deep she couldn't reach it at all.

"My husband interviewed at a placed called Verico, in Elizabeth, New Jersey. Tell me, Julia, did they by any chance approach you before Ben?"

Julia Garvey raised her blue eyes from her drink, to meet Judy's directly. Too directly. People only looked that straight at you when what they had to say was significant in some way. A revelation. Or a warning. Or a lie.

"No, Judy. I didn't interview with Verico. And you know how this community is for gossip—I would have heard if anyone else had. I think Ben must have been their only choice."

Don't ask questions, Judy heard. *I won't tell you anything.* Loud and clear.

Message received.

Dr. Julia Garvey knew something she wasn't saying.

Judy said, smiling, "I was just curious."

"Of course."

"I think I better get a drink—I'm the only one here without one. Can I bring you a refill?"

"No, thanks. I'm fine."

Judy smiled and moved toward the kitchen door. She could feel Julia Garvey's eyes on her back the whole way.

It was Dr. Garvey, then. She had interviewed at Verico, they had told her whatever they had told Ben, and she was too frightened to talk. Well, too bad. Judy wasn't done with her yet. Dr. Julia Garvey didn't have a monopoly on whatever she knew. The truth about Ben's death belonged by right to Judy, and Dr. Garvey would give up her little piece of it. Not here, at a party, but someplace, soon, she would tell Judy what she knew. Judy would stalk her and confront her and badger her until she did. That's what Judy Kozinski was good at, remember? Persistence in the pursuit of facts.

In the kitchen Mark Lederer, without Caroline, was helping himself to another scotch and water. Judy said, "Hello, Mark."

"Hello, Judy. Want a drink?"

No *How* are *you?* Judy was so grateful she smiled at him. "Please. Vodka and tonic. Why is there such a lull here at the alcoholic epicenter?"

"Everyone's in the family room, including my wife, admiring the Christmas tree."

"They have it up already?"

"Nobody does Christmas with the gusto of atheists. The kids want ours up next week."

Judy laughed. "How are your kids?"

"Same beautiful strident bitches." Mark's eyes glowed; he adored his daughters. It was one of the most attractive things about him, an otherwise slight, homely man with a long face and soft belly. "Dare I bore you with the obligatory picture?"

"Bore me."

Mark pulled out his wallet. The three girls clowned for the camera, the oldest in her junior high cheerleader outfit, the ten-year-old sticking her tongue out, the little one proudly standing on her head, impossibly small sneakers wobbly in the air. "They look so lively," Judy said. "It's a wonder they don't just tumble out of the picture entirely."

She suddenly became aware of Mark's stillness beside her.

She looked up from the picture in her hand. Mark gazed down at his daughters, every muscle in his body clenched into stillness. The anguish on his face cut so deep he looked like somebody else. For only a moment, and then the anguish was gone although some of the tension remained in his body, residue electricity.

"Mark?"

"Coming right up. Vodka and tonic." He put the picture back in his wallet and turned to the kitchen counter so decisively that Judy recognized what she was being told. Whatever was wrong with one of his girls, Mark didn't want to discuss it. Leukemia? Bone disease? God, it was always so much worse when it was a child.

Judy said, only partly to change the subject, "Mark, how well do you know Julia Garvey?"

"Julia? As well as most of us know each other. Which is to say we argue passionately about things scientific, and have trouble filling ten minutes with any other kind of conversation."

"Is she happy at NIH?"

"I assume so. She's not doing spectacular work, but it's solid. Why?"

"I think she knew Ben better than she admits."

Mark made a soft, warning noise and looked past her. Judy turned around. Caroline Lampert stood in the doorway.

The two women stared at each other silently. Then Caroline hurried away.

"Can I get you . . . get you some peanuts? Judy?"

"Everybody knows, don't they, Mark? About Ben and Caroline?" The words came out steadily; she was astonished at their steadiness.

"Judy, honey . . . you've had such a rough time. . . ."

Clumsily Mark put one arm around her. A detached part of her mind noted that he was as awkward at this kind of scene as all the other men she'd ever met. With the exception of her father.

"Oh, God, Judy, it's so damn hard to know what's the right thing to do. . . ."

"It's all right, Mark," she said clearly. "It wasn't your responsibility, or anybody else's, to inform me of Ben's doings."

"Oh, God," he said again, and she was surprised, in a detached kind of way, by the pain in his voice. It matched the look on his face when he'd stared at his daughters' picture. So this anguish wasn't even for her, but for the mysterious problem with Molly or Ruth or Rosie. She smiled a little. So much for assuming that she was the center of everybody's thoughts.

"I'm going to mingle," she said. "Want to come?"

"In a minute."

"Mark, did you interview at Verico before Ben did?"

She'd surprised him back into stillness. He took his arm from around her shoulders. When he spoke, his voice had changed, to one as clear and controlled as her own. "No."

"I think Julia Garvey did."

He didn't hesitate. "No. She didn't."

"How do you know that? How?"

Mark gazed at her. His face was smooth and blank as a peeled egg. "Because she told me last June that she'd received an offer from Genentech, a good offer, but nothing could ever induce her to leave NIH. She's as firmly entrenched there as I am at Boston Biomedical. Neither of us would even consider another offer at this point in our careers. And Julia has eventual hopes of the directorship of the National Center for Human Genome Research."

"She might have changed her mind since June."

"Julia isn't changeable. Private, but not changeable."

Yes, Judy could see that. *Had* seen it. Uncompromising rectitude. So Dr. Garvey hadn't been a serious candidate for Verico, and Verico wouldn't have said anything damaging to anyone except a serious candidate. The woman's slight uneasiness had come only from

Judy's blunt-instrument probing of her privacy.

"Shall we go to the food table?" Mark said, his face still blank. "There's supposed to be a great *caponata*."

"Sure."

But once in the dining room, Judy couldn't eat anything. Out of the corner of her eye she glimpsed Caroline Lampert retrieve her coat from the hall closet and slip quietly out the front door. Good. Let the bitch slink away.

"And on some have compassion, making a difference . . ."

Get out of my head, Daddy.

From the family room came the sounds of hilarity. Judy took a deep breath and clutched her drink. There was nobody else at this party whom Verico might have interviewed, but she still had the obligation of mingling and smiling. At least for another hour or so. And even though both Julia Garvey and Mark Lederer were "firmly entrenched" beyond even entertaining an offer from a biotech firm, there were still more names on Judy's list. Microbiology was a small world. A few of those scientists would be at Christmas parties in Boston or New York or Philadelphia, parties to which Judy could get herself invited. Everybody would want to do something for the widow, even a widow whose husband had only infrequently let her into his professional world.

And in January there was a major biotech conference in New York, at the St. Moritz. Everybody would be there, even the West Coast scientists. Judy could arrange to attend as press.

In the family room somebody started to play a piano. Oh, God, not singing. "Joy to the World," no less. Resolutely, she clutched her drink and started forward to put in the obligatory hour.

Nineteen

ind that cable," the blond girl said to Wendell. She didn't smile. The cable was a thick bundle of a lot of little cables tied together, snaking across the narrow hallway. The girl, Wendell figured, was something like a roadie for a rock group, even though "Albany Right Now" didn't go on any road and the girl sounded snooty when she warned him about the cable. He didn't bother to answer. She was just a roadie. *He* was going to be on TV in ten minutes.

"Nervous?" asked Jake Peterson, the reporter who'd been writing articles about Wendell for the newspaper. One little article had come out; the big one, Peterson said, wasn't ready yet. Wendell shrugged. The palms of his hands felt slippery.

"Just remember," Peterson said, "you've got an important message to bring to the attention of the public."

Wendell didn't answer. He already *knew* that. Peterson was watching him real close, smiling faintly, which pissed Wendell off. So Peterson had coached him, all right, but this was still Wendell's show. And it was happening in a real TV studio, with cables on the floor and everything, not some little hole-in-the-wall operation like "The Rick Abrams Hour."

"They're ready for you in the studio," the snotty girl said. She had a fat ass. Wendell had a sudden sharp vision of Saralinda, slim and sweet.

The studio was a large room with black ceiling and walls, two cameras on dollies, and a fake-looking living room built on a low platform. The talk show hostess was already seated. She was in her forties but still a stunner, with that classy look you saw on department store mannequins. Wendell scowled at the technician who attached his mike.

Then he couldn't stop scowling. "Relax," the hostess smiled. Fuck that. Peterson said this was an important message, right? You didn't relax about what was important.

God, he wanted a drink.

"Mr. Botts? Did you hear me? I said thirty seconds till air."

"Yeah, sure."

The red light went on.

"Welcome to 'Albany Right Now,' the city's most timely television news magazine. I'm Rebecca Johnson, and we're so glad you're here. Joining us later will be State Senator William Kerber, updating us all on firearms legislation in New York State, and Vivian Jones, author of the best-selling *The Bagel Diet*. And with me right now is Mr. Wendell Botts, who has a shocking and important story to share. Wendell, you were a member of the Soldiers of the Divine Covenant, the religious group that has a compound just outside the village of Cadillac, in Marion County."

"That's right." His throat felt dry.

"And you lived in the compound."

"They call it a camp."

"The camp, yes. When was that?"

"I left two years ago." He'd left for prison, right after David was born, after the alcohol had attacked Saralinda and Penny. But Peterson had said the hostess wouldn't bring that up. Wendell could see Peterson now, just beyond the cameras, his hands thrust deep in his pockets, his eyes missing nothing.

"And you're here to tell us . . . what?"

The woman's smile was encouraging, not like that asshole on the radio. Wendell said, "I'm here to tell you that there's things going on out at the camp that shouldn't never go on anyplace."

"What sort of things, Wendell?"

"Animal sacrifice."

"You mean that for religious reasons, animals are being slaughtered on an altar? In front of the congregation?"

"Yes." He saw again the little outdoor amphitheater made from a natural hillside, under hard stars. Sacrifices took place at night.

"What kinds of animals?"

"Woodchucks. Rabbits. Birds." He remembered the call-in on the radio show. "And sometimes a cat. A cat that strayed in from someplace."

The hostess looked grave. "You saw these sacrifices with your own eyes, Wendell, when you lived in the camp?"

"Yes. I did." Despite his nervousness . . . the camera kept moving, and the red light he was supposed to look at kept moving with it—he recalled Peterson's coaching. "I heard the animals squeal and scream when the Elders drew the knife across their throats. That's a terrible sound you don't forget."

"Are there children in the camp, Wendell?"

"There sure are. Two of them are mine, and I want them out."

Peterson was gesturing wildly. Wendell reached into his pocket for his wallet. "See? These are their pictures. Penny is almost five and David is two."

The hostess held up each picture to the camera. Penny's hair was tied up in two high ponytails; David grinned. "They're darling. I can see why you're concerned about them—any parent would be, witnessing such cruelty. What have you done about getting them out of the camp?"

"My lawyer's working on it. We're doing everything we legally can. But the animal sacrifice isn't the only reason I want my kids out of there."

"Go on," the hostess said, her face all concerned and waiting, like she didn't know what he was going to say next. But of course she did. He'd already told her people all about it, and they'd told her. Wendell drew a little away from her on the sofa. None of these people were honest, he had to remember that. They were helping him for their own reasons. He made a little pause before speaking, like Peterson had taught him to.

"I think the Soldiers of the Divine Covenant are practicing human sacrifice in Cadillac."

The hostess's eyes widened. "That's a very grave charge, Wendell. What proof do you have?"

"Three things. First, there were thirteen recorded deaths in the camp from last April to now, out of, oh, maybe five hundred people. You can check the *Cadillac Register* obituaries. That's a death rate of over two and a half percent in eight months, or nearly four percent a year. If people were dying at four percent a year in Albany, the city would be completely empty in thirty years." The figures were Peterson's. "That isn't a natural death rate. And all of the deaths are supposed to be from natural causes—not even taking into account that some of a death rate is supposed to come from accidents or violence. These were all—every single one—supposed to be natural."

"And how many of those were autopsied?"

"Six. The doctors said they were all heart attacks." Peterson again. Reporters had ways of finding out things.

"But if they'd been human sacrifices, as you said, with their throats cut—"

"That isn't the only way to make a human sacrifice," Wendell said. "How do we know how thorough those autopsies really were? You can put an AC current through water, for instance, and electrocute somebody without leaving no external sign of injury. And if the authorities didn't have any reason to suspect anything when they did their autopsies . . . And that doesn't even count what might have happened to bodies hid in the limestone caves all underneath Cadillac."

"But you have no proof of any of that. And even though a four-percent death rate is startling, the small sample size—"

"My second reason," Wendell said, rolling over sample size the way Peterson had taught him, "is that the Soldiers think human sacrifice is justified by the Bible. They're capable of it. Believe me, I *know*. They believe completely in Leviticus."

"Which says . . ."

Wendell recited carefully. None of that St. Cadoc reincarnation stuff, Peterson had said, but quoting the Bible was okay. Wendell paused where Peterson had taught him to. " 'For the life of the flesh is in the blood: and I have given it to you upon the altar, to make an atonement for your souls: for it is the blood that maketh an atonement for the soul.' That's the one they use to kill animals and let their blood run out over the ground."

"And you know that your children have witnessed this bloodshed."

"What would be the effect of that on a kid? I want my kids out of there. Oh, God, I want them out!"

The hostess's face, which had been watching him like he was a dangerous dog, softened a little. She still held the pictures of Penny and David. Wendell saw Peterson hold up three fingers.

"But my third reason, Rebecca . . ." This was the first time Wendell was supposed to use her name—". . . my third reason is that the Marion County Medical Examiner thinks there is something to the human sacrifices at the camp."

"Dr. Richard Stallman," Rebecca Johnson said. "He's been a previous guest on 'Albany Right Now.' But what makes you think the authorities are suspicious of the Soldiers of the Divine Covenant?"

Wendell paused again. "Because last week they exhumed two of the bodies of people that died in the camp in August."

Rebecca Johnson had known this was coming—Peterson said it was the reason she agreed to put him on the show. But now she looked as upset as if it was all news to her.

You couldn't trust a one of them.

"Exhuming a body is very unusual, isn't it, Wendell?"

"You bet. It's almost impossible to get permission. So why did the county exhume not one but two bodies that died in that camp? Unless they screwed up the first autopsies, or unless there's something fishy going on?"

"That's a good—"

"You bet it is! It's a damn good question! And nobody's given me an answer yet, not the so-called authorities—although we called 'em, you better believe it! And not the Elders in the camp, who won't even talk to me, when it's my own kids in there that I'm worried sick about! And not Saralinda, my ex-wife, who's got so-called custody because of some trouble I got into a while ago and they don't ever forgive a man in the Soldiers, no, no matter what the Bible says plain as day, black and white, let the ones without no sin cast the first stone, you're supposed to forgive the sinner . . ."

Peterson was frowning at him now, and drawing a zip across his own mouth. Wendell ignored him. This was what he'd come to say, this was a rush like the one he'd got on the radio show, better than a scotch even, the rush he was entitled to with all the crap he'd gone through. He was entitled to it, and he was going to say what he'd come here to say, all of it.

"And forgiveness is the key here, Rebecca, make no mistake about that. What I done was wrong, but the Lord forgave me, and I've straightened my life out, no help from the camp and my ex, Saralinda, who doesn't see no need to ask forgiveness because she never thinks she does anything wrong. Isn't that something, Rebecca, somebody who never does anything wrong, ever? But the Lord knows better than that, he knows that although

I regret bitterly my own mistakes, she's partly to blame because she drove me to them. Always acting like I wasn't a good enough Soldier, wasn't holy enough, wasn't man enough to live like the Elders. . . . She drove me to what I did, Rebecca, and has she ever apologized to *me?* That's what their religion comes to in the camp, they're always right and everybody else is fucking *wrong . . .*"

Something was wrong. Rebecca had moved to a chair at the far end of the stage, her back to Wendell. Wendell was talking, but so was Rebecca. And he could hear her better than himself. The cameras were both turned toward her, too, and then one of them turned instead toward a young man who mounted the shallow steps to the stage, carrying a white telephone.

Rebecca Johnson took the phone and set it on a little table in front of her chair. The young man left. Beyond the cameras, Peterson leaned against the wall. Wendell shook his mike; it had been turned off.

"Dr. Stallman, welcome to 'Albany Right Now,'" Rebecca Johnson said into the phone. "This is an unexpected pleasure."

"It's not a pleasure," said a deep voice, clearly irritated. The voice filled the studio. "It's a public service. I feel an obligation to set the record straight before your viewing public gets the wrong impression."

"Certainly, Doctor," Rebecca said. Even though he could only see her from behind, Wendell knew how to read that back: straight, leaning a little forward, shoulders lifted. Old classy Rebecca was fucking delighted with this call.

"First, let me categorically contradict Mr. Botts's inept assertion that autopsies performed by this office are less than complete. Each one we do is thorough, complete, and professional. Those are our standards, and I defy anyone to produce any evidence to the contrary."

"We hear you," Rebecca said. She half-swiveled in her chair. The camera followed her. Her eyes gleamed.

"Second, Mr. Botts has clearly demonstrated his ignorance of even the most basic medical principles, which disqualifies him to comment intelligibly on our work. For example, it's just not true that electrocution leaves no external sign of injury. *All* electrical injuries, no matter how they're produced, cause a characteristic burn. This consists of a central pale area with a bright red peripheral zone where blood has been pushed by the heat generated in the electrical charge. Mr. Botts clearly is no doctor, and should not comment on medical concerns about which he knows nothing."

"We hear you, Dr. Stallman," Rebecca Johnson said again.

"And finally, I want to make perfectly clear that the two bodies exhumed at Cadillac were nothing more than a failsafe precaution, an acknowledgment that certain persons have been raising issues about this office which are so completely unjustified that the best answer seemed to be to double-check our own work. Which we did. The two subjects had both died of myocardial infarction—heart attacks. That's what the original reports said, and that's what the follow-up teams found. Is this clear?"

"Oh, completely," Rebecca said smoothly. "And it's clear, too, how much this matters to your office, in your rush to clarify it."

Her voice was grave, but Wendell saw her eyes dance. Beyond the camera the young man who had brought the telephone waved frantically. Dr. Stallman's voice said abruptly, "Thank you for allowing me to set the record straight," followed by the click of a telephone.

Rebecca looked directly into the camera. "And so you've heard both sides of these grave charges, viewers— charges of animal and even human sacrifice at a religious compound in Cadillac, exhuming of bodies for reautopsy, children in danger, death statistics and protests by the county medical examiner. What do *you* think should be done next—if anything? 'Albany Right Now,' bringing you the issues that matter in the city we love. Next, Vivian Jones on losing weight through delicious low-fat recipes based on bagels. Stay with us."

The red lights went off. The young man who'd

brought the phone and an older man from the control booth both rushed up to Rebecca Johnson. Peterson advanced purposely on this group. A technician came onstage to unfasten Wendell's mike, calling over his shoulder to the cameraman. The white telephone, still on the table on stage, started to ring.

"But what about my *kids?*" Wendell said, but the technician motioned him offstage and motioned on a woman carrying a paperback book with a bagel on the cover, and nobody seemed to even hear Wendell's question at all.

JANUARY

Often the use of informants is of limited value.

—*Task Force on Organized Crime, 1976*

• • •

Informants are very key to investigations. . . . They are probably the lifeblood of an investigative effort, particularly against organized crime.

—*William Kossler, in a Senate subcommittee hearing on organized crime, 1989*

Twenty

Jeanne Cassidy stood in front of the mirror in her dorm room, a single, studying herself. The mirror was spotty, tarnished, and streaked with something that might have been beer, or Coke. The mirror was also too small to see herself full length, but Jeanne could see enough.

It made her shudder.

Damn Jeff! Why did he insist on going to such a cheesy thing as a "Winter Ball"? Give us a break. The student union decorated with cutout paper snowflakes, a few wilting white flowers, and a melting white candle on every table. A rock band that probably practiced in a local garage. Strictly high school. And her dressed up as if this were actually a glamorous occasion, in her floor-length black sheath and Lancôme "Paris Red" lipstick and taupe eyeshadow and long gold earrings. The first time she had dressed up like this since Las Vegas. The first time she had worn any makeup at all since the night that Sue Ann . . .

Jeanne put her hands over the mirror, as if she could

block out her own reflection with just her palms and spread fingers. As if she could block out Susie's reflection, standing there beside her in a yellow sweater jammed over pasties, her rhinestone earrings touching her shoulders, mascara smeared from crying.

Nothing could blot out Susie's reflection. Nothing. Ever. Jeanne saw it in every mirror she passed, every darkened window, every shiny spoon bowl. She saw it in her dreams.

Her phone rang.

"Jeanne? You ready, babe?"

"Yes. No. Five more minutes, Jeff."

"You got it."

Jeanne looked again at herself in the mirror. Her short hair, back to its natural red, was brushed into a halo around her face. Makeup made her eyes look twice their size. The black sheath clung. Jeff had never seen her like this: glamorous. Glittery. She looked like everything she had never wanted to see again.

Susie's reflection gazed at her from the depths of the mirror, white to the lips. *"Carlo's dead. And now I'm dead, too."*

Jeanne clasped her hands in front of herself, hard. She closed her eyes to shut out Susie's image. In the hall outside her room people clattered past, hurrying for the elevator, laughing and chatting.

"Listen, Sue Ann, I just remembered, I have a Tampax in the car—"

"No! Don't leave me!"

But Jeanne had. She had left Susie. If only she could go back and do it over, do it differently, do something to help Susie—

Do something. Do. Something. Yes. If she could do something different to help Susie. . . . But there was no way to help Susie now. Susie was dead. And anything Jeanne did might only endanger herself as well.

But Jeanne was already dead. If she had to go on looking at Sue Ann Jefferson's reflection in every smooth surface, go on waking in sweats every night, go on having her heart pound every time she crossed a street . . . then she, Jeanne Cassidy, was already as dead as Susie.

"No! Don't leave me!"

The phone rang again. Jeanne ignored it. She couldn't remember the name of the man who had questioned her in Las Vegas. The FBI agent. Carter? Connors? It had started with *C*. His first name had been Robert, she remembered that. In Vegas she'd known so many men by only their first names.

Cavanaugh. Robert Cavanaugh.

The phone was still ringing. Jeff again. Jeanne lifted the receiver an inch, set it down, lifted it again. She touched 1-555-1212.

"Directory Assistance. What city, please?"

"Washington, D.C."

"That's a different area code. Dial 1-202-555-1212."

"Thank you." Her voice sounded calm in her own ears. She got the number, keyed it in.

"FBI Headquarters."

This was Saturday night. "I'd like to leave a message, please. For an agent. When he comes in on Monday morning."

"Name, please."

"I'd rather not leave my name."

"I meant the name of the agent." The voice was patient.

"Robert Cavanaugh."

"I'll transfer you to VMX."

A moment later she heard his voice, pleasant but economical. "This is Robert Cavanaugh. Please leave a message." Beep.

Jeanne licked her top lip. She deepened her voice, projecting from the diaphragm, disguising herself the way a Vegas actor, temporarily working as a busboy, had taught her. "The FBI should know that Carlo Gigliotti and Sue Ann Jefferson were both killed by the same people. Carlo's people. Miss Jefferson knew something dangerous that Carlo had told her. Cadoc. Verico. Cadaverico."

Jeanne hung up. Twelve seconds. They couldn't trace

that, could they? On TV, they always needed longer than twelve seconds.

The doorknob to her room rattled violently. She always kept the door locked. Jeff pounded on it. "Jeanne! Open up! Are you all right?"

Jeanne stood a moment longer, calm, staring at the phone. Then she opened the door.

"What's the idea of tying up the phone? I thought you were . . . Jesus Christ. Look at *you*."

Jeanne, smiling, let him look. She moved her shoulders a little above the strapless dress. Funny how fast it all came back, when you needed it. Jeff's face looked stunned.

"Let's go," she said. She picked up her beaded evening bag, clutching it tightly.

"You look . . . *incredible*," Jeff said.

"Thank you," Jeanne said. She flicked off the light, and Susie's reflection disappeared from the mirror.

Twenty-one

Overnight, snow had blanketed Boston. Judy Kozin-ski lay in bed, listening to the radio. Fighting in Liberia. The funeral of Supreme Court Justice William Taylor Fogel. Celtics lose to the Knicks. Winter storm activity along much of the Eastern seaboard.

She sat up in bed, pushed aside the curtain, and rubbed a clear spot on the window so she could see what she didn't want to see. Bright skies for two weeks, and then the night before you needed to drive someplace, pow! "Winter storm activity."

At least a foot of snow blocked her driveway. It would take her an hour to shovel it. And more snow was coming down. Driving between here and New York would be horrendous.

Judy chewed on her bottom lip, and made a decision. She leafed through the phone book.

"Amtrak? When is your next train from Boston to Penn Station? An hour and fifteen minutes. Terrific. I'd like a round-trip ticket, please, returning on a morning train Saturday." She gave her name and credit card number, and then dialed Natick's only cab company. Half an hour to shower and dress, thirty minutes into Boston with somebody else doing the driving, and at least fifteen minutes to spare.

"Sorry, lady, it'll be at least an hour wait for a cab. We've got reservations called in before you."

"But I'll miss my train!"

"Sorry, lady."

"Look, I'll pay double the fare."

"Sorry, lady," the voice said, and now it sounded offended. But, then, dispatchers didn't share in driver windfalls; she should have remembered that.

The Boston cabs would probably take even longer. If she could get one.

"Look," Judy said, trying to sound both reasonable and impressive, "this is Dr. Kozinski, I'm with the Whitehead Institute for Biological Research at M.I.T. It's very important that I get to New York today for an international scientific conference at the St. Moritz. Very important. I know you have reservations ahead of mine, but if I miss this train, they'll have to reschedule my paper."

"Oh, well . . ."

"I'd really appreciate it. Scientists from all over the country have flown in to hear this paper. It's on a new way for genetically altered viruses to penetrate selected disease cells via receptor-specific envelope proteins."

There. Snow them with verbiage.

Her eyes filled with tears.

"Well, I guess I could maybe . . . okay, I'll have a cab there in twenty minutes."

"Oh, thank you. You have no idea how much I appreciate this. Really."

"I'm a big fan of science. Did you ever see *Invasion of the Body Snatchers*?"

"Ummm," Judy said. There was always a price.

Her suitcase was open, half packed, on the bedroom chair. She threw another blouse into it, yanked her nightgown over her head, and caught sight of herself, naked, in the dresser mirror. She stopped.

Underneath the dresser were several dozen dust bunnies. Judy fumbled through them and pulled out a digital scale, equally dusty.

One hundred eighteen pounds.

The scale must be broken. She couldn't have lost that much. It was true that all her clothes hung on her, but they'd been a size sixteen to start with . . . *118*?

She twisted this way and that, studying her naked body in the mirror. Trim hips, almost flat belly. Round, medium-sized breasts over a narrow rib cage. Slowly, sadly, Judy smiled. Ben would have loved the way she looked at this weight. Now she looked like all the other women he'd admired.

In the back of the guest room closet she found a pair of wool slacks and a blue silk blouse in size six. She hadn't worn them in a decade. Judy pulled them on. They fit perfectly. She stood looking at herself in the mirror, not smiling, running her hands over her slender hips. She wanted to laugh. Cry. Curse. Show off to Ben. Show off to somebody. No. Never again.

She had wasted eight minutes of the twenty before the taxi arrived.

Well, she could still make it. Five-minute shower, five minutes to dress and throw her makeup into the suitcase. She could comb her hair and put on lipstick in the cab. Piece of cake.

She soaped herself in the shower, rinsed off, and flung open the opaque fiberglass door, reaching for a towel. A man wearing a ski mask stood in her bathroom, holding a gun.

"I don't think so," he said quietly. "Sit down in the bathtub, please."

Judy screamed and started to climb over the side of the tub. He grabbed her firmly by her naked shoulder and two extended fingers did something excruciatingly painful to the side of her neck. She screamed again. He eased her into a sitting position in the tub. Some part of her mind registered that he wore gloves.

"You killed my husband!"

"No," he said quietly. "I didn't. Push down the tub stopper, please, and turn on the water."

She stared at him, terrified. He waved the gun at her. Through the ski mask the whites of his eyes looked horribly bright. Unthinking, Judy crossed her arms in front of her naked breasts.

He lowered the tub stopper himself and turned on both hot and cold water, full force. Gently, almost as if trying not to alarm her, he pulled the shower cap off her head. Then he reached for the hair dryer, on the sink counter behind him, and took an extension cord from his pocket.

"Nooo," Judy moaned, and clamored to her feet. Once more he did the thing with her neck, and this time the pain was so bad she swayed on her feet and thought she might vomit. Everything in the room dimmed. He moved his free hand to her arm, still wet from the shower, and eased her again into a sitting position in the tub.

He plugged the extension cord into the wall and the hair dryer into the extension cord.

She couldn't move. Every time she tried, a nerve in her neck pulsed and her vision went dim. She was going to die. This was what Ben had felt, then, in the seconds before this man had smashed his skull with a hammer. No, not this man, he'd said it hadn't been him. Some other man. She couldn't think. She was naked in her bathtub, and the fully dressed man had turned on her own hair dryer. She heard the noise it made, a whirring, no it wasn't a whirring she couldn't find the right word for it, Daddy would know Daddy knew everything there had never been a man who knew as much as Daddy until she'd met Ben, who'd died just this way as this man or some man loomed over her, making the world explode in her ears into deafening sound, looming closer and closer, falling toward her—

—falling—

—falling sideways onto the bathroom floor, the hair dryer still whirring in his hand.

A second man stood in the doorway, holding a gun.

"FBI, ma'am. Are you all right?"

"I'm dead," she said, not thinking, not able to think. The water reached the top of the tub and overflowed onto the body on the floor. Immediately the water began to turn red, and only then did she realize who was dead, and who was not, and that, once more, it was somebody else besides her. She was shivering, and naked, and alive.

She reached out and turned off the faucet.

Alive.

Her, and not Ben.

And given a choice, that's exactly what she would have chosen. Her and not Ben, who *should* be dead for hurting her so much, for getting her into this in the first place, for not being what she had thought he was and needed him to be. Rage at Ben filled her, choked her, so that she almost couldn't see the man lying on her bathroom floor. It was the most powerful rage she'd ever felt, and she moaned and wrapped her arms around her naked body.

"Ma'am?"

"I'm not dead," she said, and this time he didn't reply, but instead reached over and gently pulled the extension cord from the wall so that the hair dryer stopped its obnoxious whirring, and silence fell.

Twenty-two

When it happened, Cavanaugh had already learned, it all happened at once.

Monday morning, a few minutes before 8:00 A.M., he picked up his mail, went to his cubicle, and called his VMX messages.

"The FBI should know that Carlo Gigliotti and Sue Ann Jefferson were both killed by the same people. Carlo's people. Miss Jefferson knew something dangerous that Carlo had told her. Cadoc. Verico. Cadaverico."

Cavanaugh stopped dead, his interoffice memos suspended in hand.

"Robert, this is Jerry Mendolia. I'm trying to locate the Ianiello file folder. Ralph said you took it to—"

He hit REPLAY.

"The FBI should know that Carlo Gigliotti and Sue Ann Jefferson were both killed by the same people. Carlo's people. Miss Jefferson knew something dangerous that Carlo had told her. Cadoc. Verico. Cadaverico."

She wasn't as good at disguising her voice as she thought. *"I'm taking another taxi to the airport and wait-*

ing there until I can get a flight to East Lansing, Michigan, where my parents live. I'm enrolling at Michigan State for the semester, and I'm getting my degree. If you want me, you can call me there."

Jesus Edgar J. Christ.

But what the hell had been her name?

He did a 180-degree turn and sprinted for the elevator to Records. He didn't make it because Felders appeared in his path, just materialized there solid as a wall. Felders looked serious.

"Listen, Bob, your agent on Judy Kozinski is on the phone. Priority one."

Cavanaugh stared at Felders. His lips felt suddenly dry. "They took her out."

"They tried. Dollings killed him. Looks like a pro, but Dollings didn't recognize him. The local cops are headed out there now."

"I'm on my way," Cavanaugh said. He felt his chest tighten. This was it, then. Verico really did lead somewhere. It really did.

He said rapidly to Felders, "But there's something else. Remember that hit-and-run killing last August in Vegas, Carlo Gigliotti's showgirl girlfriend, the same day he was knocked off? I was out there anyway, I interrogated the dead girl's best friend about anything Carlo's girl might have told her. Nada. She told me she was getting the hell out of Vegas to go back home to East Lansing, Michigan. Well, I just got an anonymous from her on the VMX. She said Gigliotti blabbed something dangerous to his girlfriend. 'Cadoc. Verico. Cadaverico.'"

Felders's face changed from its serious look to its feral one. "How do you spell that?"

"No idea."

"What was the girl's name? The one who called you?"

"I can't remember. But she said she was going to attend Michigan State."

"Go on up to Natick. Call me in an hour from the plane. I'll have everything I can for you. And Neymeier can run those words through all his dictionaries."

Just then Neymeier himself stepped out of the glassed-in analyst area. He seemed taller and weedier than ever, perhaps because he was dressed in a thin dark-green suit whose pant legs drooped over his loafers. "Yo. Robert. Got something."

"Something? *Now?* What?"

"In the early edition of the *Boston Globe*. Kid disappeared last evening, then found unharmed in the toy section of a K Mart several miles away. Six-year-old girl. Program flagged it as one of the names you gave me on the Verico thing."

"What name?"

"Dr. Mark Lederer. At Boston Biomedical Research Institute."

Felders's eyes gleamed. "Boston. Great. You can talk to him while you're up there, Bob. Since you apparently didn't learn anything from him the first time you interviewed him."

Mark Lederer. Cavanaugh remembered him well. He'd been absolutely convincing that he knew nothing about Verico. Absolutely convincing.

"Save the price of flying up twice," Felders said. "Duffy always appreciates economy of motion."

He called Felders just before the plane landed at Logan, from a phone beside the flight attendants' galley.

"Marty? Robert. What have we got?"

"Listen, the fingerprints just came in—the local team took them right away and the lab rushed through a preliminary check. The guy Dollings shot is John Paul Giancursio. One conviction, attempted robbery, 1983. Suspended sentence—he was just a kid then. He's been photographed with Michael Callipare."

"A pro." The lack of a real record was key. Only the second best stayed that clean. The very best never got their fingerprints on file at all, and they were never seen with anybody.

"Almost certainly."

"But the Gigliottis, not the Callipares, are the ones with the connection to Eric Stevens at Verico."

"Tenuous as it is," Felders said. "And Carlo Gigliotti was the one knocked off in Vegas. But it's possible Giancursio was a specialist who worked for more than one family. Gigliotti's girlfriend's name was Sue Ann Jefferson, and the friend you questioned was Jeanne Catherine Cassidy. She *is* enrolled at Michigan State in East Lansing."

"Who can we send to talk to her?"

"Natalie Simmons is already in Chicago, she'll go. Natalie can blend in on a college campus. Neymeier's data banks show that *cadaverico*, C-A-D-A-V-E-R-I-C-O, is Italian for 'deathlike' or 'corpselike.' But 'Cadoc' isn't in the language programs, no matter how he spells it. Neymeier's still checking news banks and so forth."

Cadoc Verico Cadaverico. Cadoc a-biotech-company deathlike. Cadoc truth-company corpses. It was like one of those spurious mathematical proofs that showed how two plus two equaled five. It almost meant something, but not quite.

A stewardess said, "Time to take your seat, sir. We're beginning our descent."

Cavanaugh said, "Has the Kozinski place been swept for bugs?"

"Yeah. It was bugged, and the phone was tapped. The phone tap's still in place, on the off chance we get something."

"How is Dollings?" He was new, just a few months out of the Academy at Quantico.

"Sounded a little shaken. First time for him. For you, too, right?"

"I didn't have to shoot anybody," Cavanaugh said, annoyed.

"True enough. Did you read the *Globe* piece on the Lederer kid?"

"It wasn't in the edition at the airport. The paper must consider it filler. Fax me whatever you got to the Boston field office."

The stewardess said, "Sir, I have to insist you take your seat. The captain has turned on the seat-belt sign."

Felders said. "What about Mrs. Kozinski?"

"I want her in protective custody."

"How do you think she'll react to that idea?"

"I don't know," Cavanaugh said. Judy Kozinski was a material witness; theoretically he could detain her, under guard, in a federal detention center. Material witnesses had far fewer rights than people accused of crimes. Hardly anyone realized this. Cavanaugh didn't want to be the one to bring it to the attention of an hysterical widow. Neither did he want anyone else shooting at Mrs. Kozinski before he found out what she knew that had aroused the Relatives' sudden interest.

Felders said, "Listen, one more thing. Dr. Julia Garvey called. She says she'll only talk to you."

When it happened, it happened all at once.

"If you don't sit down," the flight attendant said severely to Cavanaugh, "I'm going to have to report it."

"I'm sitting, I'm sitting," Cavanaugh said. "Bye, Marty. Tell Dr. Garvey I'll contact her as soon as I can." He went hastily to his seat, but the flight attendant continued to frown at him all the while the plane taxied at Logan.

Boston was choked with snow. Salt trucks had saturated the roads, and his rental car threw up heavy gobs of dirty slush. He drove carefully, glad he didn't live here but impressed by how efficiently the city mobilized for bad weather. In Washington, two inches of snow shut down everything except the rats and the drug dealers.

Lieutenant Piperston, the Lithuanian Catholic who had warned him about the unpredictability of gently raised Irish-Catholic girls, met Cavanaugh at the door of Judy Kozinski's house in Natick. When Cavanaugh had been there in August, bright orange and yellow flowers had bordered the walk. Now he couldn't even see the sidewalk under what looked like more snow than Washington would get all winter. Hopefully.

"Agent Cavanaugh," Piperston said quietly. He hadn't changed: short, bald, intelligent-looking. Neither had the Kozinski living room, filled with books and pottery and plants. A uniform stood guard at the foot of the staircase. Cavanaugh had seen at least three more outside.

"Hello, Lieutenant. Apparently we're not done with the Kozinskis."

"Apparently not," Piperston said. "The ident team is just finishing up in the bathroom upstairs. Your man is in the study with Mrs. Kozinski."

The study was where Cavanaugh had interviewed her last time. Economy of motion, Felders had said.

Cavanaugh went upstairs to the bathroom first. The victim/would-be-killer lay on his back on the bathroom floor, covered with blood which had already dried to a dull brown-red. He had black curly hair, regular features, and a nice tan, which he probably got vacationing in Vegas or Mexico or the Carribean. The perks of murder. If they could have gotten the guy into court, he'd have looked better than the lawyers.

The medical crew arrived to remove the body, and Cavanaugh went downstairs to the Kozinski study.

Dollings sat on the small sofa beside a strange woman. Cavanaugh scowled at Dollings, although this certainly wasn't the way he'd planned to greet the younger agent, whose jaw was clamped together too hard. But Dollings should know how important security was here. Cavanaugh said, "Where's Mrs. Kozinski?"

Dollings looked surprised. "Right there."

Cavanaugh hadn't recognized her. Immediately he felt stupid. But he remembered a short, fat brunette on the edge of violent hysteria. This was a slim redhead dressed in close-fitting slacks and a blue blouse. She was pale, and her hazel eyes looked enormous, but there was no hint of hysteria about her. Instead there was an indefinable air of calm sorrow, as if she had strong feelings but had them in control.

Like Marcy.

He said, "Mrs. Kozinski, we've met. I'm Robert Cavanaugh, FBI."

"Oh. *FBI*."

"I beg your pardon?"

"I remembered wrong. I thought you were Department of Justice."

So she remembered him. It gave him a small ridiculous glow. "Mrs. Kozinski, I know you already told Agent Dollings and the local police what happened here. But I'd like to ask you some additional questions. Who did you talk to or visit yesterday or this morning? Including phone calls."

She took a moment to think, to make her answer complete as possible. "Yesterday I didn't visit with anybody, unless you count the checkout girl at Wal-Mart. Yesterday afternoon I talked on the phone to my dentist, to make an appointment, to the post office to stop delivery for four days while I'm away, and to my mother in Troy, New York."

"You were going away for four days? Where?"

"New York."

"Business or pleasure?"

She hesitated a moment. "Business. I was going to attend a scientific conference that my husband would have gone to."

Bingo. He was annoyed that he didn't know about the conference. What was Tamara Lang, supposedly his science advisor on this case, doing with her time? "Did you tell either your mother or the post office clerk where you were going? Did you tell anyone?"

"No. My mother would just—oh, wait. I told the cab company this morning. I wanted to give them a reason to let me budge."

"Do what?"

For the first time, she smiled faintly. " 'Budge.' You know, like kids standing in line and one of them cuts in way ahead of his place and all the others yell, 'Teacher, he budged!' Don't kids say that where you come from?"

"No." Cavanaugh said.

"Well, anyway, I wanted to budge in the list of people waiting for a cab. So I told the dispatcher that it was important I get to a microbiology conference at the St. Moritz in New York." She looked at him steadily. "You're telling me my phone is bugged, aren't you? Or my whole house? By whoever tried to kill me?"

He couldn't see any advantage in lying to her. Not yet. "Yes."

"So who *did* try to kill me?"

"Do you have a room reservation at the St. Moritz?"

"Yes," she said. "Who tried to kill me?"

"And how did you make that reservation? By phone, or mail?"

"By phone, but not this phone. I stopped and made the reservation on Thanksgiving Day, from a pay phone on the Mass Turnpike while driving from my parents' house in Troy back here to Natick. I needed to take some sort of action that very day. *Needed* to. And I needed to go to that conference."

"Why?"

"Mr. Cavanaugh," she said calmly, "before I answer any more questions, I'd like to know what the FBI involvement is here. Also, who is trying to kill me, and why. Plus whatever you know about who killed my husband."

Cavanaugh studied her. He was having trouble believing this was the same woman he'd interviewed five months ago. Something had happened to her in between, something internal. He remembered that she was a journalist. Whatever had happened inside her had let her bring her professional skills in line with her personal life. She was bargaining with him, in the currency in which journalists bargained: information. Only, unknown to her, he held the better bargaining position: He could use whatever she told him, but she was going to be prevented from using whatever he told her because she was going to be immobile in protective custody, where she would be safe, and where she would stop messing up his investigation.

He said, "The Bureau is interested because we think Verico, where your husband interviewed, has connections to organized crime. He may have been killed because of that connection. The attack on you may have come from the same source."

She didn't flinch, but she sat down, in slow motion, on

the sofa behind her. It made her look very small. Her eyes never left his face. Cavanaugh sat down, too, to avoid looming over her.

"What connections? Between Verico and . . . and organized crime?"

"We don't know yet. Probably it has something to do with Verico's scientific work. What did Eric Stevens tell you on November 18 when you went out to New Jersey to talk to him?"

Her eyes widened, then narrowed. He saw her putting it together: Dolling's presence to rescue her from the killer, Cavanaugh's knowledge of her trip to Verico, the tapped phone call saying she was going to New York.

"They . . . somebody . . . didn't want me asking questions at the microbiology conference."

He watched her carefully. She would be capable of lying, if she was any good as a journalist. But he didn't think she was lying just yet.

"I asked Stevens what had upset Ben so much, and who else he'd interviewed to head Verico."

Cavanaugh felt a surge of annoyance. Amateurs. Blundering in and tracking up the pristine ground. "And what did Stevens say?"

"He said he thought Ben had been upset for some personal reason, and that the Verico candidate list was confidential."

"And then you decided to ask around yourself and see if any of your scientist friends had interviewed there."

"Yes," she said quietly. "Although they aren't really my friends—they were Ben's. But until this morning, I'd only asked at parties. No place I could be overheard, or traced. So that means that whoever knows something will be at that New York conference, and the . . . those people don't want me to go there."

"Not necessarily," Cavanaugh said. She couldn't be expected to see all the angles, but if she couldn't, why the hell was she trying to do his job? Journalism wasn't law enforcement. "It could be that you already talked to the right candidate, and the Relatives are simply afraid of who you'll talk to *about* whatever you learned."

She said, "The relatives?"

Now it was himself he was annoyed with. Felders's term had just slipped out. Because he was trying to one-up her, which happened because he'd been annoyed with her meddling in the first place. This kind of cycle was how agents made mistakes.

Judy said, "Now I've told you what I've been doing, it's your turn to—"

"You haven't told me all of it. Who did you talk to about interviewing at Verico, and what did they say?"

"Your turn first, Mr. Cavanaugh." The hazel eyes met his steadily, with no attempt to hide the shade of sorrow there. Which meant she'd made some kind of peace with it. A rare thing. Judy Kozinski struck him as very unusual, which was a good reason to tell her nothing.

Except where she might be useful.

He said, "What do these words mean to you, Mrs. Kozinski? Cadoc. Verico. Cadaverico."

She frowned. "Say them again."

"Cadoc. Verico. Cadaverico."

"Nothing. I mean, 'Verico' does, obviously. And *cadaverico* sounds Italian—couldn't you look it up?"

"We did. It means 'deathlike' or 'corpselike.' "

She said, with a strange mixture of expressions flitting across her face, "So it's a joke of some kind. About Verico causing death and corpses."

"I'm afraid so. A grisly kind of joke. But 'Cadoc' doesn't mean anything to us, and the whole sequence of words doesn't help much."

"Should it? What is it?"

"Something we learned applies to Verico."

"Applies how?" she said. Now she looked like a journalist, Cavanaugh thought: alert and open, ready to track down facts. Which he was not going to give her. She had also started lying. She knew more than she was saying about some part of the three-word puzzle. The word "Cadoc"? Or the phrase as a whole? Cavanaugh knew when people were lying to him. He'd known when Jeanne Cassidy had lied, all those months ago.

So how come, if he was so good at lie detection, he'd missed Dr. Mark Lederer?

Dollings came in with papers. His jawline had relaxed a little. "These came for you by courier from the field office. Faxes from Washington."

"Mrs. Kozinski," Cavanaugh said formally. "I'd like you to come voluntarily with me to a federal detention center. For your own protection. You could still be in danger here."

"No," she said instantly. "I'm going to the microbiology conference in New York. It starts this afternoon."

"No, you're not. We need to ask you more questions, and we can't allow the people who tried to kill you once to try again."

"In a crowded hotel? When I'm with other people every minute? Just escort me there safely, and I'll be fine."

She clearly had no idea what the Relatives could do. But then, why should she? She was an amateur.

"Mrs. Kozinski, I could force you to stay in a detention center, as a material witness to a federal crime, for at least a short while. I could also detain you for questioning under suspicion of withholding information concerning a felony. I don't want to do either of those things. I do want to keep you safe. I think we can best do that in a detention center, but if you won't come, I'm going to at least assign a federal marshall to your house here."

She didn't go to pieces. Despite himself, Cavanaugh was impressed. She looked at him levelly and said, "I'm not withholding information. I don't have any more information. And I'd like to call my lawyer."

"Certainly," Cavanaugh said. "But your phone is tapped. You should—"

The phone rang.

Judy Kozinski said, her voice sharper now, "Aren't I allowed to take my own phone calls?"

"Of course you are," Cavanaugh said, irritated again. "If it's for you, Dollings will hand you the receiver. Just remember that we haven't removed the tap yet."

Dollings said to Cavanaugh, "It's for you. She won't give her name."

She? Here? Cavanaugh took the receiver. "Hello?"

"Mr. Cavanaugh, this is Dr. Julia Garvey. I'm at Dulles on my way to Boston. I'll meet you at Logan, by the United Airlines ticket counter. It's vital that I see you and only you about—"

"Stop," Cavanaugh said. "Stop. Don't fly to Boston, Dr. Garvey. Don't—"

"They're calling my plane," she said crisply. "I don't have time to argue. Be there at one twenty-eight. I have exactly what you need." Her voice fell on the last word; Cavanaugh would have sworn she shuddered. The receiver clicked.

"No!" he shouted into the emptiness. The dial tone sounded. "Who the fuck gave her this number!" Frantically he dialed Felders.

"What is it?" Judy Kozinski said. Dollings looked dumbfounded.

Felders wasn't in. Cavanaugh tapped in the code to reroute the call to Patrick Duffy, urgent. And let the phone tappers be listening, please God, if they got the last call let them get this one, too—

"Mr. Duffy, this is Robert Cavanaugh. I'm in Boston, on the Kozinski attempt—"

Duffy heard immediately that it was important. "I got the background from Marty. What do you need?"

"Dr. Julia Garvey is at Dulles. She just called here, some fuck-up at the office must have helpfully told her where I am. This phone is tapped. Garvey's taking a United plane to Logan that lands on or a little before one twenty-eight. Get our watcher at the airport to find her and bring her in to you, under safe guard. *Now.*"

"Got it," Duffy said, and hung up. Cavanaugh stood staring at the receiver.

Judy Kozinski said quietly, "All right. I'll go with you to a detention center."

Cavanaugh heard her with one corner of his mind. The rest was flooded with an intuition, the deep certain kind. They said intuition was supposed to be an agent's best resource, a personal extra that could illuminate un-expected connections and pull you out of tight corners. A gift. What they never said was how it felt when it was an intuition like this one.

He suddenly knew, beyond rational doubt, that Dr. Julia Garvey was already dead.

Twenty-three

Dr. Mark Lederer lived in a big, white-columned, fake Colonial in Newton, set among other houses built at the same time and designed by the same architect. Nearly every lawn had a swing set, now a rusting skeleton of summer, a sandbox, a treehouse, a basketball hoop above the garage. The front yard next door swarmed with kids coasting on silver platter-shaped sleds down an incline that must have dropped all of three feet. Another kid opened Lederer's door, a pretty, gap-toothed preteen in a Guns 'n' Roses sweatshirt. She smiled. Apparently what had happened to the six-year-old hadn't made the Lederers warn their daughters about opening doors to strangers. Maybe the parents didn't want them to grow up distrustful. Cavanaugh shook his head, marveling. People were amazing.

"Is your father home? Dr. Mark Lederer?"

"Dad!" the girl bellowed, startling Cavanaugh. She had a bray like a drill sergeant.

Mark Lederer came down the staircase, dressed in khakis and a sweater, towel-drying his hair. When his

face emerged from the terrycloth and he saw Cavanaugh, he stood completely still, one foot suspended halfway down a riser, his expression wiped clean as his hair.
It lasted only a moment, and then Lederer was smiling
and extending his hand, but the moment was enough.

Son of a bitch, Cavanaugh thought. Son of a bitch.

"Mr. Cavanaugh. Hello. Molly, close the door, the
cold air is coming in."

Molly shut the door, gave another of her gap-toothed
smiles, and loped off.

"I have some questions for you, Dr. Lederer," Cavanaugh said. His mind raced. Son of a bitch. And he didn't
mean Lederer.

Somehow, before, somehow, he'd let Lederer lie to
him.

"Certainly," Lederer said. "Come to my study."

"I'd rather we talked in my car."

"No, I'd prefer my study," Lederer said, which could
mean he suspected the house was bugged and wanted
to demonstrate clearly to whoever had bugged it that
Lederer was behaving as agreed.

He led the way to his study, which looked a lot like
Ben Kozinski's study with less grandiose furniture, and
closed the door. On the near wall hung a framed photograph of the three Lederer girls, all as pretty and gap-
toothed as the one that had opened the front door. They
wore homemade Halloween costumes: a ballerina, an
angel, a bunny. The ballerina stood on toe, laughing.
The angel stuck her tongue out at the camera. The
bunny held a red lollipop.

Cavanaugh said, "You told me that you never had a
job interview at Verico, Doctor."

"That's right," Lederer said pleasantly.

"We have reason to think otherwise. Someone threatened you, didn't they, if you ever told anyone what
you'd learned at Verico. And now they suspect Judy Kozinski may have talked to you about her husband's
death, and so they underlined that threat by temporarily
seizing your little girl and releasing her unharmed a few
hours later. A show of power."

"We've talked to the local police about Rosie," Lederer said. His voice was firm, and he looked Cavanaugh straight in the eye. "I told him I have no idea who took her, or why. And I'm telling you the same thing."

"Bullshit," Cavanaugh said gently, hoping to jolt Lederer into a reaction to either the comment or the gentleness. But Lederer was no Ben Kozinski. He went on smiling like a man hard to panic.

"I'm sorry I can't be of more help, Mr. Cavanaugh."

"You can be a lot more help, Doctor. And there may be lives at stake."

"I know," Lederer said, and his expression didn't slip. He didn't even glance at the Halloween picture.

Cavanaugh had a sudden intuition that he'd gotten everything he was going to get here. But maybe if he could get Lederer away from this could-be-bugged house, and push him . . . He said, "The Witness Protection Program—"

"I can't help you, Mr. Cavanaugh."

Cavanaugh looked again at the photo of Lederer's little girls. He remembered that he usually asked himself what he would do if he himself were in a witness's place.

He said abrupt good-byes, drove his car down the winding streets, and circled back as soon as he was sure he wasn't being followed. He parked in a driveway a few doors down from Lederer's. The driveway hadn't been plowed recently; no lights shone inside; a snowy magazine sat on the front steps.

It wasn't the sort of neighborhood where a strange man could sit in a car very long. Too many kids. Cavanaugh imagined the telephone conversations: *"Sue, Billy just came in and said there's a car with a man in it in the Hendersons' driveway. Aren't Jan and Don in Mexico?"* *"Let me call Connie—she and George are watching the house for Jan."* *"Ann, Kathy says—"* *"After what happened last night to little Rosie Lederer—"* *"Maybe Beth knows if the Hendersons—"*

It took only fifteen minutes before Mark Lederer was walking across the snowy yards to Cavanaugh's car.

Cavanaugh reached across the seat and opened the

passenger door. Lederer hesitated, then climbed in. Cavanaugh didn't give the scientist a chance to get in his first objection. Fifteen minutes was enough time to prepare the monologue.

"Dr. Lederer, I know you understand what organized crime can do. You're an intelligent man. What you don't seem to understand is that they *will* do it to you. You can't make deals with them. You can't negotiate, because if they perceive you as a threat, they break all promises. Instantly. They owe you nothing. If they so choose, you and all your kids are dead. And without the truth, the government has no tools to even begin to protect you.

"Please, don't interrupt, just listen. I don't think you really understand. They killed Benjamin Kozinski. They killed a man named Carlo Gigliotti, one of their own, and his girlfriend, an eighteen-year-old kid who was an innocent bystander. This morning someone they hired was shot dead trying to kill Judy Kozinski in her own bathroom.

"Do you know why they killed all these people, Doctor?

"The bystander girlfriend died because they thought she might know something. I don't even know if she did. Maybe not. Judy Kozinski nearly died for the same reason. Benjamin Kozinski did know something, and he made a sudden move: He went for a drive at three o'clock in the morning. That's all it took to get his head bashed in with a hammer. They may have thought he was going to the police. Maybe he was. Maybe not.

"Now I think you know something about Verico, Doctor. Something you learned when you interviewed there. Yes, I know you said you didn't interview there. But I'm not sure I believe that. I think you went to Verico, and nobody but you and Dr. Stevens knows what you were told there. I don't know. But whatever it is, I believe it makes you a potential liability of either the Gigliotti or Callipare families. That's not what you intended, of course. A man like you doesn't choose to be a liability to men like those. But that's what you are. And La Cosa

Nostra deals with its liabilities through murder, because they're evil.

"A harsh word, isn't it? People don't use it much anymore. Old-fashioned. Melodramatic. But there's no better word, Dr. Lederer. Evil people don't trust anyone to keep their bargains, Doctor, not even their own. And you're not their own. In the long run, they won't trust your silence. They didn't trust Carlo Gigliotti, family to them, and now he's dead. How safe are you?

"They *will* kill you, Doctor, sooner or later. When the heat's off. It will look like an accident, but you'll be just as dead as Carlo. As Benjamin Kozinski. As Judy Kozinski would have been this morning if we hadn't been watching her. They can do it—they've already demonstrated how easily they can pick up your children, if they choose to. These aren't tax cheats or savings-and-loan embezzlers. These are professional assassins and child pornographers and drug traffickers and people who send messages to each other via car bombs.

"You let your daughters open their front door to anybody, Doctor. Molly opened it, with total trust, to me. I could have been standing there with a gun. Or a knife. A knife is more silent. You would never even catch a glimpse of the man who knifed Molly. And no bargain of silence will prevent it—because *they don't keep their bargains.*

"We do, Doctor. We're your only real chance to keep your family safe. Unless you tell us whatever you know, let us protect you, and enable us to *take out* these bastards, every time that doorbell rings, you're going to have to wonder who's standing there with a gun or a knife. Every time. Every single time.

"Let us protect you. And help us do it right."

Cavanaugh stopped. Lederer stared, expressionless, through the windshield. Snow fell from the darkening sky, fat lazy flakes. Finally Lederer said, "I can't help you, Mr. Cavanaugh."

"But don't you *see*—" His mobile sounded.

He called in, not looking at Lederer. It was Felders. "Listen, Bob . . ."

"Go ahead," he said, but he already knew.

"Our man was about two minutes too late. They got Julia Garvey in the ladies' room at Dulles. She's dead. Knife."

He pictured it: the brisk, gray-haired woman pushing open the door of the stall with a firm hand, closing it, sitting down on the toilet. The killer coming in after her, and the sharpened blade. Was it one of those long ladies' rooms with a whole row of stalls? Had Dr. Garvey chosen a stall near the middle, or at one end?

He put the call on the speaker phone, so Lederer could hear it.

"Two witnesses," Felders was saying, "but one of them is an airport junkie and the other's hysterical. Not much reliable information on the perp. Male, dressed in a raincoat, brown hat pulled low. No trace of how he got out."

"Who favors a knife?" Cavanaugh said. His voice didn't sound like his own.

"Hell, they all favor whatever works, you know that. He took her purse and her coat, she'd left both hanging on the hook on the stall door, a witness said. If Dr. Garvey had any notes or anything with her, they're gone."

Mark Lederer stared at the speaker. His face had gone the same color as the snowflakes.

Felders said, "What about Lederer? You saw him?"

"Just now."

Felders said flatly, "And he didn't give you anything."

"No. But he's got it. He knows."

"Are you going with Judy Kozinski to the detention center?"

"In a little while. I'll keep you updated. And Marty— were there any signs that Dr. Garvey had time to struggle?"

"Afraid so. But not for very long. Is that significant?"

"No," Cavanaugh said. "I just wanted to know." He hung up and looked at Lederer.

Lederer said, "I can't help you."

A woman hurried, shivering, across the snow. She wore a ski sweater and boots, but no coat. In her mid-thirties, she was slender and beautiful, with a slight gap between her front teeth. Opening the passenger door, she leaned in toward Lederer. "Mark?"

"It's all right, Beth."

"Why are you sitting out here? Is this the police officer Molly spoke to? What's going on?"

"It's all right."

Cavanaugh said, "Mrs. Lederer, your husband and I just learned that Dr. Julia Garvey is dead. She was murdered at Dulles Airport on her way to see me about Verico."

Beth Lederer paled. "Julia? Dead? But we just saw her at . . . are you sure? Julia?"

Cavanaugh said nothing.

"But that can't be, we just saw her . . . she was such a quiet . . . what's 'Verico'? Mark?"

"It's a biotech company," her husband said quietly.

"I don't understand. Was Julia doing something illegal? Some . . . drug thing? Not Julia!"

"Beth, honey . . ."

"What happened, Mark? Who would kill *Julia?* Why would she be involved in anything the police would care about?" One hand clutched her husband's shoulder. The nails were faintly blue from the cold.

Either she was the world's best actress, Cavanaugh decided, or she didn't know anything. He watched her fingers wrinkle Lederer's sleeve, her face turned fearfully down to his.

Cavanaugh got out of the car. Across its roof he said, as gently as he could, "Mrs. Lederer, I'm sorry to have to say this, but we think there might be a connection between Dr. Garvey's murder and your little girl's kidnapping yesterday. Which is why it's vitally important that both you and your husband tell us anything you know."

"Know? About what? We already told the police everything about Rosie's . . . 'kidnapping'? Mark, what does he mean? We don't know anything else, do we? Mark?"

Lederer pulled himself out of the car and eyed Cavanaugh with anger, but not the kind Cavanaugh needed. This was cold, implacable anger. The kind that clammed up, not the kind that spilled its guts.

"Mark?"

"No, Beth, we don't know any more than we told the police. Agent Cavanaugh naturally hoped we did, but if there's a connection between Julia's death and Rosie, I can't imagine what it could be. It doesn't seem to me there *is* a connection. But the law has to look at all possibilities, I guess, no matter how far-fetched."

Cavanaugh watched Lederer's eyes. They never wavered. The next hour, then, was going to be another waste. And the eventual signed statement was going to be worthless. He wasn't going to be able to break down Lederer, not with his pretty sweet wife clinging to his arm and his three pretty cherished daughters sledding in the next yard. Cavanaugh held no cards stronger than that. And Beth Lederer, whom clearly anybody could break down, didn't know anything. A completely wasted hour.

He started in on it.

It was late afternoon before he called Felders again, a winter afternoon already edging toward dark. Driving from Newton to the federal detention center in Boston, he had the weary sensation that the entire city had turned gray. No other color. His stomach rumbled, and he realized he hadn't eaten since dinner yesterday. He pulled into a McDonald's, ordered a Big Mac, and called Felders from the pay phone. In the nearest booth four teenagers, arranged in couples, traded insults and French fries. "Oh, gross," one of the girls laughed. She looked a little like Molly Lederer might in another three or four years.

"Marty? Robert. Did Dollings report in?"

"He and Mrs. Kozinski are on their way to the detention center now. There was a delay in the paperwork. Anything from Lederer?"

"No. He's protecting his family."

"Subpoena him?"

"As a last resort. I don't think he'd talk even under threat of contempt. What did Natalie learn from Jeanne Cassidy?"

"Nothing. She cornered her after some class and they talked for three hours. Natalie is convinced that the 'Cadoc-Verico-Cadaverico' thing is all that Cassidy knows. She phoned you out of conscience, and she's probably just as terrified as Lederer, but that's really all she's got, Natalie thinks."

"Okay. I'm on my way to Government Center. Marty—can we get REI status now?"

"You still don't have the link to Verico, Bob. You've got crimes, but no pattern by an enterprise."

"But if Duffy—"

"Find the link to Verico, first. Maybe it *is* there," Felders said, and hung up. Cavanaugh realized that was all the apology he was ever going to get for insisting on surveillance for Judy Kozinski. As back-assed an apology as everything else.

His nose was running. He found he didn't have a tissue. Shit, not another cold. Why were some people so susceptible, and others never got sick?

Marcy never got sick.

He blew his nose and thought about calling Marcy. It was after five o'clock; she might be home from work. No. He wouldn't call. She didn't want him to. He wouldn't.

He went back to his booth and stared at his Big Mac, now lukewarm. In the teens' booth a boy fed fries, one by one, to a girl. Fluorescent light gleamed on her glossy hair. Cavanaugh's head ached. His neck hurt. His witnesses were being murdered.

He walked back to the phone and dialed the number. After the third ring, the answering machine came on. A man's voice. "Hello. Neither Marcia Gordon nor Hal Clark are available right now, but if you leave a message at the sound of the tone, we'll get back to you as soon as we can."

Cavanaugh replaced the receiver in the cradle. He

stared at the wall. Hal Clark. Marcy's boss.

He walked between the booths, past his congealing Big Mac, and out to the rental car that would take him to the federal detention center in Boston.

Twenty-four

Judy sat in the passenger seat of Agent Dollings's unmarked car. Dollings drove seriously, glancing often in the rearview mirror at the police cruiser behind them. Was the cruiser an "escort," which sounded like something visiting diplomats got, or just "protection"? She didn't know the words for this situation. This bothered her. She was a journalist. She should have her terms right.

She realized that she was probably in some sort of delayed shock.

Dollings kept checking the rearview mirror. Was it really the cops he was checking for? Did he expect more danger?

Her hands clutched the purse on her lap so tightly that the clasp snapped open. She stuffed her wallet, makeup case, and tissues back inside, and put the purse on the floor. Her hands she laced together tightly in her lap.

Dollings said, "You all right, ma'am?"

"No, I'm not all right. Somebody just tried to kill me.

They did kill my husband. I'm most definitely not all right."

Those weren't the words she'd intended to say. She didn't know what she'd intended to say. Dollings glanced again at the mirror.

"Is anybody following us?" Judy said. She hated her abrupt, jerky tone.

"Police escort, ma'am."

"I already know that. Anybody else?"

He glanced at her. "Don't worry, Mrs. Kozinski. They're not going to try again with an FBI agent and state troopers practically on top of you." He seemed to consider how this sounded, and actually blushed.

Immediately Judy felt better. She could feel her sense of humor flow back, like a returning tide. She said, "How old are you, Agent Dollings?"

He frowned. "I don't see that it's important."

"No. I'm sorry." Twenty-three, she guessed. Twenty-four at the outside.

Dollings went on frowning and glancing in the rear-view mirror. He pulled the car off the expressway and drove toward the Government Center. At a red light he held the wheel lightly with his left hand, reached for the phone with his right, and punched in a code.

"Dollings . . . about three blocks . . . yes . . . Dr. who?"

The car was too warm. And the passenger-side window was dirty. Wouldn't you think a quasimilitary agency would keep its cars clean? Spit and polish. She rolled down the window and watched the crowds on the twilight sidewalk. Government workers rushing for the metro, tourists walking back to their hotels, lugging shopping bags. They all looked a little unreal to her. People in another, safer world.

"Where?" Dollings said in another tone. "Any witnesses?"

Slowly, Judy turned her head away from the window.

"No," Dollings said. "Okay." He replaced the receiver. The light was still red. His jawline looked rigid as glass, faintly sheened with sweat.

Judy said, "Who else was killed?"

The muscles of his face didn't move. They must teach them to do that, Judy thought detachedly; the blush she had surprised out of him had been an anomaly. But there was still that faint film of sweat. He stared straight ahead, through the windshield. The crosslight changed to yellow.

"'I want to know who else died!" Judy screamed, startling herself. All at once she was two people: one yelling and hysterical, the other watching herself calmly, from a safe distance. The first Judy was suddenly swept with waves of blackness. She was going to faint. *Put your head between your knees,* the second Judy ordered, in a voice like her mother's. She did, her right hand palsied on her legs, her left clutching Dollings's arm as if she could squeeze from him by sheer force the knowledge she didn't want to hear. *Who else died?*

"Ma'am . . ." Dollings said, and jerked his arm free of her grip. Judy fought nausea. No, don't upchuck here, not here, please God, in a government car. The vertigo passed. She flopped upright in her seat, her head thrown back against the headrest, her forehead suddenly cold, and closed her eyes.

Horns barked. A siren shrieked. Judy opened her eyes. The light was green. Dollings sat in the unmoving car, half turned toward her, half leaning against the far door, his face serious. There was a bloody hole in his right temple.

The passenger door was ripped open, and Judy screamed. It was one of the state troopers. He pushed her back onto the floor of the car and looked at Dollings. "Fucking God!" he said, and a part of her mind registered that she'd never heard that particular oath before. He ran back to the police cruiser, and a moment later it shot past Dollings's car in the right lane.

Where the attacker must have been. In another car. Or on the sidewalk. And if she hadn't crumpled forward just when she did—

The second cop ran away from the car, into the crowd. Searching? For the killer? For a witness?

It had all happened so *fast.* Now other cars started to

honk, annoyed at the vehicle blocking traffic. Cars flowed around her stationary one on both the right and the left. Apparently nobody knew what had happened, or didn't care. Dollings continued to stare at her seriously, upright, his brain pierced by a bullet.

Both cops had left her alone, looking for the killer. Were they supposed to do that? What if the killer were still here, or there were two of them? What if—

Judy opened her door, into oncoming traffic. A green Mercedes passing on the right honked angrily. Judy saw the driver clearly, with such a heightened visual sense that it seemed she must remember her forever: a woman in her forties, auburn hair in a sharp geometric cut, tailored coat of beautifully cut dark blue wool, the seat beside her stacked with bags from Jordan Marsh. The woman wore pearl earrings. Her gray eyeshadow was smudged.

Judy bolted across the traffic lane to the curb. A few people glanced at her curiously, but as yet no crowd had formed. These people didn't realize what had happened. They walked away from Dollings's car as if everything were normal, flowing steadily along the sidewalk. Judy flowed with them.

She let the crowd carry her along, staying close to groups of people, not thinking about what she was doing. Just moving away from Dollings. Just being with the normal. Just blending in. One block, two. She didn't look behind her.

When she realized which way the crowds were moving, she stopped abruptly. The metro stop at Government Center. No. That's where Dollings had been taking her, that's where they expected her to be . . . what was she even doing on the *street*? Abruptly she ducked into a building.

But that was worse. The long empty corridors, the closed office doors, each with neat gold lettering and security locks . . . it was obvious she didn't belong here. She stood out. *The thing to do,* the second Judy said calmly, *is to not stand out.* She left the building and rejoined the crowded sidewalk. But not walking toward

Government Center, and not heading back the way she'd come, either. Turning a corner, she joined the people walking west. She tried to look exactly like the other women: take steps the same size as theirs, glance at street beggars with the same split-second uneasiness, carry her purse the same way—

She'd left her purse in Dollings's car.

That almost broke her. But the second Judy said, *Steady now. You can do this,* and she kept walking. At the next corner she looked at the street signs. Three streets converged in a busy intersection: Somerset. School. Beacon. She walked down Beacon.

She had no money. No ATM card. No MasterCard. She couldn't take a cab, or a bus, or a hotel room. She was exposed. Someone might still be looking for her. She kept walking.

To her right loomed the State House. Charles Bulfinch's gilded dome, huge but looking weightless, floated over the neoclassical building. The dome was sheathed in copper, Judy remembered irrelevantly, from the foundry of Paul Revere. During World War II they'd painted the dome gray, so it wouldn't attract the attention of the Luftwaffe planes that never came. This wasn't what she should be remembering right now. Her mind wasn't working right. The State House was a riot of flowers in the summer, but now it wasn't summer. Piles of dirty snow dotted the lawn. In the visitors' parking lot stood rows of school buses. Judy's mind suddenly cleared.

She mounted the State House steps and walked inside. There, gawking at the statuary and portraits in Doric Hall, she found what she'd expected: mobs of schoolkids on tour. Judy looked for a preteen group that was mostly white, mostly not in jeans, mostly carrying souvenir books, mostly looking tired. The out-of-towners. Every suburb in the state sent their seventh- or eighth- or ninth-graders to the city to trudge through the historical sites of Colonial and Revolutionary War Boston. The state was small enough for this to be a day trip. Each year her father chaperoned a similar trip to Saratoga and

Fort Ticonderoga. He was always a calming influence on the overexcited kids.

In the Hall of Flags two short boys were shoving each other with murderous expressions and very little effect. "Fuck off, you!" "No, *you* fuck off!" Judy marched up and grabbed an arm of each.

"Hey! You know what the principal said about representing our school!"

The boys glared at her, angry but not willing to shift the attack to her. Yeah, suburbanites. She hoped it was a distant suburb.

She said, "Now you just both stay with me until we get back to the buses!"

They did, muttering under their breaths. The group straggled through the rest of the tour, which was almost over. Judy eyed the adults and picked a mother acting as chaperone. These were easy to distinguish from the teachers, who didn't look nearly as rattled. The teachers were used to this. The mother-chaperones had pictured something different, a civilized cultural excursion. This mother peered fearfully, chicly groomed but both nervous and near-sighted. Judy said to her, "Can you believe this madhouse schedule?"

The other woman smiled. "I think the idea is to wear them out. Get them so tired that they fall asleep on the bus."

"Well, it's working on *me*. I'm tired out. How about you?"

The woman now had the embarrassed expression that meant she didn't remember who Judy was, and thought she should. "I'm sorry, I don't—"

"Sally Carter. John's mother. I'm filling in at the last minute, another chaperone got sick. This morning I was on one of the other buses, but the trip coordinator . . ."

"Mr. Perkins?"

"Yes, he asked me to switch because . . . well—" She rolled her eyes at the two sullen boys she still held firmly by the wrists.

The woman laughed. "*Oh*, yes. I'm Ann Browning."

"I know, we met," Judy said, and the woman looked embarrassed again.

She made a few more innocuous remarks to Ann Browning during the half hour left of the afternoon, and in the parking lot climbed on the bus with her.

The bus driver, holding a list of names, frowned. "I don't see any Sally Carter—"

"Oh, Mr. Perkins made a switch," Ann Browning said to him knowledgeably. Making up for not having recognized Sally before. "Beefing up security." She actually winked.

The bus driver, already bored, just nodded.

When everyone was seated, a harassed-looking man climbed aboard—Perkins?—and did a head count. Judy ducked down, pretending to search for something she'd dropped. The bus seat hid her; she was shorter than most of the kids. Perkins nodded at the driver and climbed off the bus.

The long line of yellow school buses pulled out.

All the way down Storrow Drive, Judy chatted with Ann about the football team. Whenever there was too much noise or too much physical activity, she disciplined kids who regarded her with the same fish stare—*I don't know you and I don't want to*—with which they regarded everybody over twenty-five.

The bus swung onto Interstate 90 and headed west. The kids actually had quieted, talking in small groups. A few, precocious or exhibitionist, fondled each other openly. Judy ignored them.

Brookline, Wellesley . . . Judy held her breath. The next town was Natick. What if the bus deposited her in her own town, where her stalkers might presume she'd go? But the bus rolled on. Framingham, Westboro . . . It was dark now. Students slept, their frantic insecurities smoothed from their faces, which looked even younger in the gloomy overhead lighting.

The buses stopped at Worcester, in a school parking lot, where kids tumbled off as if released from prison wagons. Parents waited in idling cars. Judy waved at

Ann Browning, and then set off as purposefully as if she knew where she was going.

There was nowhere to go.

It was after six. Cars pulled out of the lot. Judy walked in the opposite direction, behind the dark school, and out onto a side street. It was quieter here. Small houses glowed with window lights. A door opened, then closed, and she smelled meat frying.

Standing on the snowy sidewalk, Judy pulled her coat tighter around her. She knew no one in Worcester, she had no money, not even a dime to call anyone. She could ask to use the phone in one of these houses. But whom would she call? Her parents' phone might be tapped. Any friend she called would be drawn into danger and death. How could she do that to a friend?

Call the police.

She could do that, of course. They'd come and get her. The state troopers, or the FBI. But look what a great job the cops had already done protecting her. A ten-second margin this morning, before Dollings fired his gun in her bathroom. No margin at all this afternoon. If she hadn't doubled over, nauseous and fainting . . . Dollings hadn't doubled over. Look what a great job the law had done protecting their own.

And if she did call the FBI, did track down Cavanaugh, she would be no closer to finding out who'd killed Ben than she'd been this morning. Cavanaugh wasn't going to tell her anything he didn't have to. That wasn't his job.

If she wanted to know who had killed Ben, she'd have to find out herself. And she needed to know. Not just wanted to know—needed it, like a drunk needed liquor. Because if she didn't find out, she would never sleep again, work again, think again without Ben in the background like harsh static, the volume rising or falling but always there, interfering with any other thoughts. Unless she found out, she couldn't go forward with her life. She just couldn't.

Right now, this minute, she was safe. Nobody in the whole world knew she was in Worcester. The killers didn't know, the law didn't know. If she stayed away from the law, they couldn't lock her safely in a detention center, where she couldn't find any answers, and which she didn't need anyway because she was already safe. And if she stayed away from the law, the killers couldn't track her by tracking the cops, the way they'd done this afternoon.

Somewhere across the dark street a door opened and a woman called, "Here, Prince! Here, boy!"

Judy started walking. She could see a traffic light two blocks away. From there, she saw another light and much more traffic. At the first store she asked for a phone book, and then directions. Worcester wasn't large. In a half hour she stood in front of The Gold Exchange. GOLD AND JEWELS BOUGHT AND SOLD, the sign said. Inside was a counter, a cash register with operator lock, a man who studied her carefully through the bullet-proof window before releasing the door lock, and a machine to test whether gold and diamonds were real. Judy watched, fascinated.

The man gave her five hundred dollars for her three-quarter-carat diamond engagement ring, and two hundred fifty dollars for the gold pendant with the ruby-and-sapphire double helix. Cash.

"You find any more jewelry in your back dresser drawers, you bring it to us," the man said, the corners of his mouth turned down, and Judy suddenly realized he thought the ring and pendant were stolen.

She put the bills in her pocket. At a Burger King a block away she locked herself in a ladies' room stall and put six hundred dollars of it in her bra. There was room. She was probably a 34B now, and the bra wasn't.

She bought a hamburger, surprised to find she was actually hungry. Then she found a cab.

"I'm a stranger here," she told the driver. "I need an inexpensive hotel where I won't be asked to show a credit card—I've had some credit problems, unfortunately. Can you recommend one?"

He turned around to look at her. Judy had no idea what he thought he saw, or how he reached his decision.

"The Princess Hotel," he said finally. "Won't hassle you none."

"Is it clean?"

He shrugged. "Clean enough."

"All right. Thank you. Please take me there."

The Princess looked shabby, but not overtly sinister. The desk clerk didn't comment on her lack of luggage. Judy signed in as "Janet Chambers," a name she picked because it had no connection with any person, book, or movie she could remember. In her room she locked the door, set the chain, and wedged a chair under the door-knob. The sheets looked clean. The window, which overlooked a fire escape, was barred.

Judy sat on the edge of the thin-mattressed bed, staring at the faded wall.

She'd done it. She'd gotten herself to a safe place.

Now what?

Twenty-five

She's *what?*" Cavanaugh said.

"Gone," the field agent repeated. "She walked out. Or they took her."

Cavanaugh stared at him. He had just walked into the FBI field office at Center Plaza, after the drive through Boston's incredible rush-hour traffic. The place was pandemonium, with agents on the phones, on the computers, tense and argumentative.

"Come into my office," Lancaster said. Cavanaugh followed him. Lancaster, middle-aged with thinning hair and iron-gray eyes, wore a look Cavanaugh recognized: furious contempt, well-controlled. The fury was because Dollings had been killed. The contempt was for the fuck-ups in Washington who had given Dollings and Cavanaugh, inexperienced kids in their twenties, an assignment this big and dangerous—whatever the hell it was. The control was pure Bureau.

"Tell me what happened," Cavanaugh said evenly, matching the fury and the control. But not the contempt. He wasn't going to play those games.

Lancaster, head of the Boston Organized Crime and Racketeering Strike Force, gave Cavanaugh a concise rendition of what had happened at the traffic light near Government Center. The perps in the car had eluded capture. There were no real witnesses, despite crowds of people—no one they'd located had noticed anything the two state troopers hadn't already seen. One trooper had given chase, but the men had abandoned the car and escaped on foot before backup could arrive. There had probably been a silencer on the gun. The Boston police, who already had members on the strike force, were scouring the city for leads, and for Judy Kozinski. Dollings's body awaited autopsy.

"And in the confusion Mrs. Kozinski just walked off," Cavanaugh said. He was careful to keep his tone neutral. Two troopers had lost her. An agent was dead. The cops, as well as the Bureau, would be turning the state upside down.

"Probably nobody thought Mrs. Kozinski would run," Lancaster said. "She had no reason to, did she?"

"Just fear. She'd been the target of two murder attempts in one day."

"Suppose you tell me everything you have here, Cavanaugh. I spoke to your chief on the phone. Felders. He's sending me the case documentation. Now let me hear it from you. We can't help if Washington doesn't keep us informed." His tone stayed controlled.

Cavanaugh explained the case, starting with the EL-SUR reference on the Cellini-Denisi tape. Lancaster sat listening, arms folded across his chest, iron eyes never leaving Cavanaugh's face. He was pissed.

When Cavanaugh finished, Lancaster said, "A biotech company. To manufacture proteins."

"Organic protein molecules, yes. By way of genetically altered viruses."

"For the outfit."

"Yes," Cavanaugh said. Lancaster must come from Chicago. "Outfit" was the Chicago word.

"For no profit that headquarters can see."

"Not at this point. No."

"And no use as a weapon."

"Not an apparent use," Cavanaugh said.

"And none of this is on the network."

"We don't have REI status."

"But headquarters is expending manpower and money on this."

Cavanaugh didn't answer. Local Strike Forces were always short of manpower and money. It was a given.

"Look, I've been boring in on the outfit for fifteen years now," Lancaster said. "Fifteen solid years. In Chicago, and then with the New York Task Force, and now here. It's the same all over. The way you come up in the outfit, you earn it. You become an earner. If you're a good earner, the old men start to listen to you. The more you earn, the more they listen. *If* you say things that aren't too out of line with what the old men already know. And *if* you go on earning. There isn't any other way. Not for these guys. They think about making money and keeping people in line from the minute they get up in the morning until the minute their heads hit the pillows at night. That's all they think about. Not viruses, not DNA, not biotech. This isn't where they're at, Cavanaugh. Not a chance in hell."

Cavanaugh said evenly, "They killed Dollings."

"And that says to me that either Dollings was into something he shouldn't have been, or Kozinski was. Did you check that out, instead of this biotech crap?"

"We did."

"Kozinski, or his wife, weren't welshing on paying juice? Did he owe a lot of money? Did he gamble? Use? Were there broads? No? Well, we'll check it again," Lancaster said. "We'll find who got Dollings. This is in our district."

"Fine," Cavanaugh said. He kept his temper. He could imagine what Felders would do to him if he didn't. Felders didn't allow turf wars, or his agents to wage them.

Lancaster stared at him a moment longer. When Cavanaugh didn't take any of the offered baits, he walked to the back of the office and picked up a notebook.

"Mrs. Kozinski left her suitcase in Dollings's trunk and her purse on the floor of the car. This was in the suitcase. We assume she would have told you about it once she was safe in protective custody."

Cavanaugh ignored this jibe as well. He took the notebook. It was a journal of some type—not hers. Benjamin Kozinski's. He speed-read the opening entries, leafed through the rest. Self-important bastard. Then he came to the equations and drawings on the last few pages.

Lancaster said, "Felders said you have somebody at headquarters who can analyze the scientific stuff. Tamara Lang. We're faxing her a copy."

Cavanaugh remembered Lang: earnest, young, smart but not imaginative. She looked as if she were constantly trying for an "A" on some law-enforcement test made up exclusively of textbook formulas. He looked again at the last-page drawings. The Lone Ranger shooting a bullet from a gun: EHRLICH! The smaller bullets, all labeled with bizarre names: PETEY. THE BRONZE DANDELION. CASSANDRA. PRINCESS GRIMELDA. At the bottom of the page the single exuberant EUREKA!!! And the previous few pages of mathematical equations, jotted names of chemical processes.

"I need a phone," Cavanaugh said.

"Use mine." Lancaster didn't leave the room. Cavanaugh called Felders.

"Marty, they just told me up here that you've been sent Kozinski's notebook for Tamara Lang to look at. I don't think she's really up to this."

"So who is? Oh. You want him brought in?"

"No. You'd have to charge him with something, or at least subpoena him, he wouldn't come voluntarily. And the Relatives see Lederer come to the field office, they might think he's talking."

"You think they don't know you've already been to see him once today? How is it going to be different if you go back a second time?"

"They won't see me this time."

"Bob—use somebody else. They'll have your photograph on file. They own cameras too, you know."

"They won't see me."

"Okay," Felders said. "Your call. You sure Lederer won't cooperate?"

"Yeah. He'd let the entire Academy of Science be impaled, disembowelled, and hung before he'd say anything that would endanger those three kids."

"So what makes you think he's going to interpret the notebook for you?" Felders asked reasonably.

"I don't know."

"So—"

"So I don't know, all right? But it has to be him."

"Why not Caroline Lampert? She's a scientist, she worked with Kozinski."

"Because she doesn't know anything. She's already familiar with what they were doing in that lab, and she would have helped us if she could, but she couldn't put it together with Verico. She can't see the hidden link. She just isn't working at that level. It has to be Lederer. And it has to be on his ground."

"And it has to be you," Felders said. It wasn't a question; he wasn't arguing. Gazing at Lancaster's folded arms, Lancaster's contemptuous eyes, Cavanaugh suddenly realized how lucky he'd been in Felders.

Felders said, "Any trace of Judy Kozinski?"

"Not yet."

"How the hell did she just disappear like that? Unless the Relatives took her."

"I don't think so. I think she bolted. Gently reared Irish-Catholic girls who get a life shock can go that way."

"What the hell do you know about gently reared Irish-Catholic girls?"

"A priest told me," Cavanaugh said wearily. "Or a cop. But you got a fax of Kozinski's notebook, right? Show it to Lang. And in the morning, let Neymeier have it to run through his data correlation banks. Maybe there's a technical article someplace that will shed light. Anything new on Garvey?"

"Nothing so far."

"On Giancursio? Who might have hired him?"

"No leads."

"On Eric Stevens and the rest at Verico?"

"All leading the regular lives of the solid ordinary citizen."

"Caroline Lampert?"

"Ditto," Felders said. "We put an agent on her this morning. No one from the Relatives has tried to approach her."

"Jeanne Cassidy?"

"As far as we can tell, nobody detected Natalie talking to her, and Cassidy's back to her normal college-student round without being bothered."

"Great. All quiet on the global front, except that people keep getting killed."

"Lancaster's crew will find Judy Kozinski," Felders said. "He's good. Old-line hard-ass, though. Started out as a lawyer. He giving you any flack?"

"No," Cavanaugh said.

"Don't let him. Listen, Mrs. Kozinski's an amateur. She can't get far. We're covering her parents' home, her friends . . . everything. She can't get far."

"Right," Cavanaugh said. "We've got it all covered."

He hung up and called Lieutenant Piperston, of the Natick police.

It was midnight when he checked into a Ramada. There was nothing else to do until morning. The Ramada room was decorated in brown and green, slightly faded. There were no tissues in the dispenser. Cavanaugh ripped a long swatch of toilet paper, wadded it up, and blew his nose.

Too restless to sleep, he sat at the Formica desk, opening and closing drawers. His case was coming through, but his witnesses were disappearing. Lancaster didn't trust him. His wife was living with her boss, who made four times what Cavanaugh did and wasn't responsible for the murders of a scientist and a special agent.

With a plastic pen stamped COMPLIMENTS OF RAMADA, Cavanaugh sketched. He drew a man standing over a tombstone. The man smiled dementedly, clearly losing it. There were stars in the sky, and a crescent moon. On the tombstone he printed BEN KOZINSKI. After a minute he drew a second tombstone, labeled JULIA GARVEY. Then a third: ANDREW DOLLINGS. Underneath the row of tombstones he printed THINGS ALWAYS LOOK BETTER IN THE MOURNING.

He stared at the sketch for a long time, then tore it up and went to bed.

By 7:30 he'd checked out of the Ramada and found a pay phone with a door at a restaurant on the north side of Beacon Hill. He called one of the Boston Biomedical names that Neymeier had researched for him, a woman with no kids and an ambitious publication record. The kind who would be in the lab early.

"Dr. Sandra Ormandy?"

"Yes. Who is this, please?"

"I'm trying to reach Dr. Mark Lederer."

"You have the wrong—" she started to say, and then it hit her. Why was he addressing her by name on her line if he was trying to reach Lederer?

"I know this is not Dr. Lederer's number. My name is Robert Cavanaugh; I'm with the FBI. I need to talk to Dr. Lederer on a line that is not his. Will you please call him to this phone, without saying anything to anyone else?"

In the quality of her silence he heard her weighing his words. Was this the truth? Something sinister? A student prank? Did serious graduate students in a field like biotech go in for this kind of hoax?

He and Lancaster had done some weighing of their own. If the Relatives had tapped the Boston Biomedical line, it was probably at the trunk. That meant that theoretically they could monitor every conversation on every line, but they probably wouldn't. The Bureau wasn't the only one with manpower issues.

Dr. Ormandy apparently decided Lederer could look after himself. "Just a moment, please."

It was a long moment. Maybe Lederer wasn't even in the building. Maybe Cavanaugh had judged her profile wrong and Dr. Sandra Ormandy was cavorting up and down the halls laughing, "Guess who's on the line for Mark? The fucking feds!" Maybe Lederer was having breakfast someplace with Judy Kozinski. Maybe he was already dead.

He picked up the phone. "Mr. Cavanaugh?"

"Thank you for answering, Doctor."

"I don't think we have anything else to say to each other. I thought I made that clear."

"I need to show you something. It's very important, and it's not more of the same. I promise you. This is scientific information, and you will want to have seen it," Cavanaugh said, and knew that probably wasn't true. Not in the long run.

"So why not bring it out to the house, the way you've done before?"

"No, not at your house."

The silence on the other end was long.

"At least four more lives hang on this, Doctor," Cavanaugh said, picking a number out of thin air. "On your looking at this particular scientific information, right now. That's all you have to do. And nobody will know I've been to see you."

Another long silence. Cavanaugh knew he could say, "I can subpoena you, Doctor," but that would be the wrong approach here. Absolutely wrong. Lederer would clam up. Call a lawyer, and never budge. He had that capacity.

Cavanaugh suddenly remembered Jeanne Cassidy, clamming up tight, sending the postcard only months later.

This time, they didn't have months.

"All right, Mr. Cavanaugh. I'll have building security escort you to my lab."

"Not yours. Another one, belonging to somebody you don't work with. On a different floor."

Another long silence. Then, "I think maybe that's a little paranoid. Nobody unauthorized gets in here."

Right, Cavanaugh thought. And all your little lab rats will turn into Cinderella's coachmen. "Give me a floor and room number, Doctor. And please ask Dr. Ormandy—Dr. Ormandy, not you—to tell building security that at ten o'clock she's expecting a reporter from the Framingham *Weekly Record*."

"The what?"

"Dr. Ormandy is from Framingham," Cavanaugh said, and ignored the mean little satisfaction it gave him. He doubted the Relatives had anybody inside the building. But they might have the reception area bugged. And they would call the *Weekly Record* and discover that, yes, the paper sent out Daniel Anderson to interview Dr. Ormandy, who was a local girl made good. Cavanaugh hadn't been wrong about Piperston; he had all the right contacts in Boston's western suburbs, and he was efficient. When Cavanaugh had called last evening, Piperston had known immediately how to set it up.

Lederer said quietly, "All right, Mr. Cavanaugh. Ten o'clock."

Cavanaugh dawdled over breakfast until 9:00, then went into the men's room and prepped. Mustache, beard, large and slightly crooked nose. Brown contact lenses. Body pad, which added fifteen pounds, and sloppy trousers that added another five. The pants slopped over his shoes. Yellow tie. He didn't look disreputable: just careless. A man who was already in his thirties and no higher than reporter on a third-rate suburban weekly, usual province of returning housewives and retired teachers. He carried a clipboard with yellow legal pad and a cheap tape recorder.

At 9:50 he walked from the parking lot to Lederer's building. The security guard eyed him carefully.

"Dan Anderson," he said breezily. "To see Dr. Sandra Ormandy. I'm a *reporter*," leaning on the last word, laying on the self-importance. "She's expecting me."

"Sign in here. Someone with be down to escort you," the guard said, still studying him. Cavanaugh ignored the scrutiny. He was playing to an unseen audience, not to this square badge. The respect that Felders had taught him to have for local law enforcement didn't extend to rent-a-cops.

A frazzled-looking girl in a white lab coat appeared a

few minutes later and led him to a second-floor room. He guessed she was too young to be Dr. Ormandy. On the stairwell—either there was no elevator or the girl just didn't offer it—Cavanaugh sneezed. The girl turned to look at him.

"It's not a cold," he said quickly, remembering NIH. "I'm just allergic to rodents. There won't be any rats in the room we're going to, will there?"

"No."

"Well, that's good, because I'm allergic. Like I said." The girl turned away, shaking her head.

She left him in a very small anteroom to a larger lab. The tiny space was crowded with lab equipment, computer monitors, tables, glassware, refrigerator. No rats. A moment later, Lederer came in, also in a white lab coat. Cavanaugh saw that here, in his own domain, he had a natural authority that owed nothing to pose. He didn't blink at Cavanaugh's disguise.

"All right, Mr. Cavanaugh, what do you need to show me?"

"This." He pulled out Ben Kozinski's notebook. "Especially the last few pages. Take your time with it, Doctor. Say anything you think would be useful. But we desperately need a link between Ben Kozinski's work and whatever you think Verico is capable of producing. You may be the only one in the country who can see that connection." He didn't add that Julia Garvey had seen it, and died.

"I already told you," Lederer said, "I have no idea what Verico is or is not doing. I have never been there."

"Yes, Doctor. But take a look at that notebook and see if it tells you anything at all that you're willing to tell us."

Lederer started reading on the first page. He grimaced slightly. Cavanaugh watched him for a while, but Lederer didn't look up. He was evidently going to read it all, in order. Methodical.

Cavanaugh got up and studied the lab.

On a table was a beaker full of a clear liquid. It looked like water. A glass rod protruded from the beaker. Cavanaugh stirred it, then realized he probably shouldn't have. What if it was an important experiment? He took his fingers off the rod, then felt an absurd impulse to wipe it for prints.

"Dr. Lederer, I stirred this. I'm sorry." God, this was how he'd felt in Bio 101. In which he'd got a C. The As came only in history and English.

Lederer looked up and actually smiled. "That's all right. It's being discarded."

"What is it?"

"Don't you know?" He walked over to the table, stirred the liquid, and lifted the glass rod from the beaker. To Cavanaugh's surprise, the "water" turned out to be sticky as molasses, clinging to the rod in long, hair-thin threads. "This is deoxyribonucleic acid. DNA."

"That?"

"That," Lederer said, and returned to his chair and Kozinski's notebook.

Cavanaugh stared at the beaker. That was *it*. The stuff that built human beings. The stuff that made them born tall, or male, or beautiful, or athletic, or genius, or twins, or color blind, or with a hole in the valve of the heart. The stuff at the base of every cell of every body of every human being in the world. The stuff that made Tay-Sachs or diabetes or Huntington's chorea or even cancer switch on after five or ten or fifty years. The stuff that scientists were cutting and snipping into something else. The stuff that got Ben Kozinski and Julia Garvey killed for how much they understood about this ultimate secret.

Cavanaugh reached for the rod again. He couldn't help himself. He lifted it out of the beaker and the long hairlike threads lifted with it, stringy as mozzarella. He stared at it.

And sneezed.

Bits of DNA blew on the force of his sneeze and spattered over the wall, the table, nearly everything else in the tiny room. Cavanaugh dropped the rod back into the beaker; liquid splashed onto the table. God, what had he done? But Lederer had said the stuff was going to be discarded, he hadn't handled it as if it was danger-ous. . . .

He heard a sound behind him. Lederer sat white as a ghost. Cavanaugh had never seen anybody that white that didn't faint a minute later. He leaped toward Led-erer, but the scientist waved him away. Lederer wasn't looking at the mess Cavanaugh had made with the DNA. He stared at Ben Kozinski's notebook, open to the last page.

"My God," Lederer whispered.

"What? What is it?"

Lederer's face went even whiter. Something else had occurred to him.

"*What?*" Cavanaugh said. "Do you know what Verico is trying to do?"

Lederer looked at the pages bent in his fist. "Yes," he said, his voice still a whisper. "And there's been work published, in just the last few months. . . . Ben wasn't the only one on this track, he was just the best . . . Goldberg at Cold Spring Harbor . . . Keith Wolfe at UCSF . . . and *my* work. My paper just two months ago . . ."

"Dr. Lederer," Cavanaugh said, "tell me what you see."

Lederer looked up at him from the chair, a man whom neither the Relatives nor the Justice Department had panicked, a cool and tough mind, now frightened dead white. "They can do it, Cavanaugh. It's completely prac-tical."

"Do *what?*"

And Lederer told him.

Cavanaugh staggered to a phone.

Twenty-six

Wendell Botts slammed the button on the remote, cutting off the TV.

"Hey, man, why'd you do that, show wasn't done yet," Charlie complained. He reached across Wendell to grab at the remote, upsetting Wendell's glass. Four Roses trickled onto the coffee table.

"Now look what you done, Charlie!" Grady said. "Wasting good booze. Wendell, don't you want to see the rest of yourself on TV?"

"No!" Wendell snarled. He reached for the Four Roses bottle, found it empty. "Fucking shit!"

"Don't have a cow, we got another bottle," Grady said. "How come you don't want to see the rest of yourself on TV?"

Charlie said, "I ain't never been on TV."

"And you ain't never gonna be, either, with your face," Grady said.

"Fuck off."

"Pass me that bottle. Wendell, how come you don't want to see the rest of it?"

"It don't help," Wendell said. He drained his glass. "*Nothing* fucking helps."

Grady and Charlie looked at each other. Wendell caught the look. The three of them had been drinking all afternoon—hell, they'd been drinking all fucking *week*, ever since Grady saw Wendell on some TV show in New York City and called up Charlie, who he'd never lost track of since they all got out of the service, and said they should go visit Wendell in Cadillac now that they knew where he was and now that he was such a fucking big celebrity. They'd been sleeping on Wendell's floor and his sofa and drinking in the afternoon and cruising the bars at night, and Grady had scored twice and even Charlie, who as a result of a bar fight in Tulsa looked like somebody ran his face through a can opener, had gone home one night with a fat redhead who tried to change her mind at the last minute but too bad about that. But despite all this, it hadn't been the same as the old days. Charlie and Grady were the same, but Wendell knew he wasn't.

Charlie said, "Nothing helps what? Christ, you're a fucking drag, Wendell. You didn't used to be like this."

"You don't know me, you fuck," Wendell said.

Charlie snorted but Grady, who had maybe three times the brains of Charlie—not that that was hard—said quietly, "Hell, you're a celebrity, Wendell, but you ain't happy. What's eating you?"

"You know how many TV shows I been on?" Wendell said.

"No. How many?"

"Seven."

"Seven?"

"Plus newspaper stories."

Charlie said, "I ain't never been in the newspapers."

"And none of it *helped*," Wendell said. Abruptly he threw his glass at the TV screen. Whiskey flew sideways in a thin sour stream, like vomit. The thick glass struck the screen and it shattered. The glass, intact, bounced on the floor among the shards and dirt.

Charlie bellowed, "What you want to go do that for,

you dumb fuck? Now we can't watch no TV!"

But Grady suddenly watched Wendell from slitted eyes.

"None of it helped," Wendell said again, and put his head in his hands.

Grady said softly, "You mean to get your kids back. None of it helped get your kids back."

Wendell didn't answer.

Grady reached for the bottle, changed his mind, left it sitting on the battered coffee table. He watched Wendell carefully. Charlie polished off another shot. The phone rang.

"Let the fuck ring," Charlie said, but Grady reached for it.

"No, he ain't . . . isn't here. Yeah, I can take a message . . . Lewis Pearson, right. From A.A. . . . I told you he isn't here." Grady looked at Wendell, who still sat with his head in his hands. Grady hung up.

"That was your A.A. sponsor again, Wendell."

"Tell him to fuck off!"

"He says he's coming over in twenty minutes."

Charlie said, "Let's take him out."

Wendell took his hands away from his face and looked at Charlie. He hadn't seen either of his friends for two years, hadn't ever expected to see them again. They belonged to another time, before he did time, before he stopped drinking, before he decided to get Saralinda back. Even before he became a fucking Soldier of the Divine Covenant. That time was supposed to be over, that drinking and cruising and drinking some more and getting into fights and going back to the base after a seventy-two barely able to stand but somehow putting in a full day of duty and proud of it. And Charlie and Grady could always put it in.

Grady wasn't big, maybe five-ten, a hundred seventy, but he was tough. And smart. Smarter than Wendell. Maybe smart enough to be an officer, if he'd wanted to. He never wanted to, and anyway by the time anybody in the marines knew how smart Grady was they also knew how much trouble he was. He got a dishonorable discharge and Wendell wasn't sure what Grady did for a living now, although he suspected. Maybe Grady was smart enough not to get caught.

Charlie wasn't smart. He was dumb, and mean, and powerful. Six-two, two hundred twenty easy, and none of it fat. Wendell had seen Charlie lift a little car, a whole fucking *car,* and drop it on the man who thought he was hiding underneath. The guy died. They'd never pinned that one on Charlie, but only because Grady was so smart.

And Wendell'd thought he'd never have to see either of them again.

But then, he'd thought a lot things, hadn't he? He'd thought that keeping his nose clean, and going to A.A., and working steady, would get his kids back. He thought that writing letters and going on TV and letting people know what was going on at the camp would get his kids back. He'd thought that playing it straight was the way to go. And what the fuck had happened? The county medical examiner does extra autopsies and—surprise!— everything turns up kosher. Protecting their asses from having screwed up the first time. The fucking media loses interest in him, once he wasn't hot news anymore. And that bastard Peterson gets his story and stops help- ing Wendell. Peterson's story was the last one, in fact, and it made Wendell look like a drip, a loser who went around whining because he hadn't had no attention as a kid.

Everybody had betrayed him.

They had—fucking *everybody.* Peterson and the talk show hosts and the medical examiner and the lawyer who was supposed to get his kids back and hadn't done nothing. And most of all, Saralinda.

Saralinda.

The thought of her still hurt him under the ribs, worse than any kick in any fight. Saralinda, with her brown eyes and sweet light body and pretty voice.... She was the best thing that had ever happened to him. But she was the worst thing, too, because if it wasn't for her stubbornness about the Soldiers, her blindness, her stupid fucking—

"*Wendell,* I said, are you listening to me, man? Wendell? That A.A. guy is still on the way over here."

Charlie said, "Let's take him out."

"Shut the fuck up, Charlie."

"Don't you tell me to shut the fuck up!" Charlie said, and if he'd been saying it to anybody else except Grady, Wendell would have dived for cover. Charlie was armed. He was always armed. But Grady could say things like that to Charlie when nobody else better even fucking *try,* because Grady had saved Charlie's ass more than once. And Charlie, dumb as he was, knew it. They stuck together.

And stuck to *him,* too. Charlie and Grady were the only ones who fucking *had* stuck. Where was Saralinda? Where was Peterson? Where was the fucking lawyer, who'd called yesterday to say Wendell's last appeal to get his kids back had been turned down by the court? "I'm sorry, Wendell." Yeah. Right. Sorry. Like they were *his* kids. Fucking lawyer didn't give a shit. The only friends he had were Grady and Charlie.

"I know you do, man," Grady said.

Wendell stared at him over the rim of his empty glass. "Know I do *what?*"

"Know you want your kids back. Ain't that what you just said?"

Wendell didn't know he'd spoke aloud. Well, maybe he had. What did it matter? What the fuck did anything matter?

Grady licked his lips. "Wendell, you know I don't never pry, don't ask no personal questions unless I think it's okay, but you and me and Charlie go way back. Am I right?"

"Fucking right," Wendell said. He reached for the bottle. God, the shit tasted good. Another lie from the rest of the world: booze wasn't bad for him. Booze was the only thing that fucking let him hang on in a world where they could just take his kids away.

Grady said, "You said you been working steady, saving every dollar, just to get your kids back, right?"

"Right."

"Well, paying them dollars to your fat-assed lawyer didn't help, am I right? You still don't got your kids?"

"Right." The word hurt, like a knife in his side. Penny. David. *Saralinda* . . .

"So maybe," Grady said, "maybe it's time to use them dollars on some other way."

He had loved Saralinda so much. So fucking much. Nobody had ever loved a woman like he'd loved her. And she had thrown it all in his face, spit on his love, turned away back into that stinking camp . . .

"Wendell?" Grady said. "You listening?"

"What?"

"I *said*—"

Somebody knocked on the door.

Charlie sat up straight, his big body alert, his chopped-up face grinning. He reached for his pocket. Grady put a hand on Charlie's arm.

"Wendell? Wendell, you in there?" Lewis P., court bailiff, Wendell's fucking A.A. sponsor. And what the fuck had A.A. ever done for Lewis? Turned him into a nosy wuss. And what had it done for Wendell?

Big fucking zero!

"Don't answer," Grady said softly. His eyes never left Wendell's face. "Don't answer, man. You ain't up to it."

Wendell glared at Grady. He jumped up from the sofa, and fell against the coffee table. "What dumb fuck put that there!" He staggered up and toward the door.

"Take him right out," Charlie said, grinning.

Wendell flung open the motel door. Lewis stood there in lightly falling snow, a big flabby man dressed in a worn brown topcoat. No hat, no gloves. His eyes were serious. "Hello, Wendell. Can I come in?"

"No, you fucking well can't!"

"All right." Lewis didn't move. "Would you come out with me for coffee?"

"I got company."

"So I see," Lewis said quietly. He looked past Wendell's shoulder into the room. For a second—a fucking weird second—Wendell could see what Lewis saw: Charlie sitting straight on the sofa, grinning, dressed in baggy jeans and boots and denim shirt, huge as a house, and Grady beside him, slim and tense, one hand on Charlie's arm and the other holding his glass. The bottle on the coffee table. The busted chair where Charlie jumped on it, demonstrating some martial arts kick. The dirty glasses and empty pizza boxes and beer bottles and blankets on the floor. Well, so what if Lewis saw all that? What the fuck did it matter? What had fucking A.A. done for him?

"Wendell, a slip isn't the end of the program. It doesn't mean you've failed or that you can't go on. You've come so far, shown such courage in fighting this—"

"Yeah, I'm a fucking hero," Wendell said, and behind him Charlie laughed.

"Wendell—"

"Get the fuck out of my face!" Wendell yelled, and slammed the door on Lewis's nagging mouth. Just like Saralinda used to nag him. No, not like Saralinda, not at all like her . . . Saralinda . . .

He clutched his middle and staggered against the closed door. Grady jumped up. "Wendell, man, you okay? Want help getting to the head?"

"Leave me alone," Wendell gasped. In a minute the attack passed. He lurched to the sofa and fell on it beside Charlie.

"Hey, little Wendell," Charlie said softly, almost tenderly.

Grady watched from narrowed eyes. Then he pushed the coffee table out of the way and knelt in front of Wendell.

"Listen, man, you want your kids back. That just shows you're a good father. A daddy's got a right to have his kids, especially when he loves them like you do. And when they're in a place dangerous for kids. Stands to reason. Now, Wendell, my man, nothing you tried so far done any good. You tried it the straight way and you got shit. Maybe it's time to try something else."

Wendell said slowly, "Maybe it is."

It takes what it takes.

Grady smiled. His voice got even lower. He didn't sound drunk at all. "You and me and Charlie . . . we could get them out. The three of us. Like the old days."

Wendell looked at Charlie. "What you got?"

Charlie laughed. "It ain't what I *got*. It's what I can get."

Grady said swiftly, "But that takes money. And for us, too, of course. But you got it, don't you, Wendell, from working and saving steady? You got it to get Penny and David out?"

"And Saralinda," Wendell said. His stomach lurched again, the way it had by the door. "And Saralinda."

"Okay. And Saralinda," Grady said. His eyes gleamed.

"Okay," Charlie said, and laughed.

Slowly Wendell became aware that somebody was knocking on the door, patiently, over and over. Lewis. Well, fuck Lewis. Lewis hadn't done dick to help him. Lewis and A.A. and the lawyer and Peterson and the media and the government—all those fucking postcards he'd sent the government! Not dick. *These* guys would help him. These guys cared. These guys were his friends.

Like the old days.

"Okay," Wendell said.

Twenty-seven

The corridors of the Princess Hotel were never quiet, not once all night. Or so it seemed. Doors opened, slammed. People argued. Heavy objects dropped— what could they be dropping at 3:00 A.M.? In the room next to Judy's, a man snored as audibly as if he shared her lumpy bed. She listened to it all, finally falling into a tossing sleep at 4:00.

She was awake and dressing by 7:00. The bathroom was down the hall; she skipped washing. Outside was a cold, sunny Thursday morning. The pay phone in the Princess lobby was sticky but deserted, if you ignored the used condom lying on the black plastic AT&T shelf.

"Cardinal John DeLessio High School. Guidance Office. How may I help you?"

"I need to speak with Dan O'Brien. Please tell him it's urgent."

"I'm not sure he's in yet," the voice said doubtfully. "Is this about one of his students?"

"No. And he *is* in—look in the faculty room. Please. It's urgent."

"Just a moment."

Judy waited. He was quick. "Hello?"

"Daddy, it's Judy. Don't say anything, please. Just listen. When I was correcting the page proofs of your book last Thanksgiving—remember? The day I made such a scene at the table?"

"Of course I remember. Judy—"

"There was something in your book about a Saint Cadoc. And a car, an automobile. I can't remember the details. Who was St. Cadoc?"

"Judy, are you in some sort of trouble? You sound—"

"Answer me."

Silence. She had never spoken to him like that before. Angry, yes, she'd been angry enough at his impractical religiosity to scream at him, but she'd never spoken like that. With that authority.

"Cadoc was a sixth-century saint, an abbot who'd been born a Celtic prince but gave that up to found a monastery. Sometimes the name is Cado or Cadaud. A very minor saint—in fact he might be a complete myth. What you remember is my story about how the name became corrupted, to Cadillac. That's the name of a small town outside Albany settled originally by Catholic missionaries and named for both St. Cadoc and a later Jesuit priest, Père Cadaud. Père Cadaud was a missionary to the Indians and was martyred by them in 1697. In the 1920s there was a small plant there making auto parts, and the town board changed the name. So what started as a tribute to a saintly life of prayer ended up as a tribute to modern commerce. Although, oddly enough, St. Cadoc himself—Judy, this is irrelevant. Please tell me what kind of trouble you're in. I'm worried sick. Honey, whatever it is, we can—"

She wasn't listening to him.

Cadoc.

And now she could see the page proofs in front of her on her father's desk, her own neat red proofreader's marks deleting extra letters, closing up unnecessary spaces, correcting spellings. St. Cadoc, Abbot.

Verico. Cadoc. Cadaverico.

It still made no sense. Was "Cadoc" meant to be "Cadillac"? But if so, how would whoever had killed Ben know about an obscure linguistic shift from Celtic saint to car-parts factory? She'd never heard that the Mafia was much into historical theology.

She'd never heard they were into biotech, either.

And "Cadillac" was all she had to go on.

"Judy?"

"Daddy, I have to go."

"Don't hang up without—"

"Don't tell anyone I called. Not even Mom. It's very important."

"Judy—"

She hung up.

The cab driver knew where the Worcester public library was, but not when it opened. Judy spent two hours in a diner, hiding behind a newspaper. When the library doors opened, she was the first one at the *New York Times Index*. There was no listing for "Cadillac" that didn't refer to the car.

But the newspaper index revealed that Cadillac had its own paper, the *Cadillac Register*. Copies through December 31 were on microfiche. Sticking her head into the reading machine, Judy flashed on Sylvia Plath putting her head into the gas oven to commit suicide.

None of that. She was alive. She was going to stay that way.

Cadillac was the site of something called the Soldiers of the Divine Covenant, a fringe group of the Catholic charismatic movement. Recently a disgruntled ex-Soldier, one Wendell Botts, had been accusing the religious compound of something or other, mostly on talk shows. The local paper, like most local papers supported by advertising, was so discreet about crime in its fair city that Judy had no idea what was going on.

The Albany papers were more explicit. Wendell Botts had made allegations of human sacrifice. Dr. Richard Stallman, county medical examiner, had made protests. Jay Peterson, writing in the *Albany Times-Union,* had

made mincemeat of Botts. St. Cadoc was not mentioned.
It still made no sense.

And it was still all she had to find out who killed Ben.

By the time the Greyhound bus arrived in Cadillac,
the sky was already orange and gold. This was the foothills of the Adirondacks, but the mountains were hidden
by low, fiery clouds. Cadillac had a two-block main
street with nineteenth-century storefronts, a diner, three
churches, a Pizza Hut, an antique store with a window
full of sad Depression-era bureaus, a Grain and Feed,
and a snowmobile dealership, and the Globe Hotel.

The Globe lobby was no more than a registration desk
in the foyer to the bar. Judy checked in under "Maggie
Davis." The bored clerk, who wore a baseball cap saying
BUFFALO BILLS, didn't even seem to notice her lack of
luggage. Her room, on the second floor, was as shabby
as last night's at the Princess, but with more dignity. The
molding was heavy dark wood, and the bathroom had
what looked like hand-painted tiles in the backsplash
above the sink. On the way back downstairs Judy
worked out that the Buffalo Bills were the football team
closest to Cadillac.

"Can you tell me where I can find Dr. Richard Stallman?"

The clerk didn't look up from his forms. "Fifty-six
Grove Street, turn left, three blocks north on Main, turn
right. But he's mostly retired. You better go by the hospital emergency room."

"It's only a femoral fracture," Judy said. He didn't
even look up.

Fifty-six Grove Street was a faded gingerbread Victorian with a bay window, wide front porch, and discreet
sign: DR. RICHARD STALLMAN, M.D. Judy rang the bell.

"Yes?" He was tall, silver-haired, as dignified as his
house. Dressed in corduroy slacks, cardigan, and leather
bedroom slippers.

"Dr. Stallman?"

"Yes. Can I help you?"

"I'm a journalist," she said, prepared to add "freelance" if he asked for her press credentials, which he

didn't. Instead he closed the door, firmly and without smiling.

Judy leaned on the bell. She kept it up until he opened the door again, coldly angry. She wedged her arm against the jamb. "Dr. Stallman, I know you don't want to talk to me. You've undoubtedly been bothered by a lot of reporters over the last few months, but—"

"If you don't leave immediately, young woman, I'm calling the police."

"—but I'm different. You *should* talk to me. I just interviewed Dr. Eric Stevens at Verico." She watched him carefully.

"I don't know any Dr. Stevens. And I repeat, if you don't leave now, I'm calling the police." The door closed as far as Judy's arm. Not enough to really hurt. Judy looked directly into Dr. Stallman's eyes.

She'd consulted the *Dictionary of American Medical Practitioners* before taking the risk of mentioning Verico. Stallman had practiced in Cadillac for forty-two years, and his father had been the town doctor before him. He was married to the daughter of a previous mayor. His son was a state senator. Stallman had a long record of selfless service and quiet charity. Moreover, his present dignified outrage looked genuine to her. He had never heard of Eric Stevens. And he *would* call the police.

Judy pulled her arm free, and Dr. Stallman closed his door.

She went slowly back down the porch steps, trying to work it out.

The people who had killed Ben had some connection to the Soldiers of the Divine Covenant, in whose camp other people were also being killed. Or at least dying in unusual numbers. That was the meaning of "Cadoc Verico Cadaverico." But what was the connection? Robert Cavanaugh had been definite that "organized crime"— that vague euphemism—had killed Ben. And the man who had tried to kill Judy in her bathroom yesterday morning—dear God, had it only been *yesterday?*—had been somebody known to Agent Dollings. Or had he?

Dollings hadn't actually said, he'd only acted as if the guy was a professional killer that the FBI already knew about. Of course, Dollings had been young and upset, even through her own shock Judy could see that. Probably Dollings had never killed anybody before.

And now Dollings was dead. Was his murder a "professional job"? Was that what one looked like?

Judy put her hands over her face. Why would a compound full of religious nuts—even killer religious nuts—be interested in the Mafia? Or vice versa? And why would a religious compound want to kill a scientist working on genetic engineering? Some crazy religious taboo, not tampering with nature, like not allowing blood transfusions? In that case, maybe Verico and the Soldiers of the Divine Covenant weren't working together, maybe they were each other's enemies. But then why kill Ben, who wasn't involved with either of them?

Because Ben had learned how Verico and the compound were linked. When he'd interviewed at the biotech company. He'd learned what was going on, and he'd died for it.

But what *was* going on? Everything Judy had read in the library about the Soldiers of the Divine Covenant said they were peaceful. They didn't believe in war, or even in guns. They preached a weird farrago of peace, vegetarianism, the coming apocalypse, home schooling, Luddism, biblical literalism, and what seemed to her, after her father's vigorous teachings, a pretty passive and wimpy approach to grace. They wore a *C* on their clothing, which might have stood for "Cadoc" or "Covenant" or, for all she knew, "carrot juice." So why were these lost lambs involved with anything the FBI would care about?

The more she learned, the less she knew.

At a Grand Union just off Main Street, Judy bought a toothbrush, toothpaste and other toiletries, makeup, underpants and socks, and all the while she made herself smile, made herself answer the checkout girl's chatter, made herself count out the money and claim her receipt. Made herself put one foot in front of the other. At the

Globe Hotel, she cleaned herself up and then made herself sit in the dining room, which was also the bar, and order a fish fry she didn't eat.

Someone at the next table sneezed, an explosion like gunfire. Judy glanced up. It was a woman in her forties, sleek and well-dressed, looking as out of place in the Globe dining room as a gazelle. With her was an equally well-dressed, bored-looking man. Why were they in a place like Cadillac? Did the reason have anything to do with her?

Judy stared at the fish on her plate. She couldn't eat. There was a cold hand pressing on her chest, squeezing her ribs. She couldn't just sit here. She couldn't. The compulsion to do something, anything, was as strong as the need to breathe. If she didn't move, didn't go somewhere, didn't do *something,* she would die. And not from the expensive bored couple at the next table.

Abruptly she stood, grabbing money from her pocket and leaving it on the table without waiting for the bill. She asked the clerk in the Buffalo Bills cap, now watching a small black-and-white TV behind his counter, to get her a taxi while she ran upstairs for her coat. He blinked at her.

"We don't have any *taxis* in Cadillac, miss."

She stopped, hand on the bannister. It was worn smooth and greasy. "No taxis? Then how do you get anywhere?"

"We got *cars,*" he said, with great disgust.

Judy walked over to the counter, reached under it to snap off the TV, and looked levelly under his Buffalo Bills visor. She said pleasantly, "Find me someone who will drive me in his or her *car,* for a fee, just like it was a taxi. Someone who wants to make forty dollars for an hour's easy work. Someone close, and soon. Do this now."

The clerk blinked. "Well, I don't . . ."

"I'll get my jacket. If there isn't a pseudocab here when I get back downstairs, I want to speak to the manager. Thank you."

When she got back downstairs, a teenage boy with

pimples stood jingling his car keys. "Forty dollars for an hour, that right? Just driving you around?"

"That's right."

"It works for me," he said, and led her to a pickup truck so thick with road salt that the blue fenders looked gray.

"Where we going?" the boy said, companionably. He seemed excited by the novelty, or the money, or by the thought that she might be crazy.

Judy said, "Do you know where to find the camp of the Soldiers of the Divine Covenant?"

Twenty-eight

Cavanaugh and Lancaster sat in Lancaster's field office in Boston, watching the speaker phone on Lancaster's desk as if it were sentient. It was 2:30 on Tuesday afternoon. In Washington, at the second tine of this three-forked conference call, were Felders, U.S. Attorney Jeremy Deming, and Patrick Duffy, head of the FBI Criminal Investigative Division. The third tine, Mark Lederer, was at his sister's house in Waltham, Massachusetts, having left Boston Biomedical early. He had first called his sister on his possibly tapped phone to tell her they needed to discuss their mother's failing health. Occasionally Cavanaugh could hear a burst of happy shouting from what sounded like a couple hundred kids.

Cavanaugh wished he could see Lederer's face. And although he could picture Duffy, who at fifty still had his black-Irish good looks but dressed like an English tailor's model, he wished even more that he could see Duffy's face. Gauge his reactions. See how well they were convincing him.

No point in looking at Lancaster's face. He wasn't convinced, and wasn't going to be. But one of his agents was dead, and Lancaster's face was pure holy war.

"Explain it as simply as you can, doctor," Duffy said. "I'm sorry to be so slow about this. We're none of us trained in biotech."

Duffy wasn't slow. Duffy had already grasped the basic situation. Now he wanted details so he could look for loopholes, possible places to position themselves.

"All right," Lederer said. His voice was calm, the underlying strain held in check. Lederer had calculated exactly how much risk he was taking, and how much he was willing to take, which wasn't much more than this careful conference call. He was balancing the importance of what he was revealing against the safety of his family. It occurred to Cavanaugh that Lederer would have made a good agent.

"Ben Kozinski was working on envelope proteins. Those are the ones that coat the outsides of viruses, including altered viruses. A virus invades a healthy cell by latching onto the outer cell wall, binding to it, dissolving the matching sections of the two walls, and injecting its viral proteins. They then reproduce safely inside the cell."

"I'm with you so far," Duffy said.

"The body fights viruses by creating T cells to destroy them. The T cells also latch onto receptor sites. But before a T cell starts multiplying itself and then destroying invaders, it has to determine which proteins are *self*, and supposed to be there, and which ones aren't *self*, and so should be destroyed. In fact, there are diseases in which the body's ability to do this fails, and so the T cells either rush around destroying their own body tissues, or else fail to destroy foreign cells."

Not unlike some law enforcement actions, Cavanaugh thought. He did not say this aloud.

"Now I have to get a little technical," Lederer said. "Stay with me. A body's cells contain two related molecules, called class I major histocompatibility complex, or class I MHC, and class II major histocompatibility complex, class II MHC. The function of these molecules is to pick up bits of material inside a cell, peptides or antigens. They then carry it to a T cell sitting on the cell surface. The T cells 'recognize' whether the material is self or not. If it's self, the T cell does nothing. If the peptide or antigen is *not* self, the T cells begin to defend the body."

Cavanaugh reached onto Lancaster's desk and picked up paper and pen. He sketched quickly:

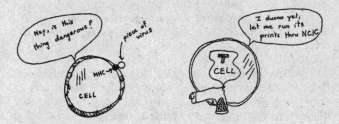

Cavanaugh thought of showing this to Lancaster. He decided against it.

Lederer continued: "A crucial point about MHCs is that the molecules are unique to every person. Each person has only two genes for each major histocompatibility class, and so, except for identical twins, MHCs are as individual as fingerprints."

Under his sketch Cavanaugh scrawled BINGO.

"What Ben was doing with retroviruses was altering their protein coats to include genetic material taken from a specific person's MHC–T cell system. This means that the process for binding the virus to the outer cell wall could occur *only* if the viral coat matches the MHC molecules. If it doesn't, the virus can't get in, and so it just sits there on the outer wall until it gets eaten by a passing macrophage."

"A what?" Duffy said.

"A scavenger cell. Your body is teeming with them."

"Oh," Duffy said. Lancaster looked wary. Cavanaugh drew another sketch:

Duffy said, "So what this means is that a virus could be made that would be able to enter only one person's cells. If you injected it into anybody else, it wouldn't affect them at all."

"Right," Lederer said.

"Wait a minute," Lancaster said, "if this is supposed to be some sort of new weapon, to be used like a poison, why not just inject poison into the target in the first place? They don't need some fancy cell-finagled version of cyanide or curare."

"There's more," Lederer replied, and now Cavanaugh could more easily hear his strain. "But first, remember that Ben, and the other scientists working in this area, aren't working on weapons. They're trying to develop a so-called 'magic bullet,' a virus that will kill only prese-lected cells, such as cancer cells. The ultimate goal, which we're not close to yet, is to have a virus that not only matches the cells of a unique individual's body, but can differentiate between healthy cells and abnormal cells *within* that body. But first we have to develop vec-tors that will express their encoded proteins within only one person."

Cavanaugh thought of Kozinski's notebook, with its little guns labeled with names: PETEY. CASSANDRA. THE BRONZE DANDELION.

"This is potentially *life-saving work*," Lederer said. He sounded almost pleading. "The scientific community has begun work to control autoimmune diseases, to sta-bilize insulin production, even to coax endothelial cells to secrete factors that would prevent blood clots from forming in arteries after heart surgery. . . . Why, *already* a biotech firm in California has synthesized a DNA that seeks out and sticks to thrombin, neutralizing it for—"

"We don't doubt that positive value of all this," Duffy said quietly. "Please go ahead, Doctor."

Cavanaugh could picture Lederer gathering himself together at the other end of the phone. Now the strain in Lederer's voice was palpable.

"The second piece of this is the work being done at Verico."

Cavanaugh shifted on his chair, leaned forward. This was it. What he'd been pressing toward all these months.

"They're working on G-proteins. Well, so are a lot of people. It's an incredibly exciting field of research."

And Cavanaugh believed him. Five months ago he couldn't have imagined getting excited about proteins, G or A or any other letter. But he'd been reading, studying. He'd glimpsed, if only at a distance, what made these guys spend seventy hours a week in the lab, as intent at chasing breakthroughs as the Bureau was at chasing criminals. He could *feel* it, even if he'd never be able to do it himself.

Lancaster poured himself a glass of water from a carafe on a file cabinet. He was frowning.

Lederer continued. "The G-protein is embedded in the cell wall. It acts as a sort of switchboard. The G-protein receives a messenger molecule from outside the cell, and it starts a series of chemical reactions that change the cell's behavior in some way. The actual mechanisms are complex, and fascinating. The result is usually to produce an enzyme that affects the body. There was a relevant article published just last month in *Science*—"

"What was it called?" Duffy interrupted.

" 'Mineralocorticoid and Glucocorticoid Receptor Activities Distinguished by Nonreceptor Factors at a Composite Response Element.' Fascinating."

"I'll bet," Lancaster said. His voice was tight. Nobody responded.

Duffy's voice was gentle, nonthreatening. "Doctor,

what was Verico doing about these G-proteins?"

"They were working with G-proteins in macrophages, which—among other things—control the production of bradykinin. Bradykinin causes heart muscle to beat slower."

"Slow enough to cause a heart attack?" Duffy said.

"If the body produces enough of it. Yes."

There was a long silence. Cavanaugh knew they were close. In Washington Duffy waited, letting Lederer choose his time and tell it his own way.

"The last piece of this is my own current work. I'd discussed it with Julia Garvey at a Christmas party, as it happened. I think this research is the reason Verico approached me to join them. My discussion with Julia may be the reason she could put all the pieces together. . . ."

And the reason she was killed, Cavanaugh finished silently. Lederer didn't say it aloud. His voice was hoarse now, although he hadn't been talking that long.

"I've been working on modifying viruses, too. But unlike Ben, I'm using airborn respiratory viruses. Flu, the common cold—they mutate much more rapidly than most organisms, which is why there seems to be a new strain of flu every winter, and last winter's variety didn't make you immune this winter. It makes it hard for the body's T cells to fight the viruses before they multiply enough to make you sick. And of course, because they're airborn, all such viruses are very contagious. I published my major findings months ago, which made them accessible to the scientific community as a whole."

Duffy said, still gently, "Put it all together for me, Doctor."

"I think Verico may have developed an airborn virus tailored to one specific individual that could cause a nondetectable heart attack."

Felders said, "Oh my God."

Making absolutely sure he had it, Duffy asked, "You mean that a scientist could infect people—say himself and his staff—with this altered virus, and it wouldn't do anything to them. It couldn't get into their cells. But they go about their lives, and infect other people they come in contact with, like with a common cold. They sneeze and cough and touch money, and the virus gets passed onto a wider and wider circle, but still nobody gets sick. Until it comes to the one person whose MHC–T cell system it matches."

"Yes," Lederer said, almost inaudibly.

"And then the virus invades his cells—"

"Probably the macrophage cells," Lederer interrupted. Cavanaugh remembered that he'd said everybody's body teemed with macrophages.

"Okay, the virus invades the macrophages. And multiplies. At some point it activates the G-proteins and they send switchboard signals to manufacture more bradykinin, and that slows down the heart muscles, and—"

"The heart stops," Lederer said.

There was another silence.

Felders burst out, "How long does it take from the first infection to the heart attack?"

"I don't know. But I'd guess only a few hours. Unchecked, a virus can reproduce itself every fifteen minutes. Exponentially."

"And nothing would check their reproduction," Duffy said. "Because the body reads this virus as a normal part of itself."

"Yes," Lederer said.

Cavanaugh said, his first contribution, "But wouldn't an autopsy show an unusual amount of bradykinin in the blood?"

"Probably not. You wouldn't need a lot. Maybe you could detect it, if you were looking for that. Or maybe you could build in mechanisms to break down the excess bradykinin almost immediately. But I assisted a coroner when I was working my way through med school. So-called 'cardiac events' are the wastebasket of autopsies. There are all kinds of internal electrical events that can cause death without physical heart damage, and that's what an autopsy would read. 'Death as a result of a cardiac event.'"

He was right. In Intelligence, Cavanaugh had seen

enough such "opinions" himself, written by coroners or medical examiners who had to put down *something*.

Duffy pressed. "What if you did deliberately look for even marginally increased amounts of bradykinin with the most sophisticated tests possible, Doctor? Would you be able to tell the difference between what the virus caused and what was a natural cardiac event?"

"I don't know!" Lederer said. "Don't you understand how unknown, how experimental, all this is? It's all new territory, new combinations of technology exploding so fast we can't control it. . . . It's possible everything I've said isn't even true. It's all speculation! Except . . ."

Except that people were getting killed over it.

Cavanaugh tried to picture it. You stand in a grocery store, buying a six-pack of beer and a loaf of bread, and somebody sneezes. Are they infected? They wouldn't know it, if the bullet virus wasn't meant for them. Is it meant for you? You reach out and take your change from the cashier—how many other fingers have touched this money? Fingers sticky with what airborn viruses? You get in your car and there's a little twinge in your chest . . . is it starting? Do you have it? Has the virus found you, the one built especially for you, your own personal angel of death. . . . This time? Next time? Transferred to me by my friend? My children? My wife? Give me a kiss, sweetheart . . .

Lancaster said, his anger almost breaking through, "This is all speculation. And with all due respect, Doctor, pretty wild speculation. There are no facts here. You don't have an informant. You don't have any favors-owed influence. You don't even have a money trail. And the bodies you do have—Kozinski, Garvey, Dollings—weren't killed with any fucking virus!"

Deming, the lawyer from Justice, spoke. Cavanaugh had forgotten he was in the office with Duffy and Felders. Deming's voice was slow, dazed, completely unlike the smart-ass know-it-all Cavanaugh remembered from last August.

"Walt. Wait a . . . minute. You mean Verico could develop this killer virus . . . *has* developed this killer virus

... and sell it to the highest bidder? Or use it themselves?"

"Yes," Cavanaugh said.

"So if the LCN had had it, say, when Robert Kennedy was prosecuting Jimmy Hoffa ... they could have just sneezed in the courtroom? And everybody breathes it in? But the virus is tailored to Kennedy's DNA, so everybody else goes on with the trial, and that night Kennedy just keels over with a heart attack? Like he died from natural causes?"

"You got it," Felders said grimly.

"No Oswald? No Dallas book depository? No Jack Ruby?"

"Not necessary," Felders said.

Deming seemed to be having trouble grasping it. Cavanaugh wished he could see the lawyer's face. Deming said, "They just take him out? *Robert Kennedy?*"

"Or Jack Kennedy," Cavanaugh said. "Or a Russian prime minister. An Arab oil prince. A South American drug lord. Murder that looks exactly like natural causes, from a distance, by anybody who can pay for it."

Felders said, "Think what this will be worth on the international terrorist market. Millions. Ultimately, billions."

Lancaster burst out, "Speculation! *Nobody's* been killed with any damn virus!"

Deming said slowly, "Monday night. Justice Fogel. He had a heart attack, he was only fifty-two. . . ."

"No," Lederer said uncertainly. "At least, I don't think so. Not yet. They'd test it first someplace ... it wouldn't be ..."

There was a long silence. Cavanaugh saw in his mind the *Washington Post* headline, an inch high: FOGEL DIES. The Supreme Court justice had been the toughest supporter of constraining the delaying tactics of convicted criminals. Fogel had fought to limit appeals, limit admissible evidence on appeal. FOGEL DIES ...

Lederer broke the silence. "Tissue samples. They'd have to have a sample of an intended victim's blood, or other body tissues. To build a virus tailored to an individual's MHC genes."

Felders said swiftly, "How much blood?"

"Well . . . just a few drops. There's all kinds of cells, including macrophages, in the blood. Just isolate and culture them."

Deming said, "Fogel was hospitalized just a few months ago. Some kind of kidney problem. It was in the papers. They would have taken blood . . ."

Cavanaugh finished for him. "So you bribe a lab technician for a sample."

"Hell," Felders said, "you don't even have to do that. Just go through the garbage. Your victim goes to the dentist, his gums bleed, he wipes them on a dental napkin. Go through the dentist's garbage. He gets a haircut. Follow him into the barber shop, get hair clippings. You see through surveillance that he cuts himself and wipes it on a handkerchief. Go to the laundry—in some cities the Relatives have a piece of all the laundries anyway. Blood is easy."

"Semen," Cavanaugh said. He'd had a few hours to think it through. "If the guy uses hookers, send him one you control. How many of them use hookers—how many Relatives, politicians, bankers? Most of them. Doctor, could you get the right cells out of come to make the virus?"

"Yes," Lederer said.

Deming, still on the concrete, the specific, said, "The women in and out of the Kennedy White House. Hell, not just Kennedy's. And blood . . . Reagan's assassination attempt, Bush's surgery, Clinton's jogging . . . and now . . ." Again he didn't finish.

Cavanaugh thought of how many people went in and out of the White House. Infect the bodyguards, the maids, the gardeners, the reporters. They won't even know they've been infected, they just caught a cold at their favorite off-duty bar, there were people in there sneezing . . . and if they don't catch cold the first time, do it again and again . . .

Nondetectable, no-risk murder at a distance.

Lancaster was staring at the wall, his eyes fixed.

"There's only one more thing I can tell you," Lederer said. His voice was weary now, the strain altered into emotional exhaustion. "They might be testing it someplace. They'll need controls, the equivalent of clinical trials . . . some population where death wouldn't be noticed much."

Deming said huskily, "A hospital? Nursing home?"

"No," Felders said. "Too much death happening there anyway. They need to know their organism caused death, not old age or some unrelated disease. They'll choose an isolated location with a healthy population distrustful of official authority, maybe even cooperating in getting around it. I can't think where."

"Any ideas?" Duffy said.

"No," Felders answered. "Cavanaugh? Lancaster?"

Cavanaugh couldn't think where, either. He couldn't think. His hand holding the pen moved toward the pad of paper, then stopped.

Lancaster said, not looking at Cavanaugh, "They could use Sicily. Small towns in the hills, they own the local police, nobody asks too many questions . . ."

Shit. Sicily. It'd be goddamn impossible to trace. They'd use their own as guinea pigs, all right, but would they go to that much trouble to transport bioproducts overseas . . .

"No," Felders said. "They do things the most direct way that will get them done. It won't be Sicily. It would be here, someplace."

Slowly Lancaster nodded.

"I'm hanging up now," Lederer said. "Don't call me again—I've told you everything I know or can speculate. I hope to God you find them before they get the virus perfected and airborne."

Unless they already have, Cavanaugh thought, *during the months we've been arguing about whether this was a case or not.* He didn't say it aloud.

Duffy's voice, coming over the speaker phone, was cool and hard. "I think," he said, "that I should phone the director, and ask him to alert the attorney general."

Twenty-nine

Grady and Charlie came back the next morning with three Cobray M-11s, wire clippers, and a ground rod with wire for an electric fence. Wendell looked at the handguns with disgust.

"Hell, those big Cobrays look tough, but there isn't a damn one of them that's accurate."

"Don't have to be," Grady said cheerfully. "Long as they look tough enough. You said the camp ain't armed, right?"

"Right," Wendell said. "They don't believe in violence." He was more sober now, but it hadn't affected his determination. If anything, he was surer. Enough fucking around with laws and groups and being a good boy. Nobody really respected that wimpy shit. He'd been begging and groveling so long, and where had it got him? People respected men who knew what they wanted and went after it. He wanted his kids.

And Saralinda.

When Saralinda saw how determined he was to get her back—how far he'd go for her—she'd respect him again, too. Hell, even the Bible admitted that much. The man was the head of the woman, and he was fucking supposed to behave like it. Timothy something.

"That ain't all," Charlie said. He was grinning like a two-year-old. After being out all night in Albany, Grady looked saggy around the eyes, but Charlie didn't look tired at all. From his gym bag he pulled two Ingram submachine guns and six military-issue hand grenades.

"Jesus Christ, we won't need all that stuff," Wendell said in disgust. "Fucking grenades! I told you, the camp isn't armed!"

"You never know," Grady said. "Although I told Charlie maybe the Ingrams was maybe too much."

"Fires seven hundred rounds a minute," Charlie said.

"The *grenades* is maybe too much," Wendell said. "They're fucking not *armed*. I told you all we needed was something to intimidate them with!"

"This will intimidate the hell out of them," Charlie said.

"I don't want my kids scared out of their heads!"

"They won't be, Wendell," Grady said soothingly. "I promise."

"What did all this cost, Grady? I gave you a big chunk of what I got saved, and I'll need . . ."

"Oh, it wasn't that much. The Ingrams are second-hand."

The Ingrams looked to Wendell about fifth-hand. But when he looked at them, he could feel the itch in his right eye, to line up the target in the site. . . . He picked up one of the Cobrays. The grip felt good in his hand.

Charlie said, "I carry an Ingram."

Wendell said, "Nobody carries an Ingram! I told you, I don't want my kids scared to death! The Cobrays are fucking enough!"

"Whatever you want, buddy," Grady said soothingly. "It's your show. We're just here to help."

"All right," Wendell said. "This is what you need to know." Charlie and Grady stopped smiling, nodded, and listened. Wendell felt a rush of power. This was how men behaved, not wimps.

Saralinda would have to see that.

"The fence is two-strand, 220 volts threaded through eight-strand barbed wire. The posts are at fifteen-foot intervals. I'll ground the wire and cut the fence—Grady, you got them other things, didn't you?"

Grady showed him the insulated gloves, rubber boots, ski masks, coils of rope, flashlights.

"Good. Today's Tuesday. If we go in at eight-thirty tonight, practically everybody will be in the Covenant Hall for evening prayer. But Saralinda—"

Charlie laughed. "They spend every evening *praying*?" Grady looked at him hard and he shut up.

"But Saralinda and the kids," Wendell went on evenly, "won't be at prayer, because it's past the kids' bedtime. They'll be in our bungalow. I'll lead us three there. Then Charlie covers us, and Grady and me slip in there and grab the kids . . ."

Grady said, gently, "What about Saralinda?"

"Maybe she'll come with me."

"What if she don't?"

"She will." She had to.

"But if she don't—"

"We tie her up and leave her on the bed," Wendell said. His heart hurt, just saying it.

"She can identify you, old buddy. Even with the ski masks."

"Well, of course she can identify me! I'm her fucking husband! Besides," Wendell added, more calmly, "she'd know it was me. Who else would bust in and take our kids? It ain't like we're the kind of people with money for ransom."

"Okay," Grady said. "Stay cool, buddy."

"Besides, Saralinda will come because she won't want to leave the kids."

"My mama left me. Not even a backward look, the bitch," Charlie said, but Wendell ignored him.

"After we get David and Penny, we slip back out the way we came in, me carrying David and you Penny. Charlie covers us again. And that's it."

Grady waited.

"If we run into anybody," Wendell went on, not wanting to think about this part but knowing he had to, "try to overpower them, gag and tie them, and hide them behind bushes or something. Don't fire unless we absolutely have to. That would bring the whole fucking congregation running. And—"

"And what? You stopped talking, buddy."

"And don't scare my kids any more than they'll already be scared. Got it?"

"Got it," Grady said. "It's only temporary, you know. In the long run, they'll be better off with their daddy than with a bunch of religious loonies."

Charlie said, "Where you gonna take 'em, Wendell?"

"I got a place, but it's better you don't know where. In case we get caught after we separate."

"We ain't gonna get caught," Charlie said. "Not this time." Looking at Charlie, the Ingram in one hand and a cigarette in the other, a camouflage vest taut over his huge magnificent body, Wendell believed him. They weren't going to get caught. He was going to finally get what was his by right.

Fake it to make it.

Grady said, "Let's draw that map, buddy."

"I already did, while you were gone. Here. Now memorize this, Charlie, all of it. We leave the cars pulled into the woods, one here and one here—"

"We got a cellular phone in ours," Charlie said. "Do you, Wendell? Because if you do and we need to communicate afterward—"

"Nobody touches the fucking phone," Grady said sharply. "You got that, Charlie? Those things get picked up for half a mile. I *mean* it, Charlie."

"Okay, you mean it," Charlie said. He lit another cigarette without putting down the Ingram.

"I got to ask you something, Grady," Wendell said, "and I want the truth. No bullshit. Can the car be traced to you?"

Grady hesitated, then said, "No."

That meant the car was hot. "Okay," Wendell said. "Just so's I know. Next thing. The grenades don't go with us. I mean that. You make Charlie lose 'em."

Grady said, "They're gone. Now get back to the map, Wendell. I want to know where every fucking blade of grass is in that camp."

Charlie said, sulky, "He ain't been inside in two years. They could of changed everything."

"Not the buildings," Grady said in his soothing voice. "Buildings don't move. Most they could do is add new ones. Now you pay attention here, Charlie. We need to know everything about that place."

He looked attentively and respectfully at Wendell, waiting. Wendell nodded; he wasn't sure why. Except that this was the way it was supposed to happen: him doing something to get David and Penny back, and the other two listening to him hard, because he was the one with the knowledge. The way it was supposed to happen, that Saralinda somehow couldn't never see.

But she would have to see, now.

"We cut the fence *here,* closest to the woods . . ."

The three heads bent over Wendell's map.

Thirty

The road turned from asphalt with ice potholes to dirt with frozen tire ruts. There had been much less snow here than in Boston. Judy's teenage driver, who had turned the radio to a hard-rock station, bobbed his head in time to Smashing Pumpkins. He didn't seem to expect conversation.

The dirt road bisected a large cow pasture, or maybe it ran between two pastures, bordered by white fencing. It was too dark to see any cows. At the far end of the pasture the road entered more woods. Trees crowded close on either side, sometimes dipping low into the cone of light from the pickup's brights.

"Just about there," her driver said.

"Turn off the radio, please."

He did. Abruptly the road emerged on the other side of the woods into another field. The pickup stopped just at the tree line. The headlights showed a cleared area in which scrub grass poked through the thin snow cover and, beyond it, a barbed-wire fence with a metal gate set between two brick posts. Beyond the fence she could just make out the silhouettes of low buildings of various sizes.

The boy said, "They aren't real friendly. And they won't let you inside, if that's what you're thinking of. And if you're a reporter, they really won't let you inside. There were reporters all over here a few months ago, when that crazy ex-Soldier was on the TV, and not a single reporter got an interview. You won't, either. It's sacred ground to them."

Judy thought wryly that he had saved all this discouragement for after he was sure of his forty dollars. She opened the truck door.

"I'm not going to go inside the camp. I just want to look at it. Wait here for me, please, but keep the headlights on."

"You said only an hour's work. You got thirty-eight minutes left. Total."

"Right," Judy said.

Her boots crunched on the frozen snow. She walked halfway across the cleared area between the woods and the gate, just to one side of the headlight's beamed path. She stopped.

Was it in there, whatever had killed her husband? Or at least connected to people in there. *Cadoc verico cadaverico.* Cadillac biotech death. She couldn't get inside the camp and even if she could, it might be dangerous, it might be suicidal. Her only protection was that they had no idea she was standing here, in the dark and cold, staring at them.

Staring at *what?* This whole connection might be a mirage, something she had made up because the human mind wanted connections, explanations. Wanted desperately to make sense out of what made no sense. She might be just as delusional as the Soldiers of the Divine Covenant, whose beliefs were bizarre but whose defenses—according to the newspapers—ran not to firearms but to fences, isolation, and contempt. So how could they be connected to whoever had killed Ben? And what the hell did she, Judy O'Brien Kozinski, standing outside their dreary camp, want from them?

I want answers.

But something else more. Behind the answers.

Judy's eyes widened in the dark. She had only just realized it. Answers, yes—but something else even more, the reason she'd been seeking answers so desperately. Five months after his murder, she wanted to put Ben's death behind her, and begin to go on.

"Put it behind her"—she never even knew what those words meant before. Ben was still *beside* her, still a palpable presence as she ate her breakfast, walked through her supermarket, drove her car, undressed for bed. It had been that way since the night he'd flown home from Verico. Constantly next to her, holding onto her, dragging at her: Ben, Ben, Ben.

The only time she'd felt briefly free of him had been the moment after a hired killer had tried to murder her, and failed, and she'd felt the intense physicality of still being alive. What kind of life was that, if you only felt alive when actually facing death?

But she *was* alive. It was Ben who was dead. And she wanted to put his death behind her and go ahead. Just a few paces ahead, at first, a few steps away from the constant dragging weight of grief and despair. Then a few paces more. And eventually he *would* be behind her, in the way her high school or college years were behind her: pictures she could see clearly still, if she turned and looked, beloved pictures, some of them—but pictures nonetheless. Not times she could return to, or even touch, no matter what she did. Irretrievable. Read Only Memory.

Her love for Ben had been real, despite his infidelities, and that love wasn't fading. The colors were still clear and bright. But she wanted to walk away from that love because it was immobile in time, and she was not.

But she couldn't do it without knowing the truth about what had happened to him. She needed answers, in order to leave those answers behind. That's just the way she, Judy Kozinski, was individually made.

She had to know if the answers were inside this camp. She stood a moment longer, staring at the dim and dreary outlines of the camp of the Soldiers of the Divine Covenant. Then she took one step forward. Then another. Now she could see a buzzer mounted on the brick gatepost. She looked back over her shoulder at the boy's truck, just discernible through the first of the trees.

Judy turned and walked decisively toward the buzzer. She'd taken only three steps when explosion and gunfire ripped through the night, and she fell to the ground.

She covered her head with her hands and tried to crawl on her belly toward the truck. But the boy didn't wait. She heard the engine roar, saw the lights leap into the darkness, and the pickup backed along the rough road. She didn't dare stand and run after it; more gunfire came from the camp beside her, and she heard the rat-a-tat-tat that television had taught her came from a submachine gun.

She cried out, and then caught herself. Calm. She had to stay calm enough to think, to act sensibly, to get out alive. Alive. She wanted to stay alive, not die yet, not die at all. . . . *Our father, who art in heaven* . . .

The gate of the camp opened and two men rushed out. Judy tried to sink down into the earth. Could they see her? Her clothes were dark, but if floodlights came on . . .

She started to drag herself by her elbows away from the gate. But floodlights would illuminate more than just the gate area . . . she might actually be safer closer to the fence, in the shadow of the barbed wire. And farther ahead the woods curved in closer to the fence. If she could just get there, where the woods almost reached the fence. . . . No floodlights yet, but more shooting. Flames suddenly leapt into the night.

. . . hallowed be thy name . . .

She was near the fence when the floodlights came on. More people ran out the gate. Judy rolled hard up by the fence. Barbed wire snagged on her sleeve, tearing it.

It could have been her face.

She tore the fabric free, got to her feet, and ran as close to the fence as she dared, hoping she was indistinguishable from its bulk. Just ahead was the point where the trees stood closest to the camp. A little farther, just a little way . . .

. . . thy kingdom come . . .

The fence was cut.

Judy stopped and stared. All eight strands of the barbed wire had been cut with clippers, which lay on the ground. Beside it was a metal peg driven into the frozen earth, connected to a wire that ran to hinged clips on the fence. Electric. It was an electric fence, and it had been grounded. Somebody had forced their way in.

She took only a second to see it. Then she was running across the illuminated space between the fence and the woods, while gunfire sounded and she expected every second to scream with a bullet in her back.

. . . Thy will be done . . .

Nobody shot at her.

A little ways into the trees sat a battered car.

Judy gaped at it as if it were the seven-headed scarlet beast of Babylon. Then she yanked open the driver's-side door. No keys. She sobbed aloud. Why hadn't she ever learned to hot-wire a car? What was she doing, running around the woods getting shot at, as if she *knew* what she was doing? She deserved to die, she was so stupid—

. . . on earth as it is in heaven . . .

There was a cellular phone in the car.

Her sudden panic left her. She felt all of a sudden icy calm, deadly cold. She leaned into the car, feet still on the ground. The floodlight that filtered through the trees weren't enough to see individual numbers, but she knew how a telephone number pad was arranged. She pressed 911.

"Hello? My name is Judy Kozinski. There are shooting and explosions at the Soldiers of the Divine Covenant camp in Cadillac, New York. People are screaming. Send police and ambulances. But even more important—and listen closely, please, this is a matter of national security—you need to call Agent Robert Cavanaugh at the FBI Headquarters in Washington and tell him that Judy Kozinski said the camp is where the biotech killers are. Tell him 'Cadillac' is 'Cadoc.' Do it."

"If you could please repeat—"

"I can't. But if you don't call Agent Cavanaugh, a lot more people will die."

She hung up, and backed out of the car. A man held a gun on her.

The gun was wobbly, because the man carried a woman over his shoulder. She hung limp and unmoving, her long hair almost brushing the ground behind his legs. The man wore a ski mask over his face. But something in the lines of his body said *despair*. The gun steadied. It pointed at her chest.

Judy said, "Don't shoot. I'm a nurse. I can help her."

The man caught his breath. Or maybe it was just a soughing in the bare branches, during a sudden pause in the shooting.

Judy repeated, "It looks as if she's lost a lot of blood. She needs help immediately. Let me see her."

He seemed to hesitate. Then he said, "Open the back door of the car."

She did, amazed at her own icy calm.

"Get in."

She did. The man put the woman on the ground, then climbed in after Judy so fast she shrank back. But he only drew a pair of handcuffs from his pocket and cuffed her ankle, just above her short boot. It felt tight. He shoved forward the front passenger seat and fastened the other end of the cuffs to the exposed metal hinge. She caught the smell of alcohol.

Backing out of the car, he picked up the woman and placed her tenderly alongside Judy, her head in Judy's lap.

"Do what you can. If she dies . . ." He didn't finish his sentence.

She suddenly had the impression he didn't know *how* to finish it.

She expected him to climb into the front seat and start the car. But instead he started back toward the camp. Before she knew she was going to, she'd rolled down the window and called, "Where are you *going?*"

Stupid, stupid. Why would he tell her where he was going? Now he would shoot her, dump her body outside the car and take off, all because she'd said one too many rash things in her impulsive life.... *Lead us not into temptation* ...

"I'm going to get my kids," he said wearily, and broke into a clumsy, defeated run.

Thirty-one

It had all gone wrong.

They went in like they planned, Wendell cutting the fence like he'd done it just yesterday. Some things you don't forget. The barbed wire snapped back but it didn't hit him in the face or hands, he was better than that. The two strands of 220-volt were grounded without so much as a tiny electrical shock. The Cobray was stuck in his belt, and Grady and Charlie were ghosts behind him, silent like they were all back at Parris Island, before all the rest of life happened to them.

The first bad feeling came when he noticed that Charlie carried the Ingram after all.

"I told you to leave that damn thing in the car!" he whispered.

Charlie grinned. Wendell couldn't *see* the grin under Charlie's ski mask, but he could feel it. "I got the other one in the trunk of the car," Charlie said, gleeful as a kid pulling a fast one. But there was no time for Wendell to argue. This was it.

He led them into the cover of the dining hall, now

dark and deserted. Across the wide bare space that Wendell had always thought of as "the parade ground," the lights of the Covenant Hall gleamed. They were all in there, praying and Bible reading. But not animal sacrificing. That happened at the other end of the camp, on a screened hillside the Soldiers had turned into an amphitheater centered on the stone altar.

It made him feel weird to be back here. Inside. On ground he once believed was holy.

"This way," he whispered, even though Grady knew which way to go, and Charlie would just follow Grady. But Wendell needed to say something. To somebody.

He led them down the streets of little bungalows, no more than shacks really, cold in winter and hot in summer. Soldiers didn't believe in putting too much emphasis on things of this world. How had he lived here for two years? How had he let his kids live here?

His and Saralinda's bungalow wasn't there anymore.

The whole section of shacks, which was close to an entrance to the underground limestone caves, had been pulled down. In its place stood a large low building with lights on in several windows. There was no sign identifying what the building might be. Why should there be? Everybody in the camp would already know.

Where the fuck were Saralinda and the kids?

Charlie slipped over to a window and peered in, sideways. "Looks like a hospital or something. Beds, and one of them bags on a pole."

"An *IV*?" Wendell pushed Grady aside. But of course it wasn't blood; a clear liquid ran from the bag on a pole to a child asleep in the bed. An infirmary. The Soldiers must have found a doctor who would agree to give no blood. Saralinda hadn't ever said.

And the doctor must have become a Soldier. No way he'd be inside otherwise.

For a wild minute Wendell thought the kid asleep on the bed was Penny, but of course it wasn't. Life was never that good to you.

Grady whispered, "So where do you think they are?"

"I don't know. Let's check out the bungalows."

"*All* of them?"

"Most are fucking dark, ain't they?" Wendell snapped. "Just look in the windows of the lighted ones. You saw the picture, right, you remember what Saralinda looks like?"

"Sure," Charlie said. "A looker."

Grady said quickly, "Then we separate. Anybody finds her, don't do nothing yet. Meet right back here in fifteen minutes."

Fifteen minutes was longer than Wendell had wanted to stay in the camp total, but he couldn't see any other way. Being here was spooking him, but under the spooking he could feel his determination still there, solid and hard. They were his kids. And his wife. Fuck anybody who said otherwise.

The three men glided through the dark streets, big shadows. Just before Charlie disappeared around the corner of a building, Wendell caught the gleam of lamplight from a window reflected off the Ingram.

In the first lighted bungalow, an old man slept sitting up in a chair next to a wood stove, a plaid blanket over his knees.

At the second, the curtains were drawn. Wendell couldn't see in. He squeezed his eyes, almost immediately opening them to see his breath cloudy in the cold air. He wanted to smash the window, shoot it out, make the thick curtains disappear like everything else in his life had disappeared. But not when you wanted it to.

Saralinda, are you in there?

He found a small stone, threw it against the front door, and drew back around the side of the bungalow, into the shadows.

The door opened and a woman leaned out. "Is anybody there?" A tall, thickset woman. "Hello? Huhhh." The door closed.

This was too dangerous. Were Charlie and Grady doing this? What if Saralinda had decided that Penny and David were old enough to be at evening prayer after all? No, she wouldn't do that. Saralinda believed in kids getting enough sleep.

Where the fuck were they?

There was only one more bungalow with lights on in Wendell's section of three streets. He glided toward it.

A single shot shattered the air.

Immediately it was followed by the bark of a submachine gun. The Ingram? Impossible, that meant that somebody else had fired *first*—He was running toward the shooting before he knew it. No, no, that wouldn't help, that would only make it worse—

A grenade exploded.

Wendell dove for the ground, covering his head. He dragged himself to the cover of a bungalow, whose lights came on. The door flung open and a woman ran out. Inside, kids screamed. Then everyone was screaming, and gunfire erupted, and there was another explosion. A building flamed.

The bastards were *armed*. The nonviolent Soldiers of the Divine Covenant, armed to the fucking teeth—

"Stop! Stop!" It was the old man Wendell had seen by the woodstove, tottering into the street, the plaid blanket caught in his belt and trailing after. Tears ran down his face. "Stop, this is sacred ground, there is no violence here! 'And the very God of peace sanctify you wholly—'"

A bullet took him in the head.

Charlie tore past, firing the Ingram. He saw Wendell and screamed, "Get out, they're armed!" Behind him a shot sounded, barely audible over the screaming, and Charlie hit the ground, rolling.

Wendell ran in the opposite direction and circled back around, toward the hole in the fence. It was longer but away from the action, toward the amphitheater and behind the farthest row of buildings. He kept out of the light and ran in a crouch. But lights were coming on here, too—why weren't all these fucking people at the Covenant Hall like they were supposed to be? Nothing was like it was supposed to be, the Soldiers were supposed to be as peaceful as St. Cadoc and fucking Père Cadaud, and instead they were fucking *armed*—why hadn't the old man known that? How could anything in this whole fucking camp happen that the Elders didn't know about, didn't control, it wasn't supposed to happen like this—

He saw Saralinda.

She stood outside a dark bungalow at the edge of camp, no more than twenty feet from the fence. He recognized her by the perimeter floodlights, which had all come on. She stood with her hand jammed against her mouth, her eyes huge, her thin sweet body almost on tiptoe with fear. Behind her, in the bungalow doorway, Penny and David in pajamas with feet clutched each other and screamed, "Mama! Come back! Mama!"

"Saralinda!" Wendell called. He started toward her, and two men tore around the corner of the infirmary, two blocks away, firing as they ran. Wendell shrank back under cover. He couldn't see what they were firing at. Then the Ingram barked from a clump of bushes, and he knew. He called, "Saralinda! Get down!"

Charlie kept firing. The first man went down, falling backward in what looked to Wendell like slow motion, a surprised look on his face. Wendell recognized him: the man who had effortlessly thrown and kicked him last summer, when he had tried to grab Saralinda. *Effortlessly.* Trained, armed . . . these guys weren't part of the real Soldiers. They were somebody else, something else, what the fuck were they *doing* here—

The Ingram was empty. Wendell could hear it. He took aim with the Cobray and fired at the second man, who went down clean and hard. But Charlie started firing again, this time with the Cobray, shooting wildly at nothing and everything, not running to the fence which meant he must be hurt pretty bad and out of his head with pain, Charlie never did have many smarts—

Saralinda screamed and fell to the ground.

Wendell emptied his Cobray into the bushes where Charlie lay, all thirty-one rounds.

When the gun was empty, he ran to Saralinda. Both kids were on her, shrieking. Wendell grabbed Penny and pulled her off her mother, and Penny turned a terrified swollen face and started hitting him with her small fists.

"Penny, it's Daddy! It's *Daddy!* It's all right, baby, I'm here now, it's all right—"

She didn't stop hitting him, hysterical. He shoved her aside and bent over Saralinda. This close to the ground there wasn't much light, he couldn't see where she was hit. He put his ear to her heart.

The ski mask stuck to the blood.

But she was breathing. He picked her up and slung her over his shoulder. "Come on, kids, let's go—"

They backed away from him, screaming. He couldn't carry them and Saralinda, too. Penny grabbed her brother by the hand and dragged him toward the bungalow.

"Okay, good, stay inside, honey, I'll be right back—"

Saralinda's long hair brushed the ground as he ran. The hole in the fence wasn't that far. And the main action was at the other end of the camp—was Grady still firing? Another grenade exploded. Her weight was so slight. The kids would hide in the closet, or under the bed. Better take Grady's car, which was probably stolen but less likely to be traced than his own. How could the camp be armed? Who had infiltrated? He should never have let Charlie carry any weapon. *"I got the other one in the trunk of the car."* The other Ingram. Saralinda needed a doctor. The camp had an infirmary now. Who had Grady killed? Penny's hair was bloody from clutching her mother . . .

He desperately wanted a drink.

There was no one near the hole in the fence, but the floodlights were bright. Wendell stumbled with Saralinda toward the woods. Then they were in the trees, safe, at Grady's hot car. And he saw a woman backing out of the front seat.

Wendell raised the Cobray, which was empty. He had another clip in his jacket. He couldn't reach it with Saralinda over his shoulder.

The woman said, "Don't shoot. I'm a nurse. I can help her."

And immediately Wendell felt the words rise to his mind, unbidden, un-fucking-*wanted,* but there anyway:

And I shall send unto you a saviour—He felt his breath catch, and for a moment all he wanted to do was cry.

The woman said in the soft, soothing voice of angels, "It looks as if she's lost a lot of blood. She needs help immediately. Let me see her."

He wanted to weep, to clutch at her, to sink to his knees and pray. But instead he put Saralinda and the nurse in the car and ran back for Penny and David, loading the second clip into the Cobray as he stumbled through the trees.

Thirty-two

No," Deming said.

He'd been saying it, in one form or another, for an hour. Cavanaugh looked at the junior U.S. attorney, elegantly draped over a corner chair in Felders's office, and resisted the urge to break his neck. So *this* was what Felders had meant by "the street cop's natural response to lawyers." Felders said that in North Carolina, where he'd served for three years, it flourished like kudzu. Cavanaugh wasn't a street cop and this wasn't North Carolina. He tried to evaluate Deming's words on content, not arrogance.

He'd landed at Dulles two hours ago, at 6:30 P.M., leaving Lancaster grim and concentrated on the search for Judy Kozinski and for Dollings's killers. The trail, such as it was, was now over twenty-four hours cold. Duffy had led the first part of this evening meeting on Verico, and while Duffy had been there, Deming had been mostly silent. Not now.

"No, that doesn't constitute probable cause, either," Deming said. He spoke through his nose, a nasal intonation that irritated Cavanaugh like a dragonfly in his ear. "I keep telling you, gentlemen, that you simply don't have enough for an affidavit of search and seizure at Verico. I'm sorry."

Felders, who'd gone in swinging axes on search and seizures when Deming had been playing Little League, gazed at the lawyer calmly. Cavanaugh wondered why Felders didn't get Duffy to replace Deming as attorney on the REI team. Of course, Felders believed in giving the youngsters their chance. If he didn't, Cavanaugh wouldn't be here, either.

In addition, Deming was right. They didn't have probable cause to search Verico.

"What you have," Deming lectured, "is a mere suspicion of a crime. Suspicion doesn't constitute probable cause. Nor is the magnitude of the suspected crime relevant to establishing probable cause."

And still Felders didn't squash him, but went on nodding his head and jiggling his elbow, listening as respectfully as if this were all new information. Biding his time.

"And of course," Deming expounded, "the fact that the director has granted you REI status does not, in and of itself, allow this investigation any additional legal status. The standard of proof for probable cause is that of a reasonable person, acting on facts leading to a conclusion of probability that the Verico premises are in fact being used to commit a crime, have been used to commit a crime, or are harboring the perpetrators or fruits of a crime. You have no facts here. Only suspicions."

Felders said, directly to Cavanaugh, "Does Verico qualify as a manufacturer of controlled substances? I can get a Control Act inspection without a warrant."

Deming said, "I don't think—"

"No," Cavanaugh said, "that would only get us an inspection of premises and of records required for substance control. Not enough."

Felders said, "An OSHA inspection? No warrant needed there, either."

Cavanaugh said, "Too limited a search. How about calling it an emergency situation? Prompt inspection of a site without a warrant for reasons of public health?"

Felders said, "You mean, under *Camara* v. *Municipal Court of San Francisco?* Do you really think that's applicable, Bob?"

"Maybe not. How about just going without a warrant under 'exigent circumstances'?"

Deming said, alarmed, "As counsel to this team, I—"

"No," Felders said regretfully, "I don't think so. Even if we called it an emergency that would endanger, we'd run into difficulty under *Chambers* v. *Maroney.* Lack of delay not sufficiently critical."

Cavanaugh said, "What if we said an important government interest would be placed in jeopardy by the requirement of individualized suspicion?"

"Now that's interesting," Felders said. "You mean like in *Skinner* v. *Railway Labor Executives Association?* No, I don't think it would hold. And we don't want to lose under the exclusionary rule any evidence we *do* seize."

"True. A forfeiture, maybe? Civil or criminal?"

"Undoubtedly our best overall legal weapon," Felders said. "But I don't think the facts would justify even an *in rem* proceeding. Let alone an *in personam* one."

Deming was silent. Cavanaugh gazed at him innocently.

"Listen," Felders said, suddenly grim. "Let's get down to work and discuss what might work. Starting with an informant. Bob, run down the Verico staff again."

Cavanaugh said, "Verico has two scientists: Eric Stevens, and one Guillaume d'Amboise, a Frenchman they hired away from Daniel Cohen's big genome project in Paris. D'Amboise is young, only thirty-two, good university record, no police record, lives alone and works night and day. That's about all the French police could tell us. We don't know if d'Amboise is part of Verico's inner circle voluntarily, or if he was forcibly recruited. But in his position, he has to know what they're developing at Verico. There's no way he could not know. We haven't had surveillance on Stevens and d'Amboise while this investigation had no formal status, but I think we should now."

"Agreed," Felders said.

"The rest of the staff consists of four research assistants, all with master's degrees, all working toward Ph.Ds. One of them has strong ties to the Gigliotti family, Christopher Vincent DelCorvo. His mother is Maria Gigliotti DelCorvo. Another assistant has real but less strong ties to the Callipares: Alfonso Ardieta. We think the other two are clean and ignorant, understanding parts of the project but not its applications. Although of course we don't really know. Their names are Miriam Ruth Kirchner and Joseph Doyle Bartlett. Both are in their early twenties. Then there are three lab technicians who apparently do routine things; they're almost certainly clean. Karlee Pursel, Elliot Messenger, Nicholas Landau."

Felders said, "Our best bet for a federal witness is one of the research assistants. DelCorvo or Ardieta. But the other two might know more than they think they do, if we present them with the right questions about the Verico records."

"Or they might know nothing, and if we approach them, our interest in Verico is clear and the Relatives move all the records and experiments out of New Jersey."

Felders nodded. They'd been over this before. Duffy had already given his opinion: Stay as undercover as possible as long as possible. Lancaster, occupied in Boston with the search for Dollings's killer, had said they should develop an informant as soon as they could. Cavanaugh wasn't about to ask Deming's opinion.

He sketched a woman holding a sword over her own head: THE SWORD OF DAMOCLES' UNCLE. The activity of sketching didn't drain off any of his nervous tension.

He said, "What we really need is to find out where Verico's killer-virus is being tested. Lederer said it's almost certainly being tested someplace. There might be duplicate records at that site."

Felders nodded. "That would help. Or if Mrs. Kozinski had told us something that we could use to establish a link between Verico and the attempt on her life."

"If Lancaster's team doesn't find her in the next day or so . . ."

"If Lancaster can't find her by tomorrow, we'd better assume she's dead. Now listen, we can proceed one of two ways. One, we might—yes, Neymeier?"

"Sorry to interrupt," the weedy analyst said. Cavanaugh glanced at his watch. Eight-forty. Why was Neymeier still here? Because he smelled something, and didn't want to be anyplace else if the something burst. Neymeier had the nose.

"What have you got?" Felders said. His feral look sharpened.

"Cadoc."

Cavanaugh felt his spine tighten.

"It's a saint," Neymeier said.

"A *saint?*" Felders said. "You mean, like, a holy person who does miracles?"

"Yup. Sixth-century. Maybe mythical. Minor data bank. Printout." He laid the hard copy on Felders's desk.

Felders, incredulous, read the single sheet aloud.

Cadoc: sixth-century saint, probably Welsh, possibly mythical. He is credited with founding a monastery near Cowbridge, of which he became abbot; with persuading St. Iltyd to renounce the world for the Godly life; with traveling as a mendicant preacher. Some stories place him as far as Ireland; Scotland; Jerusalem; Rennes, France; and Benevento, Italy. The lives of more than one saint may have become confused in this. Few written references; most reliable is probably Alban Butler, founded on Capgrave.

"What the fuck do the Relatives want with a Welsh saint?"

Nobody answered.

Felders said, "Neymeier, cross-check with the Italian

newspapers. Find out if the Pope or anybody issued any decrees or whatever they're called about this saint. In the last three years. Get somebody who reads Italian to work with you."

"Yo." Neymeier left.

"Any ideas?" Felders asked. "How the hell else might the Relatives know enough about an obscure mythical saint to make a joke about it? A joke that gets a foot soldier and his girlfriend killed?"

Cavanaugh sketched a test tube of DNA. Rising from it was the form of a holy man: long white beard, plain ragged robe with a cross on the front, legs forming from a swirl of genetically altered viruses. He labeled the sketch MODERN MIRACLES.

Then he blacked out the drawing with heavy, black, meticulous cross-hatching.

"I think—" Deming began, and the phone rang.

Felders picked it up. "FBI. Felders."

"Sir, we have an incoming call that mentions Judy Kozinski, although it's not from her. It's from a 911 operator in New York State. Do you want it transferred?"

"Yes."

"Hello? Hello?" The woman's voice was steady but nervous.

"This is the FBI, Martin Felders speaking. Please go ahead."

"My name is Carolyn Waters, I'm with the Marion County 911 . . ." She sounded unsure how to proceed. "To tell you the truth, Mr.—Felders?—I wasn't sure if this was a joke or not. A woman called about fifteen minutes ago—"

Judy Kozinski.

"—and said there was shooting at the camp of the Soldiers of the Divine Covenant in Cadillac and we should send police and ambulance. Then she said to call an agent named Robert Cavanaugh at the FBI and tell him that Judy Kozinski said the camp is 'where the biotech killers are,' and Cadillac is really Cadoc. Well, it didn't seem to make any sense, but I dispatched a squad car to the camp—they're a religious group, you know, and supposed to be nonviolent—and there really *was* a shoot-out. There's backup and ambulances there, and all the emergency personnel we could scrounge up. And when I called you I was transferred to a Ms. Victoria Queen—"

So Queen Victoria was working late, too, Cavanaugh thought. And somebody had decided this was a call for the Nut Dump.

"—and I thought that was actually a joke, too, I mean with *that name,* so I almost hung up. But Ms. Queen transferred me to you."

"Yes," Felders said. "Your 911 calls are taped, aren't they? Play me the tape."

"Yes, sir."

It started, and Cavanaugh listened to Judy Kozinski's voice. Alive.

"Hello? My name is Judy Kozinski. There are shooting and explosions at the Soldiers of the Divine Covenant camp in Cadillac, New York. People are screaming. Send police and ambulances. But even more important—and listen closely, please, this is a matter of national security— you need to call Agent Robert Cavanaugh at the FBI Headquarters in Washington and tell him that Judy Kozinski said the camp is where the biotech killers are. Tell him 'Cadillac' is 'Cadoc.' Do it."

"Do you want me to play that again?"

"No, thank you, Ms. Waters. Just don't tape anything over it. Do you have anything else we should know?"

"No, just that the reason I thought it was a joke, was that everybody around here knows about the Soldiers of the Divine Covenant, they're a laughingstock, not that anyone is openly rude of course. I didn't mean we're infringing on their right of religion or anything—"

"Thank you, Ms. Waters. We'll be in touch."

Cavanaugh grabbed Felders's atlas. "Where is Cadillac? Where do I fly into?"

Felders was already on the other phone, saying ". . . every available field agent, and tell them—"

The closest big airport was Albany, New York. Cavanaugh seized his coat. "Have me paged at Dulles about which airline."

Felders interrupted his call long enough to say rapidly, "Somebody will meet you in Albany, an agent or a local. Use this office for phone-in until I tell you different. Deming, get on the other line and arrange Bob's flight."

Deming, looking startled, reached for the second phone.

Cavanaugh said, "Double the guard on Mark Lederer's house." The Relatives would figure that Lederer had talked, that it had been an FBI or Justice raid. Whatever "it" was. Judy Kozinski wasn't the type to hire button men. Who had caused a shoot-out at a religious camp? And why did Judy think it was Verico? If they were using this religious camp as a test site for the virus, the last thing they'd want was to attract that sort of serious attention.

A quiet, isolated place, Lederer had said. Where death would not attract a lot of official attention.

Cadillac. Verico. Cadaverico.

Cavanaugh ran across the parking lot toward his car. Something tugged at the back of his mind. Cadillac, Victoria Queen, the Nut Dump . . . He'd lost it. Maybe he'd get a minute to call Vicky from the airport.

He hoped to hell there were duplicate records in Cadillac. Or something else he could get, fast, to justify probable cause.

Before the Relatives moved all the records out of Elizabeth, New Jersey.

Behind him, in the Hoover Building, Felders was on his third call.

"Don't you think *you* should have gone?" Duffy said. There was just the slightest shade of irritation in his voice.

Felders said, "Bob can do it."

"You've had him from Intelligence how long? A year? Year and a half? And this is his first real case?"

"He can do it."

"Damn it, Marty—"

"Listen, this case wouldn't even exist if it weren't for

Cavanaugh. We all wanted to close it, but he kept digging, kept insisting, kept following his hunches. His hunches were right. He's young, but he's not a screwup. He can do it."

"I'm not easy with it. It's too big. You watch him every step."

"He can do it," Felders repeated doggedly.

"Okay. But you watch him. At the first missed beat, you take over."

"Okay."

Felders hung up. Deming was watching him.

"It's called faith in your soldiery," Felders said, too pleasantly, and picked up the phone again. Deming looked at the floor and didn't answer.

By the time he landed in Albany, he had some of it straight in his mind, partly due to another in-flight phone call to Felders. Neymeier had background on the Soldiers of the Divine Covenant. This camp was the perfect place for Verico to test its lethal individualized virus. A bunch of peaceful, reclusive, weird religious nuts, who disapproved on biblical grounds of blood transfusions. Ideal candidates. Test the virus, and if it worked, the subjects would resist any medical treatment that involved blood. Lederer had said a blood sample could provide the necessary DNA fingerprints to individualize the MHC doohickies—but he'd also said that other bodily tissues would do as well. So the subjects resist elaborate medical treatment, resist voluntary autopsies, resist anything that might bring in outside, unclean officials.

And a religious compound was always full of drifting souls nobody on the outside would really miss.

But how did the Relatives get in? Say they infiltrated, pretending to be penitents. Well, why not? A religious movement got all types. They probably even got the occasional stockbroker or airline pilot or doctor. And the Soldiers accepted them.

After which the Relatives carried on their experiments inside. And armed the camp against any interference in their investment. No, it didn't even have to be that. They armed the camp because to the Relatives, conducting important business unarmed was like visiting your stockbroker naked. You just didn't do it. Even if there was no reason to expect serious interference.

But who had tried to interfere?

Neymeier had unearthed a lead. "Listen, we got newspaper background on Cadillac," Felders had said to Cavanaugh from thirty thousand feet below and a few hundred miles south. "A guy named Wendell Botts has been doing minor talk shows for the past two months. He claims the Soldiers of the Divine Covenant practice human sacrifice. Claims too many deaths for natural rate, and a cover-up by local officials. Botts's ex-wife has his two kids inside the camp; he wanted them out. No action was taken on Botts's complaints by local agencies."

"So was the attack his?"

"Could be. Ex-marine, did time for assault—that was on one of the kids—two DWIs and a drunk and disorderly, but nothing since he got out of prison. No gun permits."

"Service standing?"

"Honorable discharge. One more thing. Botts sent a postcard to the Nut Dump last fall. Queen Victoria says she showed it to you."

He remembered now. The postcard with a grinning baboon, unsigned, addressed to the director. Vicky had showed it to him months ago. *Isn't there a law? This sacrifice is true even if I can't prove it YET.*

All this time, they'd had the key and hadn't known it. How had Judy Kozinski known it?

He said to Felders, "What's the situation at Cadillac now?"

"We're in touch with the state troopers. They got there first. Our agents are on the way. The troopers got control of the camp and are holding everybody for you. They say they can't tell yet who belongs there and who doesn't."

Cavanaugh said incredulously, "They can't tell the

genuine religious nuts from the armed and trained Relatives pretending to be religious nuts?"

"For Christ's sake, give them a little time, Bob. Apparently it's a zoo. Gunshot victims, burn victims, hysterical believers, nobody carrying any I.D. They're moving everybody out, putting police guards on the hospitalized, transporting the rest, making sure the camp isn't booby-trapped. Or the caves."

"The *caves*?"

"Neymeier says the whole area is honeycombed with limestone caves. Apparently another group of them is a big tourist attraction."

Tourists. Just what they needed. "And Judy Kozinski?"

"No sign of her. Not among the gunshot or burn victims, not in the camp. As far as we know. It's a zoo. We learn anything else, we'll let you know."

"Tell the troopers, and our agents, to identify the camp doctor, or whoever is the medical personnel at the camp—nurse, faith healer, whatever—and hold him right there, under guard. Don't let him be moved to wherever they're taking everybody else."

"You got it," Felders said.

"The captain has turned on the seatbelt sign," the flight attendant said. "Please prepare for landing."

Cavanaugh was sick of seatbelt signs. He put his head against the back of the seat and closed his eyes for the fifteen minutes of rest he hadn't gotten during the flight, and didn't get now, either.

Where was Judy Kozinski?

And were her DNA fingerprints one of the ones Verico had from tissue samples?

It didn't seem likely. If so, why not kill her two days ago with a retrovirus, instead of sending a professional to her bathroom? So they didn't have an appropriate sample. Not from Judy.

From who else? Who else was already marked for an individualized, custom-built death?

"Please prepare for our descent," the flight attendant said.

Thirty-three

The pocket flashlight was pink, three inches long, attached to her keychain. Judy clenched the flashlight in her teeth, and every time she moved, her dangling keys clinked. One key for the house in Natick. Two for her Toyota. One for her parents' house. Two for Ben's Corvette. One for her grandmother's mahogany hope chest. And the keychain ornament, an embarrassing holographic rose inside plastic that Ben had given her as a joke. *My wild Irish rose.* Keys and ornament swayed and jangled from Judy's teeth as she tried to keep the flashlight beam focused on the bleeding woman in the dark backseat of the car.

Both Judy's hands pressed hard against the woman's chest. Two wads of cloth, torn from the woman's long dress, had already reddened. The third cloth, pressed on top of the other two, wasn't so bloody; the wound was clotting. But the woman's breathing remained shallow, and there was a cold film of sweat on her delicate forehead. In the front seat the two children whimpered but didn't cry out.

"How is she?" the man said over his shoulder. Judy heard the panic in his voice. *Don't die,* she said silently to the head in her lap. The keys swung and jangled.

"The bleeding's stopped."

"Good, good."

"Daddy, I want to go home." The little girl, her voice too tentative. A child who had been brought up not to ask very much.

"We are going home, baby," the man said, and now the tenderness in his voice surprised Judy. She wiped the injured woman's forehead yet again. Was the bullet still in her? Would a real nurse know how to take it out?

The only parts of this situation that she understood were the parts that mattered least. Under his ski mask, the man driving the car had to be Wendell Botts, who had so desperately wanted his wife and kids back. And now he'd gone in and taken them. Judy couldn't remember the wife's name, now dying in her lap.

No. Not dying. If Mrs. Botts died, there would be no reason to keep Judy alive. Please God, not dying.

Judy peered out the window. The car was a four-door, without driver-controlled power locks. If she hadn't been handcuffed to the front seat, she could have waited till the car slowed for a turn, flung open the door, and ran. But she *was* cuffed, Botts had a gun, and the car didn't slow much even for turns. Botts dove higher into the Adirondacks as if he were being pursued. Which, of course, he undoubtedly was. By the law. By the people who owned Verico. By, clearly, his own demons.

"How is she now?" he said hoarsely from the front seat.

"The same," Judy said. "I'm doing what I can."
Please don't die.

They drove for an hour: two, maybe not. Judy lost track of time. There was no sound from the children, who must be asleep. Around them the mountains rose higher, hulking dark shapes under a half moon. They drove past all other traffic, on roads that hadn't been salted or plowed. If this area had had the snow Natick did a few days ago, they wouldn't have gotten through at all. Judy hoped there wasn't slick ice under the few inches of snow. At some places the road sheered off into steep drops, and there were no guard rails.

Eventually they turned onto a dirt road, thickly bordered with trees whose bare branches met overhead. The car labored hard to get through, bumping and groaning. Judy put her arms around the woman to keep her from sliding off the backseat onto the floor. The little boy woke up and started to cry.

"It's okay, Davey boy, almost there . . . almost there," Botts crooned.

They stopped. Judy caught a glimpse of a small rough cabin under concealing trees before Botts cut the headlights. Finally he pulled off the ski mask. "Okay, Davey. Soon you'll be snug in bed. Just hang on, big boy." The child wailed louder.

Botts picked him up and carried him to the cabin, fumbling with a key from his pocket. He left Davey inside and came back for Penny. Her face flashed briefly in front of Judy in the white moonlight, terrified and pale. But the little girl said nothing. Temporarily cried out. On Botts's third trip, he carried in his wife. On the fourth trip, he carried something long and blanket-wrapped from the trunk, plus a huge box of Pampers. When he returned, Judy opened the door on her side of the backseat.

"No. You stay in the car."

A thrill of fear slid down her spine. Botts drove the car back down the dirt road, turning off on what must have been no more than a track under the snow. Judy could see nothing through the trees. Then he cut the lights just before the woods ended and below them stretched a smooth unbroken expanse of white, dazzling in the moonlight.

A lake. A mountain lake, cold and very deep. To hide the car, with her handcuffed helpless inside.

Botts killed the engine, got out, and opened Judy's door. He uncuffed her and pulled her from the car. His gun was in his hand.

"I need you to help me, nurse. You and me push."
He led her behind the car.

Her relief was so great she almost laughed aloud. He
wasn't going to kill her yet, after all. No, of course not,
his wife was still alive.

The rough ground, the slight upslope to the little bluff,
and the piled snow made the car hard to push. Judy
strained. Beside her Botts breathed deeply but not labored; he was in good shape. The car wouldn't budge.
What would he do if they couldn't . . . but then the car
started to move. Puffing and gasping, they forced it up
over the bluff. When it left Judy's fingers, her hands felt
suddenly weightless, as if released from gravity.

The car splashed hugely. Wendell walked to the edge
of the bluff and peered over, dragging Judy by the arm.
The unfrozen black water had closed over.

"Deep here," Botts said, with satisfaction, and she
thought, He's a talker. Maybe that would help her.
Maybe she could get him talking and he would feel he
needed her for that, even if his wife did die. And she
could help with the kids. . . .

"We should be getting back to your wife," she said,
trying to sound competent and professional. "And her
name is . . ."

"Saralinda."

"That's a pretty name. How did you two first mee—"

"Come on."

He set a fast pace, holding her by the wrist, his gun
in his other hand.

The cabin was dark and freezing. Wendell lit a Cole-
man lantern. Saralinda lay on the double bed, the kids
huddled close beside her. David had stopped crying. His
blue eyes were perfectly round in the plump baby face.
Penny had one arm around him, the other clutching her
mother's skirt, torn to make bandages. When Botts lit a
propane heater, Judy was disappointed; she had hoped
for either a fire or electricity, both of which would signal
occupancy. She didn't see a phone.

"Be warm here in a minute, kids," Wendell said, that

same tenderness in his voice. He stuck the gun inside his jacket. "Here, let the nurse look at your mommy."

Judy sat on the edge of the bed, beside the children, and felt Saralinda's pulse. It was fast, erratic, and weak. Shock? She felt Saralinda's heart, which beat with the same shallow, jumpy rhythm.

"She needs to be kept warm, for shock," she said, trying to sound authoritative. "Mr. Botts, help me get her under the covers, and move that heater close to the bed."

"How did you know my name?"

Judy's own heart skipped a beat. "I recognized you from TV."

He nodded; that seemed the right answer. But Judy wished he didn't know that she could identify him.

They got Saralinda under all the blankets. The children shivered. Judy couldn't see any choice but to put them under the same blankets. But if the worst happened, for a child to wake up next to her dead mother . . . There was no help for it.

"Penny, honey, you and David get under the covers too, where it's warm." Immediately both children scrambled beside Saralinda, snuggling close. David's baby eyes were still enormous. Judy wanted to cry.

"The real danger," she said to Botts, "is from pulmonary infection or bradycardia. We'll have to watch closely for both, and then proceed accordingly." He nodded. Snow 'em with verbiage.

The cold had seeped into Judy's bones as well.

But as the night wore on, the cabin warmed. Black curtains at the two windows kept in the light. Both children fell asleep. Saralinda never moved or moaned; was that a good or bad sign?

Please don't die.

In her sleep, Penny sneezed. Oh, Lord, what if she were starting a cold? Saralinda couldn't sustain an infection on top of a gunshot wound—could she?

Wendell Botts took a bottle of whiskey from a locked wooden cupboard and held it out toward Judy. "Drink?"

"I never drink on duty, Mr. Botts."

He nodded approvingly. "Me neither. When I'm working, I'm sober as a judge. It's only later, after work. A man has to wind down. *She* never understood that." He waved the bottle at Saralinda, but there was no condemnation in his voice, only regret and tenderness. He poured whiskey into a glass, drank it off, poured another.

If he got really drunk, she might be able to just walk out.

"I'm sure that's true, Mr. Botts. Many people don't understand the actual medicinal value of alcohol. It can aid digestion and even lung capacity."

She had gone too far, saying whatever came into her head. From fear, from panic. Botts peered at her suspiciously. She mustn't underestimate him.

"I never heard that before."

"Well, it's still in clinical trials. Actually, I interrupted you before. You were going to tell me how you and Saralinda met."

His face actually softened. "It was in a bar. Before all that Soldiers stuff come to us. Not that Saralinda was the type of girl to hang around bars even then, she wasn't, but some of her girlfriends talked her into going that night. And I was on leave with my buddies, and when I saw her standing in a corner there, quiet and little and ladylike in the middle of all them tramps, I just thought, That's the girl I'm going to marry."

She'd been right. He was a talker. "I'll bet you can even remember what she was wearing."

"Blue jeans and a frilly white blouse with a pink bow. Her hair was long and shining, like it still is now."

Judy looked away from his face as he gazed at the bed. He was a mass of contradictions. This man had attacked and firebombed a religious camp, and God knew how many people were dead because of it.

He finished his drink and poured a third. "The thing is, I never stopped loving her just like the first night. Just as much. Only she couldn't never believe that. Oh, sure, we had our rough times, who don't? But there was something in Saralinda that just plain couldn't believe that I really loved her and wanted us to be together no matter what bad things happened. It was like she didn't think she *deserved* to be loved and happy.

"Like, this one time when I was still in the marines and Grady and I come home on leave. Saralinda didn't like Grady. Penny was a few months old then, and Saralinda just met Elder Connors, that was going to get us into the Soldiers. But not yet. Grady and me went out on a Friday night, and we wanted Saralinda to go too. I even found a baby-sitter, teenage daughter of a friend of mine. But Saralinda wouldn't go. It wasn't like Penny was sick or nothing, cause then *I* wouldn't go either. The baby was fine. But Saralinda said Penny was too little to leave and wouldn't go. She didn't think she deserved any fun. That was what Grady said."

His face darkened, but he didn't reach for his third drink.

"Well, when we got home, Grady got a little out of line. I admit that. Like I said, the baby-sitter was a teenager, and a real looker, and Grady was drunk enough to try his luck. He scared her a little. Nothing serious. But Saralinda reacted like we had us a rape in the apartment. She screamed at Grady and put not only the sitter but Penny too in the car and drove the sitter home and went off herself for two days to a girlfriend's.

"I tell you, by the next morning I was nearly out of my mind. I took Grady's car and drove all over creation looking for her. And when I found her I begged her to come back, on my knees. Really down on my knees. I even sent Grady away, the best friend I ever had, why the stories I could tell you about me and Grady and Charlie . . . course Grady came back eventually. Bound to. The three of us were buddies. But I threw Grady out for Saralinda, and from that day to this there isn't anything I wouldn't do for Saralinda, including getting her out of that stinking camp. . . . I *love her.* Is that so hard to understand? Is it? Simple love?"

Yes, Judy thought. "No," she said.

"It is for Saralinda. There's something wrong with her,

some way she don't think she deserves my love. Grady was right about that. But she does, nurse. She deserves everything."

Judy looked at the woman on the bed, comatose. Saralinda's forehead shone again with clammy sweat. The wadded cloths stuck to the dried blood on her chest; Judy didn't dare remove them. Penny sneezed again and moaned. Outside, the wind began to pick up.

Wendell drained his glass. Tears stood in his eyes. "*Everything*. Saralinda deserves it all. Here, nurse." He held out the bottle. "You pour the rest of this out."

She looked at him. "Pour it out?"

"Yeah. Just open the door a little and pour it out in the snow." He stared again at his wife: pale little face, blue-veined eyelids, long brown hair tangled on the pillow. A hole in her chest.

"Pour it all out. Saralinda don't like me to drink."

Thirty-four

By the time Cavanaugh reached the camp of the Soldiers of the Divine Covenant, it was nearly midnight. Nobody appeared to be thinking of sleep. He walked slowly through the camp, looking at nothing.

It wasn't that there wasn't anything to see. Under powerful floodlights, the sights included three or four burned buildings, blackened timber soaked with water from the firemen's hoses. Taped outlines where bodies had lain in the light snow. Evidence teams all over the place, photographing and collecting and measuring. Local police posted all around the perimeter to hold reporters and gawkers at bay. Detectives, liaisons, county officials. But it was all nothing, because Cavanaugh wasn't looking at either of the things he wanted to see.

First, there was no sign to tell who had taken Judy Kozinski. It might be the Relatives, in which case she was already dead, and they might never even find her body. It might be Wendell Botts, taking a hostage along with his wife and kids, to use as a bargaining chip if he got caught. Or it might be the damn woman simply walked into the woods away from the blazing camp and disappeared, the way she'd disappeared two blocks away from the Bureau office in Boston.

Second, there were no external signs that this place had ever housed any experiments in biotechnology. No laboratory. No files. No autoclaves or lab rats. Not so much as an out-of-date personal computer. And if there were no duplicate files here, all Cavanaugh had was a local nut storming a religious compound to get his wife and kids back. Assault, murder, weapons charges, abduction—yes, yes, yes, yes. And none of it counted shit toward what Cavanaugh needed.

Unless he could pressure the doctor, who had to belong to the Relatives, into turning.

A wind sprang up, swirling snow around his feet. He pulled his coat more tightly around him and went into the infirmary.

Two agents from the Utica field office were meticulously tearing the place apart. Cavanaugh said, "Anything?"

"Not yet."

"Even a scrap of paper might help." They didn't bother to answer this; they knew. That Cavanaugh even asked it was a measure of his frustration.

Incident Control, which had been set up in the Covenant Hall, had been equally frustrating. Cavanaugh had gone there as soon as he arrived at the camp. Cadillac's chief of police, Ray Plovin, sat at a desk at one end of the room. The special investigator sent down from Albany by the governor sat behind a desk at the other end. Turf wars.

"Chief Plovin, how long do you estimate it will take your men to explore the caves under the camp?"

"Hard to say," Plovin said coldly. He was in surly middle-age, the kind of man who hasn't achieved what he'd hoped and blamed the world. Which was now going to blame him for the bloody circus in his jurisdiction. Reporters were already shouting questions across the police cordon: "Why weren't the cops even *aware* that this supposedly peaceful religious cult was actually heavily armed?" "What steps are being taken to find Wendell Botts and the wife and children he's holding hostage before more tragedy occurs?" Plovin didn't have answers. He hadn't even been made aware there was any situation to have answers *to*. He was pissed.

He snarled at Cavanaugh, "Caves haven't even been mapped."

"But the Soldiers wouldn't have been likely to go in very deeply? For fear of getting lost, collapse, bats, whatever?"

"Hard to say." Definitely pissed. Cavanaugh had already explained that the FBI had reason to think the abduction of Saralinda Botts and her children crossed state lines. Hence the involvement of the Bureau in what was essentially a spectacular version of domestic violence. Cavanaugh knew both men were too experienced to accept this. They knew something else was going on here, and they had to resent not being told what it was. By now, one or both would have discovered that Cavanaugh was with Organized Crime and Racketeering.

He turned to Special Investigator Hardesty, a tall trim man who moved like the athlete he probably once had been. "Anything I should have?"

Hardesty said, "Nothing yet from the APB on Botts, or on the getaway car. We found a car registered to Botts in the woods. Empty. No stolen vehicles reported during the last two weeks in or around Cadillac, but of course that doesn't mean anything. But the newspaper check turned up allegations by Botts that the local medical examiner, Dr. Richard Stallman, had ordered two bodies exhumed for additional autopsies in November. Both deceased resided at the camp. You want to run that down in the morning, or will I?" His tone was perfect: cool courtesy, without actual deference. A professional who did not let personal feelings color his job performance.

"I'll take it," Cavanaugh said. Felders hadn't told him about this during his call from the plane. "Stallman at the hospital?"

"No, he's retired. Fifty-six Grove Street."

Cavanaugh turned to Plovin, in order to involve him. Don't make turf wars worse. "How do I get there?"

"Back to town, east on Main Street, left at the second light," Plovin said, his voice sarcastic at this interloper who couldn't even find his way around town.

"Thanks," Cavanaugh said evenly.

Hardesty said, "We got a report from the hospital. Two of the bodies were I.D.'d by camp members as not belonging to the cult. Strangers. Both Caucasian males, twenties or early thirties, wearing ski masks, dark clothing, and combat boots. No identification on the bodies. We're requesting prints now."

"Okay," Cavanaugh said.

"Here's a preliminary list of people being held at the hospital. The rest are at the high school—we don't have that list yet, there's at least a couple hundred people. Even the hospital list might not be complete. The detectives are at the hospital and the high school now, taking statements. You'll get them in the morning. But what we're hearing so far is that camp members were shocked when some of their own suddenly produced firearms, and started using them in a competent manner in response to strangers in ski masks who carried guns. The cult members interviewed didn't think there were even any guns in the camp."

"And the guys with the guns are the camp members missing now," Cavanaugh said.

"Yes," Hardesty said. He looked Cavanaugh straight in the eyes. "Cavanaugh, you going to bring us up to speed on this case?"

Cavanaugh had already discussed this with Felders. "It's still nebulous at this point, but I'll tell you what I can. We think the LCN may have been testing out biological weapons at this site."

"The hell they were!" Plovin exploded. "There isn't anything like that in my town! This is just some wacko who snatched his wife and kids!"

Hardesty said, "What kind of biological weapons?"

"We're not sure. I need to interview the camp doctor.

Then we'll know more." He didn't promise to share the information.

Hardesty caught the omission. His voice stayed cool. "We have the doctor in a bungalow next door to the infirmary. You'll see the light on. No one has spoken with him, except to say he's being detained as a material witness. Our instructions were to wait for you."

He found the bungalow easily. It was a single room, furnished with a double bed, chest of drawers, wood stove, and a few chairs. The furniture had the solid, earnest look of homemade. On the wall was a cheap print of *The Last Supper* and a calendar with puppies on it. Two cops sat in the chairs. The doctor slumped on the bed, but he stood quickly when Cavanaugh walked in.

And the moment Cavanaugh saw the doctor, his tired senses sharpened again. The doctor was it. One of them. Cavanaugh *knew* it.

"Dr. . . ."

"Anthony Parker." He was in his thirties, heavyset. Dark smooth hair, wire-rimmed glasses.

Cavanaugh flipped his badge. "Agent Robert Cavanaugh, FBI."

Parker didn't change expression. "I think I should have a lawyer."

"Why is that, Doctor? We just want to hear what happened."

"I don't think I should talk to you without a lawyer."

Cavanaugh watched him, not saying anything, waiting to see what Parker would say next. The bastard knew. He knew a background check would turn up something . . . not a rap, but a family connection, a financial tie, something. Parker knew, too, that the others, the muscle, had all escaped or been killed and he was cut off, alone with the law. Of course he wanted a lawyer, and to hell with how that made him look to Cavanaugh.

"I understand there are no phones in the camp," Cavanaugh said. "The Soldiers of the Divine Covenant didn't believe in them. Are you a Soldier of the Divine Covenant, Dr. Parker?"

"There must be phones by now. You people . . . the

law enforcement agencies would have run lines in by now."

Which of course they had. Cavanaugh had seen the emergency cable.

"I want my lawyer," Parker said. "I'm entitled to call him!"

"Certainly. I'll have a police officer accompany you."

Parker nodded. There was a thin film of moisture on his face; his glasses kept sliding down his nose. "What am I charged with?"

"Nothing, Doctor."

"Then why must I be accompanied by a police officer?"

"This is a crime scene," Cavanaugh said, and felt deep satisfaction. Parker was jumpy, and frightened, chosen for his medical profession rather than for any natural toughness. The Relatives had run him until now, but he was their weak link. There was a possibility Cavanaugh could get him to turn. Even with a lawyer present.

He said to the two uniforms outside the bungalow, "Escort Dr. Parker to Incident Control. Tell Investigator Hardesty that the doctor wishes to call his lawyer." One of the cops stepped quickly forward; an eager beaver. Cavanaugh thought of Dollings.

When Parker returned, he said, "I called him. He'll be here in an hour."

"Fine," Cavanaugh said. "Meanwhile, come in out of this cold." He led Parker back into the bungalow, motioning to the uniforms to stay outside. They wore parkas. And he wanted to talk to Parker alone.

The two men faced each other across the handmade wooden table. Cavanaugh said softly, "It's all screwed up, Doctor, isn't it. And they'll blame you."

"I don't have to answer any—"

"I'm not asking any questions. And you aren't charged with any crime. I'm just talking to you, telling you how it is. You're an intelligent man—hell, you're a *doctor*. You thought you could work with them, control your little piece of it, collect the payoff that you figure will set you up for life. And then you'd disappear and be done with them. And maybe you could have, if nothing had gone wrong—but I doubt it. And something has gone wrong. They take out even their own, Doctor, when their own fail to get something done right. You probably already know that. And you're not their own. But you already know all this. You're an intelligent man."

Cavanaugh paused. Parker pushed his glasses back up on his nose. He didn't tell Cavanaugh to go to hell.

"They kill their own when something goes wrong, Doctor. We find them all the time. In the trunk of a car in Chicago. In the harbor in New York. On the desert in Vegas. A clean kill, if it's a made man. To show respect. If it's not a made man—well, it's pretty awful, Doctor. You can maybe imagine what they do. You're a doctor, you must know what can be done to the human body. After Frank Guelli failed to kill Tony Lupica when he was supposed to, they tied Frank up, poured lighter fluid on his face and genitals, set it afire and—"

"I'll deal," Parker said. "With you."

"Yes," Cavanaugh said swiftly. "About Verico."

"Yes. About Verico. But only after my lawyer arrives. I'm not saying anything more until after my lawyer arrives!"

So the lawyer was clean. "Okay," Cavanaugh said, keeping the elation out of his voice. This was it. The link between Verico and the Relatives. "We'll talk when your lawyer gets here in an hour."

He left Parker huddled on a chair by the woodstove and raced back to the Covenant Hall. Plovin had left. Hardesty still sat at his desk, beside a whirring fax. Cavanaugh called Felders at home. Felders answered on the first ring.

"I got it," Cavanaugh said. "The link. The doctor says he'll deal, and he already mentioned Verico to me. Reliable criminal informant, reasonably corroborated by other knowledge."

"I'll have Deming prepare the warrant," Felders said. "It'll be a pleasure to get him out of bed. Judge Gallagher'll sign it in the middle of the night if Duffy asks him to. I'll go in to Verico first thing in the morning."

"You? Personally?"

"Bet your ass. There's a 5:10 flight to Newark."

"Call me afterward," Cavanaugh said. "And we'll need subpoenas for the Verico staff."

"You got them. Bob—"

He was going to say it, Cavanaugh thought in disbelief. Felders was actually going to say "Nice work." He waited.

"Don't screw up," Felders said. "I promised Duffy you wouldn't."

"Right," Cavanaugh said.

He was too keyed up to sleep. He told Hardesty where he'd be and went to see Dr. Richard Stallman.

Fifty-six Grove was a gray Victorian house. Its bare maples thrust bleak and ash-colored branches against a black sky. Between the branches shone stars, icy and sharp. There was no odor at all in the winter air. The steps gleamed with ice and Cavanaugh gripped the wooden railing with his gloved hand, feeling the blood pulse in his fingers, the adrenalin surge through his body. Somewhere in the far distance a dog barked.

The woman who answered the door, without so much as the chain left on, was plump and grandmotherly. She wore a quilted robe and blue slippers. Her face creased with worry.

"Mrs. Stallman?"

"Yes?"

He showed her his shield. "Robert Cavanaugh, FBI. I'm sorry to bother you at this hour, but I'd like to talk to your husband, please."

"He's asleep. He doesn't hear the bell when his hearing aid is out. He takes it out at night—"

"I'm afraid you'll have to wake him up, ma'am."

"Yes, of course. Won't you come in?"

She led him into a cluttered living room. No, the right word was "parlor." *This* was a parlor: overstuffed plush chairs, faded rug with pink roses, a million little tables densely covered with picture frames and wooden boxes and seashells and candleholders and dried flowers in small vases the dim colors of Victorian gentility. How old were these people?

Stallman, when he appeared in a plaid bathrobe and leather slippers, looked older than Job, and as righteous. The moment Cavanaugh saw him, he knew that the Relatives had not gotten to Stallman. His lined, long-jawed, fine-boned face was etched with a lifetime of absolute honesty.

"Please sit down, Mr. Cavanaugh. What can I do for you?"

Cavanaugh sat. "You can tell me, Dr. Stallman, why you ordered the bodies of Anna Borlan and Ramon Morreale exhumed for additional autopsy."

The old man didn't seem surprised. "If you know that much, Mr. Cavanaugh, you know that allegations had been made that the original autopsies were inadequately performed."

"Is it usual to exhume bodies just because of allegations made in the media by a less-than-reliable person, who wasn't even a relative of either of the deceased?"

"You already know it is not," the old man said. For the first time Cavanaugh noticed that his left hand trembled slightly. "I was under court order."

"Who requested the order?"

"Police Chief Plovin."

Cavanaugh was beginning to see. Plovin, unlike Stallman, was stung that the newspapers and TV were running around—that's the way a man like Plovin would put it, "running around"—saying the police work in his jurisdiction was inadequate. Plovin would think he'd followed the book, damnit, he always followed the book, it was a damn stupid conspiracy is what it was, they wanted autopsies they'd damn well get autopsies.... Wendell Botts's crazy cause had lucked out in Ray Plovin.

Cavanaugh said, "I would guess you and Chief Plovin may have tangled before."

Stallman smiled faintly and didn't answer.

"What did the autopsies reveal, Doctor?"

"Nothing unusual."

"Nothing?"

Stallman said quietly, "I'm sure you're going to request copies of them."

Of course he was. But Cavanaugh said, watching him closely, "Doctor, did the autopsies reveal unusual amounts of bradykinin in the bloodstream?"

Stallman's eyes widened. For a moment he was completely still, thinking. "I didn't ... it isn't usual to measure bradykinin levels. It's a naturally occurring molecule, of course, and isn't commercially available as a toxin, so ..." He trailed off.

Cavanaugh waited.

"Mr. Cavanaugh, what is this line of questioning about? Why is the FBI interested in my autopsies?"

"I can't tell you that, Doctor. And I'm going to ask you not to mention these questions to anyone else, even your wife." Never had Cavanaugh been so confident of anyone's silence. Excepting Mark Lederer. "But first, is there anything else you can tell me about the medical situation at the camp of the Soldiers of the Divine Covenant? Anything at all?"

"They had their own doctor, I understand."

"Yes. I'm talking to him soon. Did you meet him?"

"No. He was a Soldier, I was told. They kept to themselves."

Cavanaugh suddenly pictured a pack of Red Riding Hoods, huddling in the woods like a circled wagon train. *The better to kill you with, my dear.* He stood up from the overstuffed chair. "Yes, I know. Anything else, Doctor?"

"No, I'm afraid not. But Mr. Cavanaugh ..." He seemed to be searching for words. Cavanaugh's senses alerted.

"Maybe you can't answer this," the old man said. "But did you people know in advance that something was going to happen at the camp? Something terrible? Because if you'd said so, I'd have told the other agent more about the local politics when she asked."

"Other agent? She? When was this?"

"This afternoon. She came pretending to be a reporter, but I could tell she wasn't any newspaper reporter. She was too . . . involved. She asked about the autopsies, too."

Cavanaugh let out a breath he didn't know he'd been holding. "What was her name?"

"Maggie Davis, I believe. Wasn't she one of yours?"

"What did she look like?"

"Small, slim, red hair, rumpled-looking clothes. Like she'd slept in them."

Cavanaugh sat down again. "Yes, we're interested in her, Doctor. Very interested. Let's go over everything you remember. From the beginning."

Stallman described the interview. Cavanaugh listened intently, but a part of him had turned sick. The Relatives would have had surveillance all through Cadillac, all around the camp. Pulled out, of course, now that the place was crawling with police and FBI. But they would have been here earlier today, as a matter of routine, and one of them could have seen Judy Kozinski stroll along Grove or Elm or Sycamore or one of these other, arboreal streets, and reported it. She had gotten to the camp, all right, to make her call to 911. But what then?

Had the Relatives grabbed her just after she made the call but before Botts took off in the car? Or had Botts taken her with him as an additional hostage? If it was the first, she was already dead. If not . . .

Stallman gazed directly at Cavanaugh. "Mr. Cavanaugh, what they were doing out there at the camp was somehow medical, wasn't it? In *my* jurisdiction. And I'll never learn what it was, will I?"

Cavanaugh was saved from answering by Mrs. Stallman's gentle voice. "Mr. Cavanaugh? You have a phone call."

Here? He followed her into the hallway and grabbed the phone off a little ornamental table.

"This is Hardesty." The cool courtesy was gone. The special investigator sounded furious. "I have a major error to report. Dr. Parker is dead."

Cavanaugh stared at the wall. That wasn't, couldn't

have been, what Hardesty had said. "Dead?"

"When he was returned to the bungalow, it appears. After calling his lawyer. One of the uniforms is also dead. The other walked out of the camp."

On the pad. Big time. Nobody had done background checks on the cops. And no cop on the pad expected to have to commit murder to justify his money. But this one knew he would be dead by the people who owned him if he didn't stop Parker from talking. So he did, and trusted they would hide him. Which they wouldn't. Cavanaugh saw again the uniform stepping eagerly forward to escort Parker to Incident Control. Too eagerly. And the thin film of sweat on Parker's nose, under his slipping glasses.

He was thinking rapidly now, trying to widen the scope of his vision of their planning. They'd bought themselves local police. They were moving fast—

He said to Hardesty, "Chief Plovin—"

"We'll look into it." The special investigator's cold fury said, *You damn well bet we will.*

"I'll be in touch."

For the second time he called Felders at home. Mrs. Stallman came back into the hall, saw his face, and said, "Mr. Cavanaugh? Can I get you anything?"

"Marty, Robert. They just took out Parker. Inside the camp. A dirty cop."

"Oh, Christ."

"Have you got surveillance on Stevens and the other eight Verico employees?"

"Not all of them. You think—"

"I don't *know.* I didn't expect this!"

"I'll talk again to Duffy." He hung up.

Cavanaugh sagged against the wall, rubbing his shoulder. Mrs. Stallman still fluttered beside him. "Can I bring you a cup of tea, Mr. Cavanaugh? Or some water?"

Stallman came out of the living room. "Bring a glass of whiskey, Mary."

"No. No, I—"

The phone rang again.

Cavanaugh picked it up, not even asking first. It was one of the FBI agents at the camp. "Mr. Cavanaugh, we found something. In Dr. Parker's bungalow, under a floorboard. It's just a list of initials, jotted in pen on a sheet of legal pad. Some of the initials have checks in front of them, others don't."

"Read me the initials with checks in front first."

"J.D., K.M., S.A.K., M.L., A.B., R.M., N.K., W.DeV., S.U., D.E.B."

A.B. That could be Anna Borlan. R.M.: Ramon Morreale. The victim list. The ones for whom viruses had been individually tailored. He said, "Cross-check S.U. and D.E.B. with the list of camp residents!"

"Collier got the list while I was calling you. He's scanning now . . . Here."

Another voice came on. "Sir? There's two possible matches for S.U. Susan Underhill, age thirty-four, and Samuel Ulster, age fifty-two. Both are at the high school."

"Hang onto them. Tell Hardesty to get them somewhere isolated and medically sterile! Immediately!"

"Yes, sir. And D.E.B. . . . just a minute, there's only one name that matches those initials."

But Cavanaugh was already there. It must have showed on his face because sweet, gentle Mrs. Stallman put a hand on his arm. "Mr. Cavanaugh?"

The agent said, "David Earl Botts. Age two years and seven months."

Thirty-five

At 7:15 A.M. on a cold Wednesday morning, three FBI agents climbed out of a van in Elizabeth, New Jersey. Martin Felders, thin even in a winter coat and hyperkinetic even in the sluggish cold, gazed at the low building. It was windowless except for the front lobby, where light shone through glass doors.

"Doesn't look like much," Abbott said.

"No, it doesn't. Where's DeWitt?"

"Few blocks away," said Marello, the fourth agent, sitting in the van beside the radio. "Stevens is still protesting."

"Let him," Felders said. He went on staring at the building. VERICO said the small, neat sign. Only that. Abbott blew on his gloveless hands. Kennan unloaded the equipment from the van.

A squad car pulled up beside the van. Two federal marshalls got out with Dr. Eric Stevens. Stevens's coat hung open, his tie had been hastily knotted, and the flesh above his collar, mottled maroon, worked up and down.

"I want my lawyer! This is outrageous, for you to

think you can come in here and—this is a scientific establishment *and* private property, you can't just—"

Felders handed him the search warrant and the subpoena duces tecum. He said, "Call your lawyer if you choose, Dr. Stevens. But you aren't being charged with anything. This is a search warrant, signed by a federal judge, for these premises, naming you as corporate officer, plus a subpoena to seize any and all documents and records for the purpose of a criminal investigation. You are requested to facilitate our entry to the building, and entitled to accompany us during our search."

"I won't! This is outrageous, Verico is an independent research establishment, our experiments can't be disturbed by people just—"

"Dr. Stevens may leave whenever he chooses," Felders said to the marshalls. He started toward the building with Kennan and Abbot. Kennan carried the pry bar and sledgehammer. Marello stayed with the van.

The lobby was small. A low counter, a few potted plants, modern sofa and coffee table covered with magazines. A second set of shatter-proof glass doors, controlled by an electronic keypad with ten digits and six letters, led to a wide corridor beyond. The single guard, unarmed, looked startled and uneasy. One look told Felders that he didn't know anything.

"This is a search warrant and subpoena duces tecum permitting these federal law enforcement officers to search the premises and seize all listed items, including documents and records. Dr. Stevens is listed as corporate officer. He's been served outside." Felders waved his hand toward the parking lot, where Stevens stood yelling at Marello and the two marshalls. "Please open the doors to the building."

The guard stared at the papers in his hands as if he couldn't read. He blurted, "I don't know the code."

"You don't know the code to get inside? What if a fire starts and you're the only one here?"

"I call the fire department," the guard said.

Felders said to the agents, "Wait another minute. I'll try again with Stevens."

He went back outside. Stevens had stopped yelling at the U.S. marshalls. He watched Felders walk toward him across the small lot.

"Listen, Dr. Stevens. Your security guard can't, or won't, open the building for us. Now, we know there's no one else inside. We know it because this building has been under surveillance for months now. You have two choices. You can either go in with us and punch in that security code, or we can open that door by force. Either way, we're going in, but if we force the door you're going to have repair bills you don't have to have."

Stevens just stared at Felders. The flesh above his collar had stopped working up and down. Instead it had gone a maggoty white, motionless. He didn't answer.

"Okay," Felders said. "Your choice." He waved to Keenan to force the door. Then he turned back to argue some more with Stevens.

But the scientist wasn't there. Stevens was already moving, running in a crouch, his hands over his head.

"No!" Felders screamed, and ran toward the building. He was too late. The explosion ripped the cold morning air. Black dirty smoke boiled everywhere, and Verico blew into a rain of wood and glass and biotech and blood.

Thirty-six

Judy's wristwatch had stopped at 11:48. Probably the quartz battery had worn out. Irrationally, it bothered her not to know whether it had stopped at 11:48 yesterday night, when Wendell Botts had been driving them through the mountains, or at 11:48 this morning, when she had lain sleeping for a few exhausted hours on a rug in the cabin. And what time was it now? No way to tell. It might be daylight outside the black-out curtains of the cabin, or it might again be frozen night.

Saralinda still lived. But her wrist pulse had all but disappeared; to find the shallow throbbing of her life, Judy had to grope along Saralinda's neck. Worse, Saralinda's hands were cold all the time now, and they'd taken on a mottling like port wine birthmarks. Saralinda's breathing had turned wheezy. Beside her the children slept fitfully.

Across the room Wendell dozed, sitting upright in his chair, his gun in his lap.

Judy rose from her own chair beside Saralinda's bed and tiptoed across the room. She was two yards away, one yard, a foot. She bent her knees and her hand reached carefully for the gun.

Wendell's eyes flew open.

She kept her hand going, her knees bending, her expression as unchanged as she could. Her hand came to rest on his shoulder and then she was kneeling beside him, looking directly into his eyes. "Wendell. I think we need to get Saralinda to a doctor."

He wasn't fooled. "You touch me again, or this piece, and I'll kill you on the spot."

She didn't really believe him. He wouldn't shoot her in front of his kids, not even when they were asleep beside their mother. But she didn't exactly disbelieve him, either. He could take her outside and shoot her in the woods, or just tie her up and leave her there to freeze, where the kids wouldn't see. He might be capable of that. He didn't look it, slumped wearily in his chair, his face a mass of pain, but he might be. He had after all stormed into a religious camp and killed people.

She repeated, as if he hadn't made a threat, "We have to get Saralinda to a doctor. I can't remove the bullet—nurses aren't trained to operate. We need an ambulance."

"Just make her hang on until tonight."

"Why? What happens tonight?"

"Just make her hang on until then!"

Someone must be coming for them. The car was at the bottom of the lake; he must have made arrangements for somebody else to pick them up. By then, twenty-four hours after the kidnapping, maybe the authorities wouldn't be expecting him to still be in the area. Or maybe two cars were coming: split up the kids. They'd be looking for a man and two kids. Make it a woman with one kid, a couple with one kid, whatever. Was he that smart? Either way, none of those plans would include her.

That's when he'd get rid of her. After she'd served his purpose in caring for Saralinda.

"I'm just afraid that without a doctor's care, she won't . . . won't make it."

"Don't say that!" he howled, and it was a genuine howl, a denial so intense that Judy scrambled backward. "She ain't going to die!"

"No, not if we—"

"She ain't going to die!"

Did he believe that if nobody said it aloud, it wasn't true? Maybe so.

Wendell said, "You just get back there and take care of her! And don't you try to walk out of here, neither!"

Judy wasn't that much of a fool. He had locked all their coats in the same wooden cupboard from which he'd taken the whiskey, and the key was in his pocket. Judy's silk blouse might be warm enough in the cabin, but not for a winter stroll through the Adirondack Mountains. And if she stripped the blankets off Saralinda, the kids would wake up.

They did anyway, an hour later. "Mommy?"

"Mommy's still sick, Penny. Let her sleep. Come on, let's get something to eat."

"I have to go to the bathroom."

She said it without hope, too scared to even cry. Wendell said, "I'll take her."

The second the door closed behind them, Judy was moving, searching the cabin for another gun, a piece of glass, anything. But there was nothing. The kitchen knives were locked in the cabinet. As she heard Wendell's boots crunching back toward the door, she snatched the fireplace poker and pushed it under Saralinda's bed. They weren't using the fireplace. Maybe he wouldn't notice it was gone.

Sunlight came with him through the door. So it was still afternoon.

Penny was sneezing. Her nose ran. "I'm hungry."

"Well, then, let's have lunch, honey. We have peanut butter! Won't that be nice?"

"Mommy, too."

"Mommy needs to sleep."

The little girl didn't argue. She never took her eyes off Saralinda.

David woke, crying, and his normal lusty yelling was

almost a relief. Judy changed his sopping diaper, gave him peanut butter on crackers and a cut-up apple, mixed some powdered milk. There was never a chance at the knives.

Wendell knelt on the rug and pulled a red metal Hot Wheels car from his pocket. "Look, Davey, I brought a car. See it go? Vroom, vroom!"

David pulled away and toddled toward the bed where his mother lay.

"No, Davey, let Mommy sleep. Come here, boy, play cars with Daddy."

"No," the two-year-old said. Judy's chest tightened. But Wendell just sat there, cross-legged on the rug, the little metal car in his hand. He turned it over and over.

Judy knelt beside him. "Wendell, listen. I know you have other plans for Saralinda. But I'm afraid that unless she sees a doctor soon—"

He raised his eyes to hers. As soon as she saw them, she backed away from him and went back to her chair. She didn't try again.

The afternoon wore on. The children lay, open-eyed but unspeaking, clinging to their mother. Every so often, Judy reached over and wiped Penny's nose. Penny's cold was getting worse. Wendell sat with the gun in his lap. He seemed to have an amazing capacity to do nothing: just sit and go blank. Judy hadn't thought criminals were like that. She'd always pictured them as energetic, restless, needing to fill up their time robbing and killing.

What did she really know about criminals? Or anything else?

During the long dragging hours, she thought often of her father. Who, if he were in her position, would now be praying to the God he fervently believed would choose the most loving action for him. Even if it were death at the hands of a crazed, sad, screwed-up nut like Wendell Botts.

When Judy was twelve, she'd fallen in love with God. That was how she thought of it now—the same collapse of ego boundaries as when she'd fallen in love with Ben, the same joyful flowing of her personality into His, the same breathless wonder that this could actually be happening to *her*. Love. It had lasted for a little over a year, and she'd seriously thought about becoming a nun. But, like romantic love, it had ended. And the trouble was, when you fell out of love with God, it wasn't like falling out of love with a husband. A husband was still there, to fight with or sleep with or patch things up with or leave. But God, after she'd fallen out of love with him shortly after her thirteenth birthday, had just disappeared. Completely gone. There was no one left to adjust to in a different way, to settle scores with, to divorce. God was just gone.

It had been her first death.

Her father, she suspected, had understood, and prayed for her bereavement.

"Wake up," Dan O'Brien whispered now. "Wake up, honey."

But she *was* awake, running down the snow-covered mountain outside, chasing after God with a .357 Magnum in her hand. She was going to kill Him, for what he'd allowed to happen to Ben. And to Saralinda. And to Dr. Julia Garvey, who suddenly appeared beside her as a ghost, whispering dryly, "No, it's science that has the answers. Not an illusory God." And Judy answered reasonably, "If He's illusory, how could I be trying to kill Him?" and kept on running down the mountain.

"Wake up, damn it!" Wendell. Botts. She wasn't with her father, she was in the cabin, her neck sore from sleeping slumped in the chair. "Get the kids ready! They're here!"

He threw jackets and mittens at her. Judy heard the cars then, outside on the snow. Penny was awake, sneezing. Saralinda still wheezed softly, but there was blood at the corner of her mouth and her skin was clammy and cold.

Judy reached across her for Penny, lifted the little girl from the bed. David didn't stir. Outside someone called, "Police! Come out with your hands up!"

Wendell Botts stood completely still, David's parka in his left hand. Judy had a clear view of his face. It sagged in on itself and his eyes grew lighter, as if they were disappearing, as if something that had given them depth had now evaporated. They turned opaque and flat, light as a mirror, reflecting only what happened around him.

He dropped the parka, shoved aside the black-out cloth, and started firing.

Glass shattered. Penny screamed hysterically. Judy hit the floor, still holding the little girl, and shoved Penny under the bed. Judy's hand felt the poker.

She grabbed it and walked up behind Wendell, who stood firing out the window, his back to her. But he must have heard. He turned just as she swung the poker, and he ducked. He grabbed the poker with his left hand and wrenched it away from her. The gun was still in his right hand. For a long second she stared at him, only it couldn't have been a long second, because he was still moving. It only felt like a long second because it was her last one, before she died. But then something clanged, and it was the poker hitting the floor. She looked at it in surprise because the picture she had in her head was that he was going to hit her with the poker, not shoot her with the gun, because of the children. He wouldn't want the children to see the blood. Under the bed Penny was still screaming. Judy's gaze, bent on the dropped poker, traveled across the floor to the bed, and just reached it before the butt of the gun came down on her head and everything, like God when she was thirteen, just disappeared.

Her last thought was that it was odd she didn't hear David screaming, too.

Thirty-seven

Cavanaugh had hoped that Botts would surrender immediately. It wasn't a ridiculous idea. This man wasn't a career criminal, nothing in his profile said he craved publicity for its own sake, he was a murderer but not a killer. So there were three choices. When Botts realized he was cornered, he might just give up. Or he might have had time to think about having committed homicide in the commission of a felony, and what the penalties were for that, and he might use his hostages to negotiate. Or, being essentially an amateur, he might panic and start firing.

If it was choice one, they could find out if Botts had Judy Kozinski, or just his wife and kids.

If it was choice two, the demand to surrender would serve as the start point for negotiations.

If it was choice three, Botts would be angrier, and that wasn't good. *Every hostage situation is a homicide-in-progress,* they taught at Barricade/Hostage/Terrorist training. But if Botts did start firing, he would start exhausting his ammunition, as well as supplying the Hostage Team with some information on what he had.

A handgun started blasting through the window at the two squad cars. Cavanaugh and the forward-area personnel stood to one side of the cabin, out of Botts's Kill Zone. Two cops in full body armor stood flat against the cabin's west wall, where they couldn't be seen from inside. Everybody watched the bullets riddle the cruisers. Okay. Now they knew.

When the fire stopped, Cavanaugh picked up the bull horn. "Wendell Botts. Please hold your fire. This is Robert Cavanaugh of the FBI. We are not going to open fire. I repeat, we are not going to open fire. Are you all right in there?"

Silence. The barrel of the gun disappeared from the window. The black curtain fell back in place.

"Mr. Botts? Please answer me. We're concerned about your children, and I know you are, too. Are they both all right? Do you need anything for them?"

More silence.

Cavanaugh could see the police sniper in position in the trees. To his right, the assault team waited quietly. He hoped to God he wasn't going to need them. Down the road, on all the roads and in the woods in between, the state police were sealing in everything on this side of the mountain, and sealing out everything else. Travelers. Gawkers. Reporters. Hit men. And whoever was supposed to pick up Botts and his hostages from this cabin where he couldn't have planned to stay very long without a car. Or was that wrong? Maybe Botts had planned to just hole up here with his wife and kids until spring, not expecting too hard a search by cops who didn't really care who joined or left a religious camp. Botts might have been thinking that way. Until it all went wrong for him.

The call had come in a few hours ago: a winter camper with a CB had come back to his car, turned to the police band, and picked up the APB. He had noticed footprints in the snow near Blackberry Lake; maybe there was something to it. He'd made the call. Cavanaugh thought winter campers were nuts, and civilians who made long-shot calls on APBs were pathetic law-enforcement wannabes. This time he could have kissed the guy, whoever he was.

There were tire tracks to the lake shore, and two sets of prints back, a man and a woman. Maybe Botts and his wife; there was still nothing to say Botts had Judy Kozinski. But at least it wasn't the Relatives, because they didn't do things that way. They wouldn't have a woman along, they would have enough men to push the car into the lake, and they wouldn't go back to the cabin anyway. Judy would be in the drowned car, and the men would be long gone. So it wasn't the Relatives.

Of course, Judy might still be in the car. They wouldn't know until they dredged. Or Botts might have already killed her. They wouldn't know that until they negotiated him out, or made the decision to go in.

The first objective was to learn who was inside the cabin.

"Wendell," Cavanaugh yelled again—God, this was so much easier with a goddamn telephone, except ten to one if they had one it wouldn't work anyway—"please answer me. Are the children all right? Do they need anything?"

"Send in a doctor," Botts called. "Send in a doctor or I'll fire!"

"A doctor is on the way," Cavanaugh called. The doctor sat five feet from him, on a fallen log. "He'll be here soon. Who needs a doctor, Wendell?"

Silence.

"If you tell us what medical supplies you need, we can give them to you even before the doctor gets here. We have medicine with us."

Silence.

Cavanaugh's beeper went off. He motioned to Collier, one of the FBI agents who'd come with him from the camp, to call in.

Botts yelled, "Send me a doctor!"

"He's coming, Wendell. He's driving up. Who needs the doctor? Is it one of the kids? Is it Penny?"

"My wife!" His voice broke.

There it was. The wife was injured. Too badly to push the car and hike back through the snow, so that the female prints belonged to Judy? Or had Saralinda Botts gotten injured while disposing of the car?

"What do you need, Wendell? What is the nature of your wife's injury?"

"She's . . . she's shot."

Which meant she was hit during the shoot-out at the camp. Or that there'd been a domestic fight and he'd plugged her since. Was that broken note in Botts's voice guilt?

"A gunshot wound, I'm so sorry, Wendell. She should get help right away. You should bring her out so somebody can look at her. Gunshot wounds should be tended to as soon as possible."

"You send the doctor in!"

"When he's here, Wendell. But you know, I can't send a doctor in to look at Saralinda with you shooting. You're a reasonable man—you can understand that I can't risk the doctor's welfare like that. I'd get in a lot of trouble if anything happened to him."

The doctor raised grave eyes to Cavanaugh's.

"You send the goddamn doctor in or I'll kill the nurse I have as hostage!" He opened fire again. This time it was a submachine gun.

A nurse? Where the hell did he get a nurse? Judy Kozinski wasn't a nurse. And there hadn't been any nurse at the camp. Unless the Soldiers of the Divine Covenant called whoever was taking care of the sick a nurse.

"No, you don't want to do that, Wendell," Cavanaugh said. God, it was hard to make shouting sound calm and reasonable. "You might need the nurse, to help with Saralinda or the kids. In fact, the nurse probably knows what would help Saralinda now. Let her tell me what supplies I should send in, Wendell. We have some medical supplies here. Let the nurse tell me what you need."

Silence.

"Just let her call out the supplies, and whatever you need, we'll get it to you."

Silence.

"Or you can ask her and tell us yourself," Cavanaugh said, but he was losing hope. Botts would have already done that himself, if he could. There was no nurse. Or she was already dead.

"Send in the doctor!"

"He's not here yet, Wendell. You didn't hear another car, did you? He hasn't arrived. But we can still help. Tell you what, can Saralinda walk? Send her out, and the agent who's trained in paramedical techniques will look at her. Send Saralinda out, Wendell. So she can get help for that gunshot wound. You don't want her to be suffering from something like that."

Botts opened automatic fire again.

The assault team drew their weapons, poised. Cavanaugh held up his hand. This was frustration fire, and it would stop very soon, because Botts wouldn't waste too much ammunition on it. But half the frustration was Cavanaugh's. Saralinda couldn't walk out, which meant she was very badly injured, or dead. The "nurse," who might or might not be Judy, couldn't call out supplies she needed, which meant she was probably dead as well. Talking about either of them just made Botts angrier, which meant Cavanaugh needed to switch to the kids.

Were they dead, too?

When Botts stopped firing, the woods rang for a moment, and then quieted. Something small scurried in the snowy bushes to Cavanaugh's left. He didn't turn his head.

"Mr. Cavanaugh," Collier said, "that was Mr. Felders. He said to give you an urgent message."

Might as well let Botts fume for a minute. Maybe he'd calm down. Maybe he'd wonder if he'd hit anybody. Maybe his kids would start crying from all the noise and distract him. If they were still alive. Cavanaugh said to Collier, "Go ahead."

The agent licked his lips. For the first time Cavanaugh noticed that he was pale. He suddenly gave Collier all his attention.

"Mr. Felders said to tell you that Eric Stevens is dead.

Guillaume d'Amboise is dead. Joseph Bartlett is dead."

Cavanaugh stared at him.

"There were agents on them. But Stevens was a car bomb. D'Amboise was found dead in bed anyway. Bartlett's apartment caught fire. All within a few minutes of each other."

Coordinated. Of course it was coordinated with the Verico explosion early this morning. Like dominos: knock down one and the others must go, too. No, wrong metaphor. More like knitting. Unravel a crucial stitch, then just keep pulling and all the other stitches unraveled, and pretty soon all that's left is a pile of kinked yarn and no one can even tell what shape it had when it was linked together.

His case had just unraveled.

No records left at Verico. No duplicate records at the camp of the Soldiers of the Divine Covenant. No place else to even goddamn *subpoena* to search for duplicate records. Both Verico scientists dead, plus one assistant to act as a warning to anybody else who might even remotely have thought of cooperating with Justice. Two agents and a security guard injured at Verico, although that was just a by-product. No traces of the viruses in the victim's bodies. And not a single Relative's name, not one goddamn capo or foot soldier, to link to what Cavanaugh *knew* had happened. No one to indict, no evidence to subpoena, nothing. All vanished.

Except a jotted list of initials that could have been anything, as far as a grand jury was concerned. And Dr. Mark Lederer. Who offered only speculation, even if he could be forced to testify, which Cavanaugh didn't think he could. Not while he had those three adorable little girls in their adorable Halloween costumes.

Cavanaugh picked up the bullhorn, put it to his mouth, lowered it. Felders's trust in him had been misplaced. He was the wrong man for this. He didn't have the experience, the skill, the ability to go after the Relatives and win. Dollings was dead, two other agents injured, and Cavanaugh couldn't even prove there was organized crime involved. It had organized itself into vanishing.

Even the danger to Judy Kozinski had vanished—at least, danger from the Relatives. They wouldn't touch her now. They didn't need to. She had identified the bridge between Cadoc and Cadillac, but it was now a bridge floating in empty space, with nothing at either end. They had tried to take Judy out to keep anyone from discovering that they were into biotech. Well, the Bureau had discovered it anyway, and the Relatives had moved from killing to preserve secrecy to killing to obliterate evidence, and Judy wasn't evidence. She was superfluous. They would leave her alone now.

If she hadn't already been killed by Wendell Botts, who wasn't organized crime but rather a disorganized pathetic asshole.

No sound had come from the cabin in several minutes. Wearily, Cavanaugh picked up the bullhorn.

Every hostage situation is a homicide-in-progress.

"Wendell? I'm asking again about your kids. Is David all right? We think he might be sick. There were medical records at the religious camp. . . . Listen, we want to help, Wendell. If your little boy looks at all sick, sneezing or sniffling or anything, he could have the same thing so many others have died of at the camp. You were absolutely right about that, Wendell, you were right all along, and I want you to know that. There was something going on at the camp, only it was a new kind of disease instead of just another traditional sacrifice, and we think that your little David might have—"

The door to the cabin opened.

Thirty-eight

Judy felt the floor first. She was sprawled across it, face down, every muscle slack, as limp as if she lay on top of Ben after making love. But she wasn't on top of Ben. Both her hip bones pressed through her slacks onto the rough wood. Her toes felt relaxed, separate.

Then she felt her headache, and the limpness vanished. The headache almost blinded her, a sharp chisel chipping relentlessly at the side of her head where the gun butt had struck. Her fingers groped for the spot, and came away bloody. It hurt to move.

Gunfire exploded around her, and she moved anyway.

No, not around her—*away* from her. Wendell fired out the window with a submachine gun he must have had locked in the pantry. His handgun bulged in his belt. Penny, still under the bed, shrieked almost as loud as the gunfire. Judy covered the back of her head with her arms. Every small movement made the chisel pierce her head. Then she realized that no answering shots were coming *into* the cabin. No one was firing back.

Had Wendell killed them all? Who was out there? Was it really the cops? People from Verico, come to try to get her again? The accomplices Wendell had been waiting for? But he wouldn't be shooting at his own accomplices. Or maybe he would. There apparently wasn't supposed to have been shooting at the camp, either.

Please God, let it be the cops!

The submachine gun stopped snarling, but Penny went on shrieking. Judy turned her head to see the little girl's terrified face under the bed, her pink mouth stretched wide open, the pupils of her eyes huge and flatly shiny. Her small face was as white as her mother's.

Who was not wheezing anymore. And David wasn't yelling along with his sister.

She heard a voice outside: amplified, maybe a bullhorn. But she couldn't make out the words over Penny's shrieking. She started to crawl across the floor towards the bed.

The bullhorn stopped. Wendell stood motionless at the window. Judy glanced at the pantry. Yes, he'd taken the second gun from there, and he'd left it open. The knives were in there.

She raised herself to her knees. Blackness washed over her, and for a minute she thought she would faint. She fought off the faintness: *not now, not now*. She staggered to her feet, any noise she made covered by Penny's howls.

Three kitchen knives, all sharp.

Judy took the sharpest and turned toward Wendell. Her head hurt so much that she saw him lined in red, like a silhouette against a lurid fire. Outside, the bullhorn blared again, words incomprehensible over Penny's terrified shrieks.

Suddenly Wendell yelled, "Send in the doctor!"

He turned his head and looked at the bed. Judy caught his face in profile, one-eyed, like some comic-book monster. But he didn't look monstrous. His ordinary, slightly pudgy face was so twisted with grief and despair that for a moment she actually didn't recognize him. What if he kept on turning, saw her creeping toward him with the knife . . . she thrust it behind her back. But he didn't turn around. Instead he turned back to the window.

This time, standing, Judy caught some of the bullhorn words over Penny's howls: ". . . hasn't arrived . . . Saralinda . . . gunshot wound . . . help . . ."

Robert Cavanaugh. It was Robert Cavanaugh.

Gladness leaped in Judy, just as painful to her head as movement. The room dimmed again. She put out one hand to catch herself, but there was nothing but air. She felt herself stagger sideways for a few running steps, and then her knees struck the side of the bed. The knife clattered to the floor. Wendell opened fire with the submachine gun and it clattered inside her head, obliterating everything else.

When the gunfire stopped, she was collapsed on her knees against the side of the bed, near the foot, her forehead resting on the rough bedspread. With an immense effort she raised her head and looked directly across Saralinda's thin, covered form to her face. Saralinda was dead.

Beside his mother, David lay dead, too.

Judy gave a low cry and reached across the dead woman for the little boy. His face was rosy, even flushed, and his small body was still warm in her arms. But in his open eyes his pupils stared wide and fixed, and his head flopped back on his chubby neck. Judy clutched the bed post with one hand to keep from falling, and cradled David with the other. At her feet, Penny still howled. Judy started to cry.

Slowly, Wendell Botts turned his head toward the sound. The machine gun was quiet now, and so was the bullhorn outside. Wendell took a step toward Judy, the gun dangling from his right hand. Then another step. Then a third, jerking toward the bed as if he were pressing forward against an immense wind, a gale only he could feel. Judy looked away from his face.

He took David from her, and held the little body against his chest, circled and supported with his left arm. Judy could see a wet spot on the back of David's pajamas, at the edge of where his plastic diaper would be. Wendell looked across his son's body at his dead wife.

Outside, the bullhorn had started again, and this time Judy could make out nearly all the words, losing only a few to crescendos in Penny's howls: ". . . looks at all sick, sneezing or sniffling or anything . . . have the same thing . . . died of at the camp. You were absolutely right about that, Wendell . . . right all along . . ."

Then she couldn't hear any more because louder than the bullhorn, somehow louder than even his daughter's terror, Wendell's voice filled the room, even though he wasn't yelling, wasn't even talking all that loud. "I am the resurrection and the life . . . he that . . . believes in me . . ."

Judy reached over and took the machine gun from Wendell's fingers. He didn't even resist, just went on in that terrible voice, holding his dead baby, staring at Saralinda as if he would never see anything else again. Judy reached over a second time and pulled the handgun from his belt.

". . . he that believes in me, though she's . . . though she's dead . . ."

She laid both weapons on the floor and fished Penny from under the bed. The little girl clung to her, her shrieks mounting. But when Judy had her pulled all the way out and Penny saw her father, her howls suddenly ceased. Her arms tightened around Judy's neck so hard that Judy had to shift her, or else strangle.

". . . though she's dead yet shall she live . . . I am the resurrection. . . ."

It was an effort to bend down. But she did, and felt along the floor for the guns. Her fingers encountered the barrels first, so she lifted the guns by the barrels and let them dangle from her left hand: one short barrel, one long. The barrels were very hot. They started to slip from her palm. She clutched harder.

". . . the resurrection . . . the fucking life . . ."

With Penny wrapped around her arms and legs, and the guns slipping from her left fist, she opened the cabin door and staggered through.

Late-afternoon light slanting across snow almost blinded her, after the darkness of the cabin. Her head pounded so hard she thought she might vomit, or faint, and it was a moment before she could see anything. She lurched forward. Then there were men in body armor running toward her, reaching her, trying to take Penny from her. Penny screamed and clutched tighter. The men gave it up and hurried them both forward, stumbling through the snow, surrounding her like a screen. When the guns slipped through her hand, someone else grabbed them. Dimly she saw other men run forward, weapons drawn, their faces transformed into machines in goggles and helmets. She understood.

"No! Don't shoot him! He doesn't have any more guns!"

But she was wrong. A single shot fired inside the cabin. The assault team sprinted forward. Judy stumbled, and Agent Cavanaugh caught her, still holding Penny, as the sun disappeared below the bare trees.

MARCH

All things come alike to all; there is one event to the
righteous and the wicked.

—*Ecclesiastes 9:2*

Thirty-nine

Cavanaugh sat in the sunshine at a picnic bench at McDonald's. In front of him was an underdone Big Mac, overdone large fries, and a Classic Coke that, as far as he could tell, didn't seem to have anything wrong with it. He didn't touch any of them. Instead he stared somberly at the eighteen-wheelers rolling past on the Massachusetts Turnpike. He wore sunglasses, jeans, sneakers, and a parka that was too warm zipped up and too cool left open. He was the only one at the turnpike rest stop who was sitting outside. It was March, the week before Easter, two weeks after his thirtieth birthday. Patches of dirty snow still dotted the McDonald's parking lot wherever the sun couldn't reach.

A vacation, Felders had said. "Listen, Bob. You need a vacation."

"I don't want a vacation."

"Take one anyway. Everybody else needs a vacation from you."

Cavanaugh had to admit there was probably some truth in this. In the two months since Wendell Botts had shot himself in the cabin on Blackberry Lake, Cavanaugh had done essentially nothing. Which fit, after all, because nothing was what he'd ended up with after all the months he had been working on Verico.

"So the bottom line is, we don't have anything," Duffy had said quietly. "The Boston Strike Force is working on Dollings's murder, the New York Southern District Task Force has the bombing at Verico and the related murders of the Verico staff. And on Verico itself, on the virus REI, we have nothing." Cavanaugh had come to hate Duffy's equilibrium, mostly because he knew that he'd never have it himself. Like Felders, he minded too much.

He had never minded anything as much as not having a name to link Verico to. Not having a witness. Not having any evidence which of the New York or Boston or Las Vegas families had run Verico. Not having a scrap of documentation. Not having an autopsy report that showed anything. David Earl Botts, aged two, had died of "an unspecified cardiac event."

They had nothing. Except, of course, fourteen corpses: Dr. Benjamin William Kozinski. Dr. Julia Sanderson Garvey. John Paul Giancursio. Agent Andrew Richard Dollings. Grady Donald Parnell. Charles Ernest Moore. Dr. Anthony Parker. Cadillac Police Officer Edward Royston, disappeared, no body found. Saralinda Smith Botts. Wendell Botts. David Earl Botts. Dr. Eric Stevens. Dr. Guillaume d'Amboise. Joseph Doyle Bartlett. Plus three Soldiers of the Divine Covenant, inadvertently killed at the firefight at the camp. Plus all the bodies, exhumed and unexhumed, in the Cadillac cemetery. And all of it added up to nothing.

Cavanaugh took a bite of his Big Mac. It tasted terrible. "You're driving everybody crazy, Bob," Felders had said. "We can't move, and you know it, and that's that. Give it up." But Cavanaugh had seen the rage in Felders's eyes. And behind the rage—way in the back, under the legal codes and all the rest of it—the fear.

At division meetings, he saw the same rage, and the same fear, in Patrick Duffy's eyes. They knew, as well as Cavanaugh did, that somebody, somewhere, still had the records of the virus. It was still out there.

He put down the Big Mac and tried a french fry. Blackened on the tip, burned tasting. And dry.

On the Mass Turnpike, more trucks streamed past. How many of them worked indirectly for the Relatives? How many worked directly? God, he hated vacations.

"See another city," Felders had said. "London. Paris."

"I've never been interested in Europe."

"Then see America, for Christ sake."

"I see America," Cavanaugh had said. "I see it every day in the field reports. I see it up close and personal when I get on a plane and go where some case is breaking. I see it in the newspapers, three of which I read every day, front page through classifieds. I don't want a vacation."

"Christ, there must be something you care about!"

"I care about law enforcement. And the proper care of law-enforcement machinery."

"Then go see some goddamn cared-for law enforcement machinery in a museum somewhere!"

And Cavanaugh had. Consulting a guidebook, he'd discovered that the top floor of Faneuil Hall held the Ancient and Honorable Artillery Company of Massachusetts Museum, with arms and artifacts of the country's very oldest militia. In Boston. Which would take him within reasonable calling distance of Natick. Reasonable for someone just passing through. On vacation.

"All right," he told Felders. "I'll take a vacation."

So now he sat at a McDonald's at the Ludlow rest stop, more defeated than he'd ever been in his life.

"It's still out there, Marty."

And Felders had said, very low, "I know. And so does Duffy and Deming and maybe even the director. But even if we had a case, there's no saying we could stop it. Even if we put a dozen, two dozen, two *hundred* dozen people behind bars, the information itself could still be out there. Somewhere."

"I'd feel better, though, if we put two hundred dozen

of them behind bars," Cavanaugh had said. "We'd have done something."

"Tunnel vision, Bob."

"I know. But at least we'd have—"

"Give it up, Bob. Take a vacation."

Cavanaugh drank his Coke. Another seventy miles to Natick. He hadn't called ahead. Why not?

Just because.

He wondered if she had nightmares, too. Well, for her it would be expected. None of this—murder, abduction, firefights—was supposed to happen in her life. Like most people, she'd planned it that way.

This was the first time in his life that he had nightmares.

Cavanaugh crumpled up the uneaten Big Mac and fries in their greasy wrappers. He drained the Coke, hoping it had a lot of calories. In the last two months he'd lost ten pounds.

A man walked toward the picnic bench from the parking lot. Automatically Cavanaugh scanned the parked cars to match the guy with his; there wasn't too much choice. Probably the blue Cavalier. Basic, cheap. The man was short, maybe five-seven, a hundred forty, young. Although under the baseball cap and sunglasses it was hard to tell.

"Robert Cavanaugh?"

"Yes?"

The man shifted his weight nervously. Cavanaugh scanned harder. No bulges under the light blue windbreaker or close-fitting jeans.

"Agent Cavanaugh? Of the FBI?"

"Yes."

"I need to talk to you." A nervous lick of the lips, a glance at the interstate.

Cavanaugh felt some inner machinery start to hum. "Go ahead. I'm listening."

"Not here. In your car. Or mine. No, yours."

Cavanaugh weighed the risks. His hunch said this guy didn't know what he was doing. Nervousness, not entrapment. He went with the hunch.

In his own car, Cavanaugh said, "Take off the cap and shades."

The man did. He was in his mid-twenties, with the myopic eyes and prematurely receding hairline that Cavanaugh associated with a certain kind of student: intense, dedicated, nerdy, and smart as hell. The machinery in Cavanaugh's mind hummed faster.

"You don't know me. But you know of me. I've been trying to find a way to get to you for a month. My name is Saul Kirchner."

Kirchner. *Research Assistant Miriam Ruth Kirchner.* Cavanaugh felt his hands tighten on the steering wheel, made himself loosen them.

"Miriam Kirchner is my cousin. Well, second cousin. We're a large family, and pretty close to each other. She worked at Verico. That was—"

"I know," Cavanaugh said. "Did your cousin send you to me?"

"Yes. She said to find you away from Washington. She said to wait at least a month. She said not to call her in that whole time, or ask any more questions. This was all at a family wedding, actually, a few days after Dr. Stevens and Dr. d'Amboise died."

Were killed, he meant but didn't say. Saul Kirchner was being very careful. He was afraid that he was being watched. The ones left alive at Verico *would* be watched, of course. But you couldn't watch everybody. You couldn't, for instance, watch all of a research assistant's second cousins in a large, close-knit family that held gala weddings.

Cavanaugh said, willing his voice to calm, "What did she give you for me?"

"A computer disk. But it's not with me now. And I'm not going to tell you where it is until I know what you'll do to protect Miriam. She's very important to me."

Cavanaugh looked at his earnest, young, myopic face, and suddenly remembered Jeanne Cassidy. Making her anonymous phone call to Justice because her conscience wouldn't let her stay quiet any longer. Taking the risk, despite firsthand knowledge of what could happen to her. Like Miriam Ruth Kirchner. If Cavanaugh wanted, he could have this pompous young man under subpoena and emptied of whatever he knew by nightfall. Cavanaugh didn't want to.

Instead he said, choosing his words carefully, "We have a witness protection program. When it's fully used, it's very effective. She would be safe."

"We'd never see her again."

Cavanaugh didn't try to deny it. "There's a lot at stake. I don't know if your cousin told you how much . . ."

"No. And I don't want to know. I begged her not to do this." He stared straight ahead, through Cavanaugh's windshield.

Cavanaugh said gently, "But Miss Kirchner chose to."

"Yes." Saul put his sunglasses back on. "The computer disk is in a gym locker in Hoboken. Dancetique, on Marble Boulevard. Here's the key. Miriam says everything you want is on the disk. Names, everything. She'll tell you herself how she got it. If anything happens to her . . ." He didn't finish the threat, which in any case was idle. He opened the car door.

"Wait," Cavanaugh said. "How did you find me?"

Saul didn't smile. "I'm a computer science major at M.I.T. So was Miriam, before she switched to microbiology. She's a brilliant girl. She has—*had*—a great career in front of her. She's always been my role model, sort of. Anyway, finding you wasn't hard. You checked into a motel in West Stockbridge last night on your credit card."

Pretty soon, Cavanaugh thought, the citizens would just do the investigative work through the computers, eliminating the law-enforcement middlemen entirely.

He watched Saul Kirchner walk away. The young man's shoulders slumped. Cavanaugh wondered if he were blinking back tears.

He knew he should feel elated. Once again they had a chance. Only that, at this point—the disk might be gone, might be useless, might not be enough to indict. But if Miriam Ruth Kirchner was as smart as her smart cousin said, and if they picked her up safely, clean and fast, and if they could keep her safe. . . . No more mistakes. Not this time. Too much was at stake.

If there hadn't been so much at stake, Cavanaugh might even have been chagrined. This wasn't the way he'd imagined it worked, or the way his training had taught him it worked. Surveillance, analysis, action, teamwork—that was what was supposed to crack a case. Training, logic, dedication, persistence, skill. And none of it had kept Verico from unraveling.

But a Vegas showgirl, a homebody scientist, an obscure research assistant nobody was watching, all acting on their collective sense of what was right, picked up the dropped stitches. Maybe.

If they were lucky.

If Miriam Kirchner knew what she was doing.

If she had the guts to go through with it.

If she were the woman her cousin thought she was.

And if nobody made any more mistakes.

He watched Saul Kirchner pull his Cavalier out of the parking lot, and automatically memorized the license plate. Then Cavanaugh headed for the pay phone outside McDonald's.

It was broken.

He didn't waste time cursing. He got in his car, drove at seventy-five miles per hour to the next exit, and found a gas station. The phone worked.

Not everything could be broken at the same time.

"Marty? Robert. Listen, something just happened—"

Forty

Something always happens," Dan O'Brien said. "Something to change our picture of the universe. That's how the mystery reminds us how much larger it is than our understanding."

Judy smiled wanly and laid down another rollerful of paint along her living room wall. "Science isn't supposed to be about mystery, Dad. It's supposed to be about removing mystery. Quantify, quantify, rah-rah-rah." She made half-hearted cheerleader motions, and immediately felt stupid.

O'Brien smiled down at his daughter. He stood on a ladder, cutting in paint at the angle between wall and ceiling. "Some people go into science in order to escape mystery. Some in order to find it."

"Ben wanted to escape mystery," Judy said. Her answer surprised her. "No, it's true—he did want to escape mystery. He wanted to solve everything."

"Everything isn't solvable," O'Brien said gently. "That's why we have God."

"Well, I like people who at least try to solve things,"

Judy said, surprising herself for the second time. It was true. She liked solvers. Deducers. Decoders. As much as she liked anything right now, which wasn't much.

Outside, it was spring. A false spring, probably—Boston sometimes had blizzards into April—but the crocuses were up, and the daffodils were trying. A good time to put the house on the market, Judy had decided. Her parents had come up to help her get it ready: painting, cleaning, sorting through the junk in the basement. A Realtor was coming Thursday. Judy thought she'd buy a townhouse in the city, maybe. Or something.

"I think this color is wrong," Judy said. "We should have picked the eggshell."

"Why?"

"I don't know. It's softer. This white is too harsh."

Her father looked at her, his smile gone.

"Well, it *is* too harsh! It doesn't have to be me, does it? Can't I even have an opinion about the color of paint without you worrying that I'm still not all right? God, give me a break, Dad!"

O'Brien didn't answer. After a minute Judy said, "I'm sorry."

"Don't be. I do think you're all right, honey. So does your mother. But you went through a lot, and it's only been two months."

She laid down her brush. "If I could just think that . . ."

"Think what, honey?"

"I don't know. I don't know what I think. Is that the doorbell?"

"Your mother will get it."

"She went to the Food Mart for more coffee and bagels. I'll get it."

Judy was glad to leave the living room. Torn apart, half-painted, full of her father's loving pressure . . . no, that was unfair. He didn't actually pressure her. He was just a man of strong convictions, and he was entitled to them. Hadn't she just said she liked that? Only every night now was crowded with dreams of little David Botts, of Wendell, of Saralinda. . . . Eight months ago her nightmares had been about Ben. Now she had a whole new group of people to wake up in a cold sweat about. This was progress?

And under the images of people were the other images, the ones she couldn't even tell to innocents like her father. The tiny tiny pinpoints, almost too small to see, that drifted in the window and settled on her skin and burned through to her heart. Hers, and her father's, and her mother's, and then everyone else in the world, one by one by one. She couldn't tell her father because she had sworn she would not. Classified information. She couldn't even tell her therapist, because he would just decide it was some Freudian symbol or other and interpret it all wrong because he didn't know. The black pinpoints were real. Ben and the others like him had made them real.

Judy finally had her answers. She knew, now, what had killed Ben. And all it had led to were more questions.

Some people go into religion, too, in order to find mystery, Dad. And some to escape it. And then there's the poor bastards who can't seem to do either. She almost went back into the living room to say this to him. But there really wasn't any point. He would only agree.

She opened the front door. Caroline Lampert stood on the doorstep.

Judy's first thought was that Caroline looked terrible. She had aged a lot in the last seven months. Her skin had dry, flaky patches, and her hair was dull and uncared for. Ben wouldn't even want her now.

"Judy, may I come in? For just a minute? It's important."

Judy said nothing.

"I know you don't want to see me. I don't . . . I can understand that. But this is very important, and it will only take a minute." She added, lower, "Please."

Judy stood aside and opened the door.

She didn't want her father to see Caroline. Nor her mother, who would be back any minute from the Food Mart. That ruled out the kitchen, living room, and Ben's study, which was off the living room. She led Caroline up the stairs to her own study and closed the door.

They hadn't started to paint or pack in here. Judy's half-finished article for *Science Digest* was on the computer screen. The article was about a new find in human prehistoric bones; research notes from the Institute of Human Origins in California littered the floor. Red or green lights glowed steadily on the printer, fax, copier, surge protector. They all looked less bright, less like a fragmented Christmas tree, when Judy flicked the wall switch and lamplight flooded the room. She didn't ask Caroline to sit down.

Caroline held her purse awkwardly in front of her body. "I just wanted you to know that we've had a big breakthrough in the lab, Judy. Based on Ben's work. We'll publish in the *New England Journal of Medicine,* and security is tight until then because this is really important, but I wanted you to know now."

Judy forced herself to say, "What is it?"

"Ben's work. . . . The work he did on the proteins of the viral coat was aimed at tailoring them to the MHCs of cancer cells, as you know. And without going into the details, we found a method that works. A receptor-site-specific alteration to enable altered cells to attack and destroy only a specific carcinoma."

Judy said slowly, "A cure for cancer . . ."

"Well, not yet," Caroline said, the careful scientist. "But a major step on the way. We still have clinical trials, all that—"

"But it will happen. Because of the genetic engineering. A way to attack and destroy cancer tumors without touching the rest of the body's cells. It will happen."

"It will happen," Caroline said, and briefly her tired eyes glowed, and Judy saw that she'd been wrong. Caroline could still look desirable. When she glowed with achievement like this, she looked the way Ben must have seen her, all those long nights in the lab.

It surprised Judy how little it still hurt. In fact, it didn't seem important at all. She had loved Ben. He had been a cheat and an egoist and a liar. He had also created this staggering scientific breakthrough, this life-giving miracle. This mystery.

"Well, I'll go now," Caroline said awkwardly. Her glow faded again. "I just wanted you to know."

Judy said abruptly, "I know you loved him, too."

Caroline looked away, out the window. Her eyes were shiny. "Yes. I did."

After that there wasn't anything more to say. Judy led the way silently downstairs and Caroline left.

"Who was that?" her father called from his ladder.

"Oh, just a neighbor. Look, Dad, I'm feeling a little tired. I'll be down in fifteen minutes or so, okay?"

"Fine with me," Dan O'Brien said cheerfully. Judy could hear the scrape of the ladder being moved across the floor.

She went back to her study, trying to sort out what she felt. A cure for cancer. It was too big, like trying to take in the concept of an eighth continent. It occurred to her that much as she'd believed in Ben's talent, she hadn't really ever expected it to lead to anything this momentous. What did that say about her?

And out there, somewhere, the tiny black pinpoints, drifting on the wind.

The fax was whirring. Glad for the distraction, Judy picked up the first page. She expected to see additional notes from the Institute of Human Origins, but it wasn't that.

A pencil sketch of a light bulb, the kind that went on above cartoon characters' heads when they got an idea. But this bulb was made of stone. Fissures riddled the surface; moss grew on the north side. Block letters said FROM THE GARDEN OF PETRIFIED METAPHORS.

Despite herself, Judy laughed aloud.

The second sheet was a caricature of every lampooned cop in every bad movie she'd ever seen: wrinkled uniform, granite jaw, enormous badge, enormous gut. A speaking balloon from his mouth said, "No habla tabula rasa." This time it took her a minute to get it, but when she did she laughed again. The man who thought he already knew everything.

The fax whirred once more. This time the sheet was covered with quick sketches:

THE WORDS "WE GOT THE BASTARDS" IN THE MANY
LANGUAGES OF THE KNOWN UNIVERSE

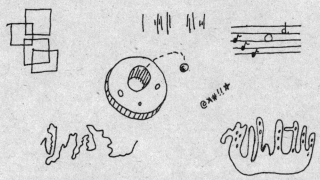

Judy didn't laugh. She peered at the drawing closely. At the bottom, in such tiny letters she had to strain to decipher them, was printed "Yes. Really." And under that, "R. Cavanaugh."

Her breath caught in her chest.

Yes. Really.

Outside the window, her mother's car pulled into the driveway. Judy watched Theresa O'Brien open the car door, climb out carrying a paper grocery sack, and vanish under the overhang of the porch roof. Beside the walk, the crocuses made little splashes of color: pink, yellow, blue.

She still had his home phone number. Someplace.

Her father entered the room, dotted with paint. "Well, you look more chipper. Working on your article?"

"Yes. No. Dad, what the hell's your definition of 'the mystery,' anyway?"

He said immediately, "A sort of cohesion below the surface of things. An unseen pattern, sensed but not fully deciphered. Or decipherable." He looked at her more keenly. "In personal as well as cosmic terms."

"Oh," Judy said, "I just wondered," and held her three papers a little tighter, and went to her bedroom to have some privacy to make the call.

Forty-one

From the *New York Times:*

ALLEGED MOBSTERS INDICTED
HEAVY-DUTY CHARGES RAISE
SPECULATION ABOUT BIOTECH

ELIZABETH, New Jersey, April 24—A federal grand jury has indicted seven men on an array of charges under the Racketeer Influenced and Corrupt Organizations statutes, including ten counts of murder, two counts of solicitation to capital murder, seven counts of manslaughter, five counts of conspiracy to terrorism, seventeen counts of obstructing justice, twenty-two counts of weapons violations, and sixteen counts of endangering the public health. All seven men are members of the reputed "Gigliotti crime family," allegedly one of New York's most powerful forces in organized crime. All seven are being held without bail.

The seven are: Salvatore Gigliotti, 47; Edward

Giovanni Gigliotti, 45; Michael J. Petruno, 40; Anthony M. Petruno, 38; Frank R. Gigliotti, 38; Joseph Paul Surace, 35; and Christopher Vincent DelCorvo, 29.

It is considered unusual for murder indictments, especially those involving alleged mobsters, to couple weapons violations with endangerment of the public health. This has given rise to speculations that the weapons involved may have been biological, speculation fueled by the fact that one of the indicted men, Christopher Vincent Del-Corvo, was until recently employed by a privately owned biotechnology company, Verico, of Elizabeth, New Jersey. The Verico facility was destroyed by explosive arson on January 12, during an FBI raid to seize records. No charges have been filed in that incident. Verico's sole owner, entrepreneur Joseph Kensington, is out of the country and could not be reached for comment.

Patrick Duffy, head of the FBI Criminal Investigative Division, declined to discuss details of the case. Duffy expressed confidence that the federal government has sufficient evidence to win

Continued on Page B2

From the *Washington Post:*

MEXICAN PRESIDENT DEAD; RIOTS IN MEXICO CITY

MEXICO CITY, April 24—Riots erupted earlier today in Mexico City when the death of President Marcos Perez was formally announced. Perez, who either died last night at Santa Catarina Hospital or was taken there shortly after expiring, had been the target of two previous assassination attempts. However, the official announcement, broadcast at 10:42 A.M. local time over national radio, stated that the cause of death was "a heart attack."

This statement was challenged by Perez's wife, Maria Carolina Perez, who was not with her husband when he died. In a press conference held this afternoon on the steps of the National Palace, Mrs. Perez said tearfully, "He was only 56 and in good health! Nothing was wrong with his heart! He had only a little cold!" The press conference was televised, and TVs had been set up in the streets around the palace. Rioting began at the completion of the press conference.

Medical authorities at Santa Catarina would not say whether an autopsy has been scheduled.

Although no charges were filed in the two previous attempts on the president's life, there is widespread belief in Mexico City that they were ordered and financed by major players in Mexico's lucrative drug trade. Perez had taken decisive steps to crack down on alleged "drug lords" operating in his country. Mexican drug profiteers, many of whom have ties to organized crime in the United States,

see PEREZ, A12, Col. 2

From the *Boston Globe:*

MAJOR CANCER BREAKTHROUGH?

BOSTON, April 24—Speculation runs high in the scientific community about a forthcoming article in the prestigious *New England Journal of Medicine.* Co-authored by the late Dr. Benjamin Kozinski, Dr. Jon McBride, and Dr. Caroline Lampert, all of the Whitehead Institute for Biomedical Research at Massachusetts Institute of Technology, the article reportedly concerns a radical new approach to attacking carcinomas through genetically engineered retroviruses. None of the co-authors would comment on the article prior to publication.

Genetic research has long been seen as a potentially fruitful field for cancer research, since most tumors show

Continued on next page

Available by mail from

THIN MOON AND COLD MIST • Kathleen O'Neal Gear
Robin Heatherton, a spy for the Confederacy, flees with her son to the Colorado Territory, hoping to escape from Union Army Major Corley, obsessed with her ever since her espionage work led to the death of his brother.

BURNING DOWN THE HOUSE • Merry McInerny
Burning Down the House is a novel of dazzling storytelling power that peers into the psyche of today's woman with razor-sharp insight and sparkling wit.

MIRAGE • Soheir Khashoggi
"A riveting first novel...exotic settings, glamourous characters, and a fast-moving plot. Like a modern Scheherazade, Khashoggi spins an irresistible tale...an intelligent page-turner."—*Kirkus Review*

CHOSEN FOR DEATH • Kate Flora
The first in the Thea Kozak series—"Thea Kozak is appealingly tough-minded... *Chosen for Death* is a first novel that sticks in your mind."
—*Washington Post Book World*

SHARDS OF EMPIRE • Susan Shwartz
A rich tale of madness and magic—"Shards of Empire is a beautifully written historical...an original and witty delight."—*Locus*

SCANDAL • Joanna Elm
When former talk show diva Marina Dee Haley is found dead, TV tabloid reporter Kitty Fitzgerald is compelled to break open the "Murder of the Century," even if it means exposing her own dubious past.